Chorus of Change

Book VIII of The Quietus of Fate

By Brian C. Kershner

ISBN: 1-942082-14-2
ISBN-13: 978-1-942082-14-9

Acknowledgements

After *Reflections in Darkness* was finished, it marked not only a new vitality in my writing, but as most of my novels, it marked changes in my own life. I thought once that *Dark Mirror* and the second trilogy of the Onea storyline was the darkest of the material that I would ever write. But as my own life evolved, and I had to come to terms with the difficulties of my own world, those difficulties of course manifested themselves in the worlds that I had created.

Where Onea had once felt small and somewhat insulated, even at its scope and size; Espre was a thriving world of countless people that hummed and moved regardless of the characters who had a spotlight shone upon them across the thirty-four chapters of *Reflections*. The scale and the scope of this new world seemed to continue to grow out of my control and out of my understanding, and yet everything fit and made sense. As I continued to write, more of the origins of the battles described in the first six books of the *Quietus of Fate*, revealed themselves and I was as much a spectator in the process as I was its architect.

Chorus of Change serves a number of purposes in the *Quietus of Fate* story, not the least of which is the major turning point in the overall understanding of the narrative of the war between Light and Darkness, shattering it into the diverse conflict that it truly is. Like all of life, it cannot be confined to simply religion, or faith, or politics, or family, or even war. Complexity is the norm, and without all facets, the composition can never truly be understood; just as a chorus without its constituent parts can never be truly appreciated.

B.K.

Table of Contents

Chapter 60

Epilogue

Appendicies

Upon the world of Espre, came the divine light,
Through which the vessels of mortality emerged,
Sheparded from the nothingness they fled untold blight,
The sins of a bloody and forgotten past purged.

Their transgressions forgiven, they sought truth,
And a place in this holy new land,
But some unbelievers demanded justification and proof,
And sought to rule what was given with an forceful hand.

Across the reaches of the divine sphere,
Armies flocked to banners of high renown,
The chosen warriors wielded faith against agents of fear,
And by the Creator's grace struck them down.

Though the war was a bloody and brutal abomination,
The victors were rewarded for answering faith's clarion,
Their sacrifice and service would form the Foundation,
Of the Divine Empire of the Creator's Chosen, Terrik Lorien.

-   *The Verses of The Word*
    From the High Priestess of the
    Church of the Creator

Prologue

Resolutions

Year Three of the Just Emperor Kaitain "Dragonsbane" Lorien,
Creator's Calendar Year 1870

Seraph Kore moved slowly through the underbrush as he approached the city of Aldere. It had been a long and arduous trip from Thorigald to Aldere, and while he could have easily passed through the magistrate checkpoints and patrols of the Imperial Legion, it would have alerted everyone to his movements. Seraph couldn't have that. Not yet. If anyone knew he was coming, they would be able to prepare. While stealth was never Seraph's strong suit, he had gone through enough training both with the Imperial Legion and with the Hunters of Thorigald to pass unseen through any woodland terrain. Though his greatest teacher was perhaps his estranged wife. However, he could not be distracted with thoughts of Chelsea, not now. Fortunately, there were plenty of wilds between Thorigald and Aldere, and Seraph took advantage of all of his training and focused his mind on his singular purpose. No fire, no tracks, sleeping suspended in trees. There was an exhilaration there that he had not felt in many years, the exhilaration of connecting to the core of his being, the essence of what he truly was. There would be no more fanfare-filled entrances, no more symbols of status or power. Seraph had reduced himself to the essentials and nothing more. His bow, his traveling clothes, a small pack of rations, and Patience; that was all he needed to complete the task ahead of him. The task was grim to say the least, but it was necessary.

Vallic had once said that necessity made killers, and Seraph's essence was revealed to be that of a killer.

Moving deftly through the last bit of tall grass, Seraph stopped at the edge of the Aldere River. Long ago, mages from the Academy of Arcane Arts in Jelan had created the river to add another layer of protection to the City of Aldere preventing invading armies from storming the capitol with force. As Aldere was situated in the very center of the Cadarian Empire, all roads literally led to Aldere. Five major roads found their start and end in Aldere, each emerging from a bridge across the Aldere River. Aldere itself was little more than an island, but it was also an island on an island. While the city of Aldere sat in a circle around the Palace of Aldere, the palace itself was separated from the city by means of a wide moat, which had only two bridges across. With its high walls and palisades, the Palace of Aldere was a nearly impregnable fortress, but every place had its weak points, and Seraph had taken great care to learn all of the vulnerabilities of the Palace of Aldere. It wasn't going to be easy, not by a long shot, but Seraph had the best chance of any who had ever tried.

Waiting in the trees until nightfall, Seraph moved to the edge of the Aldere River and slipped quietly into the water. Holding tight to the hilt of Patience, Seraph let all of the air out his lungs and sank to the bottom of the river, where even the light from the lanterns of the city did not reach. Patience did have its virtues, and so long as Seraph kept his mind clear and free of distraction he could hold his breath indefinitely and take the slow and deliberate actions necessary to make sure his infiltration would succeed. It took nearly an hour to walk across the bottom of the Aldere River to the opposite shore, and then nearly another hour to find the entrance to the Aldere sewer system. Traveling through the sewers would not be the most pleasant experience, but it would at least prevent discovery a little longer. After finding the large metal grate that covered the sewer exit, Seraph pulled out a small knife and slowly removed the bolts that held the grate in place. After several minutes Seraph found himself in the pipe leading to the sewer system, and a new feeling of accomplishment began to fill his heart.

The sewers were dark and dank to say the least, and the smell was one that could have singed the nostrils of one with even the strongest constitution. But Seraph was unaffected by the smell, the rats, and even the viscera that filled the tunnels. Patience kept his mind clear of distraction and focused on the task at hand, a terrible task that had but two possible outcomes. Neither outcome found Seraph still alive, but if he was successful, it would be a fair trade. Kaitain had to be stopped at all costs, and one life for the life of thousands was a more than fair trade. Within a few minutes, Seraph had reached the end of the Aldere sewer system and found where it adjoined the palace system. This is where things got very tricky.

Security was always important to those who sat on the Throne of Cadaria. There seemed to always be some type of threat against the Emperor, and any way to increase the security of the Palace of Aldere was considered. Long ago, the third Cadarian Emperor Morikan Lorien had his Imperial Sorcerer, a man named Dorik Aldeen place a series of enchantments throughout the lower portions of the sewer system to prevent someone from accomplishing just what Seraph was attempting. However, Seraph had the advantage of knowing the safeguards existed. Kneeling slowly at the entrance to the Imperial Sewers, Seraph silently prayed to the Creator. If his cause was just the Creator would grant his request for power, if his cause was not just, Seraph would simply find another way to accomplish his goal.

Unlike some of the other members of the Knights of the Flashing Blade who had received training in either the Academy of Arcane Arts in Jelan or at the Heart of Stone in Albitonin, Seraph was largely self-taught in his application of power. Some of it was from the realm of the arcane, learned by listening to the wizened sages of Thorigald, while other abilities had been collected during the many long and tedious political functions he was forced to attend with the excruciatingly pious Gregor Quicksilver and Hannah Ironheart. The ability to combine divine and arcane powers seemed blasphemous to some and a foolish endeavor to others, however Seraph believed that one could never had enough tools. Sometimes a hammer was required while others required something a little more delicate.

When he finally stood, Seraph could fell the change had come over him, and suddenly the subtle flows of arcane magic would be seen all around him. There was indeed a ward that stood before him, and as he slowly extended a hand toward it, a veil of divine power enveloped his body, and Seraph passed silently through the ward, the alarm untriggered. Seraph's path would now be clear. He moved quickly through the tunnels, avoiding wards where possible, and bypassing them where necessary until he stood beneath the sewer grate that would lead him to the northeast guard tower.

Dawn was quickly approaching, so Seraph quickened his pace. He chanted a silent prayer, and all sound around him was totally suppressed. The grate moved silently from its position and though it slid across hard uneven stone, not a sound escaped. Seraph smiled slowly and then pulled himself through the too thin opening to the ground floor of the tower. Most of the guards would be two levels up, sleeping, while the rotating guard would be farther up in the many levels of the tower and parapet.

After replacing the grate, Seraph moved across the small room that served as disposal area to the next room which held the towering spiral staircase that led to all levels of the tower and had exits onto the two-tiered parapet that overlooked both the city of Aldere and the internal grounds of the Imperial Palace. Moving slowly, his back hugging the wall, Seraph climbed the stairs, watching intently for any movement above him. The next level up would be the exit to the Imperial Grounds. It was not yet dawn, so the next guard rotation would not be ready to take place yet. He still had several minutes before any traffic would start. He slowed his pace as he passed the second level, the guard quarters. Looking through the always open door, Seraph could see several men sleeping soundly, knowing that they would soon be roused for their next watch. The whole of the Imperial Legion would be mobilized come morning, to ensure the protection of the Emperor and Empress-to-be during their wedding. Seraph knew it was both the best and the worst time to strike. The sheer amount of guards made it next to impossible to succeed, but the volume of men together also meant that it was just that easy for one more to go nearly unnoticed.

The third level of the tower was Seraph's first target. He moved quickly through the door and finally let a relieved breath fill his lungs. Part of him had not expected to get this far, fearing that the increased security would have all of his options limited. However, it seemed that while an attack from without was being guarded against, an attack from within was still not taken seriously. But then again, why would it be? With nearly all of the Knights of the Flashing Blade either in attendance, dead, or incarcerated and all of the Imperial Legion on alert; who could have possibly been a threat? Taking another breath, Seraph recovered a uniform from the supply closet and then donned a set of Imperial Guard armor from the sparsely stocked racks. He was able to find a tunic with the rank insignia of lieutenant on it, high enough rank to not be questioned through every movement, and low enough to not draw too much attention. It was the same rank he had achieved in the legion before returning to Thorigald to lead the Legion of Water, and so he knew almost all of the protocol by heart. Returning to the stairway, he moved up another level to the entry to the parapets. There was only one reason to stop here. The logbook that sat on the low table by the exterior door held the information about the daily ciphers and identification credentials. Seraph took note of the evening and morning passwords before moving up yet another level to the tower entrance. This would be the test. At any time there would be four guards on duty in the tower; two men to hold the entryway, and then two higher up in the high tower. One of the men in the high tower was a spotter while the other man was the signalman. Bracing himself and watching the faint light beginning to stream through the small windows in the tower, Seraph pulled back the bolt of the tower access door, and loudly swung the door open and pulled himself up into the room.

The two guards standing in the lower part of the tower turned to look at the entering man, and relaxed a little when they saw the lightly polished armor of the soldier who entered. When the new arrival was fully into the room they each snapped a quick salute to the superior officer and waited for him to speak.

"At ease, men," Seraph said in his practiced military voice. The helm would hide most of his appearance, and most were not accustomed to seeing him with a full beard. Though facial hair was frowned upon in the Imperial Legion at low rank, the higher one ascended, the more was overlooked. The two soldiers relaxed and one smiled.

"Morning, sirah," the younger of the two men said, his voice obviously accented with Rashaleb drawl, "password?"

Seraph coughed.

"Fleeting," he said without pause. "Rather interesting word for the morning. Though it is better than last night's"

The older man laughed and clapped Seraph on the shoulder.

"That it is my friend. Don't think I've seen you before? You get called back for the wedding?"

Seraph sighed and nodded.

"Was out with the magistrates rounding up the last of those bandits who were harassing the shipments from Lordhill. We got back in just last night, and of course we don't have any time to sleep before we have to be on duty this morning. Most of my squad is in the west tower, but they called me over here because I'm the most experienced spotter of the group."

Seraph had heard enough rumors and gossip during his travels to create a plausible enough story to fool those he would come in contact with. Traveling with a magistrate meant that he would not be in command, and so his name would not be important, and with all the bandit activity, there were too many groups of legionnaires traveling with magistrates to be able to pin him down to one company.

"Guess I better get to it," Seraph said quickly. "It's almost dawn."

Both men nodded, and Seraph pulled the latch back on the upper hatch and then slid through the thin opening into the high tower. Neither man responded to his appearance, and when Seraph moved up to the man who was manning the position that looked down over the courtyard, only then did his appearance elicit a reaction.

"You're gonna have the best seat in the house," the young sergeant said softly. "I'm going to be stuck on the parapet making sure that there are no riots."

Seraph chuckled.

"At least you won't have to worry about keeping yourself awake."

It was a common joke among spotters. The sergeant pulled himself from his vantage point, nodded softly to Seraph and moved toward the portal.

"I stand relieved," he said in a practiced military tone.

"You are relived sir," Seraph echoed. "I have the post."

The sergeant snapped a quick salute, and within a moment was gone. Several minutes later the morning crew would arrive in the tower, another spotter and another signalman. While the replacement spotter was a bit surprised to see Seraph, there was little protestation. It was assumed by all that the increased scrutiny caused by the Imperial Wedding would result in some redundancy in positioning. Seraph would now bide his time. The signalmen would only check in if there were a problem, and the spotters would not be required to take any action at all unless there was a threat. He was now in a perfect position. There would be no shift change or check-in until after the wedding was complete. Once again, Seraph chanted silently to himself, letting the bubble of silence extend slowly until it enveloped the entire upper tower. Moving quickly before the signalman could act, Patience's blade found the tender flesh of the signalman's throat, followed quickly by that of the spotter. Seraph did not relish killing both of the innocent men, but it was a small price to pay for what had to be done. However, as he quickly moved to keep the blood of the men from dripping to the floor below, Seraph felt a pang of guilt fill his heart. He had just committed cold-blooded murder. He was now a criminal in the worst sense of the word. There was no war or duty that shielded him from the responsibility of his actions. There was only the act. A wave of sadness and revulsion passed through Seraph before he shut it away quickly and returned to the post that gave him the best view of the courtyard. In just a few minutes the wedding precession would begin, and his target would come into view. What happened after that would not matter much, because Seraph knew he wouldn't live long after. Everything that he had ever loved had been taken from him, so he no longer needed to live. At the very least, Dominique would be free. That was enough. That was the price of love. A price Seraph was more than willing to pay.

* * * * * * * * * * * *

Dominique Arais stood in her private chambers and slowly wiped two tears from her eyes. This was supposed to be the happiest day of her life, however, the man that she wanted to marry was not the man she was set to wed. Seraph was long gone from her now, and her fate was sealed. She was to be the Empress of Cadaria, the most powerful woman in the whole of the Empire, and she could not help but feel sorrow because of it. In her few months in the palace, she had begun to see the politics of the Empire, as well as the politics of the Imperial Palace. They were not one and the same; in fact they were far from it.

Kaitain was a man of passion to be sure, but his passions and rages seemed to move from one subject to the next without any seeming pattern. The only constant was his obsession with the Knights of the Flashing Blade and that of an item called the Dragon's Tear. Dominique had only been able to get minor pieces of information out of Kaitain in the dead of the night when he was either half-asleep or utterly drunk. Kaitain's abuse of the drink had deepened in the days leading up to the wedding, and was threatening to grow out of his control. Because he was the Emperor, no one dared to caution him as to the amount of alcohol he was consuming, and everyone made as many allowances as they could. To that end, Kaitain's impulses also raged out of control. His sexual cravings were deviant at the least, and pathological at the worst. None of the ladies-in-waiting or servants of the Imperial Palace were safe from his desires, and more often than not, his bed was filled with someone other than his wife-to-be or his mistress the Imperial Sorceress. Dominique took some solace in that, knowing how violent he was becoming in his lovemaking. It was becoming less lovemaking and more rape as his anger deepened with the Flashing Blade and the poor progress against the dragons and the Dark Gods of Mythryn. He was clearly distracted and disturbed, and the vacant cold expression in his eyes often brought a terror to Dominique that she had never felt in her life.

While Kaitain had his rages, Marlae Lorien had her diversions. It had become no secret to Dominique that Marlae hated her soon to be step-mother. However, this hatred was petty and merely a footnote compared to her hatred of Irene Drage. Marlae resented Dominique because of her beauty and her new position, nothing more. The Celestial Princess as she had begun calling herself desired nothing more than to be the center of everyone's attention, and she fancied herself the uncrowned ruler of the Empire. However, Marlae felt that Irene Drage was encroaching on that title. Irene had begun to consolidate her power, that much was sure, and with equal power to that of Marlae as the Voice of the Emperor, the divide widened between the two women. Dominique wondered if Marlae would be an ally against Irene, or if she would be better served to let the princess fight the war herself and then simply deal with the victor. However, Dominique did not believe that even with all of her methods and tools at her disposal that Marlae would be a match for Irene Drage.

Irene was an enigma to be sure. One minute the woman was cold and calculating and the next she would be warm and inviting. She knew where the power in the Empire was and how to seize control of it, but at times she would stand back and let Kaitain make the moves. It was a brilliant strategy most of the time. Kaitain's rages would ruffle feathers, and Irene would swoop in to calmly sooth them. She was becoming more popular with the nobles of the different kingdoms, but Dominique knew that Irene's true enemies were in Jelan. That would be a rift that would have to be exploited if Irene was going to be removed from power.

Sighing to herself again, Dominique watched as her ladies-in-waiting entered the room and began the process of dressing her for her wedding. She had already been up for several hours, bathing and being primped and polished. Chelsea and Quyhn had been at her side almost immediately helping to add some sanity to the mass of insanity that seemed to be descending upon her. The three women had spoken often over the last few days, talking of changes that needed to be made, and if Kaitain could be brought back to his senses. The consensus had been the same. Irene Drage would have to be dealt with. One way or another...

Finally the dressing was finished, and Dominique took a long moment to look at herself in the mirror. The white dress clung to her lithe frame tightly, showing off every curve and feature, and the veil covered her face slightly, her features still visible. Her long blond hair hung gently to one side, light and brilliant in the morning sunlight. The dress had been altered slightly so that more of her long legs would show, and the seamstress had been nearly shocked when the slit was increased even more to show the frilly garter that circled her left thigh. It would be enough to drive Marlae insane, Dominique thought as she looked at herself in the mirror, and would leave an impression for years to come on the assembled guests. When Dominique turned to face Chelsea and Quyhn, both in their brides'-

maids' gowns of pale blue, she smiled lightly. Dominique was determined to make this a day that no one would ever forget, and she vowed to herself to make the best of her new station in life. Taking a deep breath, she led her two closest friends in the world out the door and toward her destiny.

* * * * * * * * * * * *

Irene Drage stood in her private chambers looking out at the growing crowd in the courtyard. This was the day that she had been waiting for. Once the Emperor was married and utterly distracted by his new wife and his wars against the Flashing Blade, dragons, and Dark Gods, Irene would be left in total control of the Empire. When she turned to the mirror, her face was not what greeted her. In the mirror stood a form that was as familiar as her own, but terribly beautiful and corrupt at the same time. Dark brown hair hung from her head, framing her cold pale features, her bright green eyes flashing a cold furious fire. Her black lips were pursed into a cruel smile.

"It's almost time, Irene. Almost time to take our rightful place. This man will serve his purpose for just a few more days, and then, it will all be ours."

Irene smiled at the voice she had known as the thoughts in her mind for so long. It was this strength that had led her to her mastery of magic, this strength that had made her the Imperial Sorceress.

"Once all is said and done my dear, the Dark Gods will tremble before us, and they will have to bow to their new master. I will make them pay for what they did to me, and you will make the Academy of Arcane Arts pay for what they did to you."

Irene smiled and laughed along with the form in the mirror before pulling her cloak around her and leaving her room for the courtyard.

* * * * * * * * * * * *

"Citizens of Cadaria," the priest from the Temple of the Creator said loudly, causing a hush to fall over the hundreds of people who had been lucky enough to gain admittance to the Imperial Gardens where the wedding was to take place. "We are gathered here today to witness the joining of the Just Emperor Kaitain Lorien with the Beauty of Aldere, Dominique Arais."

There was a small cheer from the crowd that lasted several moments before the priest raised his hands again and the crowd fell to a quick hush of anticipation.

"Here in the sight of the Creator, it is my honor to join these two in the bonds of marriage, and to give them the Creator's blessing to lead us into the New Year stronger than we were before. In the face of the war with the dragons of Espre, and the constant looming threat of the Dark Gods and their foul spawn, the strength of Cadaria stands before us now, and with the Emperor of Cadaria supported by his lovely Empress and family, there is nothing that can defeat the Just Emperor's Might."

A cheer went up from the crowd the next moment. Kaitain raised his hands in triumph and turned to look at his bride. Dominique was beautiful, perhaps more beautiful than he had ever seen her before. He could feel Marlae's stare piercing through her soon-to-be step-mother, and inwardly he stifled a smile. Dominique would be good for Marlae, a distraction of the highest order. Looking out at the assembled crowd, Kaitain felt the pangs of anger grow inside him. Most of the Knights of the Flashing Blade were missing. Only Chelsea Zarova, Jaccob Aldora, Orren Eldrath, and Vallic Ultiv had arrived in time for the wedding. Bernhardt was well on his way to Jelan now with a full detachment of the Imperial Legions in tow. Devlin Rannoch, Gregor Quicksilver, Leonora Wastri, and Hannah Ironheart were fugitives from justice. Natalia Pressen was on her way to Mythryn. Tolon Morr, Xaran Firesoul, and Seraph Kore's whereabouts were unknown. Only four of the Knights of the Flashing Blade, the Emperor's sworn defenders were present, a fact that would not escape the nobles and other important guests for long. Of course, Irene had been quick to explain away most of the absences, but the escapes of Gregor and Leonora were a huge blight that hung on Kaitain's heart and mind. They would prove to be problems in the long run, problems that would have to find a quick resolution.

The priest's words rose above the din once more, this time, he reached out and took hold of both Kaitain and Dominique's hands and pulled them together.

"The Love of the Creator is absolute, and while the love between a man and a woman cannot hope to match that of the Creator, when it binds two hearts and souls together on this world, it is the most pure and powerful that we as humans can ever hope to achieve. The Just Emperor has felt this love before only to have it taken from him by the Crawling Plague. Now, the love of this beautiful woman, Dominique Arais will try to soothe that wound and bring wholeness back to the heart and soul of our beloved Emperor. May they rule together for a hundred years, and may happiness and love fill the halls of the Imperial Palace, along with the laughter and footsteps of their progeny."

Another raucous applause rose from the crowd. The priest raised Kaitain and Dominique's hands and turned them both to face the assembled crowd.

"From this day forth, let Dominique Arais be known as Dominique Lorien, Empress of Cadaria, and heir to the Throne. She is and shall ever be the beauty of Aldere, the wife of the Just Emperor Kaitain Lorien, the savior of Cadaria."

As the crowd cheered, an arrow appeared from the nothingness and slammed into Kaitain's chest, sending a plume of blood spattering into the air. The cheer was instantly pierced by screams of shock and horror, some people frozen while others scattered, angry shouts from men and soldiers alike filling the air. Dominique knelt beside Kaitain, blood trickling from the corners of his mouth as he coughed, pain etched on every feature of his face. Irene Drage and the members of the Flashing Blade would circle the fallen emperor a moment later, protecting him from the invisible threat. Dominique could not take her eyes off of her husband. She could see the light fading from his eyes, and as she looked up and found Marlae looking down at her father, she thought for a moment she saw a wicked smile come to her face.

* * * * * * * * * * * *

Seraph Kore cursed. The bow fell from his grip and the arrow that had been nocked and ready to leap toward the Emperor's vulnerable chest clattered harmlessly to the ground. He had been betrayed…. robbed of the kill that had been rightfully his. Now there would be no other choice. He would have to make sure the Emperor had met his end.

Chapter LII

Into the Spotlight

Year Three of the Just Emperor Kaitain "Dragonsbane" Lorien, Creator's Calendar Year 1870

Vallic Ultiv knelt beside the bed of Emperor Kaitain Lorien looking down at the gaping wound in his chest. Luckily for the young man, the arrow had missed his heart by a fraction of an inch; otherwise there would be no amount of power that would have pulled the Emperor back from the brink of death. Concentrating, Vallic could feel the dark evil power rolling from the wound. There was poison on the tip of the arrow, that much was certain, and it was an organic poison the likes of which Vallic had never seen. But with some effort, and with the assistance of Orren Eldrath, the poison had been removed and the wound in the young man's chest would begin to knit. However, there was no telling if there would be any lasting effects from the poison. For all Vallic knew, Kaitain would die anyway in a matter of days.

It took some effort for the Imperial Guard to keep back the throngs of people who were trying to get to the Emperor and Empress. Some were well-wishers who were trying to check on their fallen leader. However, there were just as many others who were most likely trying to make sure that the young man was dead. After Vallic had ensured that moving Kaitain would not cause further damage, the members of the Flashing Blade lifted the Emperor carefully and moved him slowly through the courtyard back to his private chambers in the Imperial Palace. Kaitain was in an immense amount of pain to be sure, and Vallic silently cursed to himself that Hannah Ironheart was not there. Very few members of the Flashing Blade were adept at healing the injuries of others, and Hannah was a master. Vallic did have some skill, but it was limited and crude. However, he did what he could to make sure that his Emperor was comfortable.

To her credit, the newly-minted Empress Dominique Lorien never left her husband's side, and she continued to nurse him through the night and into the next morning. Kaitain's night was filled with agonized moans and brief moments of delirium-filled consciousness. Through the night, Marlae Lorien, the Celestial Princess took much of the duties of the court on her shoulders, but much of her time was spent in battles of will with the Ethereal Sorceress Irene Drage. They each seemed to have a different notion on how to find and punish the would-be assassin. However, though the Imperial Legion had scoured the whole of the capitol city of Aldere, nothing was found to indicate who had been the one who fired the nearly lethal shot. Several guards were found murdered in both the north and east towers of the palace, but other than that, there were no signs of escape. The assassin could have been anyone, and the person now could have been anywhere.

When morning finally dawned, Dominique Lorien emerged from the chambers of her husband the Emperor and she made the long slow walk to the audience chamber where the captains of the Imperial Legion as well as the still-loyal members of the Flashing Blade waited. This was to be her first audience as the Empress, and a feeling of dread filled her as she ascended the dais and looked down over the assemblage. Only a few hours before, all of the people in the audience chamber had been above her in status, and now she had the power to end their lives with but a single word. But that was not her way, nor would it ever be. While Marlae Lorien chose to lord her power over those around her and constantly display herself as their betters, Dominique chose to rule from a position of quiet strength rather than with an iron fist. Looking down on the group, Dominique met Chelsea's eyes. It didn't take much for Dominique to know what the older woman was thinking, and the horror and fear of the thoughts had filled Dominique since the attack. Seraph could have been the assassin that much was clear. The shot was well within his ability to make, and with his experience and familiarity with the Imperial Palace of Aldere, it would not have been difficult for him to gain admittance to the palace or to one of the towers. There was no doubt that the shot had come from either the north or the east tower, but at this point, no one could say which. Not a single member of the mass that had gathered for the wedding had seen the arrow until it was too late, and neither of the spotters from the western or southern towers had spotted anything out of the ordinary. Finally, Dominique suppressed the uncertainty and fear in her heart and let her voice catch the still air in the audience chamber.

"Emperor Kaitain Lorien has been gravely injured, and though the efforts of Vallic Ultiv and the healers here in the Imperial Palace were prompt and effective, it seems that our beloved Emperor is not out of danger yet. From what I have been told, there was an exotic poison of some type coating the tip of the arrow, and that poison has begun to attack the mind and the body of the Emperor. It is unclear as to whether it will drive him to madness or death first, but the healers as well as myself will continue to tend to him in the days ahead."

There was a wave of shock and awe that resounded through the assemblage. These people that stood before Dominique were soldiers, life-long and hardened. However, in these times, they would have turned to the Emperor for strength and comfort. Never in the history of Cadaria had the Emperor suffered an infirmity of any kind. Even up to the end of his life, Ender Lorien, though his body was ravaged by the Crawling Plague, ruled with determination and wisdom. Now Kaitain Lorien lay in his bed, unable to lend his voice or wisdom to the battles which raged throughout Cadaria.

"Have no fear," Dominique said firmly, her voice suppressing all of the fear and uncertainty that filled her, "the Emperor no longer walks alone through these halls of power. With the help of the Voice of the Emperor, my daughter, the Celestial Princess Marlae Lorien, and the wisdom of the Ethereal Sorceress Irene Drage, as well as the council of the members of the Knights of the Flashing Blade, I shall lead the Cadarian Empire until such time as my husband the Just Emperor Kaitain Lorien recovers from this cowardly attempt on his life."

The captains of the Imperial Legion sent up a cheer, and the tension was broken. Smiles came to the faces of most of the soldiers, and the feeling of pride began to swell in them. However, the tempered reaction of the Knights of the Flashing Blade went unnoticed to everyone but Dominique.

"However, it is clear that whoever launched this attack upon the Emperor will not be content with his failure. There is no doubt in my mind that whoever is behind this will strike again, and may not be content with merely eliminating the Emperor, but will undoubtedly now expand his package of targets to include myself as well as Marlae and Irene. To that end, I have no choice but to levy the following decrees."

Dominique braced herself. The next words she spoke would make her an enemy of many, and would further exacerbate the situation throughout most of the Empire. However, in the days ahead, there would be no choice.

"Through their actions, Leonora Wastri and Gregor Quicksilver have shown themselves to be traitors to the Throne. As Leonora Wastri has already been stripped of her title, so too must Gregor Quicksilver be relieved of his position as the Ruby Knight. Also, through his actions, the Onyx Knight, Devlin Rannoch has also made himself an enemy of the Empire. A standing order to arrest these three criminals is now decreed. They are to be brought to justice by any means necessary, even if it means their deaths."

Dominique found her eyes going back to Chelsea's. There was sadness there, but it was balanced with an acceptance of the inevitable. Leonora was set to be executed and she escaped the Imperial Dungeon along with Gregor with the assistance of Devlin Rannoch. The transgression could not pass without retaliation. Dominique's hands were bound. If she did not take an action in the name of the Emperor, she would inevitably look weak when Marlae or Irene were forced to take the same action. The only way to stake her claim to the power of the absent Emperor was to deal with the difficult problems in a quick and concise manner.

"The Imperial Legions will continue to assist the regional armies in their battles with the Dragons of Espre, however, no longer will the Imperial Palace be without a full complement of soldiers to protect all manners of entrance and exit. There shall from this moment forward be roving patrols at all hours, and the captains of the Imperial Guard shall be held responsible for any failings of those under their command. The Emperor was wounded during his wedding while the majority of the Imperial Guard stood watching. The fact that you are retaining your positions as well as your lives should impress upon you the severity of any failure after this day."

All of the members of the Imperial Guard in the room snapped to attention and then saluted their leader. Dominique in a few quick words had captured command of the most imposing military unit in the whole of Cadaria, and Chelsea found herself suppressing a smile. There was far more to this woman than anyone could have guessed, and while Chelsea knew that she was a rage of emotions on the inside, the calm and powerful outer demeanor was impressive to say the least.

"Finally, each of the remaining members of the Knights of the Flashing Blade will receive new orders following this audience. You shall report to my chambers in one hour to receive these orders. However, this one I shall make known now. Lady Chelsea Zarova, Garnet Knight of the Kingdom of Fire, Saldarine, from this day forth, you shall be the personal guard of the Empress of Cadaria, charged with protecting me from all harm both within and outside the borders of Cadaria. Do you accept this charge, Lady Zarova?"

Chelsea took a single long stride forward and then went to one knee with her head bowed. After a moment, her head rose, a smile on her face before she spoke.

"I shall protect you with my life, my Empress, as I know the rest of the Knights of the Flashing Blade shall."

Without prompting, the other assembled members of the Flashing Blade fell to one knee the next moment and let their voices hit the air the next moment.

"So say we all."

Chelsea rose, and let her voice ring out again.

"Long live the Empress!"

The other Knights of the Flashing Blade rose, and let their voices join with those of the Imperial Guard.

"Long Live Empress Lorien!"

Dominique folded her hands before her and then sat slowly onto the Throne of Cadaria. It was a simple gesture that spoke louder than any words could have.

* * * * * * * * * * * *

Marlae Lorien sat on the edge of her bed as Rhain Feirbran brushed her hair slowly. Despite herself Marlae found herself smiling. She looked across the room where Gabriel Shadowfall stood stoic, his eyes constantly scanning the windows and the door of the room to ensure that no invisible assassins could take advantage of the chaos and attack his charge. Gabriel was very adept at his duties, nearly as adept at ignoring the two nude women in the room. Though Marlae would have normally taken the opportunity to tease Gabriel with their blatant sexuality, this was neither the time nor the place. Her sainted father lay dying on the other side of palace. Though the practiced exterior of the caring daughter was able to squeeze out a few tears of sorrow, inwardly the smile deepened. Already word of the chaos in Albitonin was beginning to reach her ears, and before the end of the day, the Empire would have to deal with Hannah Ironheart and the rebellion that she was brewing in the Kingdom of Stone. Marlae had no doubt that within a few days, Gregor Ironheart, Leonora Wastri, and Devlin Rannoch would join this little rebellion and it would begin to gain momentum, if Hannah could keep the unrest alive through the news of the assassination attempt. It was a precarious time for Cadaria, and Marlae was confident that she could turn all of this uncertainty to her advantage.

"A very interesting morning, my Celestial Princess," Rhain said giggling like a little girl.

Marlae felt her smile widen.

"A perfect morning," Marlae hazarded.

From all the years that they had been together, Marlae knew that Gabriel would never breathe a word of the thoughts that Marlae expressed. And in the days to come, that discretion would be tested more and more.

"Now that my new mother is taking a more active role in the Empire and being seduced by the trappings of power, she will have no choice but to continue the agenda that my father began. At the same time, she will have to try and wrest the power away from that bitch Irene and that should allow me to act with impunity. If the rebellion in Albitonin begins to spread, I will be able to slip away from the palace and set up a new government of my own there. Then Cadaria will be mine."

Marlae smiled all the more when a knock came on the door. With practiced speed and efficiency, Gabriel moved to the door with weapon drawn and opened it enough that he could see into the hallway. The point of his sword was at the lower opening of the door and could have been plunged forward in an instant if there was a threat. Though his own life may have been forfeit in the process, at least his last breath could have been used in protecting his charge. However, there was no threat on the other side of the door, just a young page delivering a message. When Gabriel closed the door he held the message in his hand and looked down at it puzzled.

"Well Gabriel," Marlae said impatiently, "bring it here. I am sure it is some important business from the Empress."

Gabriel stood silent for a moment, his eyes still locked on the parchment in his hand.

"Gabriel!"

The Princess' shrill voice broke Gabriel from his disbelief and quickly he looked up and carried the parchment over to Marlae. Without a word, she snatched it from his grasp and looked at her guard with disdain. It was very unlike him to be so impudent. She would have to remember to punish him for that later. After a moment of glaring, Marlae looked down at the parchment and quickly read the words. She would read them several more times before their meaning would pierce the disbelief. Rhain sat patiently behind Marlae waiting for the words to be spoken.

"So," Rhain said finally, "what is it? Some idiotic decree from the Empress?"

Marlae didn't react to the jibe.

"It's a summons," Marlae said finally.

"A summons?" Rhain asked.

Marlae stood and took a step toward Gabriel.

"From the Empress of Cadaria. Gabriel Shadowfall is called to appear before the Empress to receive a commendation for his years of service to the Throne as the personal protector of the Celestial Princess Marlae Lorien as well as to receive his new appointment to position of Ruby Knight of the Kingdom of Blood, Zevarit, member of the Knights of the Flashing Blade, and wielder of the sacred weapon Valor."

When Marlae and Gabriel's eyes met, a lifetime of words could not have expressed what passed the moment before Gabriel turned to leave. Perhaps for the last time.

* * * * * * * * * * * *

Irene Drage stood in her private chambers fuming. The attack on the Emperor was intolerable, but now the fact that this woman, this pretender was trying to take everything that Irene had worked so hard to cultivate was maddening. Irene had the power at her disposal to crush the life out of Dominique with a thought, as well as the rest of the members of the Knights of the Flashing Blade. Then nothing would stand in her way. The Empire would be hers once the little wretch Marlae was eliminated. Of course there were other members of the Lorien family, but there were already plans in the works to make sure that they would disappear. Emperor Kaitain Lorien did not suffer fools lightly, and he had no tolerance left for his younger brother or niece. Geoffry Aramour had been given the assignment the night before the wedding, and Geoffry assured Kaitain that it would look like an accident. Now, the timing would be even more perfect. It could look like an assassination attempt against the whole Imperial Family, and would stir up more paranoia and chaos. Suddenly

Irene felt a presence all around her. It was powerful to be sure, and then suddenly the presence became more palpable. She was no longer alone.

Spinning around, Irene found herself face to face with a very young woman whose face was familiar but one that Irene could not place. She was slightly shorter than Irene, with bright blond hair that was pulled back behind her ears and hung down to just above the tops of her shoulders. Her bright blue eyes shown out, but there was no sparkle of life in them, they were cold and distant. The young woman's skin was very pale, nearly lily white, what flesh could be seen outside of her thick armor. The plates of the armor were made from what looked like skin and bone, and though horrific, seemed to fit this woman like a second skin. Irene felt a cold shudder pierce her as the two women's eyes met. However, Irene was confused when the young blond woman smiled.

"I see you are already plotting to finish what we have begun."

The young woman's voice was willowy and light, but there was an underlying power, a demand of respect for her words.

"Who are you? How did you get in here?"

The young woman stood proudly for a moment and then put one hand upon her hip before answering.

"Oh yes, I do forget," the young woman said slowly, "you don't have access to all of the information as you should yet. But all in due time I suppose. I am the Fallen Angel Seraphina Masile. Daughter of the Forgotten Dark Goddess Talisia Masile, the leader of the Hand of Chaos. I do believe you have had some dealings with some of our agents in the past, most notably Torda Safrick, our Master of Secrets."

Irene's eyes went wide at the realization. She had accepted the help of Torda and others ever since her ascendance to Imperial Sorceress without question. It was almost as though she knew these people and inherently trusted them. Perhaps this Seraphina would hold the keys as to why.

"So, this Hand of Chaos, you are a part of it?"

Seraphina smiled.

"In the absence of my mother, I am in command of the Hand of Chaos. We have thus far been operating in the shadows, and for a time we shall continue to do so, at least until others have had their way with Cadaria."

Irene was puzzled.

"What do you mean?"

Seraphina smiled and eased herself into a chair near one of the wide bay windows on the east side of the room.

"Did you like our little demonstration New Year's morning?"

Irene's eyes went wide again, and then suddenly she let the arcane power fill her to the brim. This woman sitting before her had been at the heart of the assassination attempt on the Emperor. However, when Irene tried to lash out, she found herself restrained. She could not strike this Seraphina down, no matter how she tried. It filled her with confusion and dread, but there would be no choice but to listen to the words of the self-titled Dark Angel.

"Yes, the Hand of Chaos was responsible for the assassination attempt on Kaitain Lorien. But believe me, Irene, if we had wanted him dead, he would not have made it out of the courtyard alive. For now, Lexa has accomplished her task and struck a blow that will keep Kaitain out of the equation as long as we wish."

After a moment to reflect, Irene sat on the edge of her bed staring out the window. None of this made sense. Why did the Hand of Chaos want the Emperor out of the way when they could have easily just killed him? Who were these members of the Hand of Chaos, and who was this Dark Goddess that they supposedly served? Was this Talisia Masile really a Dark Goddess the same as those who fell from the Heavens? Or was she simply a powerful witch masquerading as a goddess to ensure the devotion of her followers?

"Why?"

It seemed the only logical question, and it also seemed to be the only relevant question to ask. There was so much that Irene wanted to know, but for now, sticking to the relevant points would be the only way to find out anything at all.

"That is the simplest of all to answer my dear Irene," Seraphina said smiling, "Kaitain is consolidating power and would prove a very formidable enemy for our friend Dorovar. We can't have that. We need Cadaria fractured, distracted, in chaos so that Dorovar's servants can do their horrible deeds and cause more fear and panic. Eventually the Knights of the Flashing Blade will defeat the last of Dorovar's servants, but it will be too late to prevent Dorovar's escape from his prison. When that occurs, the Dark Gods of Mythryn will have no choice but to come to the aid of Cadaria and fight as best they can to defeat Dorovar. They will eventually succeed I am sure, but not before my mother, Talisia Masile has her revenge upon her siblings. Then, Kaitain will become a valuable tool that she will use to crush all of the Dark Gods, and then she will lay claim to this world with only her faithful at her side."

The simplicity of the plan was striking. Without the Emperor to steel the wills of those in the Empire, there would be unrest and chaos. Regional governors would take command of their armies and be caught fighting their own battles against the dragons until there was nothing left of the Cadarian Empire but a fractured countryside. Finally, when the servants of Dorovar, the others like the Gray Man and the woman Famine, arrived in Cadaria, they would kill and destroy until this Dorovar was released. There would be nothing left for Cadaria to defend itself with, and the Dark Gods would have no choice but to leave the protection of their citadel and join the fight. Once they were exposed, away from their precious Mythryn, they would be vulnerable.

"And where is your mother, how will we be able to find her when it is time?"

Seraphina stood and motioned for Irene to join her. After a moment, Irene stood with Seraphina before the mirror and looked in horror as the alien face and body looked back at her again. However, the horror was instantly quenched when Seraphina put her hand on Irene's shoulder.

"She is already here, my dear little sorceress. And you have her to thank for everything you have ever achieved in your miserable little life. You are ours now Ethereal Sorceress. Welcome to the Hand of Chaos."

Trumpets Sounding

Year Three of the Just Emperor Kaitain "Dragonsbane" Lorien, Creator's Calendar Year 1870

Sitting in her personal chambers above the Heart of Stone, Hannah Ironheart read over the scrolls containing the news from the far corners of Albitonin. It had only been three weeks since the assassination attempt on the Emperor at his wedding, and the Empire seemed to be threatening to tear itself apart. So much had happened in such a short amount of time, Hannah was still trying to process it all in her mind. Full-scale riots had ripped through the entire kingdom of Albitonin, and it had taken the full efforts of not only the Army of Stone, but also as many volunteers as could be mustered to bring everyone back to order. But, all of the work had been worth the time. Albitonin was united again under a single banner, and under a single leader. Of course there would be a few pockets of dissent here and there, but they would be handled easily by the faithful. Much of the clamoring had died down when Gregor and Leonora had made their way to the Heart of Stone to lend their support to Hannah. Devlin too had been a welcome sight. With four members of the Knights of the Flashing Blade leading the charge for change, there was a veil of legitimacy to the movement. More importantly, there was hope that the voices of change would actually be heard with the four champions at their head.

Hannah put the scrolls to the side and her mind began to wander. There was so much going on in Albitonin, it was enough to keep her distracted and away from the thoughts of her niece and the woman named Camille. The dark goddess that should have died, but somehow still lived. Neither Tess nor Camille seemed willing to talk about what transpired after her fall from the top of the Heart of Stone, but it seemed that both women were somehow changed by the events of that fateful morning. Camille seemed more pensive and somehow diminished. She had rarely spoken before the confrontation with the creature calling itself Death, now she spoke to no one other than Tess. Tess seemed to have developed a stronger will. There was a distance, a coldness that had enveloped her, and the young woman's poise was that of a woman much older. A new weight had fallen on her shoulders, one that Hannah didn't think she would ever come to understand. However, her niece was safe and seemed to be content with helping the rebellion take shape.

Death was another issue in and of itself. The creature had not been content losing the Heart of Stone to Camille. Its rage had been felt in the countryside of Albitonin, and would eventually spread to the neighboring kingdoms. The death toll was already in the hundreds, and it would be in the thousands before the month ended. There seemed to be no stopping Death from his appointed rounds, and inwardly Hannah prayed for another miracle. However, in her heart, she did not feel that one was forthcoming. Finally, a knock at the door saved Hannah from her reverie.

"Enter."

Hannah's voice sounded sterner to her than she intended, but the weight was starting to take its toll. While she was comfortable leading a flock of the faithful to the word of the Creator, she did not know if she was capable to lead men and women in a war against the very Empire that she once served. To take arms against the Imperial Guard was nearly a suicidal undertaking, but one that seemed more and more necessary as the days passed. Two years under Kaitain Lorien had brought nothing but pain, misery, and death. The reign of terror had to be stopped, no matter the cost.

When the door finally opened, Hannah was relieved to see the face of her husband. Gregor looked much older, and it seemed that he too had gone through a great deal at the behest of the Emperor. Though Hannah and Gregor had not spoken about the events of his mission to the Dark Continent, Hannah knew that what he had found there was not nearly what he had expected. Few in the world could read the man known far and wide as the Ruby Knight, but for Hannah, it was as easy as looking up and seeing the light of the suns.

"Are you ready, Hannah?"

Gregor's voice was calm and his tone measured. For two days they had been debating who was to announce the intention to take control of the Empire, and Hannah had continued to insist that Gregor be the one. However, Gregor's point was a valid one. He had been stripped of his position, disgraced, not by the Emperor that they were seeking to unseat, but by the new Empress, a woman who by all rights had been thrust into a situation beyond her control. She was not some reckless youth driven by guilt and rage. She was, as far as anyone could determine, a woman of high moral character who was doing her best to hold a fractured Empire together through sheer will and determination alone. And to her credit, she seemed to be succeeding. Most of the kingdoms that had been hit hardest by the dragon attacks and the ravages of the Crawling Plague and the Wasting Disease seemed to flock quickly and easily to Dominique Lorien's soft touch. Already Rashaleb, Pellatori, Celidar, Saldarine, Hedorah, and Bellnoc had voiced their open support for the Emperor and Empress. They would not be swayed easily. As was its custom, Iltorp gave its support to the recognized ruler of Cadaria, but they could be swayed if Vallic Ultiv was brought into the rebel camp. Menoris was strangely silent, largely Hannah had theorized due to the disappearance of the Tiger's Eye Knight, Xaran Firesoul.

Zevarit was a kingdom divided in and of itself. Most of the kingdom still wanted to support Gregor Quicksilver regardless of the crimes he was accused of by the Emperor. However, with the appointing of a new Ruby Knight, a man who seemed to have not only the credentials but also the reputation from his years of service in the Imperial Guard, some elements in Zevarit seemed willing to remain loyal to the Emperor. Gabriel Shadowfall the man as well as the reputation could cause serious problems for any rebellion's start and duration in Zevarit. The Kingdom of Blood divided was no good to anyone, certainly not to Hannah's growing movement.

Oradrim had no such issue however. The Empress had named a new Jade Knight, however, the Kingdom of the Soul had been quick to reject any pretender to the position and had quickly levied their support behind Leonora Wastri and the growing rebellion in Albitonin. The Empress had not been pleased at the news to be sure, but she had yet to send any troops in any case to stop the dissent. Dominique had been very wise thus far in avoiding any open confrontation regardless of the calls from the Imperial Legions and the Ethereal Sorceress to the contrary. It was a race thus far, a race to curry as much favor and breed as much support as possible before any conflicts began. There would be many battles to come, many crossings of swords and many harsh words spoken, however, now was the time to build and prepare. Oradrim was a small kingdom in the scheme of things, but their dedication to the cause would never be questioned.

However, as Hannah thought about the support the cause was getting, she began to feel a sick feeling in the pit of her stomach. So far with the exception of the support of Thorigald, who willingly joined Albitonin under the orders of the rogue knight Seraph Kore, the lines seemed to be drawn across spiritual boundaries. The more spiritual and religious kingdoms, Albitonin, Oradrim, Galateria, flocked to Hannah's banner, while the more militant and practical fell in behind the Emperor. That more than anything concerned Hannah. If the Empress wished, she would be able to characterize the rebellion as a hand-full of religious zealots who wanted nothing more than to turn the Empire into a theocracy with the high-priestess dictating moral law to the people. Skeptics would fall in line quickly, and only the most devout of motivated would not be swayed by the argument.

"To be honest Gregor," Hannah said finally, "I'm scared to death."

Gregor quickly closed the door behind him, walked across the room, and sat lightly on the window sill. After a light scratch of his beard, he sighed and then shook his head.

"Rebellion is a bad business, Hannah, and if there was any other way, I would gladly take it. However, the Dark Gods are not going to tolerate any more of Kaitain's meddling, and believe me, they could level Cadaria before we knew what happened."

Hannah reached down and took hold of Spirit and felt its power rush through her. More and more she was using Spirit as a crutch to steady her nerves through the difficult days, and the dependence was beginning to grate on her. Never before had she doubted her course in life. She was a dedicated servant of the Creator who had never faltered in performing her duties. No, when her direction in life was no longer clear, the steadiness of her convictions brought little comfort. If anything, her beliefs fought against her at every turn. Duty, honor, dedication, all of these betrayed her need for the safety and welfare of those around her. How could she remain loyal to an Emperor who let those under him die by the thousands for no reason? Kaitain seemed to thirst for blood, and war was his preferred method to get it. How long before there were no wars to be fought? How long until he had to find more savage and brutal ways to spark the conflicts that he seemed to thrive on? No, no matter the cost, Kaitain had to be stopped, and Hannah would not be able to live with herself until he was. There would be no peace in her heart, no comfort in her prayers.

"I need to know what happened on Mythryn, Gregor." Hannah said finally. "We've been avoiding it since you got here, and I can't do that any longer. If you are insistent on me being the leader of this rebellion, then I have to know what we are up against."

Gregor sighed.

"I think you should talk to your niece. She would be able to tell you more than I. But what I can tell you is that the Dark Gods are far more powerful than we were ever led to believe. Both Leonora and I have felt the touch of their children, and their power pales in comparison to the real Dark Gods. Even that woman Camille who revived those touched by Death cannot compete with their powers."

"Are you afraid of them, Gregor?"

Gregor looked up at Hannah for a moment and met her eyes. Hannah had expected an instant response of defiance. Gregor was a prideful man, perhaps more than a pious man should have been. He would never let fear stain his honor or show fear in the face of an enemy. But finally Gregor nodded.

"I fear them as I would fear the power of the Creator, Hannah. The Creator's power could unmake us all, and I know this whether or not I have seen it in action. However, I have seen the power of the Dark Gods, up close and personal, and I know they could unmake us."

Gregor stood and took a long step toward the door as Hannah pondered his words. Most devout members of the Church of the Creator would have called Gregor's words blasphemy, but Hannah knew better. Gregor did not speak so lightly, and more than likely would never speak those words again.

"At least for now the Dark Gods are on our side," Hannah said finally, heading for the door.

Gregor stopped short and turned to face Hannah. There was a different look in his eyes now. It wasn't fear, or anger, or even sadness. It was a quiet fire of determination and barely controlled rage.

"Make no mistake Hannah," Gregor said coldly, "the Dark Gods are only on their own side. We may share a common enemy now, but the implication is clear. Once Kaitain has been defeated, if we were to make the same provocative moves against Mythryn, they would not hesitate to destroy us if necessary. They have their own goals and their own motivations, and I can assure you, that nothing will get between them and what they desire."

Gregor's words sent a cold shudder through Hannah, and even though she steeled herself for the task ahead, his words would not leave her mind.

* * * * * * * * * * *

Devlin Rannoch sat alone in one of the many gardens surrounding the Heart of Stone, looking down into a small pond that was fed by a fountain. The great speech that would signal the official rebellion against the Emperor Kaitain Lorien was only a few minutes away, and Devlin could not help but feel that he was in the wrong place at the wrong time.

You just had to go and be the hero didn't you? I have never in all my lives seen anyone as reckless and stupid as you are. Just think, you could be in Aldere right now, and there would be no rebellion. Gregor and Leonora would be dead, and Hannah would be all alone out here. You could have been the one that ended all of this, but no. Now you have to be sitting here in Albitonin waiting for the Imperial Legion to show up and kill all of you for treason. Well, Onyx Knight, or at least former Onyx Knight, you really made a mess out of this didn't you? Shortest reign in the history of the Knights of the Flashing Blade, at least you have that going for you.

"Old man, you are starting to try my patience."

Devlin spoke out loud even though he knew he didn't need to. Over the last few days, the voice in his head was becoming more and more of distraction. It rambled on for hours on end no matter what Devlin tried to do to shut it up. Letting his wings stretch out behind him, Devlin felt the wind crest under his leathery wings, buffeting against his body and making him feel at peace.

"You know he's right, though," a female voice said from behind Devlin.

Devlin didn't have to turn around to know the voice. Though Camille Renar didn't speak often, her voice was not one that Devlin would ever be able to forget. It wasn't often that he got to speak with those who came back from the dead, though he supposed that was standard fare for someone who was supposed to be a goddess.

"So, you can hear him too."

It wasn't a question, more a statement of fact. Ever since Devlin had met Tess Annis and her bodyguard, he had suspected that the private little voice in the back of his mind wasn't so private after all. Tess had heard the voice for sure back in that little cabin on the outskirts of Galateria, and now it was obvious that Camille could hear it too.

"The voice of the Dark Gods and Goddess are never hidden from others who have fallen. Though I find it curious that he only chooses to speak to you and not to the Council."

Devlin kept his back to Camille even as the confusion began to fill his mind. The voice in the back of his head, that had been there since the day he was born was the voice of a Dark God? It was the voice of one who had fallen from grace and been cast out of the Heavens? How was that possible? And now of course that the revelation had been made, the voice was silent.

"At least he decided to shut up…"

Camille walked closer to Devlin, and he could feel one of her hands lightly touch the crest of one of his wings. While normally he would have immediately folded them back and chided her, there was something about her touch and her manner that made his defenses fade. There was no malice in her action, no revulsion or hesitation in her touch. For her, it seemed that there was nothing wrong with his deformity, with his curse. To her, it was as natural as breathing.

"Not as beautiful or as functional as yours I'm afraid," Devlin said smiling.

In an instant her hand left his wing.

"Have you ever tried?"

Devlin laughed and shook his head.

"I didn't get any of the good abilities, I'm afraid. Just the skin and the wings, without the tail, I can't exactly balance in the air like I'm supposed to."

The next thing Devlin heard was the sound of buckles being undone and he could feel the air change around him as the woman's beautiful angelic wings were extended and caught the air. One hard push with her off-hand spun Devlin to face Camille, and he could see the mischievous smile on her face.

"Does it look like I have a tail to you?"

You should know, you've looked enough…

Camille laughed and took Devlin's hands and began to slowly beat her wings against the air. She slowly began to lift off the ground even as Devlin laughed and shook his head.

"It's no good, Camille, I can't do this."

Camille frowned.

"You're either going to do it, or I'm going to tear your arms off."

Camille pulled up hard on both of Devlin's hands and instinctively his wings extended and he flapped them wildly, trying to regain some sense of balance and stability. His movements were wild and erratic, and no matter what he tried, he could not keep up with the graceful woman.

"No," Camille said softly against the rushing wind, "slow and even, Devlin. Let the wind fill your wings and lift you. Don't fight the wind, use it."

Closing his eyes and cursing the woman in his mind, Devlin slowed the flapping of his wings to an even pace, and just as she said, he felt the wind fill the leathery pouch of his wing and as he moved, it lifted him higher into the air. A few more carefully timed beats of his wings, and Devlin was safely aloft in the sky. When he opened his eyes again, he could not find Camille. Panicked, he searched the sky around him, only to see her far below him, looking up smiling. Devlin laughed in spite of himself as the woman slowly climbed to meet him in the skies above Albitonin.

"Not very graceful," Camille said softly, "but it will do."

The two moved together through the skies for the next few minutes, oblivious to the commotion their activities were causing below. Devlin felt good, free. It was the first time he remembered in his life that he actually felt where he belonged. At that moment, soaring through the clouds, he almost felt that his heritage was not as much of a curse as he initially thought. Perhaps there was more to being a half-dragon than living in darkness, hidden away from those who feared him. Together Devlin and Camille navigated the winds around the Heart of Stone. Finally, it was Camille who took hold of Devlin's hand.

"We should be getting back. Hannah will need us on the dais."

Devlin nodded but felt sadness fill him. After being in the air, feeling the wind around him, and tasting the sky on his tongue, he never wanted to return to what he had been. He never wanted to be confined to the ground. He never wanted to be ordinary again.

"Don't worry," Camille said to his unasked question, "we have plenty of time for more lessons."

* * * * * * * * * * * *

"Red."

A flash of golden light, and the carpet below her feet became a bright red color. It clashed with the paint on the walls terribly, not nearly what she had intended. Perhaps something lighter or maybe she should change the color on the walls again.

"Orange."

Another flash of golden light, and the carpet was orange. No, that would not do at all, it did not match and it was ugly to top it all off.

"Oh, just go back to the way you were."

Tess slumped in her chair in the little cabin as the paint on the walls and the carpet beneath her feet disappeared in a flash. She had been at it all morning, and no matter what she did, there was no way to make the house look right. She had been trying to remember what her room looked like back in the Citadel of the Dark Gods in Mythryn, and no matter how she tried, she couldn't get it exactly right. Several hours passed she had given up on getting the bed right. No matter what combination she tried, the mattress never felt right. It was either too firm, or not firm enough, or it was lumpy, or too small. It was maddening that she could never access the right memories to get it to feel right. But that had been the least of her problems.

It seemed that ever since she had brought Camille back from the dead, something inside her was different. There was so much power inside her that she had to hold it back from rushing out of her like a flood. And yet, every time she held it back, she felt as though she lost part of herself. It was almost as if as more power filled her, it needed to make room for itself by removing something from her mind. The most precious of her memories were unaffected, but minute and largely unimportant details were getting lost. It was maddening at times, and freeing at others. In the end though, she supposed it would not really matter.

After a few minutes of pondering, Tess decided to try again, this time she would start with the floor and then the walls. Maybe that would make a difference. The of course she would need to fix the furniture. Just as she was about to make her first alteration, there was a knock at the door.

"Come in please," Tess said softly.

After a moment, the door opened, and the beautiful Leonora Wastri entered the small cabin. Tess smiled widely at her new friend and quickly bounded off her chair and gave the much older woman a long hug.

"Aunt Leonora, so good to see you."

Leonora smiled. While she was not fond of personal contact of any kind, she tolerated it from her newly adopted niece. It was clear that Tess had gone through a traumatic experience with Camille, and she was clinging to everything she could to make things right. And so, when Leonora became Aunt Leonora, the former Jade Knight accepted her new position with pride.

"Sorry I haven't been by to visit, Tess," Leonora said after a moment, "but Hannah has kept me very busy with preparations for today. We've had a lot of information to gather, and I am afraid there will be more busy days ahead."

Tess frowned, and then moved to sit in the big cushioned chair that she had created earlier that morning. Leonora looked at the chair puzzled for a moment.

"Did Hannah bring you that?"

Tess smiled again and bounced in her seat slightly before shaking her head.

"Oh no," she said giggling. "I made it."

Leonora just looked at Tess puzzled.

"Here, I'll make you one, so you can sit down too."

Before Leonora could protest, there was a bright golden flash, and there before Leonora where there had been nothing before, there was a large cushioned chair that matched the one Tess was perched on.

"If you don't like the color," Tess said quickly, "or if you want the cushions softer, it just takes a snap and it'll be exactly how you want it."

Leonora smiled, but did not react. She didn't understand how the young woman was capable of creating anything out of thin air, regardless of her nature as a Dark God. All arcane theory dictated that anything created through arcane means had to be created out of existing elements. There was no true creation magic, a feat reserved only for the Creator. Perhaps the Dark Gods possessed the power of true creation as well.

"I'd love to sit and chat, Tess," Leonora said quickly, "but we must attend the speech with your aunt."

Tess frowned for a moment and then stood. That instant there was another quick flash, and both the chairs disappeared. It was an amazing feat that left Leonora's mind spinning.

"Oh, alright. I guess I'll work on this place later."

* * * * * * * * * * * *

Hannah Ironheart stood on the dais outside the Heart of Stone and looked out at the throngs of people who had gathered for this speech. Many from different kingdoms had gathered to hear the words that would be the true spark of a rebellion against the Just Emperor Kaitain Lorien. There was speculation that Gregor Quicksilver would be the one giving the speech, or at least that he would be taking the lead of the offensive forces. Everyone conceded that there would be a war. Hannah hoped that her words would prove otherwise. Finally, she stepped forward and let her voice hit the air.

"Fellow citizens of Cadaria. For two years now, we have seen the rule of the Just Emperor Kaitain Lorien be anything but just. He has led us into war with the dragons of Espre, and has brought us to the brink of war with the Dark Gods of Mythryn. He has undermined the duly appointed governments of the Thirteen Kingdoms, and he has attempted in every way possible to discredit and destroy the Knights of the Flashing Blade, an order almost as old as the Lorien line. Cadaria was brought from war and turmoil at the dawn of civilization, and under the rule of this deranged boy, we are threatened to return to that chaos."

There were murmurs of agreement through the crowd, and a few shouts of support from the onlookers.

"We do not want open conflict, and we do not want a civil war. Such losses could not be measured in the face of the open war with the dragons. We all want a peaceful solution to these issues. To this end, we demand that Kaitain Lorien step down from his position of Emperor of Cadaria and allow his daughter, Marlae to take the Throne. We are not here to overthrow the Lorien line or upset the balance created nearly two millennia ago. And regardless of the propaganda being spewed from the Ethereal Sorceress Irene Drage, I do not wish to become the Empress, and I do not wish to establish a church-dominated rule for Cadaria. The Throne of Cadaria belongs in the hands of the Lorien line, just not in the hands of Kaitain Lorien. He and his appointed sorceress must be removed from their positions of power where they have brought nothing but destruction and death to Cadaria."

"Long Live Empress Marlae Lorien!" someone shouted from the crowd.

The cry was repeated until dozens shared the call. Hannah felt a great weight lifted from her heart as she listened to the support for her words grow. However, as she looked to the face of her friend and husband, her smile and relief were broken by his deep frown.

Hunters

Year Three of the Just Emperor Kaitain "Dragonsbane" Lorien,
Creator's Calendar Year 1870

Hedorah was supposedly the most civilized and upright of all of the Kingdoms of Cadaria. It boasted one of the largest mercantile districts in the whole of the empire, and it was said that all of the craftsmen, artisans, and artists brought only their best fare to be bought, sold, and traded in Hedorah. During the light of the day, and on the wide well-lit and well-traveled streets, this was certainly true. The open air market was always bustling with activity, and the shops that lined the streets had incredible fare and a wide range of prices. Thus far Hedorah had been spared the worst of all of the calamities of the recent years. The Crawling Plague and the following Wasting Disease had only seen limited cases in the Flying Kingdom, and the dragons had seemed to be almost totally ignoring the kingdom in their campaign against Emperor Kaitain "Dragonsbane" Lorien. While everyone feared the possibility that Hedorah could become another Rashaleb, whose population was wiped out by the creature calling itself Famine, so far the lack of true outbreaks and devastation had created a kind of arrogant pride within most of the citizens of the city.

But that was the public face of Hedorah. The private and darker face of the Flying Kingdom was known to those who skirted the edges of the law, and who needed those things that were frowned upon by the common man. The truth of Hedorah was that anything could be found in the back-streets and alleys of the bustling capital city. From drugs of the highest order, to slaves, weapons, and any other manner of item, all were readily available, if you knew where to look. This shadow economy also fed the prosperity of the kingdom, so the authorities usually found it in their best interest to turn a blind eye to the dealings of these dark merchants. However, this imposed ignorance had created graft and vice even within the Flying Guard, the elite troops and keepers of law and order within the kingdom. Very few were able to proclaim themselves free of the influence of any such illicit activities. The Flying Guard was commonly referred to as the best army money has bought. The perversion of the cliché was never lost on any who lived in Hedorah.

Far away from the bustle of the open air markets was the Strata district which typically housed the vendors for pack animals, horses, hunting dogs and falcons, messenger animals and the like. Nestled at the far end of a dark street was a run-down looking shop with a simple sign hanging outside the door. On the sign was carved the crude representation of an axe. Those in the know knew the man who ran this shop and all of the wondrous things that could be found inside, and those that didn't would never come to this part of Hedorah in the first place.

Jillian Corven opened the door slowly and walked into the shop, pulling back the hood of her cloak and letting her curly red hair shake loose. Blade's shop always had a strange smell to it, but the smell was never consistent enough for her to get used to it. It seemed different every time she walked through the door, but no less strange and unsettling. As Jillian expected, Blade was sitting on a rickety looking old chair in the corner of the room, his feet up on the counter, and his axe in hand, slowly sharpening it with a whetstone. Blade was a short man, standing no more than four and a half feet tall, but he was built like a bull, his shoulders broad and his chest laden with muscle. His long black beard hung to about the middle of his chest, but always looked as though it had been freshly washed. Blade's cold gray eyes were enough to strike fear into anyone, and never had softness about them, even when he laughed.

"Jillian," Blade said in a gruff uncaring tone. "Didn't expect to see you and your crew back for some time. Not many dragons around Hedorah for you to hunt. I should know."

Jillian had first met Blade years ago, purely by accident. She had just embarked on her career as a dragon hunter and she was trying her best to accumulate the tools that she needed to be successful in her hunts. The problem was that most of the tools required were either illegal to purchase for regular citizens, or so rare that finding them was nearly impossible. Jillian had heard a rumor about an eccentric man who sold and bought just about anything so long as it was strange, exotic, and unusual. So, being young and a little naïve, she went about finding this man the very wrong way, she started asking questions. And it nearly got her killed. Talking to the wrong people, in the wrong tavern, on the wrong side of town, Jillian found herself at the mercy of four men that she could never overpower or escape from. Luckily Blade had been there. Had Jillian not been choked into unconsciousness, she would probably have been impressed by the actions that left all four men broken, dismembered, and dead on the floor. Jillian had awoken that night on a cot in one of the basement rooms of Blade's shop, a new dress sitting on the chair beside her. While no one would ever confuse Blade for the sentimental type, he did have a heart and a love of strays.

"We haven't set out again yet. Heard some rumors coming from Aldere after the attempt on Kaitain. Not sure it's safe for independents to be moving around right now."

Blade looked up for a moment from his axe, regarded Jillian, and then focused on the whetstone again.

"Kinda hard to do your job with a price on your head, huh?"

Jillian wasn't sure she heard him right at first, and then slowly the reality of the words set in. It took only a few seconds for that dawning reality to become a blazing fire in her mind. Kaitain had double-crossed her. He had agreed to her terms, and in her arrogance she had actually taken him at his word. She inwardly wondered if he had drafted the order for her capture and execution before she had even left Aldere. Wordlessly, Blade reached to the table beside him, grasped a rolled up piece of parchment and threw it in Jillian's direction. The parchment landed just short, and had started to unroll and Jillian bent to pick it up. As soon as her hand found the top edge, the emblazoned script of the 'Wanted' notice became visible. She read the notice wordlessly:

Due to traitorous acts against the Throne, and for a direct assault against the body of the Emperor of Cadaria, the woman known as the Lady of Cadaria, Jillian Corven, as well as her known associates, Angelina Lynn Sydor, Kiara Aren, and Jacqueline Escandi are to be captured and brought to the Imperial Palace at Aldere. The reward for the capture and delivery of these criminals is set at ten thousand gold a piece for the associates, and twenty-five thousand for Jillian Corven, as well as amnesty for any previous crimes committed against the Throne. Rewards are to be paid for the return of the criminals, dead or alive.

"If I were a greedy man," Blade said finally as Jillian attempted to digest the words, "I would turn you in myself. But, I'm not a greedy man, and I have no use for blood money. But, there are plenty of bounty hunters and real criminals out there that could use the amnesty far more than they can use the money."

In a flash, Jillian understood what Blade was saying. The money meant nothing. Kaitain could have thrown out any total and it would not have garnered any more notice than any of the other wanted notices that circulated. However, this offer of total amnesty, forgiveness for previous crimes, could change the lives of many. Long-term criminals that had death warrants hanging over their head could erase them quickly. Skilled people who had made a mistake that led to their downfall could create a second chance for themselves. Now nearly everyone in the Empire had a reason to be looking for them, and a pretty powerful reason to try to kill them.

"This day just keeps getting better," Jillian said finally.

Blade looked up again, and finally set his axe aside and pulled his feet away from the counter.

"I can hide you and your band here for a couple of days and then try to smuggle you out with one of my outgoing shipments. I have a few crates going out on a ship to Rashaleb in a few days, and the captain and crew are trustworthy. No one will come looking for you in the Kingdom of Ice, at least not for a little while because of the disaster there, so it's probably the best place for you to lay low. Either that, or you can try to make for Lordhill, or Albitonin, or if you're really feeling reckless, you can make for Mythryn. Wherever you decide to try to make it to, the first order of business is to get you out of a kingdom still loyal to Kaitain."

Jillian was about to respond when the door to the shop opened. In her focus on the wanted notice, Jillian had neglected to realize that it had begun raining, and she was immediately assaulted by the sounds of the falling rain, the stench of the wet streets, and the fear that struck to the very core of her as the stranger entered the shop. Was this the way it was going to be from now on? Was she going to be jumping at shadows every time she passed an unfamiliar alley? Would she walk on the other side of the street just to avoid the possibility that she would be noticed and recognized? Jillian tensed but made no move as the new arrival turned and shut the door before stepping fully into the shop. If Blade knew who the new patron was, he gave no outward sign. Finally the man pulled back the hood of his cloak, shook his head slightly and stretched his back and shoulders.

"Can't you find a better place for this dump? It takes forever to get over here, and I hate the idea that I have to fend off so many robbers every day."

"You would think that the robbers would know by now that you have nothing worth taking," Blade countered.

The man snorted in reply. Finally he turned and faced Jillian and gave her a wry, almost playful smile. He was well-built and handsome, a slight start of a beard on his face, and wild black hair that seemed to have a mind of its own while not looking completely unkempt. His blue eyes were clear and had power and gravity to them and from the way he held himself, he could have been someone very important, though his common dress clashed with that assertion.

"Unsavory company you're keeping, Blade," the man said turning back to face the much shorter Blade.

"No one said being your friend is easy, Dane."

Dane chuckled and removed his cloak. Jillian saw that the man wore much simpler clothing that she had initially expected, and with the exception of the silver chain around his neck upon which hung the symbol of a sunburst with an inlaid bird, its wings outstretch, the man's appearance was that of a beggar. The man that Blade had called Dane turned fully to face Jillian and extended his hand.

"It's a pleasure to make the acquaintance of the renowned Lady of Cadaria, Jillian Corven. I am humbly at your service. Brother Dane Rhuiden of the People of the Phoenix, at your disposal."

Jillian took the man's hand reluctantly. If he was telling the truth and was some sort of monk or priest, she felt that her identity was probably safe with him.

"Careful with that one, Jillian," Blade said his gruff tone belying the comedy he tried to convey, "Dane has been known to talk the richest men and women into donating the lion-share of their fortune to his little con game."

To his credit, Dane kept the annoyance from his face.

"Spoken truly like a man with no faith."

Dane smiled and turned back to face Blade.

"Faith is the luxury of the poor," Blade countered. "Those with means have no need of faith or fate, as this world allows for the creation of both through gold."

Jillian felt sure that this conversation was continued from a much earlier time, and that these men were obviously very old friends. Dane clapped Blade on the shoulder and the two laughed, probably the first time Jillian had ever seen the stalwart Blade indulge in anything that resembled emotion. Dane hopped up on the counter and sat facing Jillian.

"I trust Blade is helping to smuggle you out of Hedorah?"

Jillian looked to Blade who simply shrugged.

"No point in keeping anything from this one," Blade said hooking his thumb back at Dane. "As a monk, he knows when to keep his mouth shut and with the resources that he has available through his order, he may actually be able to help. After all, he constantly professes that his mission in life is to help people."

Dane scowled.

"As usual, Blade has no concept of any reality outside his shop. My order is not interested in the continuation of the life that the Cadarian Empire would want us to live, especially not the one that Emperor Kaitain Lorien has started to carve out for us. No, my order is committed to a rebirth into a purer way of life, one following the precepts of the Creator, but not necessarily the religion that has sprung up around those precepts."

Blade rolled his eyes.

"Here we go…"

"Have you ever felt that life has become a faint shadow of what it could be? All of these trappings, and vice, and war. There is a simpler and more balanced life out there. One that the Creator wants us to be living, free from the influence of those who claim that they know how you should be living. We have become blinded by this world that has been pulled over our eyes. We've lost the path. The People of the Phoenix strive to lift that veil and give everyone the chance to see the truth about life."

Jillian was momentarily mesmerized. She had never considered herself a religious person, even when she was a child before her village had been destroyed. It was the only real cause of tension between herself and Kiara, who as a former priestess was very rooted in her faith. Finally Jillian was able to shake herself away from the hypnotic words and voice of the talented monk as thoughts of Kiara drew her back to the danger she and her associates were facing.

"As fascinating as this all is," Jillian said finally, "we have a bit of a problem we're facing. I'll gather my team and come back here."

Blade nodded and headed toward the stairs that led to the basement and workshop under the shop proper.

"The shipment leaves day after tomorrow. I'll make all the arrangements, and you can decide on your final destination once you get to Rashaleb."

Jillian pulled the hood of her cloak up and headed for the door. Dane hopped off the counter and wrapped his cloak back around his shoulders.

"Mind if I tag along with you? We can talk more about my order and all it is doing to help humanity."

Jillian felt herself nodding, even though deep inside she couldn't believe she was doing it. Behind them, Blade snorted.

"Another sheep for the flock..."

* * * * * * * * * * * *

Jillian was surprised at how quickly they made it back to the small residential section of Hedorah where the band of dragon hunters had their unofficial headquarters. Perhaps it was because Dane had continued to talk throughout the entire trip, or perhaps it was because the ever-strengthening rain made them keep a quick pace. Whatever the reason, Jillian was relieved to open the door to the small cottage and step inside out of the weather. Dane was more of a character than Jillian had anticipated, and his antiquated logic did have the ring of sense to it, though she would have never put voice to that opinion. His devotion to a simpler and politic-free life certainly had appeal, especially to someone of common upbringing as herself, and it was not surprising that he boasted of an order that could rival the Flying Guard scattered throughout the countryside of Cadaria. What did shock Jillian however was the fact that in all her travels she had never once heard of anyone who counted themselves among this flock, or openly displayed their symbol as Dane did. The pessimistic voice in her head wanted to call Dane delusional, but his association with Blade made that unlikely. Secretly, Jillian wondered what kind of debates that Dane and Kiara would find themselves in.

The cottage was warm and a pleasant respite from the cold rain. Hedorah was in the northern reaches of Cadaria, and though it did not share the same harsh winters that northern Zevarit and Rashaleb experienced, Hedorah's sometime volatile coastline could produce storms of such severity that they would shake structures down to the foundation. If the wind blew in from the north, the rain could nearly freeze and cut like razors. Angelina sat at the table in the front room near the fire, sharpening and polishing her blade. She was meticulous about the condition of her blade and never a day passed that she did not give some level of attention to its sharpness or finish. Jillian was just shaking the rain out of her curly red hair when Angelina looked up to regard the two new arrivals. Before anyone could utter a word, the east wall exploded inward throwing the three of them to the floor. Jillian soon realized that it hadn't been the explosion that propelled her to the floor, but rather it was Dane's impossibly fast reflexes that had somehow anticipated what was about to happen. He grabbed her and took her to the ground in a single deft motion and shielded her from the flying debris with his own body. That same fast movement got Dane to his feet before anyone else, and when Jillian finally regained her senses, she saw three people standing in the hole where the wall used to be.

Standing in the center was a young looking man whose eyes burned with a fire that Jillian had never seen before. The bright red tint of his eyes was as unnerving as his obvious fighting stance. He stood slightly hunched forward, the dark chain armor hung loose around his frame, the sword in his right hand held in front of him as though he had simply struck the wall with such force that it had yielded to the force of his blow. His long black hair flowed around him in the whipping wind and rain, streaked with red in many places. However, from the streaks of blood across his arms and chest, Jillian was sure that the red in his hair was blood as well. To the man's right was a woman dressed in white, a hood pulled up over her head, but her face fully revealed. Her golden eyes shown bright and her blond hair whipped around loosely. It seemed that the rain did not touch her though the wind did gently lift her flowing white garment from time to time. Her pale, almost ghostly features were chilling and the cruel smile on her face was unnerving. The woman to the man's left was also terribly pale, dressed in blue and red, her bored almost passive expression accompanied by searching eyes. While the other two seemed to ignore the rain, she reveled in it, tossing her head from left to right idly, feeling the way the water ran down her face.

"Jillian Corven, my mistress would like a word with you."

The man's voice was cold and hard, there was no emotion, no venom. It was the voice of a killer.

Jillian forced herself back to her feet and found the sword on her hip. Scaleripper was not accustomed to being used on humans, but Jillian was sure it would not mind the exception. Angelina was also back to her feet, crouching slightly near the overturned table. There was a line of blood on her cheek where a piece of debris had struck her, and her left arm hung limply at her side, but Jillian knew she was still capable of mounting a defense.

"I'm not sure the Lady of Cadaria appreciates this rude entrance," Dane replied, taking a step toward the trio. "If your mistress does indeed wish an audience, I would suggest that she make an appointment."

The man stood straighter and smiled a vicious smile. However, before he could speak, the woman in blue and red spoke up. Her voice was nearly a whine, childish in timbre but melodic all the same.

"Macero...I'm bored. Can't we just kill them? Kyrie said we could kill them..."

The blond woman spoke up, her voice harder, more matriarchal.

"Now, now, Orchid, you know better. We have to give them the opportunity to exercise some level of intelligence. My beautiful boy here will make sure they don't do anything stupid, and we'll take the little dragon hunter back to Kyrie."

The girl called Orchid frowned, almost pouting. Macero spoke up finally.

"Lexa is right, Orchid. We need to give them the opportunity to be intelligent. Though I can't imagine they would start now. Come quietly Jillian, and I may only kill your protector here. If not, I'll start executing your little dragon hunting band one by one until you agree to come along. And believe me, they'll suffer more horrific deaths than you could even imagine."

The quiet sneer on Macero's face spoke volumes. Just then, Jacqueline and Kiara emerged from deeper in the cottage. They both looked a little worse for wear from the explosion, but Jillian knew they were more than ready for a fight. The next second, Jacqueline charged forward, her sword raised high above her head. Her target was obviously the man Macero, but the woman he had called Lexa stepped in front of him as Jacqueline's blade arced down for a killing blow. Lexa's hand shot upward and intercepted the blade, holding it tightly in the palm of her hand. Her flesh ripped and tore against the hardened steel, but only a smile sat on the woman's face. Finally she turned the blade to the side and pushed back hard, sending Jacqueline stumbling backward. Blood streamed from Lexa's hand as she held it palm out toward Jacqueline. The streams of blood flew across the room and wrapped like a cord around her neck and forced her to the ground. Her sword clattered to the floor, both hands going to her throat in an attempt to wrest the grip of the tendrils away from her throat.

Angelina was on her feet, charging toward Lexa, and Macero's blade quickly intercepted Angelina's deft strike and forced her backwards hard, sending her to the floor and off her feet. Slowly, Angelina got back to her feet again, judging the best way to attack Macero or Lexa to help Jacqueline resist the strange attack that was slowly draining her life with every choked off breath. However it was Orchid that stepped before Macero with an evil yet childish smile.

"Can I have her, Macero? Please?"

Macero's eyes glimmered briefly, and then he smiled that cold hard smile and nodded. Jillian held her ground, unsure what to do and Kiara could be seen out of the corner of her eye trying what spells and chants she could manage to assist Jacqueline. Dane on the other hand was advancing toward Macero slowly; his hands balled into fists, and for the first time, Jillian noticed a bluish glow around his hands. Orchid advanced again, almost skipping. Angelina was caught off guard by the playfulness of her opponent, and lowered her guard for only a moment. Orchid took advantage of this and raced in, and raked her nails across Angelina's face, immediately drawing blood and sending Angelina reeling, her hand going to her face. Blood flowed between her fingers, and Orchid took a quick moment to taste the blood on her nails.

"That should make you much prettier," Orchid said sweetly. "Won't help how bad you taste though. So sour…"

Angelina growled and rushed forward, her blade slashing right through where Orchid stood. The blade passed harmlessly through her body, and then the girl disappeared, only to reappear a step behind Macero.

"Enough!"

Dane's voice resounded through the cottage above the din of the rain and wind. Macero's focus immediately shifted to the monk, and his cold smile dimmed slightly.

"We don't want you," Macero said finally. "Leave here and we may not hunt you down and rip the flesh from your bones. Leave these little girls to us, and we may forget you exist."

Dane lunged in, dashing forward, Macero raised his sword to block, but at the last moment, Dane diverted and his stiff left hand landed across Lexa's jaw, sending her sliding across the room. The grip around Jacqueline's throat was broken and the woman fell to the ground unconscious. Kiara was immediately at her side doing everything she could to help. Dane took a half-step back, reset himself and then launched forward again, this time at Macero. The man took a quick slash with his sword, a slash that Dane ducked and floated inside Macero's guard, striking him with a palm strike to the center of the chest. Macero didn't move an inch, and Dane found himself thrown across the room. The next second, Orchid's form appeared before Macero, her hand extended. Dane's strike had obviously not connected with Macero as it initially appeared. Orchid had somehow intercepted the strike and redirected it against the monk. To his credit, Dane was quickly dusting himself off and was back on his feet.

"That's a good trick," Dane said readjusting his clothing, "let's see you try it with this."

Jillian watched as a sword of pure crystal appeared in Dane's hand. The air around the sword cooled and smoked as though the blade were made of pure ice. After a moment, Dane looked to his left and smiled at Jillian.

"Should we take care of these three?"

Jillian raised her sword and readied herself for the fight ahead. She had never fought anything like these three people. She had never envisioned herself fighting people at all. Dragons were her enemies. Dragons were her prey. But now, here, faced with the prospect of ending a human life, she found that her blood ran cold. But despite herself, Jillian nodded.

That next moment, the door behind them flew open. In the doorway stood the diminutive form of Blade with an axe, whose head was nearly the size of his upper body, resting on one shoulder. His lips were curled into a cruel smile.

"I figured you would probably get into some trouble, so I thought I might lend a hand."

Chapter LIII

New Day, New Knight

Year Three of the Just Emperor Kaitain "Dragonsbane" Lorien, Creator's Calendar Year 1870

Rumors had been swirling throughout the Imperial Palace of Aldere since the declaration of Hannah Ironheart proclaimed the current Emperor and Empress as pretenders to the throne. The Celestial Princess Marlae Lorien had been all but confined to her chambers in order to prevent elements of either the Imperial Guard or other factions loyal to her father from acting against her. Though Empress Dominique Lorien had exonerated Marlae from all connection to the rebellion, there were many in the palace who felt that while Marlae had not been directly responsible for the rebellion or Hannah's declaration that Marlae was the rightful Empress of Cadaria, she would certainly be the type of person to try to profit from it. While Marlae found herself irritated by the confinement, the visits from Rhain made it somewhat tolerable. However, as the days passed, there was one absence that tugged at Marlae's mind more and more. Gabriel was gone. The new Ruby Knight has been dispatched by the Empress to try to gain support in the fractured Kingdom of Blood, Zevarit, in order to prevent it from falling fully into the rebel camp. The battle of wills between the supporters of the new Ruby Knight and those of the disgraced Gregor Quicksilver had raged for several weeks, but Gabriel's passion and charm had won over all but the most dedicated of Gregor's thralls. Now, the Kingdom of Zevarit had set itself firmly behind the Empress, but Marlae knew that if Gabriel chose, he could turn the zealots of the Kingdom of Blood to whatever cause he saw fit. He was doing his duty to his Empress, but as Marlae plotted, she believed that he would soon do his duty to the rightful Empress, Marlae Lorien.

Even as the door opened to her private quarters, Marlae found herself smiling, and when Gabriel came into view, she smiled widely and motioned for him to enter without a word. She had to admit to herself, though she would never say it aloud, that Gabriel looked dashing in his armor with the seal of the Ruby Knight emblazoned on his breastplate. Though the weight of the Sacred Sword Valor did not seem to sit well upon him, Gabriel seemed to manage well enough. He stood straight after closing the door behind him and bowed low to Marlae.

"Sir Gabriel Shadowfall, Ruby Knight of the Kingdom of Zevarit, Knight of the Flashing Blade reporting as ordered my Celestial Princess."

Marlae's smile widened. The title sounded good coming from his lips, and even better that he remembered how to properly address her. While in the past she would have taken the opportunity to tease Gabriel or perhaps find some way to entice him, this was not the time for petty games.

"Rise, Sir Shadowfall."

Gabriel straightened but remained at attention, as his practiced military service demanded. He was a soldier first and foremost, regardless of his elevated position. Moreover, he was in the presence of the woman who many had begun to believe should have been the rightful ruler of the Empire.

"Gabriel," Marlae said after a moment, "have you heard the reports of the rebellion that has been started by the former Ruby Knight and his wife the Celestine Knight?"

Marlae had chosen her words very carefully. From the beginning of the rebellion, Marlae learned through Rhain and other sources in the palace that Irene had placed powerful wards and spells throughout the Imperial Palace to alert her when the names of the traitors had been spoken. The excuse given was to be able to ferret out possible sympathizers and assassins before they had a chance to act against the rightful rulers of the Empire.

However, Marlae knew better. Irene was afraid that if there was enough support for the rebels in the Imperial lands of Aldere, that her position of power would be threatened. It did not take a scholar to know that as soon as Kaitain was wrested from power that Irene would quickly follow, and that her fate would probably not be as kind as the one reserved for the Emperor.

"I have, Princess," Gabriel said carefully. "I have just returned from Zevarit on a mission for Empress Dominique. While there are many in the Kingdom of Blood that would support my predecessor, most are content to follow me. It seems that my reputation from the years in your service Princess has been enough to hold the kingdom together and prevent it from splintering into a civil war."

Marlae nodded and moved to her wardrobe.

"Then you have heard that the rebels have declared that I should be the rightful ruler of this Empire, replacing my sainted father and angelic mother-in-law?"

The venom in Marlae's voice was not hidden in the slightest. Gabriel had known for some time that Marlae had visions of unseating her father and becoming the ruler of the Empire, however, while assassination was not out of the realm of possibilities for avenues that Marlae would explore, she was very cognoscente of the reaction that most of the Empire would have to that type of coup. Simply dispatching the Emperor was not the way to true power.

"I have, Princess," Gabriel said slowly.

Marlae measured her next words very carefully. As she reached into the wardrobe to withdraw a shawl, she carefully retrieved the small dagger that Rhain had brought her. The tip of the dagger had been coated with some exotic poison that would work quickly and cause very little pain in its victim. While Marlae would not hesitate to murder Gabriel if he gave the wrong answer to the next question, his years of service at least merited a quiet and painless death. She turned to face Gabriel and locked eyes with him.

"And if I were to leave Aldere and join this rebellion as their chosen ruler?"

Gabriel did not move, did not blink, and Marlae thought for a moment he was holding his breath. To his credit, he did not flinch or wither as Marlae would have expected many to do in his position. However, Marlae knew that Gabriel was made of stronger stuff, that much he had proven over the last few years.

"The Empire could not hope for more than the wisdom that you would bring to its new age, my Princess," Gabriel said slowly, "and your claim to the throne is as valid as any of the others being made these days."

It was an answer, but not an answer. Marlae had guessed that Gabriel would be non-committal at first, but it would only take another pointed question to force him to choose sides. But there was something more about his statement that puzzled Marlae.

"Other claims?"

Gabriel's face remained expressionless, and he nodded slightly as he responded.

"Yes, Princess. There are some within the Empire that are calling for my predecessor to take the throne, others are calling for the Emperor's brother, Lord Feyd Lorien to take the throne, or perhaps his daughter Princess Felicia. Still others whisper quietly that the Ethereal Sorceress should rule, but those voices are very few. It seems that as long as the Emperor remains in his poison-induced slumber, more and more contenders for the throne emerge. Before long, I fear, each of the great kingdoms will have their own champion for the throne."

Marlae sensed the pattern of Gabriel's thoughts and began to relax a bit. Perhaps she would not have to kill him after all.

"And who do you think should be the ruler of this great Empire, Gabriel?"

Without hesitation, Gabriel answered. He knew it would come to this as soon as he received the summons. The previous conversation had simply been a test, one that he hoped he had passed. Gabriel had known from the minute he walked into the room that he would either walk out as the vassal of a rebel or he would fall under the hand of either the Celestial Princess or her chosen assassin Rhain Feirbran.

"The throne has always been sat upon by a member of the Lorien line," Gabriel said slowly, "a member by blood. Perhaps Emperor Lorien's mind has been corrupted by the Ethereal Sorceress, or perhaps he will never rise from the poison that has placed him into a pained slumber. Without a shadow of a doubt, the Empire cannot be ruled by a wicked temptress or a whore in royal clothes."

Gabriel fought hard not the choke on the words. He had gained nothing but respect for the new Empress Dominique Lorien, but in order to remain in the good graces of the Princess, and in order to fulfill his mission, he would have to play the fool and give in to the hatred that Marlae felt for all above her in the Imperial Palace.

"Nor can it be ruled by those who would usurp the power and bring shame to the Lorien line, like the fool brother of the Emperor or his warrior daughter. In my opinion, there is only one who has a true claim to the throne, and that is you, the Celestial Princess."

Marlae smiled again as Gabriel continued.

"The Empire must be saved from itself Princess," he said softly, "it cannot be allowed to descend into the turmoil that a competition for the throne would cause. I can see no other choice but for you to take control of the Cadarian Empire and lead it through this time of strife and see us safely through to the other side."

A sick feeling turned in the pit of Gabriel's stomach. He had not wanted this assignment, he had not wanted to betray everything that he knew to become an enemy of that which he loved more than anything. But his comrades in arms had been right....

* * * * * * * * * * *

The time was late when the page came to the quarters of the new Ruby Knight, Gabriel Shadowfall. He had just recently returned from the

Kingdom of Blood and had barely had time to place his saddlebags on the bed before the page was at his door. Accepting the summons quickly, Gabriel took a moment to change out of his road-stained tunic and into one of the fancier ones that bore the crest of the Kingdom of Zevarit. He was now the representative of a whole kingdom in the Imperial Court of Aldere, and he needed to remember to respect that station and act the part. The first time he looked at the summons, he simply noted that it was a summons to appear in the Imperial Court immediately. It was only on second inspection that he noticed that the summons had come from the Empress herself. Exhaling slowly, Gabriel slung Valor over his shoulder and made his way quickly from his quarters at the edge of the Imperial City toward the Palace of Aldere.

A great many changes had taken place in the Imperial City since Gabriel had left for Zevarit. Before the attempt on the Emperor's life, the city had been teeming with activity, even at the late hours of the night. However, now the streets were devoid of commoners, and their presence was replaced by armed guards and magistrates roaming the streets. Martial law had been declared, and the magistrates and soldiers ruled the nights in Aldere. A few tried to impede Gabriel's path to the Imperial Palace, but a quick look at the crest on his chest and the massive sword over his shoulder answered any questions that the soldiers may have had. But Gabriel could not get over the palpable sense of fear that filled the city. The Empire of Cadaria was beginning to fall, and the loss of the Emperor was realistically only the latest in a series of events that could signal the downfall of an empire that had reigned for almost two thousand years.

As Gabriel made his way up the long flight of steps that led to the main entrance of the Imperial Palace, he was met by a woman who he knew quite well by reputation. Chelsea Zarova, the Wolf of Saldarine was a formidable woman to say the least, and were she not so fearsome with a weapon in hand, many would have found her beautiful face and intoxicating eyes a more fitting reputation to praise. However, Chelsea was unattainable, even for the most accomplished or powerful lords and knights of the Empire. She was married to the often unstable Seraph Kore, and was fiercely devoted to her husband. Perhaps it was this devotion that made people forget how attractive Chelsea was. However, in the moonlight of the late night, Gabriel could not see past her blond hair as it glowed in the light, or her eyes which shined like stars in the darkness.

"Welcome home, Sir Shadowfall," Chelsea said softly, so soft that Gabriel's ears could barely discern the words, "I trust your travels were safe?"

"There aren't many that would disturb a member of the Knights of the Flashing Blade while on an official mission for the Throne, Lady Zarova," Gabriel returned formally, "but I did note the increase of Imperial soldiers on the road and dragon hunters in the wilds."

Chelsea nodded and took a step closer, her voice lowered to a mere whisper.

"The Ethereal Sorceress feels that with the Emperor still suffering from the assassination attempt, all members of the royal family as well as the Knights themselves could be targets for the more unscrupulous elements in the Empire. Especially with the news coming out of Albitonin."

Gabriel nodded. So this was the purpose for his summons. Only a few days before, the word had begun to circulate that the people of Galateria, Oradrim, and Albitonin had begun to call for Marlae Lorien to be crowned Empress of Cadaria with Thorigald putting their support behind the rebellion without naming a successor. The other kingdoms had countered by giving their support to Empress Dominique and the rightful government, with the exception of Menoris whose representatives had withdrawn completely from Aldere. Gabriel felt it was only a matter of time before Menoris would be counted among the rebels as well, provided Xaran Firesoul did not shock everyone by supporting Kaitain and his wife. That would put five of the thirteen kingdoms in the hands of the rebels with Zevarit and Iltorp on shaky ground. Vallic Ultiv's ties were to his brothers and sisters in the Flashing Blade, not to the Emperor, and he could easily go either way. Zevarit was a hair's breadth from falling to the rebellion and supporting Gregor Quicksilver, and part of Gabriel felt that he had only delayed the inevitable with his latest round of diplomatic talks with the nobles of the great houses. Gabriel had earned his reputation as a soldier and as a man of honor, however, he did not have the pedigree of someone like Gregor Quicksilver, and talk would only go so far. Gregor had spent decades building up good will throughout the empire, and no words from the Empress or from a pup like Gabriel could tear that down so easily. A man like Gregor, a man who was once seen as the equal to the Emperor himself could not be dismissed to fate so easily.

"Is that why I have been summoned?"

Chelsea's face went cold, and she nodded slowly.

"There are too many ears here, my young friend," Chelsea said in a voice that could pierce stone, "follow me to the Empress' chambers."

Gabriel felt the tension pass between them as the two Knights of the Flashing Blade walked through the winding corridors of the Imperial Palace toward the receiving chambers of the Empress of Cadaria. What struck Gabriel the most was the different feeling in the palace since the assassination attempt. The palace had begun to feel like a tomb. Finally, Chelsea and Gabriel reached the white double doors of the Empress' chamber, and with two quiet knocks at the door, one of the doors opened. There was a faint light flickering from inside the room, and Gabriel waited until Chelsea had entered before following.

Inside the room, Gabriel saw Empress Dominique Lorien sitting on a gilded chair in the corner near a small lamp, dressed in a simple white dress with limited finery. She was beautiful to say the least, perhaps the most beautiful woman that Gabriel had ever seen, and she more than earned the title of the Beauty of Aldere. Sitting across the small table from Dominique was the lithe and willowy form of Quyhn Ravenheart Lorien, the ward of the Empire. She had been adopted into the Imperial family after the death of her father, and had apparently formed a very strong bond with her new mother. Chelsea and Gabriel both went to a knee after the door was closed behind them and waited to be addressed by the Empress.

"Oh do stand up, Chelsea, you know I hate when you do that while we're in private."

The Empress' voice was playful, and Chelsea stood quickly, a smile finally coming to her face. It was obvious the two women had become fast friends, despite the fact that the same man had shared their bed. Gabriel remained on a knee, his head bowed, waiting to be addressed. He could feel the eyes of the three women in the room pass over him, and after a moment, Dominique spoke.

"Arise, Sir Gabriel Shadowfall."

Gabriel stood slowly, and fell into a military attention, waiting for the next words from his superior.

"As you have no doubt surmised from your summons here, I have an assignment for you that directly has to do with your former charge the Celestial Princess Marlae Lorien and the rebellion growing in the Kingdom of Stone. Before I give you the details of this assignment, Sir Shadowfall, I want you to answer this question for me. Where does your loyalty lay, Gabriel? Will you serve the interests of the Empire and the orders of your rightful Emperor and Empress, or will you abandon your duty and serve a rebellion who believes they are protecting the empire from itself?"

Gabriel regarded the Empress for a moment and then stole a sideways glance at Chelsea. While he was not shocked to see her hand on the hilt of her sword, it still caused an uneasiness to fill him.

"Empress," Gabriel said finally, "I am a soldier. For most of my life I have dedicated myself to following the orders of my superiors and ensuring the safety of my charge, whomever that may be. I have served with distinction and with honor, and never have my loyalties been called into question. Make no mistake, Empress Lorien, I have no delusions as to why I was elevated to the position of Ruby Knight. You needed someone whose reputation was above reproach and could keep Zevarit in line while Gregor Quicksilver's defection was dealt with, but you also needed me because of my connection with the Celestial Princess because you knew she had designs upon your throne."

Dominique smiled. Perhaps she had made the right decision with Gabriel's ascension after all.

"But in answer to your question, Empress," Gabriel continued, "my loyalties are to my Emperor and to my Empress. Not because you gave me the position of Ruby Knight, not because of any personal preference I have for you or for Marlae, but because until his death, the Emperor is the rightful leader of this Empire, and he is who I am sworn to defend and to follow, even if it means my death."

Gabriel could feel some of the tension lift from the room. Chelsea moved from his side and settled into a chair near Quyhn, and Gabriel waited silently as the Empress appeared to consider her words carefully for a moment.

"Gabriel, this Empire is at a crossroads, and depending on the next few months, we could rise into light or fall into everlasting darkness. I do not know the true motives of this rebellion or of those who call the Emperor a monster. Are they doing this to further their own personal agenda? Are they fervent zealots who are pushing for a theocracy under the High Priestess of the Creator? Or are they merely misguided fools with delusions of grandeur? What's worse, is that they could actually be right in thinking that Kaitain Lorien and Irene Drage have designs that could destroy Cadaria forever. I need to know the truth, but I cannot learn this for myself, nor can any who are loyal to me. That is why I turn to you my new friend, Gabriel. There are too many voices in the wind, coming from Jelan, Albitonin, Lordhill, for me to not believe that there is some truth to the vile words spoken about Kaitain and Irene. While Jelan must remain a mystery to me, as I have no one who could act as an agent within those walls, Albitonin and Lordhill are within my power to monitor."

Gabriel nodded. He had begun to understand what was happening all around him. The Empress was in an impossible situation, caught between her duty to her husband the Emperor and her duty to the Empire. Without some real proof of the actions of either Kaitain or Irene Drage, Dominique was powerless to do anything other than follow the plans laid out by Kaitain. And if the information came too late, and Kaitain woke, any chance she had to undo his horrible schemes would be lost without direct action against him. Action that could have disastrous consequences.

"To that end," Dominique continued, "I have decided to dispatch Quyhn to Lordhill to monitor the seeds of rebellion that have been planted there, and to ask you to act as my eyes and ears in the rebellion in Albitonin."

Gabriel swallowed.

"How," Gabriel asked as respectfully as he could manage, "am I to infiltrate the rebellion in Albitonin as I have just taken over the position of Ruby Knight and spent the last few weeks rallying support to the banner of the Emperor? They will surely see me as a spy."

Chelsea smiled.

"That would normally be true my comrade," the Garnet Knight said brightly, "if not for the fact that Marlae Lorien herself will bring you into the fold as her protector. It will give you the perfect opportunity to appeal to Hannah and Gregor by returning Valor to him in order to make amends for your role in his downfall. Once the sword is back in his hands, Zevarit will break ranks and fall to the rebellion, but we expected that would happen even without your apparent defection. We will still retain the advantage, at least until Xaran Firesoul returns from his mission and pushes Menoris one direction or the other."

"If we can understand the cause behind this rebellion and the truth of the nature of my husband, perhaps we can salvage this Empire without a true civil war. Personally I do not believe that Marlae belongs on the throne any more than her father, but we must find a way to make peace in Cadaria, no matter the cost to me or to the Lorien family. You must find me the way to make peace, Gabriel, and you must find it quickly."

Gabriel fell to one knee again.

"I shall do my best to fulfill this mission, my Empress, at any cost."

＊＊＊＊＊＊＊＊＊＊＊＊

It was the dead of night when Marlae, Gabriel, Rhain, and a small detachment of Imperial Guards that Gabriel could personally vouch for stole away from the Imperial lands of Aldere toward the Kingdom of Stone, Albitonin. Even as they rode away, Gabriel could hear the voice of the Empress ringing through his mind. He would accomplish his mission, and he would help heal the wounds of the Empire, even if it meant his life would have to end.

Untenable Positions

Year Three of the Just Emperor Kaitain "Dragonsbane" Lorien,
Creator's Calendar Year 1870

Bernhardt Yeoman scowled as he looked out of the entryway of his command tent at the line of men who stood between him and the gates of the Academy of Arcane Arts. His army, thinned as it was by the recent entanglements with three separate dragon nests, had only arrived at the top of the watchtower hill late the previous day. This was to be the morning that the Moonstone Knight was to take control of the Academy in the name of the now catatonic Emperor Kaitain Lorien. However, the presence of a defense force complicated matters. Bernhardt had no love for magic or those who used it, and while the siege of the Academy would expose him and his troops to massive amounts of the foul power, the added dimension of traditional troops delaying his army while the Masters of the Academy had time to perform their more complex rituals made Bernhardt's stomach turn.

Hobbling on his recently-crafted steel leg, Bernhardt made his way over to the hastily constructed planning table and consulted his maps of the Academy and the surrounding area. A siege of the Academy was possible via multiple routes, but the use of the watchtower hill was the most obvious. Bernhardt's troops would control the high ground and his archers would have advantageous angles into the open grounds of the Academy. As the siege moved into its third and fourth day, this tactical advantage would be paramount. Once there were breeches in the walls, the inhabitants of the Academy would need to move supplies and people from safer areas to the areas of combat in an attempt to repulse the Imperial soldiers. The archers would have free reign to attempt to prevent these reinforcements from reaching their new positions.

As Bernhardt continued to look over the maps, another thought crept into his mind. The kingdom of Menoris within which the Academy of Arcane Arts had carved its home existed on a large island that was divided equally between Menoris and its sister kingdom of Oradrim. The large chain of mountains called the Mountains of Conscience divided the intertwined kingdoms of Soul and Knowledge. The unfortunate part of this arrangement was that the city of Jelan, which housed the Academy, sat on a major trade route in the shadow of the now rebel kingdom of Oradrim. Only days earlier Bernhardt had learned of the traitorous coalition of kingdoms who had sworn themselves to the banner of the so-called Celestial Princess Marlae Lorien. While those were the matters for practiced politicians and sycophants, Bernhardt worried over the proximity of his troops to a now enemy kingdom. Oradrim had never been known for the power of their army, but Bernhardt knew the capabilities of the Jade Army very well, and if they were under the leadership of Leonora Wastri, Bernhardt did not like the odds. The Academy to his front and the Jade Army to his flank, his troops would stand little chance in open combat. The other worry of course was the Army of the Tiger's Eye. While they had not openly joined the rebellion started in Albitonin, neither had they voiced their open support of the Empress as most of the other kingdoms had. Most of the trouble in Menoris had come from the disappearance of Xaran Firesoul. The word coming from the Imperial Palace in Aldere was that Xaran was on a mission for the throne. Whispers from the countryside said that he had been killed and Aldere was covering it up to keep Menoris in line. Still others told stories of Xaran negotiating with his old friends Hannah and Gregor in Kingdom of Stone attempting to broker some kind of peace accord. No one knew anything for certain, but what Bernhardt did know was that his bad tactical position could become impossible if the winds of fate decided to blow Menoris into the column with the rebels.

"This is a damn nightmare," Bernhardt growled to himself.

A few moments later, the flap of the tactical command tent opened, and Bernhardt's second in command, a man by the name of Kaleb Escandi entered. Kaleb was a promising soldier with a tactical mind that far out-paced Bernhardt's, however; Kaleb lacked the confidence and conviction in his talents. It seemed for some time that Kaleb was on the fast-track to becoming one of the greatest generals that the Iron Legion had ever seen, however once his sister Jacqueline left the legion to pursue her future as a dragon hunter, Kaleb became a shadow of his former self. While Jacqueline had been an average soldier, she had an incredible charisma and natural leadership ability that Kaleb clearly lacked. They were two halves of a perfect warrior, unfortunately contained in separate bodies. Kaleb waited just inside the flap of the tent waiting to be acknowledged by his superior. Bernhardt, while not the most perceptive man when it came to the reactions or body language of others when not in a combat situation, could feel the impatience and nervousness rolling off of Kaleb.

"Report, Commander Escandi."

Kaleb took two swift and precise steps into the tent and then addressed his commander, who was still turned away from him.

"There are three urgent communications from the Imperial Palace of Aldere, General, and an envoy from the Academy of Arcane Arts has arrived under the banner of truce to parlay with you."

Bernhardt sighed. Being a soldier had been easy. With a weapon in hand, all he needed was to be pointed toward an enemy and he was at peace. After being elevated to commander, things had not changed much for him. He was still on the front line of the army with his men, charging down the throat of any enemy who was foolish enough to face them. However, once he had reached the rank of general, things had changed. He felt more disconnected from his men than he had ever felt before. Though he bent the rules and fought and bled on the same fields as the rank and file soldiers as much as he could, the demands of tactics and diplomacy took more and more of his time away from the battlefield. Once the responsibilities of a Knight of the Flashing Blade were added, his priorities became clearer. No longer could his life be risked on simple battles for territory or over some imagined slight between feuding kingdoms. He was one of the chosen protectors of the royal family. If his life were to be lost on some trivial battle, his power would be lost to the Emperor were a threat to rear its ugly head. His zealous fervor for battle had already cost him a leg, and diminished his ability to fulfill his role, and he vowed to himself that such carelessness in execution of his duty would never occur again.

"The dispatches first, Kaleb, the envoy can wait."

Kaleb nodded wordlessly and opened the first of the dispatches.

"From the Just Emperor, Kaitain Lorien, to General Bernhardt Yeoman, Moonstone Knight of the Kingdom of Iron, Pellatori. Due to the traitorous actions of the Ruby Knight Gregor Quicksilver, Bernhardt Yeoman has been appointed as the Sword of the Emperor, effective upon receipt of this decree. The military resources of all kingdoms loyal to the true Emperor of Cadaria, Kaitain Lorien, will remain at the discretion of the Moonstone Knight. These resources are to be used in any endeavor to combat the enemies of the Throne, or to defend the lives of the royal family. This effectively puts all loyal members of the Knights of the Flashing Blade under the direct command of the Moonstone Knight; however, those orders cannot countermand orders from the Throne."

This decree was not a surprise. Bernhardt had felt it coming ever since word had come of the arrest of the Ruby Knight prior to Emperor Lorien's wedding. The Knights of the Flashing Blade were a diverse group with impressive abilities; however they were short on pure warriors. Of the thirteen members, only six of them qualified as warriors in the classic sense, though Leonora Wastri and Natalia Pressen were impressive in their own rights where combat were concerned. Of those six, Gregor Quicksilver, Devlin Rannoch, and Seraph Kore were counted among the rogue kingdoms. Chelsea Zarova had been named the personal guard of the Empress Dominique Lorien, and so her responsibilities could not allow her to take the post of Sword of the Emperor. Tolon Morr was the only other possibility, and while the young man was impressive with a weapon in hand and an enemy staring across at him in a gladiatorial arena, he was certainly no leader. Bernhardt was the only logical choice, but it didn't make the decree sit any better in the pit of Bernhardt's stomach.

"Move on to the next one."

Bernhardt's tone was gruff, and he didn't feel the need to hide his impatience or irritation from his subordinate.

"From the Just Empress, Dominique Lorien, to General Bernhardt Yeoman, Moonstone Knight of the Kingdom of Iron, Pellatori, made in the name of the Just Emperor Kaitain Lorien…"

So, the Empress is now making decrees, Bernhardt thought to himself, *how interesting. And she is using the name of the Emperor to give those decrees more legitimacy. It makes sense given the position that she's in.*

"…effective upon this decree," Kaleb continued, "Hannah Ironheart, Devlin Rannoch, Leonora Wastri, Gregor Quicksilver, and Seraph Kore have been labeled traitors to the throne. Additionally, Marlae Lorien, Rhain Feirbran, and Gabriel Shadowfall are to be detained and returned to the Imperial Palace of Aldere upon their capture. They are not to be harmed in any way. Furthermore, the armies of the Kingdoms of Albitonin, Thorigald, Galateria, and Oradrim are to be considered enemy combatants. However, full quarter is to be given to those troops wishing to surrender as well as those who are injured in combat. Those found not to have committed direct treasonous acts will be allowed to re-enter military service as members of the Imperial Army of Aldere. Those who have committed treasonous acts will be sentenced to work in the mines of Lordhill, or be put to death depending on the severity of their crimes. Any commanders whose troops do not obey this decree of full quarter shall be disciplined along with their troops, and sentenced to work in the mines of Lordhill."

The wording certainly meant that it came from the pen of the Empress, whether or not it had her name on it. The language of mercy clearly would not have come from Emperor Kaitain. He would have ordered no quarter to be given to any of his enemies, and most assuredly would have had no qualms about ordering the death of any rebel, including his own daughter. Bernhardt was actually happy at this turn of events, because it gave him much more latitude when dealing with the Academy. His original orders said that he was to assure the cooperation of the Academy by any means necessary, up to and including the execution of the Masters. There was a lot of middle ground now afforded with the offer of quarter. So much so, that it was possible that they could all escape this conflict with no loss of blood. Of course, that would all change if an army from Oradrim showed up on the field, or if Menoris were to suddenly throw their allegiances in with the rebels. However, if either of those things came to pass, it would most likely be Bernhardt hoping that the enemy would give quarter rather than the other way around.

"And the last?"

Bernhardt could hear Kaleb unroll the last of the parchments, but when the man gave no voice to the words written there, Bernhardt began to feel a little concern and fear grip him. The agonizing seconds stretched on, and finally Bernhardt turned to face his trusted second. He needed to only glimpse Kaleb's face before he knew that something was terribly wrong.

"What is it Kaleb?"

Kaleb didn't respond, he stood transfixed, his face pale as a ghost, and his body shaking from what seemed a mixture of terror and anger. The anger was betrayed by his quickly whitening knuckles that clutched the edges of the parchment so ferociously that they threatened to rip the delicate material to shreds.

"From the Just Emperor, Kaitain Lorien, to General Bernhardt Yeoman, Moonstone Knight of the Kingdom of Iron, Pellatori," Kaleb's shaking voice came finally, "due to traitorous acts against the Throne, and for a direct assault against the body of the Emperor of Cadaria, the woman known as the Lady of Cadaria, Jillian Corven, as well as her known associates, Angelina Lynn Sydor, Kiara Aren, and Jacqueline Escandi are to be captured and executed."

Bernhardt felt as though he had been punched in the throat. His breath could not be coaxed from his lungs, and only after several moments had passed could he find the strength to let a long exhale escape his lips.

"General, I have to ask..."

Bernhardt put up a hand.

"I understand that your mother is quite ill," Bernhardt said finally. "Perhaps you should take leave for a few weeks until you can get your family obligations in order. Alert your second to the situation, and post the first two decrees. Leave the third here. Then, show the emissary from the Academy into the command tent."

Kaleb stood wordless for several moments before finally snapping a quick salute to his superior and turning on his heel to carry out his orders. He stopped just short of the exit to the tent and left the final decree on a table that sat there with various other correspondences before quickly exiting. Bernhardt watched the man go with a mixture of dread and worry. This correspondence had to be quite old, and probably had been re-routed several times to find its way into the hands of the Moonstone Knight. For all either of them knew, Jacqueline could already be dead. Bernhardt knew that Kaleb would make with all haste toward Hedorah, the semi-regular base of operations for Jillian Corven and her band of dragon hunters. At least Hedorah was still a kingdom loyal to Emperor Kaitain; it would make Kaleb's passage once he left Menoris swift and less complicated, though it also meant that greedier bounty hunters would be vying to collect their prize. Fortunately, the Flying Guard of Hedorah were corrupt and incompetent. That would give Jacqueline a fighting chance.

After Bernhardt had finished writing quick orders for Kaleb to continue the veil of legitimacy for his leave, a very young lieutenant returned with the emissary from the Academy of Arcane Arts. Bernhardt wasn't sure what he was expecting when the flap of the tent opened to admit his two guests, but it certainly wasn't the pair who walked in. Perhaps it had been all the stories he had heard as a child, or perhaps it had been all of the renegade wizards and self-fashioned destroyers that he had put down over the years that had colored his impression of those who wielded the arcane arts, but he always expected older men, with lithe frames from their years of book study. Long beards that looked to be filled with soot from standing over boiling and burning spell components, their fingers irrevocably stained by one of their foul-smelling concoctions. The woman that stood before Bernhardt now was the kind of woman that could make him forget any grudge he ever had against magic-users.

The woman was short by any standard, but standing across from Bernhardt, she was nearly the size of a child; however her calm and confident aura made her a larger presence than the grand general of all the Imperial armies. Her sandy blond hair was perfect kempt, not a single hair out of place, and her strong and powerful countenance belied her striking youthful beauty. She was obviously noble-born by the way she held herself, and looked to be ready for her style of combat…fierce negotiation.

"General," the young lieutenant said nervously, "may I present the Master of Stone of the Academy of Arcane Arts, Ashinica Maupin, and the Captain of the Jelan Defense Force, Rory Blackrock."

The woman's name floated through Bernhardt's mind like a warm breeze, only for his thoughts to be frozen by the man's name. Blackrock. He was a commander in the Jade Army under the command of Leonora Wastri at last report. If he was here…

"Excuse my rude question, but I understood that Commander Rory Blackrock was a member in good standing of the Jade Army."

A small smile crept to the lips of Ashinica Maupin, and Bernhardt realized that his worst fears were becoming a reality.

"Commander Blackrock and a detachment of troops were made available to the Academy by the Jade Knight, Leonora Wastri, as a token of her thanks for our honesty and forthrightness during her investigation. She feared that some power would attempt to take advantage of our current out-of-favor status."

Bernhardt could not keep the scowl from creeping to his face.

"I'm sure it comes as no surprise to you that I have received orders listing Leonora Wastri as a traitor to the Throne, and that all soldiers from the rebel state of Oradrim are to be treated as enemy combatants."

Rory nodded solemnly, but if he had any thoughts on the situation, he kept them closely contained in his manner and expression. He was here simply as a show of force. This was a negotiating tactic plain and simple. The Masters of the Academy could have kept the identity of their defense force a secret as long as they wanted, and only revealed it when the time was right. By revealing their identity now, Bernhardt learned two very important pieces of information. First and foremost, the situation had become much more dire. With the support of the Jade Army, even in part, the Academy could mount a defense that even the full Iron Legion would have issue overwhelming. What's more, the open combat between forces loyal to Emperor Kaitain and Empress Dominique and forces loyal to Marlae Lorien on Menoris' soil would force the currently neutral kingdom to pick a side. That side would almost certainly be to rally defense for the Academy and their long-time ally Oradrim. The Masters had baited the hook, and if Bernhardt was stupid enough to walk blindly into this combat by following his orders to the letter, the Rebellion would have a legitimate victory, and a new set of resources to draw from with not only Menoris, but also the Academy.

However, the second piece of information gave Bernhardt a little hope. By revealing the identity of the defense force now, the Masters had given Bernhardt some options. He could withdraw from the field and gather reinforcements from the loyal kingdoms to make the strategic situation more balanced, and create a greater cost for the rebellious forces to defend the ground, while making Menoris think twice about getting involved. Bernhardt could also stall for time, sending to the Empress for instructions given the change in circumstances. While Emperor Kaitain would have had his head for asking for clarification on 'by whatever means necessary' orders, the Empress seemed to be much more level-headed and open to negotiation. She could intervene in this situation and try to avoid bloodshed. The downside of stalling for time was that it gave the rebel forces time to negotiate with Menoris. If Menoris were to join the Rebellion while Bernhardt was waiting for a reply, the Tiger's Eye Army could easily cut off any possibility for landing additional troops, and the combined forces could easily force Bernhardt into surrendering. If the rebels were to capture the General of the Imperial Armies, it would be a huge victory that would in the eyes of some kingdoms legitimize Marlae Lorien's bid to rule. What this ultimately meant however, was that the Masters wanted to end this conflict without bloodshed.

"Perhaps we should sit and talk," Bernhardt said finally.

* * * * * * * * * * * *

Jastra Mythryn sat at the Master's Table looking out the low window at the troops that had massed at Watchtower Hill. Hopefully Ashinica would be able to achieve her goal of diffusing the situation without bloodshed. As much as it galled Jastra to admit it, she had come to accept Alistair Ravenheart's assertions that the kinds of magic that were studied at the Academy could never be allowed to be perverted into a tool for violence. It was the responsibility of each of the Masters to make sure that never happened. However, it wasn't until Jastra ascended to the rank of Master of Energy that her eyes were opened to just how far Alistair had been willing to go to protect the sanctity of what had been built in Jelan. Jastra remembered it as if it had been only yesterday.

After her ascension ceremony, Alistair and Fiona requested that Jastra join them in the Master's Council chambers to discuss a matter of great importance.

"Jastra," Alistair had said, "we have an important charge that we have given our most sacred vows to protect. I know that over the years you have been a proponent, much as Jaccob Aldora had, of a more militant application of the gifts our talent has bestowed upon us. However, I have seen over the years a softening in your resolve that Jaccob never had, which is the reason you are standing here, and he is not."

Jastra felt almost slighted by the comment; however, she knew that in many ways she was not as talented as Jaccob Aldora, the man that in just a few weeks would be named the Topaz Knight.

"To that end," Fiona continued not missing a beat, "you are hereby charged with one of the most difficult responsibilities you will ever be given as the Master of Energy. Should the Academy ever be compromised, or turned to serve the will of an evil purpose that would pervert the tenants that all novices and adepts swear to by entering the Academy, you will have the unenviable task of completing the ritual that will suppress the life energy from all members of the Academy no matter where they are in the whole of the world."

Jastra's breath caught in her throat. They couldn't be suggesting what she thought they were suggesting. She was being tasked with the ultimate duty of killing every person that had ever studied at the Academy of Arcane Arts. Her head swam. As cold as she could be, as hard as she had worked to attain her position, she could never see herself performing such a task.

"How?"

That was the only word that would escape her throat. The nausea at the suggestion was cresting in her stomach, and the conflicting battle of rage, indignation, sorrow, and utter disbelief was rendering her nearly mute. Fiona saw the turmoil on the younger woman's face and put her hand on Jastra's shoulder.

"I know what you're feeling Jastra, and I felt the same way when Alistair informed me of my role in all of this. Each of the Masters has the responsibility and capability of bringing complete and utter destruction to the legacy of the Academy, and in the end, only two masters are actually required to complete the ritual."

"When each novice or adept joins the Academy," Alistair said solemnly, "they take an oath. This oath is not simply words to reinforce some archaic code of conduct, but it is the beginning of a ritual that ties them to the ultimate fate of the Academy. It was grudgingly put into use after a few misguided apprentices thought that the invocation of forbidden rituals could bring an end to a long-standing conflict."

"The Plain of Blood incident," Jastra said coldly, the memory of the story shaking her to the core.

"After that tragedy, it could not be allowed to happen again, either in a rogue capacity or as a result of an action sanctioned by a legitimate body. Therefore, the Masters were entrusted with the means to destroy the whole of the Academy by completing the invocation started by the oath. Three of the Masters, Water, Wind, and Energy, have responsibility for the people of the Academy. One of those Masters will drown, suffocate, or suppress the life essence for every member of the Academy who had taken the oath. The other two Masters will destroy the physical assets of the Academy which are each inscribed with a secret glyph which will reduce them to ash and dust. However, should the Stone or Fire Master be unable to complete their portion of the ritual, you, Jastra, as the Master of Energy, can also activate the physical glyphs. In truth, you have the power to destroy us all, should it come to that. It is a terrible burden that I place upon you," Alistair said regretfully, "and now you see why the Master of Energy can never sit as Grand Master of the Academy."

Jastra's thoughts moved away from the past as the door to the Master's Council Chambers opened to admit Aris Ebonsight. The young slender woman sat at the opposite end of the table and regarded her colleague for a moment before speaking.

"It's been four hours," Aris said finally, "I suppose that is a good sign."

"It's a good sign for today," Jastra replied coolly, "it does not however mean that tomorrow will see a lack of bloodshed. And should the soldiers from Oradrim fail to live up to their goal of keeping the occupants of this Academy from a fight, I shudder to think what the final outcome will be."

"A scar on the world unlike any has seen in twenty generations," a voice said from the doorway.

Fiona Ebonsight stood in the doorway with her gaze cast out the window toward the would-be invading army. She had expected a show of force for some time now, but now that it stood at their very doorstep, each moment that those troops threatened the walls of the Academy, it was a moment closer to the unthinkable resolution of the situation.

"Any word from Albitonin?" Aris asked calmly.

Fiona shook her head.

"Nothing more than the last communication that said Leonora should be here in a few days to negotiate for the inclusion of the Academy of Arcane Arts and the whole of the Kingdom of Menoris into the camp of the Empress Marlae Lorien. However, I feel that a change is about to come over this little rebellion, but I cannot tell if it is one for good or for ill. I had been tempted to seek the advice of the Maldovrin Triplets in this matter, but seeking them through the flows of magic has revealed nothing. Either they are dead, or they simply do not want to be found."

Suddenly a horn blew in the camp of the invading Imperial Army, and the soldiers began to mobilize. They were advancing toward the walls of the Academy, fully armed and ready for a fight.

Jastra hung her head and said a small prayer to herself.

"Ashinica has failed in her task, there will be war...."

Grace of the Fallen

Year Three of the Just Emperor Kaitain "Dragonsbane" Lorien, Creator's Calendar Year 1870

The Dark Citadel of the Fallen had never been filled with so much life and so much hope, and even as the Dark Gods began to make preparations for the most important council meeting since their imprisonment on the world of Espre, there were some that were not full of the jubilation and anticipation that seemed to run rampant. Sitting alone in her chambers, Midarin sat looking into her long mirror and sighed. How long ago had it been that the lines began to deepen in her face? How long had it been since it stopped hurting when she rolled over and expected her husband to be there? Pulling her hair back away from her face, she reached for the small piece of green fabric, worn by time and by use, and quickly tied her hair into a tail. As she stood again, she inwardly felt the twinges of power deep inside her, the power given to her by the Creator long ago when she joined her husband in the Heavens. She had never understood the power that he had at his disposal when he had once been called the Brother of Angels, but now that she had the power of a god at her disposal, she hated the Creator all the more. What she wouldn't have given to just be normal again. To give up everything she had, all the power, all the heroic deeds that seemed a thousand lifetimes ago, and just die….ignorant…..and happy in the arms of her husband. Even her daughter was not a comfort. Already she had watched a son die….twice, and in the pit of her stomach she knew that her daughter would fall. Camille was strong, wise, and powerful, but a life guarding Tess Annis could only end one way, and that was in death. But, it would have made Gwydeon proud that their daughter was living in the same way he had, so Midarin could take some small solace in that face. Suddenly Midarin felt a set of eyes watching her, and when she looked in the mirror she caught a familiar face. While she had expected a scowl to curl the corners of her lips, when she caught a glimpse of her own face in the mirror, she was shocked by the smile.

"It's been a long time, Midarin," the red-haired woman said brightly, "you look well."

Midarin turned and felt her hands go to her hips.

"I never thought I would ever see you again, Bryn. But then again, as the last of your kind, I suppose it's hard to just give up and die."

There was more venom in her voice than Midarin intended, and much to her surprise, Bryn's smile widened. The two women had never been friends, had never trusted one another, and for her part, Midarin would have loved to see Bryn die a painful death for what she was.

"Civility was never your strong suit, was it Midarin? I suppose that is why Gwydeon loved you as much as he did. The two of you were such a strange pair."

Midarin scoffed.

"No stranger than you and Aerith, I suppose."

Bryn moved out of the doorway of Midarin's chambers and sat lightly on the edge of a plush gray chair in the corner. She smoothed the dress down her thighs for a moment and then looked up at Midarin again.

"I didn't come here for a fight, Midarin, I came here because I need your advice and your help."

Without looking, Midarin began to sit, and the chair behind her turned quickly and slid under her. While Midarin may not have liked the powers that she had been given, she had to admit that they did have interesting uses at times.

"I'm listening."

Bryn ran her fingers through her long hair briefly and then sighed. There was obviously a great weight on the woman, and Midarin could practically feel it from across the room. Bryn had always been a strong woman to say the least. As the first daughter of the demon-god Shau-ling, Bryn had to be strong in a way that Midarin could never comprehend. She was confident, cruel, blatantly sexual in everything she did, and quite possibly the most manipulative woman that had ever drawn a breath, even more so than her long-dead sister Caris. But, like every villain and hero alike, Bryn had a weakness, and her weakness was the man named Aerith Seth. He pierced her heart deeper than any blade ever could, and though it had taken lifetimes, Bryn had found that which she had been seeking. In spite of herself, Midarin had always admired that of Bryn and Aerith. They never stopped trying to find a way to be together, even when it seemed that the whole universe was trying to tear them apart.

"You're about to hear Pike tell you about a plan to go home in the Council chambers...." Bryn started.

"I know," Midarin interrupted. "It's hard to keep a secret from any member of the Dark Gods here in the Citadel. Besides, I think everyone knew you were here the moment you used a portal to get here. There aren't that many people on Espre who know how to do that. Aerith is the only non-Dark God that I know of who can. So I figure you used one of his stones....."

Bryn shook her head. With a simple snap of her fingers, a bright green flame appeared at the tip of her index finger and danced in the light for a long moment before disappearing back into the nothingness from whence it came. A sudden spark of recognition flashed in Midarin's eyes, and her smile faded.

"I'm back."

Bryn's words were as simple and as terrifying as any that Midarin had ever heard in her life. Though Bryn for all of the time that Midarin had known her was an ally to the forces of the Light on Onea, she was still born a member of the phasia, a group filled with such evil that they nearly made slaves of the entire world. Had it not been for petty jealousy and cut-throat competition between them, they may have succeeded in dominating everything that lay before them.

"So, the Lady Fox lives again."

Midarin tried hard to keep the shock and discomfort from her voice, but was sure she failed. Long ago Midarin had been thrust into battle against the phasia at the side of the man who would eventually become her husband and a band of fresh-faced youths with the laughable goal of saving the world. How much had they lost in the attempt to save a world that had been doomed from the beginning? And even in winning they had lost everything. Their world was gone, their lives taken; even their names had been robbed from the survivors. Now they were damned; doomed to walk the world of Espre for eternity as punishment for being the heroes they never truly wanted to be. The word hero rung hollow in Midarin's mind even as Bryn began speaking again.

"But not without a price that I don't know if I will be able to pay."

Midarin was snapped from her introspective moment by the twinge of pain and regret in Bryn's voice. Never before had she heard the woman sound more human.

"What happened, Bryn?"

Bryn fell silent, then exhaled softly and raised her head as if to speak but was interrupted by the young woman who burst into the room.

"Midarin, come quick!" Lissa nearly shouted, almost out of breath.

Midarin shot up, and was about to ask a question, but abandoned it as quickly when Lissa turned and sprinted out of the room. There was a quick look between the two women before they each followed, unsure of what awaited them.

* * * * * * * * * * * *

Aryx could not believe his eyes when he entered the chambers of his daughter and her husband. For nearly two thousand years, Lissa had been without her husband Wolf, a victim of the fall from grace. But now, Wolf sat on the edge of his eternal bed, scratching his beard, yawning slightly in spite of himself. There was something different about the man now, there was more to his awakening than just his physical being pulled from the veil of slumber. Something had awakened inside Wolf, something familiar. It was then that Wolf fixed his eyes on Aryx's, and a knowing smile crept to the younger man's lips.

"You feel it too, don't you brother?"

A wave of recognition passed through Aryx in a way he could not describe. The young man sitting before him was his son-in-law, it was the man that his daughter had married, but that was only on the outside. However, the soul inhabiting the body was not that of the son of Logan and Elwyne Ranthall…it was in fact something older, stronger, and much more familiar.

"Feel what?"

Aryx's mouth was dry. He didn't need an answer to the question. Already there was a burning in the back of his mind, a flame long-extinguished burned anew. The phantom green fire flickered at the edge of his consciousness. The Blaze had returned, and no matter how Aryx tried to ignore its siren-song, he felt it as surely as he could still feel the ache in the shoulder of his non-existent arm. It was then that Lissa rounded the corner with Midarin and Bryn in tow, while Diana entered from the other side of the room. The tension in the room was palpable, but was broken the instant that Lissa breached the distance and threw her arms around her long-lost husband, tears filling her eyes and streaming down her face. Wolf held his wife against him, but as Aryx looked into the man's eyes, the caring and love that should have been there was eerily missing. Suddenly, as if struck, Lissa pulled away, the joy of the reunion shattered.

"Why isn't your heart beating?"

Lissa's shaky voice sent a shiver of recognition through Aryx's body. Wolf had called him brother…the common greeting from one member of the phasia to another. They were all children of the living nightmare Shau-ling….they were all agents of damnation. Each in their own way had been forged by the life-giving power of the Blaze, a force created by nature itself that fueled everything and yet could be turned to devour everything.

Bryn walked to Lissa's side and put her hand softly on the younger woman's shoulder.

"It's alright dear. There is nothing to be concerned about. You may see Wolf on the outside, but I don't think the boy you knew is there on the inside. Isn't that right, brother?"

A wicked smile came to Wolf's face, a smile that Aryx knew all too well. Long ago, Wolf had been given the gift of power from a dying member of the phasia, an act that had eventually led to the destruction of the world they had all once called home. The imbalance had threatened to engulf everything and wipe all the citizens of Onea completely off the slate of reality. It was only through courage and faith that the forces of light and darkness were able to save the inhabitants of their world.

"Oh, Wolf is still here, Bryn," the dark voice responded. "But he is still sleeping. This body would still be asleep were it not for the rash actions of your dear husband. Now that the Blaze burns again, I was brought back. However, I am as surprised as you that this is the case."

Bryn took two steps forward and put her hand on the man's shoulder.

"It's good to see you again, Basille."

＊ ＊ ＊ ＊ ＊ ＊ ＊ ＊ ＊ ＊ ＊ ＊

Sadrina Annis sat on her throne, her mind troubled with the words of her husband. Pike would not divulge more than that there was a way for the Dark Gods to return from whence they came, and that the woman in the red dress had opened the door. However, even as she thought, happy for her husband, her thoughts went to herself and her children. What would become of her? What would become of Darrien and Tess? Would they ascend with their father into the Heavens to take the fight to the Creator, or would they remain stuck somewhere between mortal and god? And what of her life, being a mortal? Even as her troubled thoughts began to plague her more and more, Darrien emerged from the shadows with Lord Alderin close at her heels. It was not much of a secret that Darrien and Alderin were lovers. Though Aryx would have frowned at the relationship, Sadrina found it almost amusing. Aryx and Pike had always had a tenuous friendship, and the thought of Pike's daughter and Aryx's son entering into a love affair was laughable at the least. Should Darrien and Alderin ever become joined in marriage, Pike and Aryx would truly be family, a fact that neither man would relish. As Darrien sat on her throne and Alderin took his position to her right, Sadrina looked over to her daughter and smiled.

"How are you, my daughter?"

Darrien frowned.

"I feel as though we have been forgotten, mother. All of us. The Dark Gods are plotting and planning for this grand campaign that we have only heard whispers about, and the children have been forgotten. The only consolation I take is the fact that Serrina too seems to be shut out of the big secret. It's the first time I think she has ever been on the outside looking in.'

"She is being sent away on a mission," Alderin said in his cold emotionless voice. "Another fact that grates at her."

"A mission?" Sadrina asked.

"A mission for the Council," Pike's voice called from the corridor. "We must recall the Forgotten."

The color drained from Sadrina's face. She had only heard of the Forgotten in snippets of conversations that Pike had with other members of the Dark Gods, but never had he spoken of it openly to her. Before she could find her voice, it was Darrien who asked the question.

"Who are the Forgotten, father?"

Pike smiled….a sight that Sadrina had not seen in some time, and it shook her to the core. A change had come over the man that she had married, a joy had returned to his heart, a joy that even the birth of his children could not bring to the surface.

"The Dark Gods are not the only ones who were cast from the Heavens in the Great Purge, Darrien. There were others, our old allies who were cast down as well. Serrina's parents and a few others, including Aerith and Bryn. In order for us to be successful in what I have planned, we need all of those who were cast down, and that includes all of the members of the Forgotten. That is why I am sending Serrina. She will be able to deliver her parents back into the fold. The other three will have to be pulled back by Bryn, but that can wait until after the Council meets."

"Will we be allowed to attend the session?" Alderin questioned, his voice aloof and matter-of-fact as always.

"I'm afraid not," Pike answered softly, "but not because you are being shut out. Darrien, you and Alderin must leave immediately."

Sadrina was puzzled, from the look on Darrien's face, she was not alone.

"And where am I to go, father?" Darrien asked standing and smoothing her lavender dress.

"To Cadaria," Pike said turning. "Bring Tess home."

Sadrina watched as Pike walked into the darkness of the hall, wanting to speak, wanting him to tell her more, but she knew it was pointless. Pike never divulged anything more than he wanted, and despite his change in mood, Sadrina did not expect that to change. Darrien turned to her mother, kissed her gently on the cheek and then turned to Alderin.

"We should leave for Albitonin then, and make haste."

Sadrina sat and watched as the two children of the Dark Gods walked out of the receiving hall with a purposeful stride. When the dark haunting voice pierced the silence, a cold chill ran through Sadrina's body.

"Everything is changing, my Queen," Jehna Feris said coldly, "and I am afraid that this is the last time that I will ever be able to speak to you."

Sadrina did not turn to face the ancient woman. She knew that this day would come. The Dark Seer's fate was that of pain and isolation, and that could not be prevented. Jehna had surrendered to her fate.

"I am sorry to hear that, Jehna. You are much valued and much loved in the court of the Dark Gods. We shall miss you."

There was a sigh from behind Sadrina.

"More than you can imagine, my Queen. But, I shall give you one more vision before I take my leave of this place and go to meet my fate. We all have a price that we must pay for our role in the downfall of this civilization, and mine is no greater than any other. It shall just come sooner than most."

Sadrina stood and turned to face the Dark Seer and was shocked at the woman who stood before her. Where only days ago Jehna had looked young and vital, now the age of dozens of years had racked her features. Her hair was gray, and deep lines cut into her face and body. The day before she had looked like a woman in her early twenties, but now her features were that of an eighty-year old woman; frail, wispy, and fading.

"Be not concerned by this shell, my Queen. Think of it as a husk that can be cast off like that of a serpent shedding its skin. The power within is still young. But now, heed the words of the Dark Seer, for they may save the life of yourself and those that you love."

Jehna's eyes closed and her body began to tremble for a moment before she began to speak in a low, distant voice.

"Fate is conspiring both for and against the Dark Gods, my Queen, and in the end, it will not be the power of the Dark Gods, or even the Creator that will hold sway over the fates of all. Innocence and love will be both a great aid and hindrance to the world, and through tragedy will come hope, and through hope will come destruction. Only one man may wipe away the tears of the dragon, and only one man may mend the glass heart."

Her final prophetic words spoken, Jehna Feris opened her eyes, and held the back of the throne, steadying herself from the exertion. In a practice voice, Sadrina spoke.

"I will heed your words, Dark Seer."

Jehna smiled and turned to leave. Then, she turned back, sorrow filling her eyes.

"I shall miss you, my Queen, perhaps more than anyone. One day, you shall help fulfill the legacy of my clan, of this I have no doubt, though doing so may mean the end of your life, but not your death. Trust not your eyes, my Queen, for they will deceive you. Instead trust your heart, and the hearts of those you value. Every devil has divinity just as surely as every angel has wickedness.'

With those last words the Dark Seer turned again and walked slowly from the hall, her steps drawing her ever closer to the ominous end that awaited her. And even as Sadrina watch the woman go, her mind was filled with strange and confusing words, and her heart ached with the terrible pain of destiny.

* * * * * * * * * * * *

"How is this possible?"

Aryx's frustration could be felt like a hot wind passing through the room.

"For that, I will yield the floor to our sister, Bryn," Basille spoke again, his voice sounding less and less like Wolf's with every word.

Bryn met Aryx's gaze the next moment and felt anxiety fill her. She could only guess at what had happened after she stepped through the portal, but what she did know for sure was that Aerith was still alive, somewhere, and if he was alive, that could only mean one thing.

"When you came to us Aryx, you asked us to convince Evan to come here and speak with Pike to try and avert a war. Because we thought it was such an important cause, we agreed."

"Pike would have never allowed that," Midarin said chidingly.

"Which is why we didn't tell him," Diana responded.

Bryn ignored the banter and continued.

"When we met with Evan, he was not the man that we remembered. The years without Meredith had warped his mind and made him bitter and resentful of everything that was tied to his past. We learned that Evan had actually been the architect of a plot that gave the dragons the ability to murder Pike."

Lissa and Midarin both responded with gasps, while Aryx clenched his fist gritted his teeth. Only Wolf/Basille and Diana seemed unaffected by the news.

"Of course, since we all know Aerith so well, you know he did not react well to this news."

"How bad did Evan hurt him?"

Diana's question was not one of jest. Aerith's temper was well known, and his tolerance for any plot that involved the Creator was non-existent.

"It was going to be more one-sided if it weren't for the fact that Aerith had a little memento of Onea."

Aryx smiled.

"So that's where it went….."

Midarin's puzzled look was mirrored by Lissa and Diana's. Aryx was quick to answer the unspoken question.

"There are only two little souvenirs from Onea that still survive, other than all of us. The first is Gwillim's red armor that Pike has hanging in the wardrobe in his private study. Gwydeon gave it to him just before he left to lead the assault on Aldere and to make the deal with Terrik Lorien. The other was the Dragon Sword."

Bryn nodded.

"When we fell, Gwydeon gave it to Aerith for safe-keeping. I think Gwydeon knew what was coming, he just didn't know when. So, when Aerith challenged Evan, things got out of hand, and the only option Aerith had was to use the Dragon Sword as a conduit to reclaim the powers that he gave Evan all those years ago."

It was then that a new voice entered the room.

"That would explain why I feel like this."

Lissa wheeled to see the woman who could have been her sister. Sabrina was a refugee from the Dark Mirror, much as Pike and Bryn were. On Onea, Sabrina had been the daughter of a great family, with a powerful name, and still she had been gifted with the abilities passed down from Aerith Seth, a Chosen One of the prophecies. Even as Lissa looked on her oldest friend, she winced, seeing the trickle of blood flowing for her left nostril, and the blood-stained rag clutched in her hand.

"Aerith was returned to power, and in doing so, he has restored more than just his own powers. Somehow the Blaze has been reawakened, and with it, my powers," Bryn finished.

Aryx fell silent, as did the rest of the room.

"Tell them the rest," Basille said finally.

Bryn gritted her teeth. She wasn't sure what she thought was true, but it was the only possibility.

"Aerith struck Evan down."

There were shocked gasps from everyone but Aryx. Aryx knew as soon as Bryn began the story that Evan's end had come to pass. He had felt the moment that the Blaze had returned, its seductive call filling him once again. It had been so long since he had last felt its loving power sweep through him. He resisted opening himself up to the power, to let it fill him as Bryn had.

"And that is why we are going home my friends," Pike's voice said from the corridor behind Diana.

Pike entered the room, his old axe Fury hanging from the loop on his belt. It had been absent for so long, shut away with the rest of the denied past. Now, he wore it proudly, and wore it with purpose.

"The Voice of the Creator has fallen," he continued. "One of the covenants has been broken. It's time for the Dark Gods to go hunting. When the last of the Creator's envoys falls by our hand, the Creator will have no choice but to deal with us....personally."

Final Orders

Year Three of the Just Emperor Kaitain "Dragonsbane" Lorien, Creator's Calendar Year 1870

Felicia had never seen her father scowl so much in such a short span of time. First the less-than-civil dinner with his brother, the Emperor, followed by the wonderful and yet at the same time vexing introduction to the woman that would become his sister and the Empress of Cadaria. Then there was the confrontation, Felicia would almost call it a collision, with the Court Sorceress Irene Drage. It was all followed too quickly by the assassination attempt, and then Feyd and Felicia's flight from the Imperial Court of Aldere. It seemed that the frown had almost permanently been carved into her father's ruggedly handsome features. At least there had been a few bright spots, Felicia reflected as their horses made quickly for the lands of Lordhill.

* * * * * * * * * * * *

Year Two of the Just Emperor Kaitain "Dragonsbane" Lorien, Creator's Calendar Year 1869

Feyd and Felicia had just been allowed to take their leave from the presence of the Emperor, and the door had barely been shut when the first of a long litany of curses began to emerge as a growl from Feyd's throat.

Though Felicia was hardly shocked at the behavior, she did tug at her father's sleeve in an attempt to get him to lower the volume of his rambling condemnation of his brother's behavior. Out of the corner of Felicia's eye, she saw Galen stiffen, and only then did Felicia become aware of the page who waited just within listening distance. His face had gone scarlet, but he did his level best to keep his eyes trained on the stones of the hallway and not gape at the offensive language.

"Father," Felicia intoned as softly and as carefully as she could, "remember we are in your brother's house, and that there are more ears that can hear offence than just his own."

Feyd regarded his daughter for a moment, caught sight of the page, and then glowered. There was no shame in his expression, and certainly no remorse for what he had said.

"There is no secret, my dear daughter, that I would like nothing more than if my dear brother burned in hell for the rest of eternity," Feyd said in his best dispassionate voice.

This admission brought a stifled gasp from the page.

"But that said," Feyd continued, "he is my brother, and I wish that he one day would accept the happiness that I wish for him, and would wish me the same. Perhaps his new bride will help him to discover all of the things that his heart has forgotten."

The page seemed to lighten with those words, and finally approached, the color slowly returning to his face. Not many were accustomed to hearing anyone openly speak ill words about the Emperor within the Imperial Palace, with the possible exception of the Princess Marlae. However, many allowances for her behaviors had been tolerated all of her life.

"My Lord Feyd," the page said in his most level voice, "the Empress-to-be, awaits you in the Imperial Dining Room with her retinue. She wishes to honor the most-beloved brother of the Emperor and his renowned daughter."

Feyd smiled briefly.

"At least my soon-to-be sister has more tact than my own flesh and blood."

The page paled again.

"Please extend our gracious thanks to the Empress-to-be," Felicia responded in her practiced courtly voice. "We shall not tarry in our acceptance of her invitation."

The page bowed, quickly turned on his heel and hurried off. Feyd turned to his daughter and put a hand on either side of her face, and then kissed her squarely on the forehead.

"You are far too good at these games, my dear. You have all the grace of your mother and your grandmother which I fear were lost on my brother and I. It's a shame that you cannot inherit the throne my dear, as I am sure that Cadaria would be well tended were it to fall into your hands."

Felicia looked into her father's eyes for a moment and saw true sorrow there. He had never let his defenses down this far in her presence, and he had not spoken of her mother since her tragic death. There was more to the story that Feyd would never divulge, and it had something to do with the great hatred that had grown between the brothers. Feyd did not wait for a response before taking Felicia's hand and leading her down the corridor toward their meeting with the newest members of the family.

* * * * * * * * * * * *

Dominique found herself almost holding her breath when the doors to the Imperial Dining Room opened. While little had made her nervous or self-conscious during her time in the Imperial Palace, and as headstrong as she had been in the confrontations with Irene and Marlae, the forthcoming meeting with Feyd and Felicia left her feeling completely out of place. Though she was only Seraph's mistress back in Thorigald, she had taken every opportunity to learn all that she could about courtly manner. Though the little she had gleaned in that time paled in comparison to the amount that was being crammed into her mind now. She marveled often at the grace in which both Quyhn and Chelsea handled themselves within the trappings of Imperial power, and though Marlae was selfish and self-absorbed at the best of times, the little exposure that Dominique had to her made it obvious that the trappings of power and courtly virtue were not lost one iota on the young girl. Marlae may have only been in her late teens, but she had a strength and a gravitas that belied her tender age and made her seem as though she was twice or even three times her age. In court, Dominique was sure that Marlae would prove to be a terrifying figure, and she hoped that she could acquit herself half as well as the woman who would soon be her daughter.

Dominique found that she could breathe again when the page entered the room and announced that the Prince and Princess Feyd and Felicia Lorien would be joining them in a few moments. Chelsea looked over to Dominique from where she was seated on the younger woman's right and tried to force a smile. Chelsea didn't like this situation any more than Dominique did, but for entirely different reasons. This simple lunch in the honor of Feyd and Felicia would quickly devolve into a political pissing contest as soon as the newly titled Celestial Princess decided to grace them all with her appearance. The battle-lines would quickly be drawn, and Chelsea knew that Dominique would be pulled into the fray and forced to pick a side. That was the unfortunate truth when dealing with Marlae. There was no such thing as neutral ground. Either you were on her side, or you were counted among her enemies. Severe people always found the most severe stances to take, especially when counting their allies and enemies. Chelsea was firmly counted in the camp of the Celestial Princess's enemies, and that distinction had been drawn from the moment the two women had met.

"Tell me this won't be as awful as I think it will be," Dominique said, letting a brief moment of uncertainty leak into her practiced calm exterior.

"You'll do fine," Quyhn answered before Chelsea could compose her thoughts. "At least until Marlae gets here, and then just try your best not to get painted into a corner."

Before Dominique could compose a response, the doors to the dining room opened again to admit the two people that would soon become her family. Dominique rose, with Chelsea and Quyhn quickly following suit. Feyd was the first to enter, with Felicia quickly on his heels, looking every bit as graceful as her father. Feyd had the look of his brother, the two being twins after all, but there were marked differences between the two.

There was more light in Feyd's eyes, though he looked more rugged and lived than his older brother. To a simple observer, Feyd could easily have been considered Kaitain's elder by a dozen years. The other most-noticeable difference between the two men was the bright red of Feyd's hair. Kaitain's hair was darker, closer to the brown of their father, while Feyd's hair more closely resembled that of their mother's. Dominique had seen paintings of the royal family and she knew that Kaitain's looks more resembled Ender Lorien, while Feyd was more like their mother whose name Dominique had finally learned was Meris. Where Kaitain was more thinly muscled like thickly twinned rope, Feyd's muscles were broad like those of the men who labored for hours at a forge or in the mines. However, one look in Feyd's eyes erased any doubt that he and Kaitain were brothers; the same determination, the same piercing stare, the same softness in the center of a well of will. Dominique caught herself when she began to wonder what might have happened were Feyd and not Kaitain been born seven minutes earlier.

Felicia was her father's daughter; bright red hair, angular features, and a fair complexion. To Dominique's surprise, Felicia did not wear a gown, but a tightly fitting pair of what looked to be leather pants stitched up the side of each leg with elaborate grace, and they looked to hug her hips in anything but a subdued way. The heavily embroidered green shirt appeared to be her own allowance for the finery of her station, but her dress was that of a practical woman, certainly not a princess. Then Dominique remembered what Chelsea had told her. Felicia had accepted a position among the Imperial Magistrates, a position that at times seemed to be at odds with her birthright as a Princess of the Imperial Court. This was not some appointment that was gotten through the pulling of strings or calling in of favors as Chelsea had explained. Felicia had studied and proved herself a capable member of the military and earned the promotion. Chelsea had wondered if at some point Felicia would not have made a very good member of the Knights of the Flashing Blade were she to continue on the path she had started upon.

Upon entering the room, Feyd and Felicia both bowed, and Dominique instinctively began to return the bow until Quyhn caught her by the arm and gave a quick yet subtle shake of the head. Chelsea and Quyhn then bowed to Feyd and Felicia once they had returned to standing positions.

There was an uneasy silence for a moment, and then Felicia's firm yet feminine voice broke the tension.

"Thank you, Empress, for honoring us with this audience. I look forward to calling you my Aunt, and my father and I would like to welcome you graciously into the Lorien family."

Felicia bowed again, and Feyd kept his eyes trained on the younger woman standing at the head of the table. Dominique waited for a moment until Felicia straightened, and then slowly inclined her head in a gesture of acceptance. She knew from her lessons that such a gesture was a magnanimous one, and should only be reserved for the most special of occasions. She was no longer a commoner after all. She was about to become the Empress of Cadaria.

"Thank you Princess Felicia, your kindness and acceptance is most warming to my heart. You and your father are always most welcome at my table, and I should like to have my new family as close as possible."

Feyd smiled brightly and with a simple gesture from Dominique, everyone found their seats. The meal was quickly served, and there was quite a bit of simple small talk and pleasantries before Dominique felt comfortable to launch into more serious topics that interested her.

"So, Felicia," Dominique asked, remembering not to use the young woman's title which was a request from both the father and daughter early into the meal. Dominique had wanted to extend the same courtesy, but she knew from her lessons and from the cross side-ways glance from both Chelsea and Quyhn that such an indulgence would not be permitted, "How is that you gained your station at Lordhill as the Magistrate of the land? I would have thought that such an accomplished warrior such as yourself could have had any number of more prestigious postings."

Felicia smiled in spite of herself.

"Father would have preferred if I would have taken a posting in Kingdom of Fire learning from the feared Wolf of Saldarine," Felicia started with a quick smile and nod in Chelsea's direction, to which Dominique could have sworn that for the briefest of instances a slight bit of color found its way to the reserved woman's cheeks, "but I felt that it would be better if I stayed in Lordhill to keep an eye on father."

"Word is," Quyhn added in, "that Felicia spends most of her time keeping their doorstep free of the single women from the area who are falling all over themselves to take care of the poor widower."

Feyd frowned but despite himself, found himself laughing.

"You are as quick-witted as your mother was, Quyhn," Feyd said but immediately felt as though he had misspoken. Trying not to miss a beat he added, "she was a lovely woman, and a great loss to this court. She was a good friend to myself and to my wife, and was always willing to keep her eye on Felecia when called upon."

Quyhn held her best smile.

"I wish I would have had a chance to know your wife," she said finally.

At that mention, the doors burst open, and Marlae strode proudly into the room and without so much as a by your leave, plopped into the chair at the opposite end of the table from Dominique and smiled her best predatory smile across the table at the assemblage. She was followed into the room by Gabriel Shadowfall and the woman that Dominique had learned to some revulsion named Rhain who was sharing Marlae's bed.

"Many people in this family already knew Feyd's wife quite well. Isn't that right, uncle?"

Color immediately filled Feyd's cheeks while it felt like it had drained completely from Dominique's. Dominique knew Marlae to be abrupt and vicious, but this was bold even for her. The blatant disrespect of both her entrance and the following implication could not be permitted. Before anyone could speak, Feyd stood and glowered at Marlae. Dominique saw that both Gabriel and Rhain's hands went to their weapons. The tension in the room was at a level that could explode.

"I don't have to listen to the words of an impetuous spoiled bitch who has spread her legs for more men than most of the whores in Aldere."

Chelsea was on her feet in the next moment, her hands on her weapons and edging herself between Dominique and the rest of the people at the table. Quyhn snorted, unable to stifle her laugh completely. If Dominique had any reaction at all, it was one of horror and fearful paralysis. Marlae to her credit seemed completely unphased by the insult. Instead, her venomous smile deepened.

"It seems that the rumors of your wife's wanderings before finding her way to your bed are quite a bit truer than I was led to believe. It's fortunate really that my father tired of her, otherwise she could have been the Empress and Felicia might have been the Voice of the Emperor instead of some tomboy playing at being a soldier. But then again, it seems that any common slut can find their way between Imperial sheets these days."

At the insult, Marlae dipped her finger into the bowl of soup that sat on the table before her and lazily played in it for a moment before withdrawing it. Before there could be any further response to her outrage, Marlae stood.

"The food like the company seems to be cold already. Tell my father that I happily abided his request to join this gathering of poor relations, but finding the atmosphere lacking, I retired to my chambers until needed for his wedding. Also tell him that should he find his sow bride unable to meet his needs on their wedding night, I shall make my dear Rhain available to meet his needs. After all, common is common, regardless of how much silk is heaped upon it."

With that, Marlae left the room, her head held high and her back straight as though she had just presided over a group of bowing and scraping sycophants. Rhain was quickly behind her, right on her heels, and utterly dispassionate to her mistress's display. Gabriel hesitated only a moment, an almost apologetic glance moving first from Feyd to Dominique. Just before leaving the room, he stopped turned, and gave his best crisp salute to both Felicia and Galen, and then left the room, closing the doors behind him. The silence in the room was an explosion waiting to happen, the emotions of the moment poised on the edge of the knife of self-control. Chelsea didn't move from her position, and Feyd stared at the closed doors incredulously. Finally with a sigh, he slumped back into his chair, and pushed the soup bowl away from him towards the center of the table.

"Well," he said finally, "it could have been much worse. She has been filled with so much poison and hate from her years with her father that it is only natural that she would loose some of it on us, as my brother chooses to do at every opportunity."

Chelsea finally relaxed from her on-guard position, but she did not return to her seat.

"You have my most sincere apologies for Marlae's actions, in the name of the Throne," Dominique said finally. "I wish that I could say that she would be made to pay for her indiscretions, but I think you would know such a threat would be a hollow one."

Feyd smiled a bit at that, and the bubble of stress and frustration seemed to burst at his lightening.

"That's alright Dominique," Feyd said, his attention to title lost in the moment, "Kaitain and Marlae are particular in their way of dealing with the inferior members of the Lorien family, and they are never shy with their endeavors to make us see ourselves the way they see us. Felicia is a disappointment because she chooses to be something other than a pampered and proper princess, and I am reviled because my dearly departed wife chose me over Kaitain all those years ago."

Quyhn smiled a bit.

"So good taste is a trait of your side of the family then, Felicia."

Both Feyd and Felicia laughed at the inference, and Dominique could feel her heart lighten a bit. Such abuse should not have to be suffered by anyone, but it seemed that both Feyd and Felicia took it in stride as best they could.

"You see, Kaitain, Teairra, the young woman who would become my wife, and I all were children in the royal court. Teairra's mother and father were great friends of Ender's while they were children, and Teairra's father was an economic policy advisor to the throne. The three of us were very close growing up, and took lessons together, and played together in the Imperial Gardens until we were too old to ignore the weight of our stations. Kaitain always lusted after Teairra, while she hardly thought of him as much more than a brother. Eventually Teairra and I began to look at each other less as playmates and more as lovers. But I was called to duty by my father and the Imperial legions, while my brother, the heir to the throne stayed protected within the walls and worked his charms on my wounded love. She admitted to me upon my return that she had given in to a moment of weakness but that it had only reinforced her love for me. We were married a week following my return and I took my posting to Lordhill the following month. This began Kaitain's rebellious period when he began to hate everything that the Lorien name stood for."

Felicia's face fell a little, perhaps she had not known the story, or perhaps she simply did not like the retelling of it, Dominique could not be sure which.

"Teairra's loss was a sudden one. It was not long after Felicia was born, our first year in Lordhill. She fell ill, a fever taking her quickly. There was nothing the healers could do, but she did not die in any pain. I did my best to raise Felicia, but a man does not always understand the subtleties of raising a girl, let alone raising a princess. She has too much of her father in her at times, and no amount of softening by Gabrielle Peregrim could beat the warrior out of her."

"And you wouldn't have it any other way, father," Felicia allowed.

The suddenly much older looking Feyd smiled down at his daughter, but Dominique could almost see the weight sitting on the man's shoulders. His heart was still filled with sorrow after all these years, but Dominique could tell that he could not let it dampen for a second the pride and love he had for his daughter. Finally Feyd turned to set his eyes on Chelsea.

"So, Lady Zarova," Feyd said in his most ironic voice, "who commands the Army of Fire while you are playing bodyguard to my soon-to-be sister?"

"Father!"

* * * * * * * * * * * *

Year Three of the Just Emperor Kaitain "Dragonsbane" Lorien, Creator's Calendar Year 1870

Feyd looked down the dusty road and sighed. He could never think of a time that he felt so helpless. His brother lay in his bed, his body impotent and wracked by a poison so sinister that even the best healers in the empire could do nothing but watch and hope that he would eventually awaken. The attack had been swift and precise, but Feyd found it more than a little disconcerting that the strike had not been immediately fatal. Whoever had attacked Kaitain had not been some rank amateur. This was a planned strike to make Kaitain suffer and to plunge the empire into chaos. However, Feyd was sure that the assassin and those he worked for had not planned on the strength and conviction of the Empress Dominique. Feyd had been truly impressed by her poise in the days that followed the attack and the deft way in which she inspired the subjects of the empire without seeming weak or insensitive. She would be a force to be reckoned with in the years to come, and perhaps she had the strength to bring Kaitain back to his senses and save the empire from the foolishness that had overcome him since his ascension to the throne. Though she had not initially agreed to Feyd's request to return to Lordhill, she had eventually relented knowing the importance of securing the loyalty of that pivotal province in the face of the mounting rebellion to the west. She had wanted to send a full detachment of Imperial Guards with Feyd, but she had been convinced that such a show of force would accomplish the opposite of what its purpose would have been. Dominique wanted to protect Feyd and Felicia, that much was clear, but an armed detachment of Imperial Guards marching into Lordhill just days after the attempt on the life of the Emperor would send a dangerous message to those kingdoms whose loyalties were weakened by the swirling chaos.

Near nightfall on the fourth day of their travel, the small column of riders came upon a cloaked man hobbling down the road leaning heavily on a long walking stick. He seemed to pay no notice to the riders as they slowly made their way past. But, just as one of the Imperial Guards assigned to protect Feyd and Felicia came within arm's reach of the man, all hell broke loose. The man in the dark cloak leapt into the air, high enough that he could have leapt over a man standing flat footed, and the flash of steel took the guard straight in the throat. There was a plume of blood, and the guard fell to the ground, with the cloaked man taking over control of the saddle. He wheeled the horse around, and then stood in the saddle, riding hard at the two confused guards at the rear of the column. The two guards at the front of the column were just turning when the mysterious man struck again, leaping from the saddle at the last moment as the protesting horse rammed hard into the mount of one of the guards, sending all three toppling to the ground. The assassin flew through the air, seeming to ignore the wind, and his cruel blade struck true piercing the eye of the other guard. The guard fell, and the assassin fell with him, rolling through the impact with the ground and dragging his sword with him, still trailing the gore from the fallen guard. The other rear guard had been killed nearly instantly when the two horses landed atop him, and the cry from the horses had been terrible without having the sound of crushed bone mixed with them.

The assassin turned his blade toward the royal family members, the hood of his black cloak finally tossed revealing his cold dead white eyes and a blank expression. In an instant he was moving again, his deadly precision leveled at Feyd.

Chapter LIV

Lessons

Year Three of the Just Emperor Kaitain "Dragonsbane" Lorien, Creator's Calendar Year 1870

"So Ayden," Jaccob said quietly, "I see you're not much of a drinker."

It had been many weeks since Jaccob Aldora had met the somewhat enigmatic young man who called himself Ayden Seth, and still he had learned very little about the boy. However, what was obvious was that Ayden was possessed of great power over all of the arcane forces and some tricks Jaccob had never seen before. Ayden had elected to stay in the little town of Coventry while Jaccob attended the Imperial Wedding, and though the Topaz Knight had spent nearly a month in the Imperial Capital of Aldere tending to issues stemming from the failed assassination attempt, Ayden was still at the Inn of Coventry when Jaccob returned. Though it was quite early in the morning, Jaccob was already finishing off his second bottle of ale, and was starting to feel the pleasant effects course through him. Yet, the younger man had not touched a drop, content to drink simply water.

"The boy just can't hold his liquor," a loud burly man at an adjacent table barked out. "Maybe he should go home and suck on mommy's teat for a while."

The fat man's stained shirt caught most of the ale that spilled as he laughed, and even as Jaccob was about to engage the man in an argument, Ayden put his hand on Jacob's arm and shook his head. A moment later a loud choking sound ripped from the fat man's throat. He spit the contents of his mouth back onto the table, and one of the serving girls screamed as they saw the pool of blood on the table. Blood trickled from the corners of the man's mouth, and cautiously he dipped his finger into his mug of ale, and when he withdrew it, it was coated with a veneer of thick red blood. The man then suddenly laughed and slapped Jaccob on the shoulder.

"That's a good trick, Sir Jaccob. Don't worry, I won't bother the little boy ever again. I'd hate to hurt his feelings again."

Again the fat man slapped Jaccob on the shoulder and turned away. With a simple wave of his index finger, Ayden caused the man to trip and fall face first to the ground. In the process, he caught the edge of a nearby table, flipping the contents into the air, where they all miraculously landed on his head. When the man finally stood, his hair was matted with ale, and chunks of food clung to the soaked hair. He turned to face Jaccob, and the joviality was gone from his features, and the red rage filled his eyes. Taking a step forward, Jaccob watched as the man balled a fist and gritted his teeth. Jaccob was about to reach for Temperance, but hesitated when he saw four spittoons from different areas of the common room levitate from their places and surround the man's head. Stopping in his tracks, the man looked pensive, debating his next words.

"I'm sorry for my harsh words, Sir Jaccob," the burly man said in his best apologetic voice. "It won't happen again."

Jaccob waved a dismissive hand and then turned his attention back to his mug of wine and didn't watch as the burly man fled the common room, and the four spittoons settled back to their appointed positions. Each of the patrons returned to their meals, and the upset table righted itself without any assistance from the inn's staff. As if compelled by the mess on the floor, a mop and bucket, as well as a broom and dustpan appeared from the corner and began to quickly clean the mess before disappearing back to their proper places. A few moments later, the innkeeper came to the table.

"Terribly sorry about that, Sir Jaccob. There won't be a charge for breakfast."

When the innkeeper was out of earshot, Jaccob smiled and regarded the boy who sat before him. There was certainly more to Ayden Seth than met the eye.

"But you do have a temper don't you?"

Ayden smiled.

"I don't like people saying bad things about my mother," he intoned casually. "It's rude."

Jaccob laughed in spite of himself, and finished his mug of wine before patting Ayden on the shoulder.

"You are going to be a very interesting companion in the days to come. But for now we have much to discuss."

The two men wordlessly left the inn and headed for a small stable at the edge of Coventry. Jaccob had intended to introduce Ayden to the Emperor following the wedding, however, it would now be impossible until the poison was eliminated from the Emperor's body. That possibility had been confounded at every turn. Even the most skilled healers had failed, and now that the Kingdom of Stone, Albitonin had become a rebel state, the best healers in the whole of Cadaria had been lost to the Emperor. So, now Jaccob had to continue with his mission without exact sanction from Emperor Lorien. He had had his suspicions about Ayden Seth and the story of his expulsion from the Academy of Arcane Arts in Jelan, but Jaccob had used as many of his contacts as possible and was able to independently verify the accounts of Ayden's expulsion. Even though Jaccob did not believe in luck, it seemed that Ayden's timely saving of Jaccob's life was certainly a lucky coincidence.

"So," Ayden said pulling himself onto his horse, "where to now? I mean, I must admit I expected being associated with the Topaz Knight would be much more exciting."

"As with you, my young friend," Jaccob replied flatly, "appearances are often deceiving. With the turmoil in the countryside stemming from the assassination attempt on through the tragedies of Rashaleb and the rumors of rebellion coming from Albitonin, it's amazing that the Knights of the Flashing Blade have any credibility left. I fully expect that I shall be recalled at some point and put to death for some imagined slight."

Ayden regarded his companion for a moment and winced. He thought his father was melodramatic when he used to talk about his days on Onea.

"Surely things can't be that bad."

Jaccob turned with the thought of chiding his young companion for his ignorance, but what he saw removed the words from his mind. Jaccob had been concentrating his attention on the road, but Ayden had other activities on his mind. Somehow he had removed the blanket from under his horse's saddle, tied it lightly to his own saddle, stretch the gap and tied it to Jaccob's saddle and now lay perfectly comfortable in the makeshift hammock. The scene was laughable and miraculous at the same time.

"You my young friend are nothing short of the most curious person I've ever met."

Ayden regarded Jaccob for a moment.

"Can I ask you a question, Jaccob?"

The sudden seriousness in the boy's tone sent a momentary shiver through Jaccob's back, and he slowly nodded his ascent.

"You strike me as a very intelligent man, Jaccob. So it's because of that I wonder why it is you do nothing but spend your life drunk."

"And you don't temper your words much, do you?" Jaccob mumbled looking down at the bottle of ale clutched in his hand.

Ayden rolled his head to the side and looked up at Jaccob.

"Before I went off to the Academy of Arcane Arts, a place I didn't want to be in the first place, my mother sat me down and had a long talk with me about all manner of things that I didn't want to hear. Most were embarrassing and words I didn't want to hear coming from my mother, but there was one thing she said to me that day that I have held in my heart since then. My mother is a proud woman, and has been known to be coarse in her dealings with others, but she said to me that the only words she ever regretted were the words she did not give voice."

Ayden fell silent, but his eyes did not leave Jaccob's face. It was then that a feeling hit the back of Jaccob's mind. This was not a man who would be expelled from the Academy for some misbehavior. He was too smart and controlled for that. He would know the letter of the law and he would just come to the edge of breaking every rule, but would never do anything that would warrant expulsion. There was another motivation involved.

"So who was she?"

Ayden to his credit didn't flinch. Jaccob's voice has been calm yet firm in the same time. He was confident in his assessment of the situation. Ayden had obviously been trying to impress someone. What's more, it couldn't have been one of the students, that would have been too easy for someone of his skill. After a moment, a smile blossomed onto Ayden's face.

"Another lesson my mother taught me is to never surrender information without getting something in return. So, an answer for an answer. You tell me what I want to know, and I'll tell you what you want to know."

Jaccob laughed and shook his head. He dropped the bottle of ale into his saddlebag, and for the briefest of moments took hold of Temperance to clear his head. Ayden deserved more than just the varnish of truth that time had laid upon the history of Jaccob Aldora.

* * * * * * * * * * * *

Tolon Morr walked more slowly than his legs wanted to carry him. Jerrica Maldovrin had proved to be a wonderful companion, but her aversion to horses and the slow rate of speed that she could travel at, and the increased number of rest stops that she needed had severely impacted the speed at which they could cover ground. Luckily, Jerrica was not averse to sleeping outdoors on the ground, which made things much easier in the long run. Tolon found her nearly perpetual mirth intoxicating. Everything she was seeing was both new and familiar in the same token. She had never been anywhere by herself, and as it was the travels of the Maldovrin Triplets had been extremely limited. The world both feared and revered the powers of the three women, but unfortunately the fear seemed to win out more often than not. Tolon had tried over the past weeks to assemble some type of understanding about the woman who would be his traveling companion for the foreseeable future. Though, the term foreseeable future took on a whole new meaning when traveling with one of the most gifted prophets in the whole of Espre.

"I'm sorry Jerrica," Tolon said again, "but I am just having a hard time getting all of this to make sense in my head. I'm just a fighter, and I'm afraid that my facility with information has been limited to pick up weapon and embed it in the nearest head."

Jerrica giggled, an intoxicating mix of soft chimes and the sound sunlight must make to plants. Every time she laughed, Tolon felt his insides weaken in a way they never had.

"I think you understand far more than you think you do, Tolon," Jerrica said smiling, and she took hold of his arm and rested her head on his shoulder as they walked, a posture she often took when explaining things that were so simple to her, while to him was like carrying a castle on his back while trying to swim the distance from Cadaria to Mythryn.

She held up her left hand. "You see this ring on my finger? This simple bronze band? To you it seems flawless and runs in a complete circle. That is the same way you see time, you and nearly everyone else on this world. Those of us with the gift of sight, either from the Forer line, or from some other means, like those abilities the Dark Gods have, see more than just a flawless band. We see the subtle imperfections, the warps and pits in the metal, the slight malformation that makes the circle a little less exact. Seeing what other people cannot or will not is what you call supernatural or magical. In some ways it's nothing more than being observant."

Tolon nodded.

"Alright, but seeing the future can't be just seeing the imperfections in the world around you."

Jerrica lifted her hand to his face and touched the tip of his nose lightly with her finger.

"You knew I was going to do that before I did it, didn't you?"

Tolon smiled and nodded. That had become one of her favorite methods to both tease him and tell him that he was on the right track. 'As simple as the nose on your face,' she would say. Tolon knew that he was not the smartest man in the world, nor would he ever be, but Jerrica had a way of making him feel stupid and brilliant in the same breath.

"My ability is almost the same thing. It's a mixture of seeing the world the way it really is, and the intuition gained from how the world has always worked before. The only other piece is the insight that we gain from the power in our blood. It gives us a glimpse of how fate may intervene."

Tolon stared blankly then shook his head.

"You lost me again."

Jerrica smiled.

"Events play out based on a combination of the actions of everyone and everything involved, but that isn't the only force involved. Fate, or destiny, or divine mandate, whatever words you want to use to describe it, is also an active participant in everything that happens. And sometimes that force can add just enough of a nudge to send things spinning in an entirely new direction. Some people think that is where instinct comes from anyway. The feeling you get in the pit of your stomach or the back of your mind when things are going to work out a way that you didn't initially think possible. Some people think that comes from fate. Fate touching you in a way to let you know what you should be doing. The Church of the Creator calls it the Touch of the Creator. Others like to call it Divine Inspiration. Those of us touched with the ability to See have less abstract ways of looking at it. Fate to us is as palpable as water. If you learn to see and manipulate the flows of fate, you can determine what events will transpire and how they will ripple outward and impact the things around it."

"Alright," Tolon said after a moment, "so why is it that your abilities are reduced without your sisters, and why can't you see what is going to happen to us on our journey."

The smile on Jerrica's face faltered for a moment, and Tolon felt as though he had been too blunt in his questioning. Jerrica had never been away from her sisters, and the transition was very difficult on her, regardless of the show of strength she tried to put forth.

"When dealing with the future, or anything for that matter," Jerrica started, her voice shaky at first, "a person's own experiences and bias comes into play. We sometimes interpret the visions the way we would like them to turn out, even if we don't realize that we are impacting the vision. When my sisters and I all see the same thing, we are more easily able to shed our own bias and come closer to the truth of the vision. As alike as we are, we are different enough so that the visions become clearer to the three of us."

Jerrica paused for a moment and searched Tolon's face to ensure that he was still understanding her before continuing.

"As far as my visions alone, besides the added bias, there is another factor. When someone takes an action, it is like tossing a stone into the pool of fate. The stone creates ripples across the face of time and reality, which in turn causes other ripples and makes other actions both possible and impossible. When you are standing outside the pond, you can see the ripples clearly and understand all of the possibilities. However, when you are the person taking the action, you aren't standing on the edge of the pool looking in, you are casting the stone from within the pool itself. So what is making the ripples? The stone itself, or the act of throwing the stone, or just your own presence in the pool? The closer you are to the situation, the less you are able to see. Perspective works the same for our ability as it does for your own eyesight."

To accentuate the final point, she touched the tip of his nose again with her thin, delicate fingers. This brought a laugh from both of them. Tolon was still laughing softly when Jerrica pulled away from him. She was looking off into the distance, transfixed by something. Her eyes went completely white, and Tolon knew that something was wrong.

Behind her dead eyes, all Jerrica saw was blackness. Then a flash of red sparked across her vision. It was blood, so much blood. Bodies of the broken and dying littering a field of battle. But this was no war. The dead were common people, peasants, unarmed, women, and children. It was a slaughter. In the background, which Jerrica knew to be a time after the vision she saw before her eyes, she saw thousands of men and women, their clothes in tatters, their hands and feet bound in irons as they moved to the beat of the whips at their backs. The cries of the dying in the foreground were drowned out by the sounds of the crying a suffering in bondage. Just as suddenly as the vision had come, it was over, but her vision did not return. All she could see was the field of blood before her. She knew where it was, and she knew where they had to go.

"Jerrica," Tolon said turning to face her. "What's wrong?"

"Saldarine," Jerrica said in a shaky voice, "something terrible is going to happen there. We have to go."

Tolon picked Jerrica up off the ground and cradled her in his arms, with her head on his shoulder. He would have to make up for their languid pace now, and the only way to do that was to carry her as far as his arms and his body would allow. As he began to push forward, he heard Jerrica begin to sob. It took only a moment for him to feel the hot tears touch his bare arm. What he never saw was that the tears were not water, but blood.

* * * * * * * * * * * *

Jaccob exhaled slowly.

"I wasn't always like this, Ayden," he said in an almost resigned voice, "and I never wanted to be anything more than a Master in the Academy. I hoped one day to be considered on the same level as Alistair Ravenheart and the other great masters in the history of the Academy. But the war and the suffering got the best of me, and I made a mistake. I see now that I was wrong. I wanted the Academy to become a weapon, to strike first at the Dark Gods on Mythryn, to take the fight to them. But Alistair was right, I know that now. That kind of power could be easily perverted and turned into something that would cause more destruction and pain than it could ever prevent."

Ayden was taking a much less relaxed pose, showing a bit more respect and deference to his friend than was the norm.

"But that isn't why you're a drunk. It's what changed your mind about the purpose of the Academy that causes you to drink."

Jaccob smiled despite himself, a half-smirk that just raised the right corner of his mouth.

"Very astute. But I wish I could say that the conversion of my beliefs was a pleasant experience. When I was named to the position of the Topaz Knight of the Flashing Blade, I thought it was an opportunity to further my goals. I was put in charge of a secret project sponsored by the Emperor himself, to assemble a group of men who thought the same was as I did. To train them in offensive magic, and to make them into a force that could bring the fight to the Dark Gods."

Ayden nodded.

"And that is where you are taking me. To become part of this order."

Jaccob didn't try to deny it.

"I'm taking you there only because that is where you want to go. You wouldn't be here if you didn't want to be, Ayden, and you certainly wouldn't have come to seek me out on some level of coincidence. Even if you were trying to get yourself expelled, they wouldn't have just let you go. You're working for the Masters, and they sent you to try to figure out what the Emperor was doing. I know that the rumors have gotten around about the Emperor's secret projects. There are too many eyes and ears in the Imperial Palace for it not to have. It only takes one little bird getting back to Fiona to cause a little panic."

Ayden chuckled.

"My attempts at gaining the favor of a woman did have unintended consequences. She was a little harder to impress than just reversing gravity or making some frogs appear. So I had to get my hands dirty a little. And who better to go to than the most famous fallen member of the Academy.

It made sense. Besides, I knew exactly where you would be, and I knew that you would be getting into a spot of trouble."

Jaccob looked at Ayden sternly.

"I mean," Ayden continued smoothly, "someone with your reputation for drinking and carousing would find himself in a tight spot sooner or later. I just needed to be in the right place at the right time."

The older man seemed to be placated by the explanation. But Ayden continued.

"But that doesn't tell me what makes you turn to the bottle at every moment. What is it that you are trying to erase now that you have had your change of heart about attacking the Dark Gods with arcane attack dogs."

Jaccob swallowed hard.

"Dreams. Nightmares really. Ever since I was named a member of the Knights of the Flashing Blade, and Temperance was put in my hands, they have gotten worse and worse. The drink is the only thing that keeps them away for any length of time. All I see is the death of this world. So much blood, so much death. There is always this young girl in my dreams, and she seems to be at the center of it all. Every night I get closer to seeing her face, every night I get closer to hearing what she is saying. But the dreams keep changing. Sometimes it's the Emperor with his arm around her throat and his laughter drowning out her words. Sometimes it's the Dark Gods. Sometimes it's even me, standing on a mountain of the dead as the world tears itself apart around me. Part of me wants to know who she is and what she is saying, the other part of me is the one that wins and reaches for the bottle."

Ayden nodded.

"I can understand why you would rather not know if what you are seeing will come to pass. But maybe together we can find a way to know the truth and keep your mind from tearing itself apart. Believe me, I have enough experience with apocalyptic dreams and visions to know how to understand and keep them at bay."

Jaccob laughed as though Ayden had told a joke. After all, the boy had to be joking, didn't he?

"So? Who was she?" Jaccob questioned, his eyes finding Ayden's again. "If I had to guess, I would say it was Aris. Though I'm sure that Fiona would fall to pieces if her saintly daughter ever found herself mixed up with a little trouble-maker like you."

Ayden smirked.

"That's old news. And believe me, Aris is no saint under the sheets."

Jaccob's mouth fell open, but Ayden continued.

"No, it's Ashinica that has my heart, and this mission isn't even half of the deal I had to make to get her attention. But if everything works out, Jaccob, we're all going to get what we want. Even you."

Lights in the Darkness

Feyd Lorien woke suddenly, pain rocketing through his body. For a moment he didn't know where he was, and looking around didn't bring anything back to his memory. He was laying on a cot, and no matter how he tried, he could not bring himself to a sitting position or move either his arms or his legs. There was no specific source for the pain, but it continued unabated. Sweat covered his brow, and his mouth was completely dry. There were two lanterns close to the cot that he lay on, but he could not see them from where he lay. However, because of the way the light was cast around the tent, it was obvious there were multiple sources of illumination. The dreams had been terrible, but even as he tried to remember them, they slipped away from him like phantoms into the shadows. Where was he? How long had he been here? What had happened? The last thing he remembered was riding back to Lordhill after the wedding and the attempt on the life of his brother. Suddenly there was a sound from the far edge of the tent. He couldn't turn his head toward the sound, and a level of panic began to set in. It wasn't until the curly red hair and the face of his daughter appeared that some of the fear began to abate.

"Father," she said the relief filling her voice, "I'm so happy to see you're awake."

Feyd worked his mouth, trying to say something to his daughter, but no matter how he tried, he couldn't make his tongue work. His lips felt cracked and dry, and his tongue seemed as though it were three sizes larger than it should have been. As if understanding without his words, Felicia reached out of his field of vision and then after a moment pressed something to his lips. The cold touch was striking, but the ice melted quickly adding much needed moisture to his lips and tongue. After several minutes of Felicia's attention, Feyd was able to croak out a word.

"Where?"

The rasp was barely above a whisper, but Felicia nodded.

"We've crossed the border into Pellatori, father. The road to Lordhill is not safe, and I don't think that we would be safe anywhere within the borders of Aldere. I've sent word to Connor Peregrim and our forces in Lordhill, and they know not to expect us for some time. We need to go into hiding for a while, at least until the threat has passed."

"What…." Feyd could barely force out the word, and Felicia shook her head nearly immediately.

"The assassin struck without warning. He killed our escort before either of us realized he was even there. Then he came after us."

* * * * * * * * * * * *

The assassin's movements were quick but precise, and it took only a matter of seconds for the escort of Imperial Guards to be subdued. A light wind and rain had started to pick up, and the black cloak swirled around the man's figure as he began to move again, the only light flashing from his stark white eyes and the steel he held in each hand. Felicia wasn't quite sure when the dagger found its way into the man's off-hand, but it was there all the same, and as he raced toward her, she did her best to draw her own sword to offer some level of defense. The man leapt from his position impossibly far away from her but seemed to be carried by some force, some unnatural force. He struck, his blade ringing against hers. Her horse spooked the next moment, rearing back, lashing out with its front hooves, trying to land a blow against the invisible malevolence that seemed to be taking hold. Felicia was thrown, and despite her best efforts, she was unable to tuck and roll through the impact with the ground, and lost control of her sword. Her shoulder stung, and she could feel numbness flooding into her fingers. Even if she were able to recover her blade before the assailant was on top of her, she would be able to do little to prevent him ending her life as easily as he had ended the lives of their escort. The assassin's singular focus brought him back toward Felicia and he propelled himself forward but a huge form intervened in his path. A flash of steel from Feyd caused the assassin to fall back briefly before changing the path of his charge, and launching himself shoulder first into the midsection of the mounted prince. The two men tumbled together and the horse bolted off in the direction of the tree line. Felicia heard a loud crack when the two men hit the ground, and the assassin was the first back to his feet. The handful of heartbeats stretched on far too long, and Feyd did not move. The assassin turned his attention fully back to Felicia, his pace slowed and much more methodical. Felicia was able to get herself somewhat upright, but her right arm still felt dead at her side. In the few seconds that her father's intervention had gained her, she had been able to draw the small dagger from her belt and held it in the best defensive position she could manage. Felicia was confident in her skill, but it was only a matter of time before a man of the assassin's obvious skill would be able to breach her meager defense and end her life. She only hoped that she could hold out long enough for her father to recover. The two of them together had a much better chance of escaping the conflict alive.

The assassin was five paces away from her when he finally lunged forward with all of his speed. He was almost on top of her, and Felicia could not help but flinch and close her eyes for the briefest of moments. She heard the clatter of steel on steel, and when she opened her eyes again, she did not see the cold white eyes of the assassin staring down at her, but she saw a brown cloak flapping in the wind, and the back of a man. He had sped in from somewhere and intercepted the assassin's strike. The two men now were struggling against each other trying to gain a leverage advantage. It seemed to be a stalemate, but from Felicia's vantage point, she couldn't see much. Finally the two men disengaged, and the assassin leapt backwards a few feet and regarded the new opponent with a blank and dead expression painted on his face. Switching his sword briefly from his right hand to his left, and then back again, the stranger shrugged off his cloak and handed it backwards to Felicia without looking back at her.

"Take care of your father, I'll take care of him."

The voice was calm, but utterly confident. Felicia took the cloak and scrambled over to where her father lay. She could tell he was still breathing, but his eyes were closed and his face was a mask of pain. It was clear that the fall from the horse had caused serious injuries. If they were not able to get him to a healer soon, a fall like that could end up being fatal. As it was, any attempts she made to move him could just as easily have killed him. After gently covering her father with their savior's cloak, Felicia turned her full attention back to the conflict.

The assassin had taken a more pronounced fighting stance now, his cloak still flapping behind him in the breeze, his dark hair slicked back by the increasing rain. The look on his face was still devoid of all emotion, and it was clear to Felicia that this man very well could be the definition of the perfect killer. The dagger in his left hand had been replaced to whatever hidden sheath that it had been produced from, and the sleek slightly curved blade of his sword was held low, the tip pointed more at his opponent's knee level. The sword itself was like nothing that Felicia had ever seen before. It was curved and much more slender than the traditional swords that Felicia had trained with, or those used by Imperial forces. The blade itself had one sharp edge that came all the way down to the circular guard. The hilt was also elongated, making it possible for the sword to be wielded with either one or two hands, and the grip was wrapped with a dark colored braided fabric. Despite its slender and sleek appearance, the weapon itself was obviously quite substantial, and had a fair bit of weight to it. His opponent wielded a more traditional longsword, but it too seemed to have unique quality to it. There was the slightest hint of gold glinting from a figure of some kind carved into the blade close to the guard. He too assumed a defensive posture with the blade of his sword held low, almost in a non-committal gesture.

For the first time, Felicia got a good look at the man who had rescued them. He was young, perhaps in his early twenties, not much older than Felicia herself, if older at all. The way he held himself, it was obvious that he was very familiar with a sword, and his wide shoulders and muscular arms told of many days spent practicing his trade. He wore no finery, and dressed more like a common farm hand than someone who had his obvious level of skill with the blade. His brown hair was short, cropped tightly around his ears, but seemed to have a willful streak to it. She couldn't see his eyes from the angle she had, but she could imagine that they were clear and filled with determination and singular focus for the conflict that was about to begin.

The two men edged closer and closer to one another, both ready to begin the conflict again in earnest. The distance between them was covered in a painful deliberate slowness, until their blades finally met. In the next second, both of the combatants moved in unison, drawing back their blades and swinging with all of their might at their opponent. The two blades met with a shower of sparks and the tortured sound of steel aching to taste blood. The two men leaned into each other again, fighting for some kind of leverage advantage against the other, but the two seemed to be equal in strength. They were nearly mirror images of each other in skill and power, at least in this clash of steel, and as they disengaged from the leverage duel, they began to circle one another with swords lowered again. The rain was starting to soak the ground, but the two men seemed to pay it no mind. Their footfalls were as confident as if they were on solid dry ground. The assassin was the first to strike, as he leapt at the stranger with his sword raised high and it came down with an inhumanly fast downward slash. The stranger's footwork was sound and rapid, putting him into the perfect position to parry the blow, but the strength of the strike forced him to one knee. The assassin leaned into the strike, trying to break the other man's guard, but the stranger had designs of his own for retaliation. His blade was held just above his head to block the strike, one hand on the hilt, the other hand on the flat of the blade to firm up the block. In one deft motion, the stranger lurched forward toward the assassin while at the same time pulling his arms back to an almost unnatural angle, forcing the disengagement of the two blades and sending the assassin forward when the counter-force to his strike was removed. Once disengaged, the stranger brought his sword around in a wide arc, then slashed it across the distance toward the assassin's exposed knees. As if sensing the counterattack, the assassin leapt over the stranger's head and rolled through before popping back to his feet and turning to face the interloper, who himself had found his way back to his feet.

The assassin finally let some emotion creep onto his face.

"Too good to be a farmer, no matter what you look like," the assassin growled, "but no match for me."

"Well," the stranger said in a cool voice, "you're wrong about me being a farmer. I wonder what else you might be wrong about."

This time it was the farmer that charged, marking the assassin's right shoulder as the target of his diagonal slash. The lunge was foiled as the assassin sidestepped and brought the blade of his unique sword down. The strike would have easily cleaved the head of a lesser opponent, and Felicia wasn't sure that she herself could have blocked it, regardless of her level of skill, but the farmer was obviously better than most. As soon as he saw that the strike would miss, he pulled his sword in and allowed his momentum to carry him into a roll that brought the farmer under the path of the assassin's sword. At the end of the roll, the farmer popped up to a knee and brought his sword up in time to stop the assassin from pressing his perceived advantaged into a hurried strike. The assassin instead kept a safe distance from the farmer as he made his way back to his feet. The two circled each other again, but this time with more speed. There was obviously a grudging respect between the two men for their skills, and the combatants were ready to put each other to the ultimate test. The assassin charged the farmer and their swords met time and time again as the two tried to find some small opening they could exploit to draw first blood. Felicia watched with a level of awe and fear. At the pace the two men were keeping, the first mistake could well be the last, and there was no doubt within her now that even at her best, she would be no match for the assassin.

Steel flashed and sparks flew as the two blades challenged one another for superiority. The two men were a blur of motion, dancing around one another with deadly precision. The two were moving at incredible speed, blocking slashes and thrusts that few other swordsmen could duplicate, let alone block. It was as if any moment one of the two would slip, and a strike would land that would prove to be fatal. In a battle like this, first blood was liable to be the last, as the one who slipped would end up with a sword in the heart, or the loss of a head. It would only be a matter of time. The combatants broke apart again. However, the farmer charged in a second later, but the assassin was ready. Nearly the same instant, the assassin charged forward as well. As the two combatants passed one another, both charging at full speed, time seemed to slow to a crawl. Felicia never saw either of the strikes that landed, but when the two parted, twin plumes of blood burst into the air. The farmer turned toward the assassin, his blade still held high, his common shirt torn, and blood flowing from a long wound across his chest. However, the strike had not been deep enough to be fatal. In a few days it would heal to a scar. The assassin turned as well, but his sword had already fallen to the muddy ground. The man's sword arm hung by just a few strands of muscle and sinew, and blood flowed freely from the vicious wound. Finally the assassin fell to his knees, pain not even registering on his face. Then, his eyes closed and he fell face-first into the mud. The farmer sighed visibly, and then moved to where the assassin lay, his sword never drooping. In one deft motion, he collected the assassin's weapon, and then searched through the man's cloak. He recovered a small satchel and a rolled parchment before returning to where Felicia still knelt by her father.

"We need to move now, Princess," the man said quickly. "There is no telling how many more of these assassins may be in the woods. You should abandon your intent to return to Lordhill."

He looked down at Feyd after a moment and then looked back at Felicia.

"Is there somewhere else that you can go? Somewhere that people wouldn't expect you to be?"

Felicia nodded.

"My mother's family had a small retreat in Pellatori. No one goes there anymore, and it's not even in the family name any more. But those who do keep the place up would gladly give us aid and shelter."

The farmer nodded and then turned his attention to the fallen form of Prince Feyd.

"It will be difficult to move him, but we have no choice. I'll build a litter, and you try to keep him warm. Once we're across the border into Pellatori, we'll stop and wait until he is strong enough to travel the rest of the way."

The farmer moved to stand, but Felicia's hand on his arm restrained him. He looked down at her, and their eyes met for the first time. As she partly expected, his eyes were cool and clear, and held a look of one who had seen a great many things despite his young age.

"Thank you," she trailed off, not sure how to address him. As if sensing her confusion and hesitation, he smiled.

"Wynne."

Felicia nodded.

"Thank you, Wynne. Your bravery will be rewarded."

There was another smile and slight laugh from the farmer, as though what she had said to him was utterly absurd. He moved away from the two of them into the trees to gather what was needed for the litter. He returned with two thick branches, and two smaller branches, as well as a bit of vine. He stooped by the assassin again, and without care or reverence for the dead man, removed his cloak and began to fashion the litter.

* * * * * * * * * * * *

The rain had stopped falling when Geoffry Aramour and Liandra Nightshade appeared from the tree line. Liandra quickly moved to her work, cleaning up signs of the battle, and planting soiled uniforms of members of the Army of Water around the scene. This would further the distrust of the entire Kingdom of Thorigald and fuel more speculation that the rebellion was escalating their fight against the true Emperor of Cadaria. It would have been so much better if Cole Breon had succeeded in his task and eliminated the Prince and Princess, but no matter, the milk had been spilled and this opportunity had been missed. But there would surely be others in the days and weeks to come. The bribe to the personal guard of the Prince and Princess had been sizeable, but he had done his part of luring them to the appointed place at the appointed time. Of course,

Geoffry would make sure that someone would slit the greedy guard's throat in his sleep at some point in the near future. Loose ends could not be abided, even if they served useful purpose at the time.

There was a brief rustling from the woods behind Geoffry, but he did not turn to see their source. A woman in a nearly transparent white dress emerged from the darkness. She was short by most standards, but her lithe frame was knotted with muscle and her every moved screamed of danger. Long blond curly hair streamed from her head like a waterfall, and she wore a silver band around her forehead that was incrusted with crystal. The band itself formed a V that dipped down above her nose and brought more attention to her slanted eyes. The bright blue eyes were filled with power. On each of her hands she wore a dark leather apparatus that circled her forearm and wrist, and at the back of her hands erupted three long silver talons.

"To what do we owe your presence this evening Alise?"

The girl moved with the grace of a dancer across the sodden ground, past where the body of Cole Breon lay and examined an area closer to the tree-line on the opposite side of the clearing.

"Your assassin was sloppy," she said in a hissing, almost reptilian tone, "the targets escaped, but not alone. One of the prey was seriously injured and dragged off on a litter. You've accounted for all of the guards, but two people walked away while dragging a third."

Geoffry grimaced. Someone other than the prince and princess had witnessed the attempt on their lives. That could prove problematic in the future. Alise turned back to face Geoffry.

"My father will not be pleased."

"Liandra will take up the mission. We will not fail a second time."

Alise held up a talon-laden hand and looked off into the distance, the direction that their quarry had traveled.

"This new obstacle is beyond you and your petty skills, Geoffry. Focus your attention on ensuring that the Empress does not exceed her authority."

Geoffry frowned.

"What right do you have to give me orders!"

Before the last words were out of Geoffry's mouth, Alise was at his side, one set of talons pressed to his throat hard enough to draw blood. Geoffry looked over to where Liandra stood, hoping that his charge would come to his aid, but the woman held her position, no expression on her face.

"You mean nothing," Alise hissed in Geoffry's ear. "You are a tool, nothing more, and like any tool you can be replaced. Follow your orders, or I will find someone else who is willing to follow them in your stead."

Geoffry swallowed hard once Alise had removed the talons from his throat. She moved back in the direction of the drag marks and frowned.

"Go, Geoffry. Next time you will not receive the courtesy of a warning."

Geoffry and Liandra both bowed to the woman's turned back and left the way they had come. Alise stood looking out into the nothingness for a long time. There was something strange on the wind, a smell that reeked of hope.

* * * * * * * * * * * *

Felicia concluded her story, and sat stroking her father's hair. Once they had gotten to safety, Wynne had been quick to set up this small encampment for them, and had even mixed several remedies to help Feyd heal from his injuries. It had taken weeks for Feyd to recover this much, but Fiona and Wynne had been careful not to draw any more attention to themselves than necessary. Wynne had gotten all of the supplies they needed from a nearby farming community, and what he could not get from the farms, he got through hunting and foraging in the nearby woods. Dinners had consisted mostly of freshly picked mushrooms and some manner of bird that had been unlucky enough to be snagged by an arrow fired from Wynne's antique-looking bow. Fiona had wanted to assist in the hunting, but Wynne cautioned her that she could be recognized and that she should stay with her father. It seemed that the young man knew a great deal about a great many things.

"You've been asleep for a long time, father," Fiona said as comfortingly as possible. "But now that you're awake, Wynne thinks that you should get your strength back very quickly."

As if on cue, the tent flap was pulled back, and Wynne entered holding two freshly caught ducks by the feet.

"Good," he said looking first to Fiona, then to Feyd, "you're awake. I'm sure that you'll want to try to get some real food down. After all, you've been living off of those terrible herbal concoctions since you got here. As soon as you are strong enough to get to your feet, we'll make for your family's keep."

Fiona smiled down at her father, and then rubbed his hand softly before moving over to where Wynne sat, plucking the feathers from the ducks. When she began to speak to him, her words were hushed and worried.

"What's wrong? You're never back this early."

Wynne looked past her to Feyd and then his eyes found hers again.

"Someone is tracking us, and they've nearly followed all of the false trails that I've been planting. Whoever it is, they are good. But if we have to carry your father out of here, we'll never be able to outpace the pursuit."

Felicia smiled.

"Don't worry, we Loriens are notoriously hard to kill."

Unseen Battles

Year Three of the Just Emperor Kaitain "Dragonsbane" Lorien, Creator's Calendar Year 1870

Deep in the Imperial Palace of Aldere, the sleeping form of Emperor Kaitain Lorien lay silent and unmoving in his private chambers. In the shadows, Empress Dominique Lorien sat watching, gently wiping a few beads of sweat off her husband's forehead now and then. The fever had been a new symptom of his continuing slumber, and it seemed to come and go with no pattern. At first it was feared that the fever was a symptom of some new outbreak from the harbingers of Dorovar, but the fear soon faded as it seemed to be just another symptom of the exotic poison that kept Kaitain in a slumber. It had been weeks now since the attack on Kaitain's life, and yet the slumbering Emperor required no food and no drink. Any attempts to pass food or liquid through his lips had resulted in almost instant reactive vomiting. Ever since the attack, every day Dominique had come to her husband's side, to watch him sleep for an hour before her next responsibilities pulled her away. Dominique didn't love Kaitain, would never love Kaitain, but love wasn't required to keep up the appearance of a dutiful wife. The Empire needed for Dominique to be devoted to her husband, needed her to act in his stead. Dominique was the extension of Kaitain's will, no matter what strides she made to define her own role in the world. What few saw or noticed were the intermittent looks of sheer and terrible pain that twisted Kaitain's features. This was the most well-guarded secret in the palace. Already Dominique had begun to notice subtle changes in his features. The right corner of his mouth had begun to droop ever so slightly, while the left corner was slightly upturned, as if in the start of a sneer. Only a well-trained eye could pick up on them at this point, but Dominique knew if these waves of pain continued unabated, it would only be a matter of time before Kaitain's features would become permanently twisted.

Dominique took a long sigh, and then waited for the inevitable quiet knock at the door. The hour that she sat at Kaitain's side seemed to be getting longer and longer every day, and Dominique continued to find it hard to distract her mind while sitting at his side. No matter what she tried to work through in her mind, no matter what matter of court tugged at her brain, she could not keep her mind from flowing back to Kaitain. The man had a magnetic presence, even in a deep slumber. But the magnetism was not pure, nor without repercussion. Those drawn to him would eventually meet a fate like moths being drawn to a fire. There was violence in Kaitain, the kind of cruelty and malice that would lead him to a bad end. Yet for the life of her, Dominique could not understand where the reserves of hate came from. Yes, there was resentment for some of the failures in his life, but his ascension and path to greatness were secured from the moment of his birth, which only seemed to magnify Kaitain's need to loose suffering on the world. What was worse was the fact that there were elements within the Imperial Palace that accentuated and drove Kaitain in his rages. There was Marlae, who seemed to delight in nothing more than causing her father distraction and irritation. She was a brutish and cruel child, spoiled past the definition of the word would have allowed, and vile to the very core. Marlae had hated Dominique before they met, simply because Dominique was another obstacle on the path to her place on the throne. Dominique tried to look at the attacks as nothing personal at first, thinking Marlae was only lashing out because she was there. But that quickly faded as Dominique felt the very personal words piercing her heart like hot daggers. But whatever venom Marlae found to inflict on her new step-mother, it was nothing compared to malice and contempt she reserved for her father.

Finally, the knock at the door came and Dominique stood, smoothing her dress before taking the few steps toward the door. Dominique opened the door and saw Chelsea standing just to the right of the door, waiting.

"It's time, Dominique."

Dominique nodded and walked wordlessly through the door and headed toward the main audience chamber. Halfway down the hall, Dominique stopped and turned to face Chelsea. The older woman could see the pain in Dominique's eyes, the kind of pain that had been building for quite some time.

"I've been putting this off for too long, Chelsea, and I can't see any way past this."

Chelsea's expression was blank, not knowing what was going to be the next words out of Dominique's mouth.

"What is it, Dominique?"

Dominique frowned.

"There has been no sign of Seraph since before the assassination attempt, and you know as well as I do that Seraph is one of the only people in the empire who could have made it through all of the security and taken the shot. If he weren't guilty, he would have shown up either here or in Albitonin. Now he's on the run, or worse he's plotting his next attempt to kill Kaitain."

Chelsea nodded.

"As much as I hate to admit it, Seraph is more likely to be plotting to take Aldere by force. The Army of Water would follow him to the gates of hell no matter if he was a general or a criminal. With the amount of disarray being caused by the dragons and the creature calling itself Death, any structured attack against Aldere might actually succeed."

Dominique's countenance darkened.

"What is even more troubling are the reports out of Lordhill detailing an attempt on the lives of both Feyd and Felicia during their return from

Aldere. I knew that we should have sent a full detachment with them regardless of what it looked like to the rest of the empire. I almost feel as though I am responsible for the opportunity the assassins had."

Chelsea pondered for a moment.

"You don't think that Seraph would have attempted to murder Feyd and Felicia, do you? I know that Seraph can be a little hot-blooded, but his vendetta is against Kaitain, not the whole of the Lorien family."

"He could be out of his mind with rage and jealousy, Chelsea. We both know that is not beyond him. If he has lost his mind, the abilities that are available to him make him an absolute threat to all of the Lorien family, including me and including those who protect me."

Chelsea's look was not one of shock, but one of sorrow.

"That is why we have to stop him now, stop him while we have a chance," Dominique continued. "Today I am going to proclaim that Seraph was a conspirator in the assassination attempt on Emperor Kaitain, as well as the attempts on Feyd and Felicia Lorien, and that he is to be taken into custody. But that he is to be taken alive. Also, I need someone qualified to take command of the Army of Water to ensure that they won't take any action we don't want."

Chelsea shook her head.

"Do you really think that is the best way to go about this, Dominique? It could just as easily have been one of Geoffry's assassins, or maybe a member of the Shadow Guild. I know that Seraph is the best candidate right now for the assassin, but there are too many things we don't know for you to make that kind of declaration."

Dominique's features held a grave seriousness, one that Chelsea knew would not be dissuaded by words. However, there were two factors that compelled Chelsea to continue. The first, and most obvious, was the fact that Seraph was Chelsea's husband, and despite all of his transgressions as a husband, he was a good man. And while Chelsea would agree that Seraph could and would have taken action against Kaitain, and perhaps even Feyd; there was nothing that could convince Chelsea that Seraph would have acted against Felicia. The second reason was that as Dominique's personal protector and advisor, it was her responsibility to give the Empress all of the options, no matter how unpalatable or painful they may be. Regardless of her personal entanglements, Chelsea's responsibility was still to the Empire, so long as she was still a member of the Knights of the Flashing Blade.

"There are whispers, Chelsea, the kind of whispers that can't be ignored by anyone in power," Dominique said after a moment. "Irene is quietly using the fact that we haven't found the assassin to undermine my authority in court. Now that Marlae has taken the bait provided by Hannah and Gregor and is heading for Albitonin, Irene is gathering all the power and support she can to take control. The longer that Kaitain stays asleep, the more control Irene is going to be able to gain. Then, one morning, they are going to find Kaitain dead, and Irene will seize control no matter what I try."

Chelsea's frown deepened.

"She wouldn't dare!"

Dominique shook her head.

"You know better than that, Chelsea. Irene will take any advantage she has open to her. The longer this goes on, the more kingdoms will fall to the Rebellion and flock to Marlae's banner, and the more leverage Irene has to paint me as an ineffectual ruler and a detriment to the throne. Albitonin, Galateria, and Oradrim have already fallen, and I had to sacrifice the allegiance of Zevarit to keep up Gabriel's cover. If Seraph chooses, he can tip Thorigald completely against us. Menoris will fall in a matter of weeks, of that I am sure. That gives us only the barest of majority of kingdoms still loyal to Kaitain and the rightful throne. If one more kingdom decides to go over to the rebellion, I don't believe I will see the sunrise of the next day. Irene will have all the leverage she needs to remove me from the stewardship of the throne. As it is, I wouldn't be surprised if she was behind the assassination attempts on Feyd and Felicia, but my gut tells me that was my husband's work. For the time being I will continue as I have indicated."

"Yes, my Empress."

Chelsea's bow and answer were both short.

"No, Chelsea. I want to know what you think. I want to feel like I'm not crazy."

Chelsea chewed on her words the next few seconds, deciding whether or not to give them voice. Finally, her duty won out over her restraint.

"I don't believe Seraph had anything to do with Feyd and Felicia. That has the Shadow Guild's handiwork written all over it. The Guild doesn't respect Irene, and they would not take orders from her, and they also would not act on their own against a member of the royal family. The consequence would be too grave. Kaitain has wanted to eliminate his brother for a long time, and the opportunity was too good to pass up. He was attempting to consolidate power. He could have blamed the assassination on the rebellion and turned public sentiment against them by playing the victim. The fact that Irene seems to be following the same template means that she must have been privy to the plan all along. Of course, we can't act against her, we only can try to think about her next moves and either stop them, or take advantage before she can."

Dominique nodded.

"Which is why I have to sacrifice Seraph."

Chelsea nodded and bowed slightly again.

"As you command, my Empress."

Chelsea turned to continue their walk towards the audience chamber, when Dominique's voice restrained her.

"We're not done, Chelsea."

Chelsea's puzzled stare answered Dominique's statement.

"I need you to recall both Jaccob Aldora and Orren Eldrath. I don't trust them nearly as much as I trust you, but they are both members of the Flashing Blade, so they are far more trustworthy than any of the other rank-

and-files. I know Jaccob was skulking around the palace for a time after the wedding, but I didn't have the chance to get a good read on him before he set out again. The last report I received was that he was in the company of a young man who was tentatively identified as an expelled member of the Academy of Arcane Arts. Orren was supposedly off to attend to issues in Rashaleb following the disaster. However, I don't think we can afford to let him continue on his good will mission. I wish we could recall Bernhardt from his mission to Jelan, but we need to keep up the public appearance of our disconnection with the Academy of Arcane Arts. But we need an agent in those walls. We need someone to re-establish dialogue with the Masters. Who can I send, Chelsea? Who can get me in there without information leaking to Irene or to our other enemies?"

Chelsea answered without a moment of hesitation.

"What about Quyhn?"

"She would be the ideal choice of course," Dominique said after a moment, "but she is too valuable to me in the Lordhill rebellion to pull her away for Jelan. The Peregrims are the larger threat, and they could be ready to move any time. Connor has been itching to fight back against Kaitain ever since he increased the production demand from Lordhill to finance the dual wars with the dragons and the Dark Gods. Besides that, now that there has been an attempt on the lives of Feyd and Felicia, it will make everyone there that much more paranoid. Quyhn is perfect to earn their trust since she is a member of the royal family not by her own doing, and not by blood, and also because her father and mother were so well respected. Also, Feyd and Felicia already know her, which is a huge advantage over anyone else we could send. I've already discovered that some of the resources that were scheduled to go to the army have been redirected to some other project. I have a feeling that once Jaccob is here, I will find out exactly what I want to know about that project."

Chelsea nodded in silent agreement and then refocused her eyes on Dominique. It was indeed a thorny problem, and it would not be the last in securing the loyalty of the disparate, sometime self-absorbed segments of the empire.

"Then I don't know how else we can get into the Academy. There is no one loyal to you that has the credentials to get in without attracting notice."

"What about outside the normal avenues?"

Chelsea knew what Dominique was asking, and she felt the acid rise up in the back of her throat as her stomach jumped. There were forces outside both the Empire of Cadaria and the Dark Continent of Mythryn that operated with a type of impunity. Most of them were not fans of the rule of Emperor Kaitain Lorien, but for the right amount of gold their qualms could be erased.

"Do you seriously want to go that route?"

Dominique gritted her teeth and hesitated for a moment before nodding.

"I'm not fond of mercenaries, but sometimes you do what you must. Who has the most experience dealing with the groups that operate around the Pritan Islands and the Wastelands to the south?"

"Unfortunately," Chelsea said slowly, "the two people who have the most experience with them are unavailable. Leonora has dealt with them on many occasions, as has Xaran. The person with the next amount of experience would have to be Orren."

"Not the ideal person to send on that kind of mission," Dominique said finally.

Chelsea knew exactly what Dominique was talking about. Of all of the members of the Knights of the Flashing Blade, Orren Eldrath was the least dependable, and the most likely to use his abilities for his own ends before those of the Empire. Though he was born under a celestial sign for greatness, Orren's life had been one of thwarted ambition, at least in Orren's mind. Patience was not a virtue that Orren prescribed to, and he wanted everything now, no matter the cost. He was not the ideal choice for a negotiator at any level. And, given his rocky history with the Academy of Arcane Arts in Jelan, finding someone to infiltrate the Academy would not be a good fit for Orren.

"It seems the only choice, Dominique, if you are set on this course of action."

"Then who do we target?" Dominique asked.

Chelsea glowered.

"Unfortunately there are many fringe groups that could have enough ties to the Academy that they could get in without attracting notice. Also, there are some that have been known to conduct trade with the Academy because of their specialized needs. Many of the ingredients for the research that the Academy conducts only grow in the Pritan Islands or on the continent of Mythryn. There aren't a lot of groups that feel comfortable operating in those areas, and none of them are friendly to the Empire of Cadaria. The most prominent of which we've been looking into for quite some time; the Viruci pirates near the Pritan Islands."

Dominique scowled at the name.

"I've read the reports coming from that area. Those pirates have been nothing but a headache, and seem to target nothing but our shipments."

"Very true," Chelsea offered. "It seems as though they want nothing more than to harass and destroy our supply lines. Some say that the captain of the pirate band is a woman who has some sort of grudge against the Throne, but none of that has been confirmed. Besides, none of the pirate leaders of the past have been women, and I doubt that any could unite the factions the way that this woman supposedly has. Another ghost coming out of the woodwork to shake her fist at the walls of the palace, so to speak."

Dominique nodded.

"Very well, when Orren returns, I put him in your hands. He is your comrade, and I think he will take the commands coming from you better than he would coming from me. Besides, I need to be able to deny that I know anything about this endeavor. He is to find the leaders of this band and bring them here. The standard offer of pardon of crimes should be enough to get them to the palace. From there you will have to show how much of a deft hand you have at negotiating Chelsea. I have a feeling that before long, you will be more practiced at it than I will."

There was a low growl that escaped from Chelsea's throat, but that was the end of her argument. Dominique was a talented woman, and she had grown into her role with grace, however she would be the first to admit that she had weaknesses, and that it would take some time and training to overcome them all. Besides that, with the threat of Irene still looming over all of their actions, it would only be a matter of time before Dominique would have to make some very dangerous and extremely difficult choices.

"Yes, my Empress."

* * * * * * * * * * * *

Hannah Ironheart sat in the depths of the Heart of Stone and poured over the massive amounts of correspondence that had flowed in from the rest of Cadaria since the revelation of the rebellion and the naming of Marlae Lorien as the rightful holder of the Throne of Cadaria. It had been a calculated if not dangerous gambit. It had shielded both Hannah and Gregor from denouncement as power-hungry pretenders, but had also put them at the mercy of a greedy and selfish girl who could just as easily unmake this rebellion as advance it. The hour was late when the knock came at the door.

"Enter."

The door opened slowly, and the light pierced the darkness of the hallway and illuminated the face of Leonora Wastri. Hannah smiled when she saw her old friend, but the smile faded quickly as soon as the stern look of the older woman was evident. No one was sure precisely how old Leonora was, and there were some that thought she might have been older even than Vallic, but those suspicions were unfounded. The mystery however was perpetuated by the fact that Leonora had no living family and that she herself was unwilling to discuss the matter at all.

"I wanted to say goodbye, Hannah."

There was a strangled feeling of panic in the pit of Hannah's stomach.

"Goodbye?"

Leonora sighed and nodded.

"The word from Jelan is not good. Apparently the negotiations went horribly wrong, and the army led by Bernhardt Yeoman was enticed into attacking. The small force that I dispatched to Jelan will not be able to hold long, and if I am unable to arrive in time with reinforcements, I'm afraid that the Masters will have to undertake some rash tactics. Were Alistair still alive I would not be as concerned, however the Ebonsight mother and daughter, while powerful, were not bred for conflict. They are diplomats, not warriors. I am also afraid that with the Dark Gods watching the Academy as we suspect they are, the once offered amnesty might look much more attractive after a prolonged siege."

Hannah did not like that possibility one bit. As allies, Jelan would be invaluable, even with their adherence to the code of pacifism. The members of the Academy would never use their abilities to take life unless their lives were threatened. There was security in that. However, if the Academy were to fall to the machinations of Kaitain, that policy would certainly be revoked under penalty of death. The most frightening possibility was that the Dark Gods would find some way to use the Academy or at the very least keep them away from either side of the civil war.

"Any word from Xaran?"

Leonora shook her head.

"Nothing. There are still many who believe that the Emperor had him quietly put to death under the guise of a secret mission for the Throne. I happen to believe that Xaran is still alive but is following some unknown endeavor. The problem is that until we know for sure either way, Menoris will not budge on their stated stance of neutrality in the conflict. They are contemplative people after all, and their leader will be the one to push them in a new direction, either through his word, or proof of his death."

"I only hope that your suspicions are right, old friend, and that Xaran is alive and will come back to us when he can."

Leonora nodded and turned to leave, but hesitated. Hannah could tell that something was on the woman's mind. Even though Leonora was notorious for keeping her own council, there were times when even she could not hide her thoughts. Something was weighing on her, something more than the budding conflicts across the lands of Cadaria.

"What is it Leonora?"

Hannah's tone was firm, but compassionate. Leonora turned, her face suddenly deathly serious. The worry was clear in her eyes, but it stayed in her eyes.

"I would caution you to tread lightly with your niece. There are abilities at her disposal that worry me beyond words. I know that she is the child of a dark god, but that does not explain the things that I have seen her do. And it should worry you that in the most holy of your places of worship to the Creator that she was able to bring Camille back from the dead. I don't pretend to understand what the Dark Gods are capable of, but I have to believe that even that is beyond them. There has to be something reserved for the Creator alone."

Hannah considered Leonora's words for a moment, but the older woman continued.

"What is more is that she seems to be becoming more and more comfortable with her abilities, and more casual with using them. She is touching her power to rearrange furniture, changes the colors of walls and floors, and that kind of irresponsible flaunting of such power is a dangerous road to travel. How long before she is no longer content with just renovating her room? How long until she starts testing the very bonds of reality and the limits of her whims and convictions? How long before we can no longer put up any resistance to her abilities?"

The implication in Leonora's words was clear, and despite herself, Hannah could not find a counter-argument. Hannah too had been frightened by what Tess had been able to accomplish. Bringing Camille back from the dead had been an act of grace to be sure, the kind of miracle that before that day Hannah would have called the touch of the Creator. But it had not been the Creator that day that had intervened on behalf of the winged woman. There was a more primal power that was exhibited that day, a power in the hands of a fragile girl who didn't have the first inkling of what was at stake. Perhaps the situation was even direr than Leonora was putting into words. As if seeing her hesitation, Leonora cleared her throat.

"This may not be a battle any of us can win," she said finally. "We may all be too far along the path. But I would say, have a care when dealing with her, but do not make mention or create policy with her in regard to her powers. The last thing you need to do is breed any contempt in a child with that kind of power and no inhibitions in using it. Though it would not be out of the realm of possibility to need to determine how best to remove the threat from the board, should it become necessary."

Hannah did not have enough time for the shock to register on her face before Leonora spoke again.

"I shall send word once I have reached Jelan and apprise you of the situation there. Were I you, I might pray that I reach my destination quickly and that the walls of Jelan are still standing when I do."

The door closed behind Leonora gently and Hannah was left with an even more empty feeling in the pit of her stomach. The suggestion in Leonora's words had been clear, Leonora wanted Hannah to have a contingency should it be necessary to kill Tess. The thoughts brought a shiver through her unlike any she had ever felt, and suddenly the Heart of the Stone felt more like a tomb than a place of worship.

* * * * * * * * * * * *

Tess lay in her bed, suddenly uncomfortable. She had heard what Leonora had said, and she had felt her aunt's response in her mind.

This will not do, Tess thought coldly, a frown coming to herself as she pulled the covers in tighter around her lithe form, *this will not do at all.*

Memories in Blood

Year Three of the Just Emperor Kaitain "Dragonsbane" Lorien, Creator's Calendar Year 1870

Macero stood stoic, his eyes taking in the forms and dispositions of his opposition. Kyrie had obviously not expected this level of resistance from the little dragon hunter and her band, and certainly did not expect the intervention of the two male interlopers. Though Macero didn't doubt the abilities of either Lexa or Orchid, he did wish that he had not been so against Lucian accompanying them on this journey. His cruelty would have come in handy. But, Macero and his band were not without assistance should it come to that. The Hand of Chaos certainly had plenty of assets in a corrupt kingdom like Hedorah to make these would-be heroes tremble and curse their maker. He took another beat to take in the condition of those that stood against them. Jacqueline and Angelina both had wounds to their faces, but still were in fighting shape. Kiara had thus far remained removed from the battle, but she was a healer, not a fighter, so she posed little in the way of a threat. The monk on the other hand was more than a threat. Macero could smell the power rolling off of him, and yet the impression was clear that only a fraction of what the man was capable of had been revealed. There was something disturbingly familiar about the crystal sword he now held in his hands, not to mention the symbol that hung from the silver chain around his neck. The new arrival, Macero knew his name to be Blade, a well-known trader in questionable goods, was not much of a threat, despite his opposing visage. Jillian Corven, her sword in hand, was only troublesome because she would have to survive the second act of this conflict. Macero growled to himself, he did not like to work with such restrictions.

"Can I kill them now, Lexa?" Orchid whined impatiently. "They're causing too much trouble."

The blond woman looked back at Orchid and then over to Macero and smiled. Even after all these centuries that killer look still caused the icy cold of death to well up in the pit of Macero's stomach. It had been lifetimes since Lexa had come to him on his deathbed in a little village on the edge of Rashaleb. He had developed a fatal fever while exploring a cave and becoming stranded in the cold for two days. As his fever dreams ravaged his mind, he only vaguely was aware of the woman's presence at the side of the bed. At first he thought her an angel, until he saw death in those glowing golden eyes.

* * * * * * * * * * * *

Year Seventy of the Just Emperor Terrik "Godslayer" Lorien I, the Creator's Calendar Year 120

Macero Vasin lay on the bed, his body soaked with sweat, but while his body was burning with fever, he was freezing on the inside. The thick blankets were thrown over him, sodden with sweat, and still Macero continued to shiver. Hours ago the village healers had left, their pronouncements of Macero's impending death lost to his ears. The dreams had him, dreams of death and pain, dreams of torture and betrayal. The walls of his little cottage distorted and seemed to loom in on him, wanting to snuff out the last embers of his life. After what seemed like days of burning and freezing, Macero could feel a calm spreading through him. He had thought for an instant that death had finally taken him, and that his suffering was finally at an end, and when his eyes opened, the glare was too much to see anything. When the forms began to coalesce into something recognizable, Macero again thought he was dead and was being lifted up into the Creator's Court. The woman who looked down upon him radiated light. Her form was lithe and beautiful, garbed in a flowing white gown that clung to her while revealing nothing. Her blond hair seemed immune to gravity as she bent over him staying in its beautiful wreath around her face. Her lips were curled into a smile so soft and disarming that it filled Macero with a warmth that could have been missing from his life since the day of his birth. Her porcelain while skin was tinted with the slightest hues of pink at her cheeks, but then Macero's eyes found hers. The golden glow was equally disarming and disturbing, but as he fell deeper into the well of her gaze, the warmth within him disappeared, only to be replaced by the cold of the grave. Panic began to overwhelm Macero but his arms and legs would not respond to his will. His eyes tried desperately to break contact with the woman's but even they could not be compelled. His mind was a prisoner to his rebellious body. Then she smiled, and all resistance within him melted.

"Relax my beautiful boy," her melodic voice intoned with a softness and sweetness that disarmed the last of Macero's trepidation. "You have nothing to fear from me. I have come to take away your pain, and give you a gift that was given to me lifetimes ago."

Macero tried to move his lips, tried to form some kind of response, but his jaw would not work and his tongue lay dead in his mouth. Any attempt that was left within him fled when one of her long slender fingers pressed against his dry and cracked lips.

"Shhhh, little one. No need for words now. This is a gift that I am giving you. A gift that the great Dorovar gave to me long ago when I was suffering. He released me from my pain, he released me from the suffering of this life. I was lost, going nowhere in my misery. My body was not my own, as I had sold it to hundreds of men, my soul a patchwork of misery, shame, and self-loathing. And though I walked the streets, I was already in death's grasp. Then I heard the whisper on the wind. Out of the corner of my eye, I saw a beautiful woman, her eyes brilliant green and penetrating, looking right through me, right through to my rotting soul. Her body and hair were white, but not the color white, but as though all color had been drained from her, and the white was all that was left. She was like smoke had solidified into a person's form. I was drawn to her as a starving man would be drawn to the smell of food. She said not a word, but her gaze spoke volumes. Her hand touched my cheek and I felt as though I was warm for the first time. When her hand withdrew from my cheek, I could feel the heat remaining, but it was different, it was viscous and oozing, and when my own fingers touched my cheek, they were coated with blood, and I knew in that instant it was mine. But I was not afraid. Her hands found my wrists, and again when she withdrew her hands, blood began to flow freely from where her fingers had been. It was then that the whispers found me again, a name repeating over and over, not on the wind, but as the wind itself. Dorovar, the voice said. And there was peace in that name."

Macero shuddered when the name caught the air. He shuddered with a cold so profound that he felt as though he would never be warm again. But the woman's eyes held him, kept him safe, perched on the edge of a knife.

"I knew in that instant that the woman's name was Jerah, and that she was the servant of Dorovar, and that she would deliver me from my suffering into the glorious service that was at the foot of Dorovar. That I would become a shepherd of the night, saving the souls of the wretched and abused, freeing them from the confines of their misery and lifting them up into a choir so beautiful and powerful that the whole of creation will tremble at their beauty. And the love and gratefulness of the souls will be felt in a song that will uplift all who hear it, freeing our master Dorovar from his prison and lift him to the heavens where his love and benevolence will reshape reality and end all suffering and pain. Jerah gave me this gift in Dorovar's name, and when her lips met mine, all pain left my body. All fear and misery and doubt, all self-loathing and shame were obliterated by her touch. I vaguely remember standing beside her, looking down at the husk that had once been my life. The broken shell of the whore had risen up this resurrected angel of mercy that sits beside you. My life before ended, and now I am Lexa Silenti, the Silencer of Shame and Misery."

Suddenly Macero became aware of another presence in the room, a powerful presence that seemed to be everywhere at once. That patient and overwhelming smile returned to Lexa's lips as her eyes finally broke contact with Macero's and looked to the other side of Macero's bed. Unbidden, Macero's glance shifted and he found the face of the woman who could only have been the Jerah that Lexa had described. Stark white against the color of the world, she was almost two dimensional; standing out from reality, denying its control over her. Her face was passive, neither comforting nor disturbing. Those shocking green eyes found his, boring into his soul. All at once he knew that she was speaking to him, but there were no words, just feelings, emotions, flashes of consciousness. But the overwhelming thought was not a thought at all, but a presence, heavy like an anvil in his mind. Dorovar. There was no choice, no options to weigh. He was to become like Lexa, a Shepherd of the Night. Before he knew what was happening, Jerah had bent low, her lips finding his, her hand wrapping around his wrist. Her lips were soft, almost like a light breeze across his face, but then a new taste found his parched mouth. Blood. But there was no panic. No reservations. He gave into the kiss as he gave into sleep.

The next thing Macero knew, he was standing beside Lexa, looking down at a haggard form lying in sweat-soaked covers on a pitiful bed. He looked so peaceful in his slumber of death, the faintest trickle of blood flowing from his nose and the corners of his mouth. Macero knew that the suffering of that man's life was over, and that his soul would find peace in the choir. Lexa looked over to him and smiled.

"Hello, my beautiful boy. Jerah says that you are to be called Macero Furiae, the Extinguisher of Fury and Pain. Together we shall build a choir powerful enough to shake the Creator from his throne in the heavens."

Macero could feel the cold smile curl his lips as the two set off together.

* * * * * * * * * * * *

Orchid was growing impatient, a situation that did not bode well for any of their opposition as Macero knew well. She had been a sweet girl once, before she became a shepherd, but the change had made her vicious and unrelenting in her duty. She reveled in every kill, in the smiting of the enemies of Dorovar. Carnage was her gift to him for freeing her from the torment of her previous life.

"The women are yours," Lexa said finally. Whatever fondness Macero had for Lexa, he knew what she was. The centuries had proven her to be an assassin on the order that could never be replicated by any mortal. The focus and attention to detail made her undetectable and unstoppable.

Macero knew when that part of her had taken over. That same stare of death that had greeted his waking eyes when he was still a mortal had filled the golden glow now; impassive, impersonal, and impregnable.

Orchid's smile had venom that the most vicious serpent would envy, and she turned her attention to Jacqueline and Angelina. Macero's eyes locked on the new arrival, Blade, while Lexa seemed to let her dead gaze float over to the monk.

"Your fates have been sealed," Macero said finally. "Resistance will only bring suffering. Surrender to what is to come, and perhaps your souls will be judged worthy to join Dorovar's choir."

The monk's face hardened.

"I should have known."

He shook his head and the sword of crystal fell to his side, and then clattered to the ground for a moment before disappearing. In a simple gesture with his right hand, Orchid flew backwards and slammed against the wall so violently that she slumped, unconscious. His fists then balled again, this time wreathed with green flames.

"I don't know what Dorovar or his puppets want with the Lady of Cadaria here, but I can't and won't allow you to spread that evil here. I know what you are now, and I will not allow your touch to spread to any life under my protection."

Macero took a step forward and pointed his blade at the monk's chest.

"Strong words for a mortal. Give me your name before I make you suffer for your impudence."

"My name is Dane Rhuiden, and it will be the last thing you will ever hear."

Lexa cursed at the speaking of the monk's name, at the sound distracted Macero for a moment, and that opened seemed to be all Dane needed. He dodged in, impossibly fast, under Macero's outstretched arm, and landed a solid blow to the center of his chest. On impact the flames around the man's fists flared, and Macero could feel himself burning from the inside out. Another blow quickly followed to Macero's right side, just under his ribs, and then a third, and uppercut to his chin. Macero staggered back, pain wracking his body, and the burning intensifying. Dane could see Lexa's white form flash in from the corner of his eye, but it seemed that both Jillian and Blade expected the move. Jillian's sword and Blade's axe met in the space where Lexa's head would have been a split-second before it would have been there, but the blond woman proved to be a cagey opponent. She ducked under the twin strikes and a single elbow strike to Blade's chest sent the older man crashing into the wall, the axe ripped from his grasp. Jillian too was unprepared for the counter attack, a quick back-hand catching her across the cheek. Her knees rebelled against her will and she toppled to the ground. Jacqueline and Angelina rushed to Jillian's side, while Kiara helped Blade back to his feet.

Lexa and Macero combined their efforts, feinting strikes, flowing together as though they were of one mind. Wordlessly the two struck, countered, and dodged as they tried to penetrate Dane's defenses. Even against the two of them, the monk seemed to be keeping up, not fully on the defensive, but also lashing out with attacks that landed far more often than they missed. The pace was maddening, and Macero felt that there was no way that this one man should have been able to keep up with them. Before long the others would find a way to coordinate their strikes and this Dane might find a way to be victorious. That was not an acceptable outcome. Macero feinted out away from another of Dane's too-precise strikes and could feel Orchid beginning to stir in the back of his mind. Just as Lexa could communicate with Macero by thought, so too could Macero touch Orchid's thoughts. In a matter of moments, Orchid would recover fully and she would summon the reinforcements. Suddenly Dane stopped dead in his tracks. Lexa darted in and connected with a hard right that landed square on the stunned man's jaw and sent him sprawling to the floor, skidding to a stop at Kiara's feet. The whole room suddenly went cold, and Macero felt a familiar presence fill the room. The air seemed to shimmer for a moment and then coalesced into the form of Jerah. Macero had not seen the woman in nearly five hundred years, not since she helped welcome Orchid into the fold. Wordless as always, Macero was filled with the direction that Jerah needed him to follow. They were to retreat. Much as Macero wanted to press the advantage that her distraction had created, he would not violate her will under any circumstances. He had seen what disobedience to her will had wrought. Lexa too seemed to want to continue the fight, but without a word, she collected the still awakening form of Orchid and fled through the hole in the wall of the cottage. Macero lingered only a moment longer before he too retreated, but not before locking eyes one last time on the monk who had caused this failure. He would have his revenge on this man, no matter the cost.

* * * * * * * * * * * *

Jillian watched with horror as Dane suddenly stopped in his tracks and then was sent reeling by a blow that she knew should have shattered his jaw at the least, and possibly would have snapped the neck of most people. The two monsters, as that is the only sane word that could have been used to describe them should have been all over the fallen man, snuffing out the threat that was both fantastic and unexpected at the same time, however, they stood mute, just watching. That was when the cold descended on the room and the other woman just appeared. It was as though reality blinked and all of a sudden she was there. Waves of cold seemed to radiate from her with every breath, and the stark white of her appearance was startling and frightening. She stood in the center of the room, totally expressionless, and it seemed that the light and the warmth of the fire avoided her, creating this pocket of near nothingness. Her eyes never left Dane's fallen form, and without looking, Jillian knew that his eyes were locked on hers. Without a word, a look, or anything resembling communication, Jillian watched as Lexa and Macero collected Orchid and then fled the cottage. They were winning, and yet they chose to flee without their prize. Jillian's head felt as though it was spinning. She felt rather than saw Jacqueline make a move toward the mystery woman, only to have Blade wrap his large hand around her forearm and hold her away from action. The wordless exchange between Dane and the mystery woman lasted only a few moments more before the woman just winked out of existence again, as though she was never there at all. It was as though in that moment, the whole of reality just exhaled. It seemed as though Dane suddenly remembered where he was because he scrambled to his feet and took in the condition of the others in the room. There were lots of cuts and bruises, but most of the damage seemed to have been done to their pride.

"We have to get out of here now. The Flying Guard will be on their way, and I know that they will not be willing to listen to reason, especially not with arrest warrants out for the lot of you."

Shock radiated from Jillian's fellows, but there was no time for explanations.

"Dane is right. We need to get out of Hedorah, and as quickly as possible."

Kiara was the first to offer a suggestion.

"The Temple of the Creator here has access to the river from an underground dock. We should be able to find passage there. I still have friends there, regardless of my status within the order."

"The less people that know we were here would be preferable, but I don't think the Order of the Creator will find much sympathy from the Flying Guard since the head of the order is now the leader of a rebellion," Blade mused, stroking his beard and recovering his axe. "The quicker the better, no time to gather anything more than what you already have on you."

There were nods of ascent all around, and the group of them made their way into the darkening night, shrouded by the increasing torrent of rain.

* * * * * * * * * * * *

High above Hedorah, the Gray Man Pestilence stood looking down at the growing storm, the Flying Guard flooding through the streets like ants, searching for the dragon hunters and their accomplices, but like the unmotivated lot that they were, the search would only last as long as it was profitable, and then they would sink back into their pits of vice and stupidity. The whole mission had been a failure, but the exercise had not been fruitless. As he stood watching, the form of Jerah appeared. The rain seemed to avoid her, not a single drop touching her features.

"An interesting turn of events," the Gray Man intoned, "would not have expected him to be here, and certainly not with her."

Jerah's placid expression did not change.

"Perhaps he has discovered the softer side of the so-called Lady of Cadaria. Not many would be immune to his charms should he wish it to be so."

There was levity in the Gray Man's voice, something uncommon for him. Jerah's attention turned fully to the man, and whatever levity may have been in his expression suddenly faded. Revulsion filled him, and he fell to his knees. She extended a hand toward his head, and blood began to pour from his mouth, nose, and his eyes. As soon as Jerah turned her eyes back to the city, the onslaught was over, and shakily Pestilence found his way back to his feet. The implication was clear. Such words would not be permitted by the First of Dorovar's servants. She was older than all of them, older perhaps even than Dorovar's imprisonment on this world, and she brooked no defiance. It was understood that she was the extension of Dorovar outside of his prison, and her whims and orders held the same weight as though they had come from Dorovar himself. Her children, the ones she had saved were loyal to her and they would stand against the heralds were it to become necessary, and no amount of the power given to Pestilence would make him a match for Jerah or her brood. Pestilence had the power to give death, but Jerah and those she touched were death.

"There is only one place they can go from here, if they follow the river," Pestilence said once he was able to find his voice again. "The bay will be too crowded with Imperial vessels for them to make much headway, and for now Iltorp to the west is loyal to the Empress. They will have to make their way to Zevarit."

"I disagree," came a male voice from behind them.

Pestilence turned to see the forms of Macero, Lexa, and Orchid walking up the hill toward them. Pestilence did not like Jerah's brood, not in the least, but at least the much more irritating Lucian and the insufferable Kyrie who held his leash were not present.

"They have no choice by to pass through Iltorp. They will be making their way toward Albitonin, it will be the only safe haven for enemies of the Throne. The prices on their heads will surely grant them sanctuary. We should be able to catch up with them in the Plains of Steam between Thorigald and Saldarine, as it is the quickest path to Albitonin from Iltorp."

Jerah looked first to Macero and then to Pestilence. There was a slight inclination of her head, so slight that it would have been imperceptible to anyone who did not know to look for it. For Jerah that allowance was like a shout from a normal person. Pestilence smiled widely.

"Track them and drive them toward Saldarine. Our newest herald will be glad to take care of them, and they can be the first to feel the iron grasp of War."

Chapter LV

Death and Justice

D eep in the night, Gabriel Shadowfall watched the small fire burning, but its heat could not erase the growing cold in his mind and in his heart. The chill that ran through him was more than just the deepening cold of the early spring evening, it was the position that he had found himself in. For years he had been the loyal servant of the Imperial Family, never doubting that he was right in his dedication to the Lorien line and all that they stood for. But over the past few months, doubt had begun to creep into his mind. Ever since the Crawling Plague and the Wasting Disease had ravaged the countryside, it seemed that the Cadarian Empire was on a collision course with destruction. What made matters worse was that it seemed that Emperor Kaitain Lorien wanted the destruction, and was doing everything in his power to hasten its coming. First it was the ill-advised war with the dragons of Cadaria, a foe that was immensely powerful and seemed to care for nothing but death and destruction. How could one fight an enemy that had no fear, and wanted nothing more than to destroy every vestige of the human race for the inconvenient nature of its existence? Then, just when the war with the dragons seemed manageable, Emperor Lorien pushed for a war with the Dark Gods of Mythryn.

The Dark Gods were a strange lot. For all of the talk in the halls of the Imperial Palace of Aldere that the Dark Gods wanted nothing but the utter domination and subjugation of Cadaria, the peace had held for almost two-thousand years. However, as soon as Gabriel was elevated to the position of Ruby Knight he learned more of the 'truth' that was hidden from the general public. While the Dark Gods had been content to sit in their kingdom on Mythryn, the past emperors of Cadaria had not been happy with the arrangement. It seemed on several occasions, agents and assassins from Cadaria, as well as mercenaries from the Pritan Islands to the south had been sent with the laughable mission of killing one or all of the Dark Gods. Even Knights of the Flashing Blade had found themselves tasked with this insane mission, including Ivan Quicksilver, the father of Gregor Quicksilver, and predecessor of both Gabriel and Gregor's in the role of the Ruby Knight. Gregor himself had been sent to Mythryn to take up his father's failed mission, but unlike Ivan, Gregor returned. Or had he? There had been a great deal of speculation in the Imperial Palace that it was not in fact Gregor Quicksilver that returned from the Dark Continent, but was in fact an agent of the Dark Gods. It was these rumors more than anything that had held together the coalition of kingdoms that were still supporting Emperor Kaitain and the Empress. Now though, with Marlae and Gabriel's defection to the rebellion in Albitonin, Zevarit and perhaps some of the other kingdoms would support Marlae as the rightful Empress of Cadaria. Either way, the seeds of a bloody civil war had been planted.

Looking through the faint light of the dwindling fire, Gabriel let his eyes wander to the litter that held the Celestial Princess Marlae Lorien and her personal protector and plaything, Rhain Feirbran. For all her jibes and her taunts, Gabriel could not help but admit to himself that somewhere along the line, he had fallen in love with the Celestial Princess. But it was a love that could never be anything more than a pain in his heart that could never be healed. Marlae was outside of his reach from the moment of her birth, and no matter how much Gabriel could ever achieve as a knight, her protector, or a member of the mythic Flashing Blade, she could never be his. She was a princess, the next in line to the Imperial Throne of Cadaria, and her fate was to marry another of royal blood, or a hand-picked suitor who could bring additional power and influence to the family. The man who ruled at her side would be Emperor of Cadaria, a position that could never be held by a rank-and-file soldier of the Imperial Legions. It would take someone with the pedigree of a Lord Peregrim of Lordhill, or even someone like Jaccob Aldora, someone with family of an elevated nature to be considered as a match for Marlae. Gabriel was nowhere near that league. His parents had been poor, and he had come from a long line of farmers and soldiers. None of the men in his family had ever served with any kind of distinction, and it was this lack of distinction of family and name that had allowed Gabriel to earn his position in the Celestial Princess's service. However, through his service to her, he had begun to add respect to the name of Shadowfall, until he had earned, though dubiously, the title of Ruby Knight of the Flashing Blade. All he had was his service and his reputation, a reputation he was now putting on the line by lying to Marlae. He was a spy.

The word caught in his mind like a barb around his throat. For the entirety of his life, spies had been the most loathsome of people. He understood their necessity, but those who skulked in the shadows, lied for a living, and killed by stabbing others in the back with either dagger or a well-spoken secret, were never to be trusted and were probably better off dead. It had been a hobby of his early in his career to research the so-called Shadow Guild. They were supposed to be a secret group of assassins and spies that carried out the assignments that were too sensitive or secret to be entrusted to rank-and-file soldiers. It was said that they were used by the Emperor and the agents of the Imperial family to conduct assassinations of rival families and any enemy that dared to stand in the way of the Cadarian Empire. While Gabriel had gotten close to a few of the Shadow Guild operatives over his career, he had never been able to get close to one of their masters. In time though, he had planned to use his position as the Ruby Knight to learn all he could about the Shadow Guild and find whether they were an honorable group, if assassins could have any honor, or if they needed to be destroyed. Now that the Emperor was incapacitated, Gabriel wondered who was in control of the Shadow Guild, and who was really giving orders. Could the Shadow Guild themselves have been behind the assassination attempt on the Emperor? Could the Shadow Guild be responsible for the seemingly senseless attacks against the royal families in several of the kingdoms? Could it be the Shadow Guild and not the Dark Gods who were truly responsible for the Crawling Plague and the Wasting Disease?

Suddenly there was a rustle from the woods behind Gabriel. In a clean, quick motion, Gabriel stood, pulled the massive length of Valor from its sheath at his back and let his weight rest on his back leg with the tip of the Sacred Blade pointing in the direction of the sound. For a few moments there was nothing. Then Gabriel suddenly realized that it was not simply the lack of the rustling sound, but there was nothing at all. No sounds of wildlife, no birds, no insects. It was as if all sound from the forest beyond had suddenly been erased. Only the crackling of the fire and the light snoring of one of the guards near the fire broke the dead quiet. A few moments later, the rustling returned. This time it was louder. There was something large moving a few feet in front of Gabriel, and it was coming right toward him. Gabriel stood his ground, but could feel the nervous sweat begin to bead on his forehead. Thinking to himself, he wondered if he should wake the small detachment of guards that had accompanied the Celestial Princess and her retinue, but if it were nothing more than a boar or some other animal, it would look foolish for the Ruby Knight to sound the alarm over nothing. He would wait. More seconds passed, and the thing had not yet emerged from the underbrush. Then, finally, Gabriel caught sight of the thing that was coming for him and fear gripped his heart. He tried to call out, tried to rouse the guards sleeping just a few feet away, but his throat contracted and no sound would emerge.

Parting the underbrush, a black-gloved hand came into the soft firelight. The armored arm that followed it seemed to drink in all the light, and not even a dull sheen emerged in response to the flickering fire or the bright moon above. Gabriel had heard stitches of information about the new threat to the Empire of Cadaria from the reports that had made their way out of Albitonin. This creature that stood before him, this mass of black armor with a cruel smile permanently twisted onto his lips was called Death. Finally the fear gripping his mind and heart was erased by the power of the sword Valor, and Gabriel felt himself steeled by the power that began to flow into his arms and body from the Sacred Sword.

"To arms! To arms!"

Gabriel's call rang through the small clearing and moments later the whole area was alive with movement. As the creature Death stood silently at the edge of the clearing, the guards who slept around the small fire stood and gathered their weapons quickly to face the threat. One of the flaps of the Princess's litter fluttered back, and Rhain appeared, dressed in only a tight fitting half-shirt and a pair of nearly transparent underwear. Her hair was slightly tousled, but her eyes were free of whatever diversion had held her moments before, and the look of a killer was there. Cold, precise, and sober. Her long sword was held tightly in her right hand, and her left was wreathed in a glow of dancing fire. When the last of the Celestial Princess's defenders had arrayed themselves against him, Death laughed a deep maniacal laughter that sent chills through everyone that heard it.

"You shall all perish here," Death said with a low rumbling voice that had a slightly metallic quality. "But you need not. My master simply wants the little would-be Empress destroyed. The rest of you may go, and tell everyone that you meet that Death is coming for them, and all shall blissfully enter the Choir of Souls at my hands."

One of the guards to Gabriel's left charged. His sword arced downward in a quick, precise motion and struck Death on the shoulder. There was an unnatural ring of steel striking metal, and the blade shattered on contact. Dumbstruck, the guard stood blinking his eyes. Death reached out with his free hand and seized the guard by the throat. The guard began to convulse the next moment, his skin turning snow white as all the life was sucked out of him by the will of the beast. As soon as it had begun, it was over, and the dead guard's corpse fell to the ground.

"You see, my little insects?" Death mocked. "You cannot hope to damage me. My armor has been forged by the will of Dorovar, and your puny weapons could never hope to pierce the skin of His chosen messenger. You shall all fall here. Your lives are forfeit, and your Princess shall meet the cold death she deserves at my hand."

The other guards charged the next moment, all of their training abandoned to fear. Gabriel could not have stopped them even if he wanted to. The slashes and thrusts were largely ignored by Death, and one by one they fell to his touch or to his haze-enshrouded black blade. When all the guards were gone, Death advanced several steps before a massive ball of flame slammed into its chest. Death fell back a few steps then pawed at the slight scorch mark on the front of its armor. Gabriel looked to his right and saw Rhain standing there, another ball of flame forming on her left hand, her blade already wreathed in dancing flame as well. Gabriel knew that the woman had sorceress ability, but had never seen it put into practice.

No wonder the Celestial Princess valued the woman who used to be a whore so highly as her protector.

"So," Death cooed mockingly, "the little girl has some ability with magic. An interesting development, but ultimately fruitless. You do not have the kind of strength or control it would take to destroy me little girl."

"We'll see about that," Rhain said with all the venom she could manage.

The next moment, another massive ball of flame lurched from her hand, and sped toward its intended target. This time though, Death was ready. It held up its hand and caught the flame against his palm. For a moment, nothing happened, then the ball of flame began to smoke and sizzle, until all the heat was drawn from it, and all that remained was a hard ball of ice. The creature sneered and sent the ball hurtling toward Rhain with impossible speed. There was no chance for the woman to get out of the way, and it was only on reflex that she was able to get a hand up herself. A stream of fire erupted from her outstretched hand, engulfing the ball of ice. However, her reactions were slightly too late to protect herself from damage. Some of the remaining shards of ice survived the torrent of flame and sliced through her hand, leaving bloody trails of shredded flash. Rhain cried out in pain and slumped to the ground, clutching her wounded appendage. Gabriel stole a glance at her hand, only to wince at the sight. Three of her fingers had been sheared off at the knuckle, and there were holes shot clear through her palm. Gabriel guessed that whatever remained of her hand would have to be removed in an attempt to save her life. But now there were more pressing matters. Not taking his gaze from the abomination, Gabriel ripped his shirt with his free hand and knelt beside Rhain. He quickly wrapped the wounded hand as best he could and looked into the shaken eyes of the woman.

"Get to the Princess. Get her out of here if I fall. Run as fast and as far as you can and do not stop no matter what."

Rhain's expression was blank.

"Do you understand me? Protect Marlae!"

Finally the haze was broken and the fire retuned to Rhain's eyes. She nodded curtly and shakily returned to her feet and moved toward the litter.

It would not be easy getting Marlae out of the battleground, but if anyone could accomplish the feat, it would be Rhain. All Gabriel had to do was buy whatever time he could. He would fulfill his charge to protect the Celestial Princess at the cost of his life.

"So," Death said after a moment, "all that is left is the little boy with the big sword. Do you think that chunk of steel makes you a better fighter? Do you think it makes you a bigger man? Does it make up for the inadequacy and failure in your heart?"

A wave of revulsion, fear, and self-doubt swept out from Death and pounded against Gabriel's soul. Every failure and misstep in his life flashed through Gabriel's mind, and he felt his knees buckle for a moment. But Valor held him up, held him together for those dangerous few seconds. Power and purpose flooded him, and Gabriel took two steps forward and brought his legendary sword to bear.

"You are stronger than most, Ruby Knight," Death allowed, "but you are nothing compared to the real Ruby Knight. But you know that don't you, Gabriel. You are a pale shadow of the man Gregor Quicksilver. You are not even enough of a man to carry his piss bucket."

The taunt washed over Gabriel, but had the opposite affect than was intended. The jibe was supposed to reduce Gabriel's resolve and make him doubt his own self-worth. But Gabriel knew that he was put in his position as the Ruby Knight for a purpose. He was not filling the shoes of the great and powerful Gregor Quicksilver. He was blazing his own trail as the trusted messenger, spy, and operative of the Empress of Cadaria, Dominique Lorien.

"Come, creature," Gabriel taunted in return, "let us see if you fight as well as you talk."

Gabriel charged the next moment, Valor crashing down on the unholy sword of Death. It felt like Gabriel had struck an anvil with his blade, the unyielding strength of Death's weapon holding his own strike at bay. The two immortal pieces of steel struck at each other as the moments wound forward, strike flowing into parry, flowing into strike. Death pressed forward every advantage, driving Gabriel back with the sheer strength of its strikes. It was only the power granted by Valor that was keeping Gabriel in the fight, but he was hopelessly overmatched by the creature. Death whirled in, the flat of its blade striking aside the guard of Valor and its armored elbow slamming into the side of Gabriel's face. The pain exploded in Gabriel's head, and he could hear the bones in his cheek and eye socket shatter. Blood poured from his mouth and nose as he toppled to the ground. Defeat had been absolute. Gabriel could not defend himself even if he wanted to. The vision in his left eye was gone, clouded over by blood. He could not feel the left side of his face with the exception of the hot blood that coated it. Sprawled on the ground, Gabriel groped for the hilt of Valor, trying desperately to continue the fight, but even if he could find his blade, he doubted that he could make it back to his feet. But as long as there was life within him, he could not abandon his charge. Death had begun to walk past his fallen form as Gabriel's hand finally brushed the hilt of Valor. There was a surge of energy and power that pulsed through him, and Gabriel could feel the pain within him begin to lessen. With only partial red-tinged vision, Gabriel forced himself to his feet.

"I'm not dead yet monster."

Gabriel's words were slurred, and it ached to talk. Perhaps his jaw had been cracked as well by the blow, but it didn't matter. Death turned and locked its gaze on Gabriel. A shudder ran through the Ruby Knight, as he knew in that moment that his life would only last a few seconds more. Suddenly the beast moved, and it moved faster than Gabriel could perceive, and as the strike came, Gabriel's eyes closed instinctively waiting for the quick pain that would mean the end of his existence. But the pain never came. There was the sound of steel against steel, and when Gabriel opened his eyes, he saw that another blade had intercepted Death's strike. It was a bright golden blade that seemed to pulse with power.

"You did pretty well junior," a man's voice said after a moment, "but you should probably let the professionals handle this one."

Death retreated a step from the stranger, and kept his sword held in defensive posture. There was a look like surprise in the creature's face, but with the permanent cruel smile, it was hard to read the beast's true expression. At that moment Gabriel's knees buckled and he fell to the ground, and got his first look at his savior.

The man could not have been more than thirty from his features. He wore simple clothing, with a long flowing cloak. There was a start of a beard on his cheeks and chin, and his features were fair to go along with his short black hair. However, when the man's head turned to look down at Gabriel, there was an age and wisdom there that could only have been present in someone who had seen their share of both life and death.

"You ok kid?"

Gabriel bristled a little at the thought of being called a kid by a man who easily could have been several years his junior, but he begrudgingly nodded and forced his way back to his feet.

"You are not here," Death said finally, pointing the tip of his blade at the young man. "You cannot be here. I do not see your life, I do not feel the beating of your heart. You are not alive! You are not here!"

There was panic in the creature's voice, almost fear. Gabriel could not understand what was happening.

"Oh, I assure you I am quite alive," the man said after a moment. "But, I can understand why you might be confused. You know, if I would have run across you a few hours ago, things might have been different. But, you know what? I'm feeling much better now."

The man held the bright golden sword at his side, relaxed and seemingly defenseless. A moment later another sword appeared in the man's other hand, this sword had the appearance of two dragons intertwined to serve as the sword's hilt, with the etching of a dragon in flight carved into its blade. Gabriel would have had to be a fool not to feel the power radiating from this sword, and the puzzle of the newcomer deepened as the moments passed.

"You shall die here!"

Death seemed to have lost all of its smug composure over the last few moments, as if the very existence of this man was an affront to everything that it was created to do. With an unearthly cry, Death flew forward, its sword held high. The thunderous attack came the next moment, and was calmly and quickly batted away by the man's golden blade. The parry was effortless, and Gabriel knew that had that strike been targeted at him, Gabriel would have been dead in a second, even with Valor at his disposal. More blows came from Death against the mystery man, and each one in turn was deflected or dodged as a master would handle the attacks of a novice. Finally, Death dropped back several feet, a clear look of confusion and exasperation painted on its stark white face.

"How? Who? What are you?"

The man released the hilt of the golden sword and it disappeared as though it were never really there. After a moment, he scratched his chin and smiled a lopsided and playful smile.

"I'm the beginning of the story, in every sense my dead friend. And I am no one to be trifled with. Go back and tell your master that when he is ready to make war for real I will be here to take care of him and every one of his servants he brings with him. But in the mean time I will not trouble myself with his errand-boys. You tell Dorovar, that if he wants a fight, Aerith Seth will be here to oblige him."

Death stood silent for a moment, and then that hideous laughter rang out again.

"You dare to challenge the great and powerful Dorovar? You must be a fool! To stand before the one who shall rule this universe would certainly mean your death. The true god shall….."

Aerith cut off Death's tirade with a raised hand.

"Don't you guys ever come up with any new material? If you knew how many times one of you over-dramatic types in the black with the master plan had told me that I was going to die, you would probably be as bored with it as I am. So, why don't we just do each other a favor and skip the 'you're going to die by my hand' bit. Either you are going to go run away and go back to your master and tell him of my insolence, or you are going to stay here and try to kill me. My recommendation personally is that you run away so I don't have to kill you and dirty my blades. But either way, I'll be happy to accommodate you."

Just then, Death surged forward and took Aerith by the throat. The piercing smile was back upon the creature's lips and as it squeezed, the laughter poured from its mouth. The hard and powerful laugh pierced Gabriel's heart with such dread, that he knew the stranger was dead. There was no way that this man Aerith could survive the touch of the creature known as Death, and Gabriel would be left alone again to face his fate. But the laughter trailed off, and instead of the twitching lifeless form of Aerith Seth laying on the ground beside Gabriel, Aerith still stood, with Death's hand still gripping his throat. The look of confusion returned to Death's face. A second later, the blade of the Dragon Sword slashed upward, piercing through the rock-hard armor and severing the hand from Death's arm. The creature fell back, a black smoke emerging from the wound instead of blood. Aerith reached up and extracted the hand from his throat and cast it to the ground. As soon as it struck the earth, it shattered into a thousand pieces and then melted away to black smoke.

"How? That is impossible!" Death shrieked. "You should be dead! How can you resist the Will of Dorovar to join the Choir or Souls? How can you resist the call of Death?"

Aerith just smiled.

"Maybe it's because I've been dead already. Twice. Now, are you going to run along and tell your master I'm waiting for him, or do I have to kill you and wait for the next one and hope it's more intelligent than you are?"

Just then Death snarled and evaporated into the night. Gabriel was looking right at the creature, and then suddenly, it just wasn't there. Gabriel heard Aerith let out a deep sigh before he knelt beside Gabriel.

"How are you doing there, kid?"

There was no mocking in the man's tone, but Gabriel didn't like the word kid, no matter how endearing it was meant to be.

"It looks worse than it is," Gabriel managed. His voice was still distorted by the injury, but Valor was working its magic and healing his wounds, if slowly.

"You know, I can help you with that. Healing was never my strong suit, but I have picked up some tricks from some pretty good healers over the years."

Gabriel waved the man off and tested the strength in his legs before taking a step towards the litter that held the certainly shaken Celestial Princess and her wounded bodyguard.

"I don't know what I can do to repay you, Aerith," Gabriel said after a moment, "but I assure you that the thanks of the Celestial Princess can go quite far in these troubled times."

Aerith cocked his head and his smile widened.

"You know, I've had a lot of luck with princesses in the past. Almost married one once. Guess you could say I'm married to one now."

Aerith clapped Gabriel on the shoulder and walked with the younger man toward the litter.

"Tell you what," Aerith said after a moment, "why don't we go check on your princess and get her where she's headed. We can worry about the thanks later. Besides, I have a feeling sticking close to you could be a lot better than me hunting for Dorovar on my own."

Gabriel stopped for a moment and faced Aerith fully.

"Are you a Dark God?"

Aerith chuckled.

"Kid, they don't have a name for what I am."

One Good Turn...

Year Three of the Just Emperor Kaitain "Dragonsbane" Lorien, Creator's Calendar Year 1870

Ashinica Maupin sat on the extremely uncomfortable folding stool and tried her best not to scowl at the monster of a man who stood across the table from her. No matter what Bernhardt Yeoman's reputation, he was an imposing figure to be sure, and with the addition of the scars and prosthetic leg, his visage was that much more impressive in a truly horrendous way. Ashinica had done her homework before entering into these negotiations, and she knew everything that there was to know about Bernhardt Yeoman. He was a hero, a valiant warrior who fought for duty, not for any seeking of glory. His appointment to the Knights of the Flashing Blade was embarrassing for him, as he never saw himself as anything more than a soldier, and it seemed that in the engagements since he was going out of his way to prove that he was worthy of his new title. But whatever lingering doubts may have been in the man off the battlefield, on it, he was a force of nature. The reports of his battles against dragons in the Kingdom of Iron and elsewhere were already reaching legendary status, and were the kind of tales that could win battles before a single sword was drawn. Perhaps Bernhardt had not yet reached the level of fear-inducing respect that Gregor Quicksilver had, but he was well on his way. Out of the corner of Ashinica's eye, she could see the Sacred Weapon Gravity stood up against the table, its great bulky head resting on the ground. The War Hammer was legendary like all the Sacred Weapons, but the stories of it crushing the skulls of dragons in a single blow had elevated it to something akin to myth. What was impossible for a tenacious man like Bernhardt when Gravity was in his hand? And this was the man that Kaitain Lorien sent to secure the allegiance of the Academy of Arcane Arts. Battle was inevitable, as it was what Kaitain wanted.

"Sir Bernhardt," Ashinica said softly, but her words firm and pointed, "I have been empowered by the Council of Masters of the Academy of Arcane Arts to speak on their behalf as well as on behalf of all of the students housed within the Academy's walls. I would like to know your intentions, and what you have been authorized to do in the name of the Emperor of Cadaria."

If this were a fight, Ashinica had landed the first blow. Bernhardt was impressed by the weight her words held even in her quieted tone, and knew immediately that she would be formidable were this to be an actual negotiation. But, Bernhardt was not empowered to negotiate, and the orders he had were explicit. But there was something unnerving about the tact the woman was taking, and the way that Rory Blackrock stood behind her, slightly to her right, a cold impassive look on his face. Above and beyond all was that this woman, despite her diminutive frame was the Master of Stone, which meant that she was not to be trifled with.

"My intentions and my orders are explicit," Bernhardt said firmly, "the Emperor of Cadaria, Kaitain Lorien, has commanded that the Academy of Arcane Arts be placed under the direct military control of the Iron Legion. The Masters' Council will surrender their positions until such time as their loyalty to the Throne can be verified."

Ashinica nodded, as though she knew that would be the answer.

"And what will become of the students of the Academy once the occupation has begun?"

"Those who are willing and old enough for military service will be assigned to regiments on the front lines of the battles against the dragons still present in Cadaria. If necessary, conscriptions notices will be issued for those who will not willingly join the ranks with their fellows."

Ashinica nodded.

"May I speak frankly, General Yeoman?"

Bernhardt nodded, waiting for the assault that was to come.

"You do realize of course that these orders essentially make it possible for Emperor Lorien to have all of the Masters put to death if they do not fulfill his vision of what the Academy of Arcane Arts should be? He can say that we are all disloyal, have us removed, and put in place those who are willing to conform to his vision, like your confederates Orren Eldrath and Jaccob Aldora, both of whom were dismissed from the Academy for their radical and militaristic views. And the very idea of forcing children to become members of your military is insulting, whether they are willing to do so or not. Your word conscription has an analog you know, and that is slavery."

Bernhardt opened his mouth to reply, but Ashinica continued.

"What's more, in violation of the decrees set down by the first Cadaria Emperor, Emperor Kaitain has formed his own training program for those with arcane ability in hopes of creating a fighting force that could stand against the Dark Gods. Which in itself is a violation of the peace accord with the Dark Continent. Your Emperor imposes his will by any means necessary, and in doing so has fractured this empire. If you continue to serve him, and insist on carrying on this charade, then we in Jelan have no choice but to resist you by any means necessary. With all of the power at our disposal."

Ashinica let her words linger in the air for a moment before she continued, her voice gaining an ominous growl.

"And believe me, General Yeoman, we will destroy ourselves and any who are foolish enough to be within our reach before we allow our powers to be used for any of the purposes of a power-mad boy."

* * * * * * * * * * * *

Year Two of the Just Emperor Kaitain "Dragonsbane" Lorien, Creator's Calendar Year 1869

Ayden Seth sat in the dining room of the Academy of Arcane Arts well after lights out chewing a bit of salt pork and drinking a larger than decent mug of ale. Breaking into the kitchen was no challenge, and he had been doing it since his first month at the Academy. In fact, no matter what different locks and wards the cooks and kitchen staff tried, things just kept disappearing from the larder. At least Ayden eventually learned not to take more than just for himself, and to keep his drinking to a more reasonable amount. Showing up to class with a headache and feeling like he was going to vomit every moment was not the best way to keep his thievery quiet. But he wasn't the first to think of sneaking into the kitchen, nor would he be the last. And to be honest, it was all a bit pedestrian for him. Unlike most of the students at the Academy, with the possible exception of Aris Ebonsight, Ayden began his lessons long before he ever set foot in Jelan. From the time that he could stand up straight, his mother had been after him to learn everything that he could, because as she put it, he would need to defend himself. His father had been more interested in making sure that Ayden knew that his wits and not his abilities were the most important thing, and that caused more than a few arguments between his parents. Not that they needed much of an excuse to argue. Ayden loved his parents dearly, but they were probably two of the most annoying people he had ever been around. They never agreed, they constantly yelled at one another, and they had the terrible habit of kissing and groping each other no matter who was around. They were in love and it was disgusting because they were his parents.

He went to take another drink to wash the thought from his mind, but found the mug empty. He thought that another mug-full wouldn't hurt, so he let the mug fall from his hand. It stopped short of hitting the table and floated toward the still open door that led to the kitchen. Ayden didn't have to see the mug or the barrel of ale that sat in the corner of the kitchen to will the actions that would refill his mug. In fact, he put his feet up on the table and stretched while the process took place nearly unconsciously in the back of his mind. The mug was just returning to the table when a voice shattered the silence.

"I should have known I would find you here."

Ayden fell backward, his feet suddenly dislodged from their position on the table. The chair fell out from under him, and he momentarily lost contact with the mug of ale that floated a foot away from him. As though dropped from an invisible tray, the mug tipped, sending the ale in all directions, spilling towards the floor. The distraction lasted for only a moment, and in the blink of an eye, Ayden was suspended in mid-air, as was the mug, the chair, and the spilling ale. The mug righted itself and the ale seemed to just find its way back to where it had been before being momentarily freed from the confines of the vessel. The chair slid itself back under Ayden, and he was back in his reclined position, mug in hand by the time that the owner of the distracting voice had fully entered the dining hall.

"Can I get you a mug, Aris?"

Ayden didn't have to look at the woman's face to know that she was frowning at him.

"Students are to address me as Master Ebonsight, especially those who know they aren't supposed to be breaking into the kitchen after lights out."

Ayden looked at Aris and smiled.

"You never made me call you Master Ebonsight in bed."

The mug wrenched itself from Ayden's grasp and upended itself above his head. The contents flooded out, but instead of pouring all over Ayden's head, the ale disappeared a fraction of an inch before soaking his hair, and then reappeared above Aris' head. She had no time to react, and in a matter of instants, was soaked in the strong liquid. Her shriek of shock echoed in the empty chamber, and Ayden nearly fell again laughing. The door to the dining hall opened again, this time admitting the diminutive Master of Stone, Ashinica Maupin. She surveyed the scene for a moment and then shook her head. Aris should have been fuming, but she herself was laughing, the strong smelling ale soaking through her robes. Ayden had resumed some level of self-control, but his face was also flushed from the uncontrolled fit of laughter.

"This is the very reason that you are going to be a serious subject of conversation in tomorrow's Masters' Council meeting Apprentice Seth.

Behavior such as this is unbecoming of a man of your obvious talent. And if you weren't so lazy and actually applied yourself, you could be the rival of any of the Masters that has ever served this academy."

Ayden opened his mouth to retort, but Ashinica's strong stare stopped him short, but could not prevent his smile from widening. Ashinica looked over Aris for a moment and then spoke again.

"Get yourself cleaned up Aris," Ashinica said finally. "I'll make sure the troublemaker here finds his way back to his room without taking any detours."

Aris was still chuckling to herself when she left the room. Ashinica turned her full attention to Ayden.

"Alright," she said in a tone that would brook no defiance, "let's go."

Ayden got to his feet the next moment, thrust his hands into his pocket, and strolled casually toward the door. When he was within arms-reach, Ashinica took hold of him by the elbow and led him out of the dining hall. If anyone would have seen the two of them walking through the corridor, it would have been a humorous, if not overly common sight. Ashinica was a full head and shoulders shorter than Ayden, and could have just as easily been a little girl tagging along with her older brother as the Master of Stone disciplining a student. She led him down a series of dimly lit corridors before final stopping at one of the wooden doors. With her free hand, she pushed the door open, and as soon as enough of it was open, she pushed Ayden through and then followed a moment later, the door closing behind them without intervention.

The room was well-appointed, and definitely had a woman's touch. There were a few tapestries hanging on the walls, nothing lavish, but certainly they brightened up the room, and had a starkly feminine appeal. Two large wardrobes stood on one side of the room, one stood open, filled to capacity with gowns and dresses, mostly of autumn tones and muted colors. Ayden was standing with his back to the door when Ashinica entered her chambers, and before he could turn to face her, she pushed him hard in the back, sending him stumbling forward.

"Sometimes I don't know if you are stupid or just reckless," the Master of Stone said firmly. "What if it had been Fiona or Jastra and not Aris that found you helping yourself to a late night snack? I don't think they would have taken as well to having a mug of ale dumped on their head."

Ayden spread his hands and opened his mouth as to give an explanation, but Ashinica continued.

"And what the hell were you thinking doing that anyway? I heard what you said to Aris, and that was perhaps the cruelest and stupidest thing you could have said. There is enough gossip floating around about you and your conquests, and the last thing you need is for anything getting back to Fiona. You'd be lucky if all you were was expelled. She just may lock you in a room with Jastra for five minutes and let her do her worst. Our volatile Master of Energy already thinks you are the lowest form of life."

Ayden cocked his head to the left slightly and smiled his infamous lopsided grin, a lock of his hair falling across his face.

"Come on, Ash, it was funny."

Ashinica frowned. It grated on her how he shortened her name. It grated on her that she actually liked it, and it grated on her even more that she was starting to appreciate Ayden's rather unique sense of humor.

"Funny or not," she said finally, "it wasn't very smart. I don't get it Ayden. I know you don't want to be here at the Academy, but you stay anyway. I know you aren't learning that much, other than how to annoy your teachers and make yourself look more and more like a lost cause."

Ayden sighed.

"Not another apply yourself speech, please." The levity in his voice was gone.

Ashinica shook her head.

"No, not another 'apply yourself' speech. I know better. But Ayden, really, what is it? They are going to move tomorrow at the Masters' Council to expel you, and to just be rid of you. These last few weeks your stunts have gotten too close to being over the line."

Ayden threw himself backwards and floated over to the bed where he perched just at the edge. Ashinica watched unsurprised and walked slowly to keep a consistent distance between herself and the young man. She had never been sure of Ayden's age, but there was no doubting that he was certainly not the sixteen years that his records indicated.

"This is just because I made Jastra's undergarments disappear from her body and reappear on her desk."

Ashinica shook her head.

"Not just," she said trying not to laugh, "but that certainly didn't help. Jastra has never appreciated your disruptive tendencies. She thinks that you have no interest in learning and because of that you are not making it possible for those who really need the help to get it."

"Ash, you've always been very careful not to ask me about my past, or why I'm here. You don't ask about my parents, and I don't ask about your Imperial Family connections. We work because we know where the line is. I'm still here in the Academy because I know where the lines are. But I'm here for one reason and one reason only. My father made a deal with Alistair Ravenheart to enroll me here, to try to help me learn to control my abilities. It wasn't to teach me anything new. It was to make sure when the time was right, I was ready to do what needed to be done."

That was the most Ayden had ever said about his past, and Ashinica knew that their trust had gotten them to a new level. Maybe it was frustration at having to keep so many secrets that had brought him to this point, or maybe she had finally broken through some of the walls that he so meticulously kept.

"So you have a destiny."

Ayden laughed. When he looked up and found her eyes, there was a mixture of emotions there. Some of it was the playful youth that was behind all the pranks, more than that was a power that no one got to see unless they happened to catch Ayden in an unguarded moment.

"You make me sound like I'm important when you say it that way. We all have destinies; some are just more boring than others. When some random villager dies, no one ever said that he fulfilled his destiny to be fat and lazy. And just because someone has a destiny, it doesn't mean that they will make a difference or even fulfill it the way everyone thinks they will. My father had a destiny, and his destiny insured that hundreds of thousands of people died horribly. My mother had a destiny too, and she fulfilled it by starting wars and burning the homes and villages of innocent people. I am the child of two monsters, but because in the end their monstrous acts ended up creating something good, they are regarded as heroes. But they are still monsters. My father is a talented killer. He puts a smile on and tells jokes, but when everything is tallied up in the end, all of your emperors put together couldn't have been responsible for more death than my father. My mother could show Fiona ways to use fire that she has never dreamed of, and create wonders that would dazzle every student here. But those same powers were used to destroy more than you could ever imagine."

Ashinica stood transfixed. This level of openness from Ayden was unprecedented, and perhaps he had just reached his limit for keeping secrets, and Ashinica just happened to be in the right place at the right time.

"If I have a destiny, Ash," he said finally, "it's to be a monster just like my parents."

For the first time, Ashinica saw tears streaming down Ayden's cheeks. She took his face in her hands and pulled his head to her chest and held him tightly.

"I could destroy you with a thought, Ash," Ayden said, the tears still flowing freely, "I could tear this whole place down, and there would be nothing that any of you could do to stop me."

The silence between them held for another few minutes before Ashinica finally pulled his face up and her eyes met his again.

"You're not a monster, Ayden. I don't know what it is that your parents have done, and I don't know why, but the sins of the parents are not inherited by the children unless they choose to go down that road. You are still here not out of any obligation, but because you want to be. I like to think that part of the reason you stay is because of me. But at the end of the day, you know what it is that you are capable of, and you make a conscious choice not to use those abilities for anything more than your tricks and games. That alone proves that you are a good man, and if you continue on this path, your destiny will bear out that you were a good man and not the monster that you could have been."

She hugged him tightly and held him as close as she could, until she felt his hand gently squeeze her butt. She pushed him away and playfully slapped him on the cheek.

"Maybe I was wrong, maybe you are a monster."

He smiled and laughed finally, the boyish sparkle returning to his eyes. Ashinica sat on a small chair across from where he perched on the bed, and leaned back, her legs crossed.

"So they're really going to talk about expelling me tomorrow?"

It was not such a new thing. The subject of Ayden's disposition had been a matter of some conjecture for quite some time, but he had always been able to escape expulsion by some measure.

"I'm not sure it's really going to matter. Forces are conspiring against the Academy of Arcane Arts, and we may need you and your abilities to help defend our walls if the time comes. The Emperor will move against us before too long, either to seize control or to simple destroy us in favor of the mages that he is training secretly."

Ayden stared blankly.

"The Emperor has his own academy? I know we agreed you wouldn't talk about Masters' Council business, Ash, but this isn't exactly a small thing here."

Ashinica waved her hand dismissively.

"Even if the Emperor has his own academy, there is no way that he can turn out enough of a force to make a difference. Besides, we have greater threats to worry about. One of the Dark Gods delivered us a message when Lady Leonora was here demanding that the Academy of Arcane Arts remain neutral."

Ayden's blood ran cold. He had heard the rumors, but that was all they proved to be were rumors. The Masters denied and obfuscated very effectively.

"Do you know the name of the Dark God?"

The question caught Ashinica by surprise.

"Does it matter?"

Ayden stared at her, suddenly serious again.

"Serrina."

Ayden frowned and then rubbed his chin and then forehead hard. He looked up at Ashinica with this annoyed expression, and then looked down at the floor again. It was obvious he was debating something internally. Finally, as though he had reached a decision, he looked up again.

"Serrina isn't a Dark God, well not exactly. She's the daughter of two of the Forgotten. They were gods who were exiled from the Heavens shortly after the rest of the Dark Gods fell. Serrina was born here on Cadaria like the rest of the children of the Dark Gods. Well, most of them anyway."

For a moment Ashinica forgot to breathe. It was only when she realized she was staring her mouth agape that she steadied herself, closed her mouth slowly, and cleared her throat.

"How is it you know so much about the Dark Gods and their children?"

Ayden smiled.

"Because my parents are part of the Forgotten too, well, kind of. It's complicated. Then again, there is nothing that isn't complicated where my father is concerned."

Ashinica wanted to laugh. She wanted to think it was another of Ayden's elaborate pranks. But the look in his eyes told her it was no joke.

In a strange way it all made sense. His level of aptitude, the secret deal that kept him in the Academy.

"Your parents are Dark Gods?"

Ayden shook his head.

"I know what you're thinking, Ash."

She looked at him a little fearfully.

"Ok, let me rephrase that. I know what you must be thinking. Don't worry, the Dark Gods can't read thoughts, at least none of them that I know about. But I'm not here as a spy or anything. My mother wanted me to learn how to make the most of my abilities because they were developing so quickly, and she didn't want me coming to the notice of Pike and the rest of them. My parents have wanted nothing to do with the Dark Gods since they came to this world, and we all just kind of keep to ourselves. It's not the most dazzling existence, but at least it's quiet. But what I said before about my father wanting me to be ready for what is going to happen, that part is true. He's known for a long time that it was only a matter of time before the Dark Gods and the Cadarians would be at each other's throats, and he just hoped that we could stay out of it as long as possible. Maybe we've passed that time."

Ashinica recovered from her shock, and her mind suddenly whirled back into motion.

"I have the perfect idea, Ayden, and I think you are the only one who can make it happen. The Academy is in danger, and if I'm right, we can prevent it from falling, but only if we are willing to sacrifice."

This time it was Ayden who stared blankly.

"I'm going to suggest that you be expelled and sent on a secret mission on behalf of the Master's Council to find out the truth of Emperor Kaitain's academy. When the Imperial Army gets here, I'll make sure that I'm the one sent to negotiate. That way I can provoke them into attacking us."

Ayden stood up straight.

"Are you out of your mind!"

Ashinica frowned.

"The Dark Gods want us to stay neutral. They're obviously watching us. After you leave the Academy, you're going to send a message to this Serrina, and you let her know that the Academy intends to stay neutral and accepts their offer of amnesty, but only if the Dark Gods act in good faith and assist in the defense of the Academy."

"Do I have a choice?"

Ashinica smiled.

"Depends on if you want to sleep alone tonight or not."

* * * * * * * * * * * *

Bernhardt snarled. He was not used to being spoken to in such a manner.

"You can't be serious. You would destroy yourselves rather than submit to the laws of the Emperor of Cadaria? You know that even saying such things is treason."

Ashinica stood and smoothed her dress.

"Obviously you have made up your mind, General Yeoman. We shall await you in the Academy, should you make it far enough to see the grounds."

With that, Ashinica and her escort turned and left the tent. She was no more than two paces out of the tent when Bernhardt screamed in frustration and brought the full weight of Gravity crashing down on the planning table, shattering it completely. He stormed from the tent the next moment, shouting in all directions to signal for an all-out attack.

On Immortality

Year Three of the Just Emperor Kaitain "Dragonsbane" Lorien, Creator's Calendar Year 1870

The Dark Content of Mythryn by all measures was a fearsome sight to behold with its dark shrouded shores, tall cragged mountains, endless swamps and vegetation that grew black and cold from the lack of sunlight. The fact that anything could grow in that desolate hell was a testament to the sheer force of will that life has to exist. Xaran Firesoul stood on the beach at the south-eastern tip of the peninsula closest to the Pritan Island chain and for a moment was happy he could not see the darkness that he felt pressing in around him. Mythryn did not feel like death, as many would have surmised. However, it did feel cold, hostile, and most of all, angry. That wasn't the only anger that Xaran felt. The dagger given to him by the Council of the Winds hung heavily in the small satchel at his side. It was as if hate had been given a shape. The dagger thirsted for blood. It thirsted to destroy. More than that though, it hated. It hated all life around it, and hated the very nature of the living universe. And now Xaran was here to help the dagger do its gruesome work. Xaran was going to kill a god.

Pulling his hood up over his head, Xaran moved forward across the moribund land, grasping his Sacred Weapon Faith, and using it as a walking staff. The contrast between Faith and the dagger was incredible. Both radiated incredible power, but while the dagger was pure hate, Faith has more of a calming and placid personality. It knew where it was needed, it knew the work that was ahead of it, and though most would have assumed a resigned posture, Faith needed to complete its task. It needed to be useful. Not because it was the weapon's lot in the grand scheme of creation, but because it knew that its power could be useful and wanted to set the right path. And now, Faith was pulling Xaran in the direction of the great palace that served as the home of the Dark Gods.

* * * * * * * * * * * *

Half a continent away, Natalia Pressen hid her small boat under some nearby foliage and stealthily moved up the shore. The trip from the mainland of Cadaria had been nightmarish, even without the minor inconvenience of the pirates that had tried to capture her. They soon learned the error of their ways. It of course had only been an accident that had caused the powder kegs in the hold to be ignited, but at the end of the day, there was one less pirate vessel patrolling around the Pritan Islands. Fortunately, the slavers' ship's hold had been empty.

Over the next ridge, Natalia could hear the movement of armored men. She had paid careful attention to the written reports that Gregor Quicksilver had given about his experiences on the Dark Continent, and while Natalia did have impressive fighting skills, she was not arrogant enough to believe that she could wade deep into the lines of a detachment of dark soldiers and survive. Guile would have to be her ally. Taking a deep breath and clutching the hilt of Perseverance tightly, Natalia whispered a quick incantation to silence her foot-falls and then began to run at full speed toward the location of the Citadel of the Dark Gods.

* * * * * * * * * * * *

All eyes were locked on Pike as he continued into the room and sat on a stool in the far corner. Basille, in the body of Wolf, stretched his neck slightly and then got onto his feet. Lissa caught her doppelganger husband and held him as the atrophied muscles began to slowly repair themselves through a small utilization of Blaze energy. Finally, he wordlessly nodded to Lissa and was able to support himself again on his own two feet. Aryx nervously rubbed at the nub of his arm at his severed shoulder and then frowned.

"Do you know what you're saying?"

Pike let his head droop for a moment in frustration and then raised it again, smiling.

"Of course I know what I'm saying, Aryx. We can finally finish what we started."

"You mean what Gwydeon started," Midarin corrected.

A little color leapt into Pike's cheeks, but he didn't lash out.

"Your protectiveness of Gwydeon's legacy is touching as always Midarin, but in this case, it is totally without context. We all fought in the war against the other gods, we were all cast down, so whether or not it was Gwydeon who struck the first blow, or the fact that he was just acting on the advice of our old friend doesn't matter. What matters is that now we have the opportunity to get back to where we belong and make things right. We have to make the Creator atone for what Emries did, and what he was going to let happen again with Dorovar. There have been far too many atrocities committed in the name of the Creator, and they cannot be allowed to continue, no matter the cost. Gwydeon would want that."

Bryn looked back and forth between Pike, Aryx, and Midarin before finally clearing her throat. It had been a long time since she had felt this far out of touch with reality. Perhaps she had let herself become too comfortable in the role of wife and mother. Hopefully the ruthlessness that served her as a member of the phasia would be a simple behavior to recover.

"So, since we're all former Oneans here, would someone please enlighten me as to what this grand plan of Gwydeon's was? Remember Aerith and I didn't fall. We made a deal, a deal for our lives and that of my granddaughter. Granted it turned out to be quite a torture living with that man for centuries, but all in all I can't truly complain about the life we were able to build together. But no deal is worth watching another world burn. I couldn't live with that."

Pike looked back at Bryn and then over to Aryx.

"What do you think?"

For a moment Aryx was caught off-guard. Since Pike had taken over leadership of the Dark Gods, he had been single-minded in his leadership and opportunities in furthering the goals of the so-called Dark Gods. He was able to unite not only all of the clans of Jeresei under Aryx's leadership, but because Diana still had the ability to utilize the powers of Nightwing, the Shadowwalkers also quickly fell into line. The army that Pike had built was nothing short of impressive, and if unleashed, could have easily overtaken all of Cadaria. It was more powerful and organized that Shauling could have ever managed at any point in the history of Onea. The fact that Pike even bothered to show restraint after all the years of harassment was commendable. But now the day was rapidly approaching where that restraint would no longer be needed, and Pike could continue down the path that he was born to walk: the warrior, conqueror, and destroyer; perhaps even live up to the name of god.

"Since a covenant has already been broken with the death of the Voice, it's only a matter of time before all of them will have to be broken. We're not bringing any more fire down upon ourselves by speaking now."

Pike nodded.

"Wait," Sabrina said holding up her hand. "What about Aerith? If you say anything now, it could remove any protection that he has against the other heralds."

"As if that wasn't erased when he killed the Voice," Lissa countered. "The Wrath and the Will are probably already hunting him."

"The Voice attacked him," Sabrina responded with frustration thick in her voice. "Aerith had no choice but to defend himself any way that he could. Because Aerith is and always has been an agent of neutrality, he might not have been targeted. However, if you break the Covenant of Silence, the Creator will have no choice but to look at all of us, even the neutrals as a threat. Think of Rael and Trece, think of Erika and Jerrard, think of Taya."

"I have no doubts that Aerith can take care of himself," Diana said after a moment, "but I am concerned as to what might happen with him in Cadaria unchecked by Bryn's more grounded nature. He is just as liable to start a war as he is to prevent one. His better natures do seem to lend themselves in that direction."

"Are you saying my husband has a tendency to get himself into trouble without me?" Bryn scoffed.

"Aerith doesn't know how to do anything else," Pike mumbled.

"Joke all you want," Sabrina said finally with an edge of anger in her voice. "But I intend to help Aerith if I can. I still have a large fragment of his power. And before any of you think that we would be better off without Aerith, never forget that without his intervention, and that of Evan, that none of you would have survived the end of Onea."

Sabrina turned to leave, but Bryn caught her by the shoulder.

"If you are intent on helping Aerith, go to the cottage and get our old friend and his traveling bag. Snag will help you find him." Then she lowered her voice to a whisper. "If you have Aerith's powers again, you know what is at stake now. We've put far too much time and effort into this. Don't make me kill you by upsetting our plans."

Sabrina nodded, and a moment later had dissolved from view. It was an interesting trick that Sabrina had learned, that to this point none of the other Dark Gods had been able to duplicate. She could simply will herself to be someplace else. It was like using a portal, but without traveling from one place to another. Sabrina simply was in one place one moment and in the other the next. It was a truly fascinating ability that had been the basis of a great many arguments and disagreement in the Council of the Dark Gods.

"She is too much like Aerith," Lissa said finally.

"You make that sound like an insult," Bryn countered.

"Enough of that," Midarin cut off Lissa's retort. "If we're going to tell stories, let's be quick about it. I don't expect that the Creator is going to let his forces just sit and wait for our next move now that the Voice has been killed. The Will and the Wrath should be on their way already, not to mention several hundred lesser emissaries."

Pike nodded with finality.

* * * * * * * * * * * *

The Citadel of the Dark Gods was in sight. Natalia had been able to avoid detection thus far, and her luck seemed to be holding. This was the tricky part. Strangely enough, the palace did not seem to be that heavily guarded. Maybe the Dark Gods didn't expect another attempt on them so soon after Gregor's attempt met with failure. Or maybe these talks of truce and understanding were actually true. It didn't matter now. Natalia had a mission, a mission that she intended to carry out, otherwise she could end up in exile like Gregor, or worse, dead. The trek from the coastline had been fast and relatively without incident, though some of the local wildlife did get a little closer than she would have ideally liked. Thought Natalia was not sure what type of magical defenses or detection abilities were around the Citadel, she had no choice but to use another incantation. This one however would allow her to leap to great heights and quickly scale the tallest towers of the Citadel in an attempt to find a mostly unguarded entrance. If they discovered her now, it would not matter. The enemy would not be able to rush her en masse, and so her increased agility and prowess with the blade would allow her to survive anything before reaching the heart of the Dark Gods' domain. Natalia took a deep breath, whispered the incantation and then leapt.

* * * * * * * * * * * *

Xaran Firesoul felt the terrible ominous power emanating from the structure before him like a great ocean wave that crested high before crashing down destructive wrath on a beach. Xaran had made little to no attempt to be stealthy in his approach to the Citadel. If anyone had paid him any notice, it had been passing and mostly ignored. Even the heavily armored soldiers that marched past seemed to care little for his being so close to the haven of the Dark Gods. Deep in his heart Xaran found the total lack of concern both strange and disconcerting. Perhaps the Dark Gods were so assured in their invulnerability that they cared little whether all of the Knights of the Flashing Blade were on their shores. While normally Xaran would take some comfort in such preposterous confidence, after hearing Gregor and Leonora's accounting of their combat with children of the Dark Gods, there was no comfort to be found.

Steeling himself against the seeds of fear that were trying to implant themselves deep in his heart, Xaran reached into his pack and found the belt given him by Khalas, the belt called Kadaan. Fastening it around his waist, a new power felt like it would overwhelm him.

I know you to be Xaran Firesoul, an ancient and powerful voice said in his mind, *and I know you to be a good man. I have been entrusted to you for purposes of assisting my race in the destruction of their enemies. I will not allow my powers to be used in any capacity that may bring harm to my brothers and sisters. If need be I will turn my powers against you and destroy you from within. If you understand and accept this, we shall work together. If not, consider your life forfeit and I will devour you now.*

"Patience, Kadaan," Xaran said in his mind, "*I have no intention of betraying the trust my friend Khalas has shown in me, or the mission that I have been placed on for the Council of Winds.*"

We shall see, blind man.

Xaran could not help but smile. Trust these days was becoming a more precious commodity than anyone could have ever imagined, even the cynical Vallic. Spreading his arms from his body and gripping Faith tightly, Xaran felt himself begin to lift into the air, buffeted by the winds around him. The Citadel of the Dark Gods awaited, and inside, the leader that Xaran sought. In his pouch, he could almost feel the malicious soul of the dagger salivating.

* * * * * * * * * * * *

"Gwydeon had a plan," Pike said somberly, "a plan so simple and so insane that there was no way to ignore it. We had all watched our world pulled apart because of an ancient war between two of the old gods. And the Creator did nothing to stop it. It was like the fights Gwydeon and I used to get into when we were kids. I would say something about his mother, he would hit me, and then we would roll around on the ground a bit yelling and screaming at each other before one of our parents would pull us apart and tell us to fight it out properly or to just let it go. The Creator had essentially sanctioned our destruction. But we had no idea how terrible it was until we all ascended. The Creator had allowed this to happen on hundreds of other worlds, snuffing out millions and millions of other lives. We just wanted to bring another point of view to the table. But Gwydeon had been around Logan and I too much I guess. He got an audience with the Voice, and Evan tried to be as gracious as he could, but eventually it degraded to a war of words. Meredith had to pull the two of them apart. That was when the Wrath stepped in. In all our time we had never seen the Creator's enforcer. Once Gwydeon did, he snapped. He attacked Evan, he threw everything to hell."

"What set him off?" Bryn asked.

"Korrd was the Wrath."

Bryn shook her head.

"The Creator has a worse sense of humor than Shau-ling ever did."

"It gets worse," Pike continued, "it seemed that anyone Halicon or Emries had tapped was fair game to be repurposed by the Creator. We learned later that most of the phasia found places in the new regime. No matter what happened to any of us, Gwydeon could not live with the thought that somewhere Taron, Jeroch, or Draven were left to their own devices, acting in the Creator's name. We were going to change things. We decided then and there that we would topple the Creator by taking away his favorite creations. We learned about Dorovar, and the dragons, and the deal that had to be made for their home. Gwydeon suggested his own expulsion and got his wish. He was cast down, and with the help of a little intervention from an old friend who I won't name right now, he landed in the right place. Gwydeon knew he would sacrifice himself to the Cadarian Emperor. He knew that his action would make it possible for things to play out the way we needed them too. Unfortunately, what we didn't expect was that the Creator had plans for this world. "

"Espre is an experiment," Aryx cut in. "The gods wanted to find out what was stronger, faith or chaos, and they made a bet on it. So the Creator made this world as a playground for their game. Gwydeon launched his rebellion when he found out. Naturally we all joined as we couldn't stand to see another world and more people needlessly suffer. We've been thwarting the game where we could."

"But why take your names?" Bryn asked.

"A god's name gives it power," Diana said finally. "Take the name; you take a measure of the power. Giving our names to the mortals defused our power and made it possible to marginalize us. Eventually it will dissipate completely and we won't be much of a threat to the Creator's power."

"But Gwydeon had a plan for that too," Pike responded. "We learned that after we got here. The Creator got careless. He let Liette come here with full memories of her time on Onea, and eventually manipulated her way to being the first Empress of Cadaria. She was the one who engineering the agreement between Cadaria and Mythryn, and she was the one who helped to enforce the peace. She was just waiting for the right time. She passed down a great secret through her descendants, a weapon of some kind that will help us defeat the Creator once all the covenants are broken. That is why I had Jehna here. But I wasn't able to get anything out of her before she disappeared. Now we have to track down the Maldovrin Triplets and make them tell us about this Legacy they are protecting."

Aryx stood and craned his neck to each side.

"I'm not the warrior I once was Pike, and you know that I have no love left for war, no matter how righteous this one seems. Diana and I will volunteer to seek out the Maldovrin Triplets and learn any information we can about the Legacy. Besides, I think some of our old friends would be more cooperative if I was away from the primary battlefields."

Pike nodded.

"Thank you Aryx. Though even with one arm I'd love to have you with me in a fight, you're probably right. Time is of the essence though old friend."

"We'll make preparations and leave in the morning."

Diana followed Aryx out of the room without a word.

"Midarin, once Jerrard and the others get here, we'll set out for the hunt. Bryn, you are welcome to tag along if you like, unless you intend to go with Sabrina and find out what Aerith is up to."

Bryn scowled.

"If I intended to go with Sabrina, I would have done so already. I came here for a reason, Rhuiden, and I intend to continue on that path, no matter the cost."

Pike took a step back as though he were struck. No one had called him by his name in almost two-thousand years, and though it seemed alien to his ears, a power surged in him at the mention.

"I'm sorry, Pike," Midarin said after a moment. "But I have to follow my own path now. Gwydeon knew this day would come, but he could not bear to sacrifice another world to make things right for what happened to ours. Whatever overtures were intended by sending Tess to the Cadarians was obviously a failure. I am going to speak to their Empress, and I am going to put an end to this war one way or another so we can focus on the Creator."

Pike stood with his mouth agape.

"That's a mistake, Midarin, they can't be reasoned with. If you go there, you'll be forced into a battle, and you'll be declaring war."

Midarin shook her head.

"Your course of action makes war a foregone conclusion. I can only hope that this Dominique Lorien and her advisors will be more reasonable."

Pike shook his head.

"Then let us make our preparations, all of us."

Midarin left the room with a nod, followed by Bryn hot on her heels. Basille and Lissa stood looking at one another.

"What about him?" Lissa said pointing at Basille.

"Lissa, I need you to keep things on track here. Alderin and Darrien should return soon with Tess and Camille. While I am gone, Sadrina will need your support to keep things moving forward on our agenda. You will act as the leader of the Dark Gods in my stead."

Lissa nodded, her eyes never leaving the man that should have been her husband.

"Basille, you will stay here and act as council to Lissa. I'm sure you have plenty of reason to be here, and I'm even more sure that information will be invaluable as the days pass."

Without another word, Pike left the room and a confused Lissa staring at his retreating form.

* * * * * * * * * * * *

Natalia lowered herself through a narrow passage into what must have been a ventilation conduit. She could hear arguing below, a heated exchange between what had to be two female voices. All of the other entrances she had tried had led to areas of the citadel that seemed to go nowhere or in circles. Natalia, despite all of her training was starting to grow impatient and a little angry. It seemed the longer she was in the citadel, the angrier she became. She found herself unconsciously holding the hilt of the dagger on her belt, the dagger that was supposedly powerful enough to kill a Dark God. She could have circled back and tried another approach that possibly would get her closer to her goal, but her patience had seemingly run out. Natalia tumbled forward through a simple metal grate, twisting, drawing both her sword Perseverance and the dagger in the same swift, deft motion, and then landed in a crouch at the far end of what must have been a bedroom. Across the chamber from her stood two women, one in a tight fitting red dress and the other in a green shirt and simple warrior's pants. Both had their hands on their hips and were facing each other as though they were in the middle of some kind of shouting match.

"You picked the wrong time to interrupt me, girl," Bryn said violently. "Now I'll have to take my frustration out on you."

* * * * * * * * * * * *

Pike rustled through his wardrobe and hurriedly pushed clothes and other belongings into a simple satchel. While part of him dreaded abandoning Sadrina to the thankless task of running the Dark Continent without him, the other half knew that in the long run, this was the only way. If their plan worked the way it was supposed to Sadrina would have to live the rest of her days without the man she called husband.

"You are the one who leads the Dark Gods."

The strange male voice forced Pike to turn around. The simple robed man stood before him with a dagger drawn. How had Pike not heard him come in? Both doors were still closed, and so were all of the windows.

"I am. I suppose the Emperor of Cadaria sent you here to kill me? Are you one of the Knights of the Flashing Blade?"

Xaran frowned.

"Who I am is of no importance. While I do not relish the fact that I must kill you, I take some comfort in the fact that your death will save countless lives."

Pike sighed.

"If you only knew how wrong you were. But come, Knight, it's been a while since I've had any entertainment."

Pike held his ground as the robed man charged, intended to take the blow and then retaliate quickly. At the last moment, and great wave of force crashed into Xaran forcing him from his feet and slamming him into the far wall of the bedroom. He was up the next moment, dagger in hand and ready to charge. He lunged forward at unearthly speed, but the dagger never connected with its target, it was countered by a long thin blade. Xaran was sent flying again, this time though he twisted in mid-air and landed on his feet. The blond-haired woman in loose clothing, who had intervened, shoved Pike backwards and took a very familiar fighting stance.

"You always were a proud idiot," the eerily familiar voice said. "That dagger can kill you."

She looked back at him, the blue eyes shining brightly. Pike fell backwards, Fury clattering from his grip.

"What's the matter, Pike," Eldar Merin said turning her attention back to Xaran, "you look like you've seen a ghost."

CHAPTER 55

Chapter LVI

Heroes and Villains

Year Three of the Just Emperor Kaitain "Dragonsbane" Lorien, Creator's Calendar Year 1870

The patrol of the Imperial Guard led by a Magistrate seemed to be taking their time in patrolling the area, and Seraph Kore hid in his mostly concealed perch high in a tree, watching. Avoiding the patrols was not difficult all in all, especially not for a man of his skill, but all of these cat and mouse games were adding too much time to his journey and significantly increasing his level of frustration. It had been weeks since the debacle at the Imperial Palace, and escaping Aldere took far longer than it should have. He expected the increased security and patrols, but it seemed that they were concentrating their searches in the exact places where Seraph was moving. He tried in vain to change his escape route, but each time, the patrol net seemed to tighten around him. A week into the journey, he had decided to take the extremely long route north, through the border into Iltorp, and then down into Thorigald. The danger in going through Iltorp was clear. Very few, if any, people passed through the Kingdom of Iltorp without the Serpentine Knight, Vallic Ultiv knowing it. At this point in time, there was no reason to fear Vallic, but then again, there was no reason to take any chances. Once across the border into the northern reaches of Iltorp, the journey would get much easier, and the patrols would not be nearly as consistent or troublesome. That was part of the bureaucracy that benefited Seraph in his endeavor. As a rule, Imperial Guard contingents could not cross the border of one kingdom into another without the presence of a magistrate. Even more binding was that the Imperial Guards of Aldere had no power in one of the Great Kingdoms, and had to give way to the proper army of the kingdom unless they had a mandate of action from the Emperor. Only a Knight of the Flashing Blade could supersede these laws, and even then it was likely to cause an incident. Rationale said that the laws were to prevent the armies of the Great Kingdoms from taking liberties in the border cities, but no one truly believed that. The true purpose of the law was to prevent any unilateral action by the Emperor against his people. The Great Kingdoms retained the power over the people that lived within the kingdom, and so far that arrangement had benefitted everyone. However, Seraph had seen the power-mad manner in which Emperor Kaitain had carried himself over the past two years, and it was only a matter of time before those last protections of the people were dissolved in favor of Kaitain's direct intervention.

Seraph saw himself as a patriot, taking the fight to an oppressive leader who did not have the best interests of the people in his heart. The wars against the dragons and the Dark Gods proved that. There was no reason for such action, and yet despite all of the evidence that the Emperor had at his disposal, he would not see the folly of his ways. Granted, Seraph had a personal score to settle with the Emperor for the way that he had humiliated not only himself, but his wife Chelsea and his lover Dominique. And now Dominique was the Empress and she was continuing the poor decisions made by Kaitain. Perhaps once Kaitain was dead, she would be able to see reason once again.

"But what if she isn't?" His mind said back at him. *"What if once Kaitain is out of the way, she still insists on these wars and these tactics? What will you do then?"*

Seraph tried to shake the thoughts away, but they would not relent. It was his worst nightmare and one that would not leave him, no matter the time or the distance. No matter how hard he tried, he could not see Dominique or Chelsea as his enemy, but the warrior part of his brain persisted. If they stood with Kaitain, if they stood on the side of everything that was wrong with Cadaria, would he have the strength to cut them down as well? Would he have the strength to kill everything that he held dear?

CHAPTER 56

Would he have the strength to hold the torch and burn the whole of Cadaria to the ground?

* * * * * * * * * * * *

A month had passed when Seraph was finally able to stop in a small farming town for supplies and to sleep in a real bed. His training in the military had prepared him for long stretches on the most meager of rations, but everyone had their limits. He knew, as he walked into the small inn's common room that he stunk not only of the road, but of the blood of the many animals that he had killed for his sustenance. No matter how many times he had washed his clothes in the rivers and streams that he had passed along the way, there were still blood stains, and there was still the smell of death that wreathed around him like a fog. Perhaps there was something fitting about that. In order to keep his identity secret, he had let his beard and mustache grow, and they were both quite thick at this point. His hair had also become a bit shaggy and was certainly unkempt. The innkeeper balked at his appearance at first, but a handful of gold coin was enough to assuage any of the man's concerns. A room was made available quickly, as was a basin for washing and a hot meal. He would take dinner in the common room to catch up on the news since he had been out of contact, but the most important thing was to be more presentable. The innkeeper offered to fetch some clean clothing for him, for a price of course, and another handful of coin seemed to be enough for the man. The unspoken conversation also included buying the innkeepers silence about his unconventional guest.

Once bathed and in some decent clothes, Seraph flung himself down on the thin mattress and shut his eyes. In his dreams he had visions of Dominique and Chelsea, of the attempt against Kaitain and where it must have all gone wrong. The practiced reflexes of the soldier woke Seraph from his light slumber when he heard the creak of the floorboards outside the door to the room. Great weight was causing the boards to protest, and Seraph rolled off the bed and took hold of Patience as the door was kicked opened by an armored boot. A spear was aloft almost before the soldiers could see into the room, and from his position on the floor, all Seraph could see was the spearhead pierce the mattress and the bedframe. It lodged itself in the floor, and had Seraph still been asleep in the bed, the spear would have gone right through his chest with little effort. Surprise had been thwarted by Seraph's practiced paranoia, and as he found his way back into a crouch from his prone position, he took hold of the bedframe and with a single smooth motion lifted and tossed the whole of the bed toward the door. The soldiers had not moved out of the doorway yet, and were surprised by the counter. But Seraph was not going to make the same mistake the soldiers made. The bed would only buy him a matter of seconds, and he intended to make use of every one of them.

Seraph charged toward the door, only a heartbeat behind the bed itself. As he reached the doorframe, he slid forward on his stomach, the blade of Patience bared and ready to strike. Taking a page from Chelsea's book of tactics, Seraph let his momentum carry him past the legs of the man in the doorway, taking time to strike at the back of his leg, severing the tender unguarded tendon there, bringing a loud cry of pain from the man. The wall was not far past the soldier's legs, and Seraph rolled himself into a ball and crashed into the structure back first. There was a soldier behind him, and two directly in front. That made a detachment of four, including the one who had crumpled to the ground in the doorway, bleeding profusely and crying in pain. Seraph kicked out hard with his legs, one food finding the knee of the soldier behind him. He was close enough to the soldier that the impact with the man's knees propelled Seraph forward. Half-way to the next guard, Seraph was able to gather his feet under him and coiled like a spring, he struck, his shoulder ramming hard and fast into the third soldier's knee. The armor there was unrelenting, but the strike had enough behind it, that Seraph heard the wrenching of the joint. His shoulder hurt too, but more damage was done to the soldier than to himself. The blow unfortunately had also forced Seraph back down to his knees, which gave the final soldier a clear strike at his head. However, the man did not have an unobstructed path to his target, as the soldier with the dislocated knee was in his path. The spear in his hands however would have been long enough to finish Seraph once and for all had the knight not been thinking a few steps ahead. As soon as he could move once again, Seraph charged forward, his momentum carrying him not toward the final standing soldier, but at the one he had crippled only a heartbeat earlier. This time Seraph's strike was higher, his damaged shoulder ramming into the breastplate of the soldier, lifting him off of the ground, and barreling the two of them forward into the spear-wielding man. Together the three of them fell to the ground,

Seraph's weight driving the crippled solider into his fellow, a muffled cry coming from the crushed man. Seraph picked up the spear from the ground and drove it hard through the throat of the soldier on top of the pile, impaling the man below him as well, and then driving the point into the floor, pinning the two together.

A sharp pain wrenched through Seraph's body as the steel tip of a spear erupted from the front of his left thigh. The soldier he had kicked had managed to quickly recover from the assault and struck true, his spear entering the back of Seraph's leg and emerging from the front. Blood flowed freely from both sides of the wound, and the soldier did not waste time celebrating his strike. He wrenched the spear to the side, twisting the spearhead in Seraph's leg, the pain forcing the knight to his knees. Any ordinary man would have passed out from the pain and the loss of blood. But Seraph was not an ordinary man, especially with the Sacred Weapon Patience in his hands. Patience struck the haft of the spear the next moment, breaking it in half, and Seraph forced his way back to his feet, despite the pain in his leg. Pushing off with his good leg, Seraph charged the shocked soldier, and thrust the point of Patience into the breastplate of the soldier. The metal was no match for the weapon and the force of the blow, and blood flowed from the mouth of the soldier as he gurgled and died from the vicious wound in his chest. Seraph fell back to his knees and pulled the spearhead from his thigh, a cry of pain held behind clenched teeth. Only one of the soldiers was still alive, but the pain from his injured leg had already forced him into unconsciousness. If he did not receive help soon, he would bleed to death in a matter of minutes. Rather than let the man suffer, Seraph quickly slit his throat.

Hearing the clattering of more armor coming down the hall, Seraph threw himself back into the small room, and recovered his bow and quiver from where it stood in the corner of the room opposite the door. Seraph sat with his back to the wall opposite the door and nocked an arrow onto his bowstring and waited. From a seated position, his shot would not be as accurate as it would have been if he were on his feet and had all of the normal power behind him, but he had to make do with what the situation presented to him. The first gleaming helm came into view a moment later, and Seraph let the arrow fly. The soldier didn't even see it coming, and it struck true, catching him in the throat and sending him falling to the ground on top of his hamstrung fellow. The other three sets of armored boots came to a stop, and Seraph reloaded quickly and waited.

"Seraph Kore," one of the soldiers called from the hallway. "You have been accused of high treason and are implicated in the assassination attempts on Emperor Kaitain Lorien, his brother the Prince Feyd Lorien and the Princess Felicia Lorien. For these crimes you are condemned to death. However, the Empress Dominique Lorien has given orders that if you will surrender yourself, you may be given a trial where you have a chance to confess your crimes and avoid execution. However, if you resist, all armies and magistrates loyal to the throne are to end the threat you pose by any means necessary."

Seraph growled.

"Your fellows weren't good enough to extend the offer to come quietly," he said trying to get a sense of the position of the men in the hallway. "They seemed quite content with killing me in my sleep."

There were hushed voices from out in the hallway that Seraph couldn't pick out the words of.

"If you come quietly, you can present your case to the magistrate. I'm sure that will be taken into account when the murder of four members of the Army of Steam are added to the charges already leveled against you."

There was hesitation before the next words, and Seraph took the opportunity to rip his shirt off and fashion a crude bandage around his wounded leg.

"You have the numbers stacked against you. Surrender now, or we will have no choice but to overwhelm and kill you."

Seraph smiled.

"Nice try, but you forget who you're dealing with. A small town like this, your maximum garrison is ten troops, and I've already killed five. There are three of you out in the hall, which makes eight, and you probably have one waiting outside my window in case I try to get out that way. If you were half as smart as you think you are, the tenth you sent on the fastest horse you could find to summon reinforcements from the nearest garrison. But it'll be three or four hours before any help comes, no matter how much you say I'm wanted by the whole of the Empire. So, the way I figure it, it's just the four of you against me, and even though I'm wounded, I don't like your odds. But then again, if you all rush me at once, you might get lucky."

Seraph reached up on the table to his left and pulled down the old oil lamp and sat it beside him. The troops outside the door were hesitating, and his words had the desired effect. It was buying him time. Obviously he had killed the officers in the first foray, and all he had left to deal with were soldiers. If he were facing down a detachment of the Army or Water or the Army of Fire, that would be a problem because he and Chelsea had always bred self-determination and initiative into all levels of the military. However, the Army of Steam was not commanded by a military man. Vallic for all his talents showed little interest in leading an army, and so there was a lot of following the leader that took place, and the lower the rank, the less initiative was shown. They weren't corrupt like the Flying Guard, but the Army of Steam was not known for a lot of independent thinking.

In the next few moments, Seraph cracked open the top of the oil lamp and removed the wick, wrapping it around the tip of one of his arrows. A flint and steel had fallen from the table when he pulled down the lamp, which made things that much easier. Seraph heard the shuffle of armor outside the door, and he knew that in a matter of seconds the soldiers would make their final push. Pushing the open oil lamp over to his side, Seraph quickly struck the flint and steel and ignited the wick wrapped around his arrow. He tossed the lamp onto the fallen bodies in the doorway the next second, the glass shattering and sending the oil spraying in all directions. The flaming arrow was upon the heap the next second, sending sheets of flame racing across the bodies, the floor of the hall, and up the walls. One of the soldiers was brave, and leapt through the flaming doorway, but he had underestimated the speed at which Seraph was able to reload his bow. The arrow slammed into his throat, bringing a muffled cry and the crash of armor slamming to the floor. The soldier's sword skidded across the room and landed at Seraph's feet.

Using the wall behind him for leverage, Seraph forced his way back to his feet, and pulled the bow over his head so that the bowstring fell across his chest, and the bow itself was across his back. He recovered the soldier's sword from the ground, and hazarded a look out the window. As he expected, another soldier stood looking up at the window in case Seraph chose to use that as a means of escape. Out in the hallway the two remaining soldiers were calling out for water, and their focus had been momentarily shifted to trying to save the inn and its patrons. Seraph bent and took hold of the corpse of the soldier who had rushed him, and using every ounce of strength he still had left in his wounded leg, pulled the armored man up onto his shoulder. With one hard push, he sent the body flying through the window. There was a cry of shock from below, and the soldier on the ground was unable to avoid the swiftly falling corpse. Despite his armor, the weight was more than the man could take, and he was crushed with a sickening sound of cracking bones and dislocating joints. At least death had been swift.

Had his leg been intact, Seraph would have had no trouble leaping from the second-story window, but as it was, it took him longer to lower himself out of the window to the ground. Unfortunately, he ended up with cuts to his hands for the effort. Seraph wasn't sure if it would impact his ability to use the bow, but there was no time to worry about that. One of the soldier's horses was tied nearby, and it took Seraph only a few moments to force his way into the saddle and make his way to the south away from the growing conflagration that engulfed the inn. Within a matter of days, if he had any luck left at all, he would reach the border of Thorigald, and he would be able to set everything right. It ached in the pit of his stomach that he had been the death of more innocent men, but he tried to reconcile it in himself that they had struck first, and he had no choice in the matter. Despite his attempts, he did not have an untroubled night sleep the rest of his journey to Thorigald.

* * * * * * * * * * * *

The capitol city of Thorigald communicated that it was the capitol city of the Kingdom of Water with painstakingly over the top detail. Every courtyard had a pond or a fountain, and there was a small stream running down the center of every major street. Some called it excessive, and others felt it was more than a little ridiculous. But then again, most felt that the royalty's obsessive adherence to the namesake of the Kingdom was another way to keep themselves visible in the everyday lives of their subjects. It was this obsession with status and reputation more than anything which continued to fuel the ancient hatred between Thorigald and Saldarine. No one was still alive who remembered the slight that started the war between the neighboring kingdoms, and no one was still alive who was offended by the slight. It had devolved into a conflict for the sake of conflict, and it had done nothing but added to the death and desolation of the two kingdoms. Nowhere else in the whole of Cadaria were there more meaningless deaths than in these two deadlocked and obstinate sets of royals. This day however, there were more pressing matters for the royal families of the Kingdom of Water. Ever since the decree marking Seraph Kore as a traitor to the Empire, there had been a growing cry among the populace to break away from the rule of Aldere and embrace the rebellion that grew daily in the kingdoms of Albitonin and Galateria. However, thus far the royal families had not committed one way or another. The other issue that was created by the public disgrace of the Emerald Knight of the Flashing Blade was the void at the head of the Army of Water. Though not tactically as sound as many of the generals under his command, Seraph was a natural leader, and his charisma on the battlefield had inspired his men into winning many battles that may well have been lost had he not been there. There was no denying Seraph's impact while on the field of battle, and there was no doubting the love and devotion that his record had instilled in his men. That was the crux of the problem that faced the royalty now. At least a dozen of the generals that served in the Army of Water had been offered command of the army, and all of them had declined the promotion. At this point there was no one left who was credible enough to have the position.

The debate over what to do about the issue had raged all morning, and the royals were about to break for lunch when the doors to the meeting room burst open, and two dozen members of the Army of Water in full armor flooded into the room, fully armed. There were cries of outrage and confusion from the collected royals, but those shouts died in throats when the figure of Seraph Kore limped into the room. He was freshly shaven and wore the uniform of his station, but his left leg was heavily bandaged.

"Seraph," Lord Myrick said after calm had filled the room again, "what is the meaning of this? You know that by being here you are putting us in a delicate situation. You are a traitor to the throne, and if we do not take steps to turn you over to the Imperial authorities, we could be seen as casting our lot in with the rebels in Albitonin."

Seraph seemed to consider for a moment.

"And what is wrong with that? The Imperial Throne says that I am a traitor. That my crimes are no different than those committed by Hannah Ironheart, Gregor Quicksilver, Leonora Wastri, and Devlin Rannoch. It seems that there is an open season on the members of the Knights of the Flashing Blade. How did we, the protectors of the Emperor, and the protectors of the Throne of Cadaria become the enemies of everything we hold dear? One reason, and one reason only. Kaitain Lorien has gone insane."

Another of the royals stood and pounded the table.

"That doesn't give you the right to attempt to assassinate the Emperor or his family."

Seraph shook his head.

"I make no apologies for attempting to kill Kaitain, other than I failed. As for Feyd and Felicia, I had nothing to do with that attempt, and if I had to hazard a guess, I would say that that blood is on Kaitain's hands alone. The man is threatened by anyone who could challenge his power, and he had not been shy about eliminating his rivals."

Lord Myrick spoke again, this time with a commanding tone.

"I'm sorry Seraph, you give us no choice. Guards! Arrest Seraph Kore, and take him to the dungeon until such time as we can open formal parlay with the Empress. We must demonstrate that we are loyal subjects of the Throne, and have no intention of throwing ourselves in the same pit of vipers as Albitonin and Galateria."

The guards all held their position. Seraph frowned and turned his back to the collected royals.

"I'm sorry it had to come to this. I was hoping that you would be willing to see reason and the folly of your actions. But I see that you are the same cowards I always thought you were."

Seraph took several steps forward until he was standing in the doorway. He never turned back, but spoke over his shoulder.

"Make sure none of them leave this room alive. Display their bodies in the square and then send out a proclamation declaring that the Kingdom of Water is now detaching itself from the Empire of Cadaria and joining our brothers and sisters in Albitonin in open revolt against Kaitain Lorien."

"Yes, Lord Seraph!" the soldiers replied in unison.

As soon as Seraph left the room, the doors were closed and barred. Seraph barely heard as the killing started.

If Bad be the Raven...

Year Fifty-Six of the Just Emperor Ender "JustHand" Lorien XI, Creator's Calendar Year 1850

Deep in the southern reaches of the Kingdom of Steel, Celidar stood a wide forest range that ran to the very jagged cliffs at the coastline. The entire southern reach of Celidar was covered with forest, from the coast to the border of the Kingdom of Gold, Bellnoc. This forest range had been the subject of the greatest conflict between the neighboring kingdoms, as Bellnoc wanted to harvest the wood from the forest within Celidar's borders to fuel their smelting operations. The confrontation escalated to the point that armies had amassed on the borders between the two kingdoms. But cooler heads had eventually prevailed, and Celidar had agreed to provide a set amount of lumber to the Bellnoc foundries every year, provided that Bellnoc agreed to cover a significant amount of Celidar's Imperial taxes. Celidar was one of the poorer kingdoms of Cadaria, marked by upheavals in the royal families, assassinations, and otherwise bad management. Finally, with the coffers nearly bare, and the royal families populated with drunkards, dullards, and deviants, Emperor Ender Lorien turned to an unlikely man to fill the role of Lord of Celidar. Ender had befriended a middle-aged man by the name of Jerrard Mistic during one of his tours of the logging camps in the south of Celidar. He was a very intelligent man and had turned his small logging operation into one of the most productive and prosperous in the whole of the kingdom. Naturally that had created a lot of jealousy of him with the royal families, and there had been a fair amount of sabotage attempts over the years. However, nothing was able to derail Jerrard's endeavors, and through all of the hardships, he and his family flourished. One of the occasions of the Emperor's visits to Celidar, Ender invited himself to the home of Jerrard Mistic and his wife.

The home itself was small, but comfortable. It was nestled in a small clearing just near the cliffs that lead to the Great Waters that separated the continent of Cadaria from the Dark Continent of Mythryn. The Emperor arrived with a smaller than normal retinue, only a half-dozen Imperial Guards and the Amethyst Knight of the Flashing Blade, Heremon Tal. As Ender walked through the door, Jerrard and his wife Erika were waiting, and Ender noticed that Jerrard had changed from his work clothes into what must have been the man's finest clothes, a black shirt that buttoned up the left side of his chest rather than straight up the middle, and a matching black set of pants. His wife, her long brown hair flowing as though it had never gone a day without being washed, wore a subdued blue gown, but its finery seemed more than a bit out of place considering the common nature of the dwelling. Jerrard bowed deeply, and his wife dipped into a low, and obviously practiced curtsey.

"Emperor Lorien," Jerrard said, his head still bowed, "you honor us with your Imperial presence."

Ender looked over the two for a moment before taking a step forward and putting his hand on Jerrard's shoulder.

"As much as I am flattered by this reception my friend, it is you that I should be thanking for this opportunity. Please, both of you rise."

Jerrard hesitated for a moment, not out of any level of uncertainty, but as a last show of respect before he stood straight, his smile wide and genuine. Erika straightened a moment after her husband, and motioned toward the foyer where very comfortable looking chairs had been arrayed around a low table.

"Would you care to sit, your majesty?"

Ender was puzzled at the address for a moment, but chalked it up to nervousness or perhaps an unfamiliarity with protocol. These were after all simple people who lived in a relatively isolated part of the Empire. Ender hesitated for a moment and then nodded to Heremon, who signaled out the door to someone unseen by the Mistics. After a moment, a striking young woman entered, with a baby cradled in her arms.

"Since you were kind enough to host me for this meeting, I thought I might bring along a bit of my family as well. Jerrard and Erika Mistic, may I present my wife and the Empress of Cadaria, Meara Lorien, and the little bundle that she has cradled in her arms is the newest addition to the Lorien family, Princess Marlae Lorien, my son Kaitain's daughter."

Jerrard and Erika went into their reverent bow and curtsey again, but this time did not wait to be prompted before standing straight again. This time when Erika motioned toward the chair, Ender, Meara, and Heremon followed the unspoken suggestion and found places. Jerrard waited until their guests were seated before finding a seat himself. Erika remained standing.

"Can I offer anyone refreshment?"

Ender shook his head.

"Unfortunately, I left the Imperial Poison Taster back at the Royal Palace in Celidar. I'm sure you understand that it is merely protocol and not a reflection upon you. Heremon here would not allow me to eat or drink anything even if I wanted to. He is a crusty and ill-tempered old man."

Heremon bristled at the characterization for a moment, and then smiled stroking his long white beard which while well-trimmed stretched down to the middle of his chest.

"Few would guess that we were nearly the same age, my Emperor," Heremon said firmly, his voice rich and full, "were only I to still look twenty years younger than my seventy-four year old frame. The women would have to lock their doors to keep me away."

Ender's smirk was echoed by Meara's soft laughter. Jerrard looked at the woman briefly, to take in her features. He had never met the Empress, in all the times that he had personally met with the Emperor she had never been with him. Her skin was fair, but with a considerable tan. Jerrard could not tell if that was her natural skin tone, or if perhaps she loved to walk in the sun so much that it had permanently colored her skin. Her cheekbones were high, her chin thin and rounded, which caused her lower jaw to appear slightly set back from the upper, which allowed her full lips to always have a pouting quality. Her brown hair was long with slight curls throughout it. It was her eyes that were the most striking. Dark like the sea, but clear and full of wisdom. She cradled the baby in her arms, who gurgled and giggled alternatively, sometimes reaching out and taking long strands of her grandmother's hair to play with between her fingers or run across her toothless gums. By this time, Erika too had found a seat beside her husband and watched the scene before her with passive grace.

"My friend Heremon here would be the last to tell anyone that when I was thirteen, and my uncle Kaldawyn, the tenth Lorien Emperor, was killed while trying to battle back the beasts in the southern borders of Galateria, I was probably the last member of my family who was ready to take the throne. I was impulsive, not very bright, and could barely hold a sword."

"At least you're not impulsive fifty-six years later."

That comment from Meara brought a roar of laughter from Heremon. Ender too, to his credit, chuckled softly.

"Be that as it may," the Emperor continued, "Heremon was a few years older than I, and an exemplary member of the Imperial Guard. He was assigned by Ivan Quicksilver to be my tutor in all things related to the warrior that I would have to become to defend my throne from the threats posed by the Dark Gods and all other manner of beast in the world. Little did I know that I would come to wish that all of the threats I had to deal with could be dismissed with a wave of the Imperial Sword. It is the other manner of threat that brings me to your home this day, my friend, and I will understand if you want nothing to do with the proposal I have for you."

Jerrard sat back a little in his seat and nodded.

"Political issues then?"

Ender laughed.

"Would only I could dismiss such things by saying they were only political issues."

Erika stood the next moment.

"I shall let you discuss this important business. I should check in on Serrina and make sure that she is well."

Ender looked embarrassed for a moment.

"I was unaware you had children. I'm sorry, that was quite rude of me not to inquire, or even think how this visit might disrupt your lives."

Jerrard waved a dismissive hand.

"We have two children actually. Our oldest is Erika's daughter from her previous marriage. He was killed while trying to save her life from bandits. She did not take her father's death well and has been estranged from us for some time. The last we heard was that she had caught on as a crewman on some trading vessels in the Pritan Islands. Our other daughter is our first child together. Serrina is only a few years old, but is growing very fast."

Meara stood and clutched the baby close to her.

"Perhaps I can accompany you, Erika. You can give me a tour of your home, and perhaps Serrina and little Marlae would like to get acquainted."

Erika smiled and nodded, and the two women moved to a room deeper in the home. Ender watched his wife go, and as soon as she was out of sight, Ender leaned forward in his chair, almost conspiratorially and spoke in a much quieter tone.

"Jerrard, how much do you know about the ruling families of the Kingdom of Steel?"

Jerrard frowned.

"I know that they are not derelict in collecting Imperial taxes, or the local taxes for that matter. I also know that there is a fair bit of disharmony between the families."

Heremon smiled.

"You have a gift for understatement my young friend. The royal families of Celidar are the worst collection of scum in the entire Empire. The Lord of Celidar is a weakling who is at the mercy of his whore of a wife and their two sons, one of which is a drunk, the other of which has a penchant for molesting stable-boys. The other branch of the family is lorded over by a senile old man and his brutish pig of a son who I think would rather sleep with his horse than with his wife. The wife is the only sane one of the bunch, as she was an arranged marriage from one of the royal houses of Bellnoc. Unfortunately, her attempts to deal with the insanity around her have turned her into a habitual user of hallucinogenic herbs."

Jerrard couldn't even register shock. What Heremon was saying was so outlandishly treasonous, that had the Emperor not been sitting within arm's reach, Jerrard would have thought the man was out of his mind.

"Heremon may be overstating things a bit," Ender allowed, "but suffice it to say that the situation in the royal families of Celidar is not conducive to the long-term health of either the kingdom or the Empire."

Jerrard leaned back further in his chair, trying to take in everything that had been said.

"Which brings me to the purpose of my visit here, Jerrard," Ender continued. "There is a little known and seldom used power granted to the Emperor of Cadaria. If a royal family of one of the Kingdoms of Cadaria has been deemed in dereliction of their duty to the Empire, or are in any other ways rendered incapacitated, the Emperor of Cadaria is empowered to appoint a steward of the Kingdom which after a period of fifteen years of successful stewardship will become the new royal family. Now, if you were to consent to my proposal, Heremon here would ensure that the current royal families would in fact be deemed in dereliction of duty, and you and your wife would be named as Stewards of Celidar, in direct service of the Emperor."

Jerrard looked down at the floor for several moments, and then looked back up into the eyes of the Emperor.

"Why me, if I may ask?"

Ender looked over to Heremon and then back to Jerrard before speaking again.

"Heremon has been keeping his eye on your for quite some time, and you have done everything within your power to not only stay within the letter of the law, but you have also gone out of your way to be discreet and keep your secrets close. Therefore I know that when you are placed in a position of power and authority, the information that is made available to you will not be misused."

Jerrard nodded.

"And if I choose to not accept this proposal? What happens to my family and I?"

Heremon was the one who spoke instead of the Emperor.

"Don't worry, Jerrard. You haven't heard anything that would put you in danger, and this offer would not be put to you if the Emperor did not feel confident that you would accept it."

"But were you to think it too dangerous," Ender continued, "I would have your family relocated to another one of the Kingdoms of Cadaria, and make sure that no harm would befall you."

Ender stayed silent for a moment.

"But I'm not going to have to do that, am I, Jerrard?"

Jerrard sat, looking down at the floor for a long moment, before finally looking up smiling.

"No, your majesty," Jerrard said finally, "I don't think you'll have to do anything like that."

Ender smiled. A few moments later, Erika and Meara emerged from deeper in the house. The two women were laughing amongst themselves, but the baby Marlae was crying.

"A problem my dear?" Ender asked.

Meara smiled.

"No problem, my husband. Little Serrina simply took exception to having her hair pulled and gave Marlae her first spanking."

Ender laughed out loud.

"And if I know my son, it may well be the last."

* * * * * * * * * * * *

Year Three of the Just Emperor Kaitain "Dragonsbane" Lorien, Creator's Calendar Year 1870

The Royal Palace of Celidar was bustling with activity. Ever since the fire had ravaged the largest part of the capitol city, the Army of Steel had been on high alert. What made matters worse was that the Amethyst Knight, Tolon Morr, had gone missing and had not been seen since well before the assassination attempt on the Emperor. All of the requests for information about the whereabouts of the Amethyst Knight had been met with the same response. He had been dispatched on a secret mission for the Emperor and there was no information available on the nature of the mission or on the Knight of the Flashing Blade's whereabouts. The Empire of Cadaria was dissolving as the weeks passed, and the Empress Dominique Lorien was trying her best to hold it together. Thus far she had been able to count on the royal family of Celidar, the Mistics, to keep the peace and stay loyal to the throne.

Jerrard Mistic retired for the evening, his head spinning from the latest reports from within the Empire. The rebellion to the west was growing in strength, and the bloodshed throughout the whole of the empire grew in magnitude every day. Thus far the worst to befall Celidar has been several outbreaks of the Wasting Disease and the Crawling Plague, but the death toll was nothing when compared to Rashaleb or Aldere. Most of the violence and death within the Kingdom of Steel was largely man-made. Tensions started to escalate after the tragedy in Rashaleb which reduced the capitol city to a ghost town. Thousands of refugees fled to the south, across the border into Celidar, causing many of the locals increased fear and anxiety. That was when the fires and the rash of unexplained deaths began. The locals began to blame the refugees, and some of those confrontations escalated into violence. Before long, Jerrard had no choice but to close the border to Rashaleb, but he did so with a heavy heart. He understood fear. He had seen it in the faces of many over the centuries that he had been alive. Under his rule, the Kingdom of Celidar had more prosperity and peace than it had in the past three hundred years, but the populace was still fearful and remembered the many lean winters under the ineffectual rule of the former royal families.

Jerrard sat on the edge of the bed rubbing his temples. His long straight black hair did not have the sheen that it once did, and he was starting to gray at the temples more than he liked. As the years dragged on, he started to feel thinner and less substantial, as though he was being stretched with every day that passed. He also didn't feel as vital as he once did. He heard rustling behind him, and knew that his wife had entered the room. She had always walked very softly and gracefully, but his enhanced hearing had become practiced in picking up her footfalls. There were few people who could sneak up on Jerrard, but Erika still managed now and then after all of these years.

"Difficult day, my love?"

Her tone was both supportive and filled with good-natured pity. Jerrard was bred to be a statesman, but he never relished the position. His care was neither for riches or power, but only to ensure that the people under his rule were never mistreated. His father had taught him that. Despite the fact that Basille Mystic was born to create misery and to bring fear to the world of humans, he treated those that he ruled with kindness and respect. He was an irony and a contradiction, but Basille knew as Jerrard did that power was neither a reward nor a curse. For those with the strength to wield it, power was a necessary tool to ensure the safety of others. Ender Lorien had been the kind of man that wielded power in that way. However, his twisted son was the other sort of man. The man who used power more like a club, to get what he wanted at all costs. Power makes people suffer when it is applied without care, and that was the lesson that Kaitain Lorien embodied with every breath that he took.

"No more difficult than any other day, my love," Jerrard responded, trying to keep his voice as light as possible. "But the news coming from the rest of the Empire continues to trouble me. The rebellion in Albitonin continues to grow in scope and power. There was apparently an attempt on the lives of Feyd and Felicia Lorien just days after the attempt on Emperor Kaitain, but details are not clear as to whether or not both survived. They both seemed to have just disappeared off the face of the empire. Calls are going up through the rebelling kingdoms that Marlae Lorien should be crowned the Empress and that her father should be deposed."

Erika sniffed at the idea.

"I doubt that spoiled girl would do anything but further her father's agendas. I think all decency in that branch of the family tree ended with Ender."

Jerrard looked up at his wife and smiled.

"Perhaps you're right. But that doesn't change the fact that like it or not, if Kaitain does not wake from this slumber, or if the rebellion is successful, Marlae is the rightful heir to the throne."

Erika sat down beside Jerrard and held his hand lovingly.

"But none of this is new, Jerrard. What is bothering you so much today?"

Jerrard exhaled slowly.

"The rumors say that Jelan has been attacked by the Iron Legion, and that the Army of Water in Thorigald has been mobilized to take Saldarine by force. Some are even saying the Seraph Kore killed the Lord and Lady of Thorigald and seized control of the army by force. This does nothing except support the Empress's decree that Seraph was behind the assassination attempt on Emperor Lorien."

Erika nodded.

"And I'm sure that the Empress has sent envoys to ensure that you are going to stay loyal to the Throne in the face of all this uncertainty."

Jerrard nodded.

"I've gotten no less than three such letters. And with the absence of Sir Tolon, the people are getting more restless. They don't know which way to turn and are looking to me to shepherd them through this situation. If the Iron Legion is indeed attacking the Academy of Arcane Arts in Jelan, then our western border could very well be in danger. The disposition of The Army of Ice is already in question, and with the amount of refugees we've taken in and the forces I've had to deploy to seal the border, I wonder whether or not we could weather an assault if we were to shift our allegiances."

"There is another option," a new voice said from the darkness in the corner of the room.

Jerrard was not startled by the voice and watched as the slender figure of his daughter Serrina stepped out of the shadows. Serrina was a beautiful young woman, and the spitting image of her mother in nearly every way. Her hair was a bit fairer than both of her parents, a more sandy brown than the jet black of her father. But one look into her stark blue eyes marked her as her mother's daughter. She smiled as Erika stood from the bed and embraced her.

"Hello mother," she said after Erika kissed her lightly on the cheek. "Father."

Jerrard smiled to her, but did not leave his place on the bed.

"From the way you arrived," Jerrard said finally, "I trust this is not a social visit."

Serrina scowled.

"Were this not a matter of great importance to the Council, father, I would not be here. You've made it very clear over the years that as long as I am working for the Council, I would not be welcomed back into your house."

Jerrard sighed hard.

"You made your choices, Serrina, just as Taya did. She wanted revenge, and there was no other way that she could get it but to go rogue and start making the Cadarian Empire suffer for the injustice that she felt the whole of the Empire visited upon us. But you, you hold this vendetta against a girl who was no more than a baby the only time you set eyes upon her. A spoiled little girl wronged us, and you wanted blood. That is why you went against my wishes and joined Pike in his damned crusade. And now, I can only imagine that you are here to once again ask us to leave the lives that we have worked so hard to build, to shatter the peace that our blood helped to create in order to fuel the whims of a power-mad fool. I have seen what Pike will become if left to his own devices, and there is nothing about him that is better than Kaitain Lorien. They are two men cast from the same mold."

Erika turned back to her husband and could not keep the sadness from her eyes. She was happy to see her daughter again, no matter the reasons for her visit.

"Things have changed father," Serrina said coldly, "and I'm sure you've been too busy helping these filthy mortals to notice. One of the Heralds of the Creator has been slain, and the first of the Covenants has been broken."

All color drained from Jerrard's face. It couldn't be.

"Which Herald has fallen?" Erika was the one who found her voice first.

"The Voice was slain. He fell by Aerith Seth's hand. Pike has sent me to bring you back into the fold, and reunite the Forgotten with the rest of the Dark Gods."

Jerrard hung his head. Then finally he shook his head back and forth very slowly, twice.

"I'm sorry, Serrina. If Pike is going to war with the Creator, he can do it without me. You are too young to know what all of this means, and you are too blinded by hatred for the Cadarians to know what Pike's plan is going to do to this world. I won't see another world burn because of the recklessness of those with power enough to know better. I lost too much. We lost too much, and I won't lend my aid to an endeavor that will cause the indiscriminant death of thousands."

Serrina frowned.

"I should have known you would turn out to be a coward."

Erika looked as though she had been struck, but Jerrard held out his hand to her. She took it finally and Jerrard stood.

"Serrina," he said after a moment, "I didn't raise you to be blind, and I hope I did not raise you to be a fool. Pike is not a leader, and he will never be. He thinks too much with his heart and his lust, and not enough with his head. And for some reason, those around him will not give voice to their objections which is the most disappointing aspect of all of this. Aryx knows better, so does Diana, and Midarin, and the rest of them. But as long as Pike is leading this charge, it is doomed to fail. You can tell him I said that, and you can also tell him that as long as he is leading the Council, Erika and I will stay here, and we will continue to do what we can to keep the promise of peace that Gwydeon gave his life for."

Serrina scowled and turned to go, but Jerrard's voice rang out again, ominous and sad.

"And as for you, my daughter, whether you believe it or not, your mother and I still love you very much. And the last thing we want to see is your life sacrificed on the altar of Pike's thirst for vengeance."

How Deep the Rabbit Hole

Year Three of the Just Emperor Kaitain "Dragonsbane" Lorien, Creator's Calendar Year 1870

Quyhn Ravenheart sat looking out the small window in the carriage and watched the countryside go by wordlessly. So much had happened to her in the short time since her father's death, and there had been few if any opportunities to come to terms with any of it. Since as far back as she could remember, she was a girl living in the middle of a dream, one that she never wanted to awaken from. Her father and mother were both wonderfully loving people who ensured that she wanted for nothing while at the same time helping her to learn the value of every opportunity that came her way. Her father had been the great Alistair Ravenheart. He was the headmaster of the Academy of Arcane Arts in Jelan and was loved by his students and the Emperor alike. Because of her father's connections, Quyhn at one time or another had met every member of the Knights of the Flashing Blade, and had also had dinner on more than one occasion at the Imperial Palace at Aldere. She had met two emperors, and their extended families. Her mother, while not as powerful or as connected as her father, was a formidable woman in her own right. She was descended from one of the royal families of Cadaria and fostered to the Academy of Arcane Arts when she was just a young girl. Once her mother and her father found one another, sparks flew, and there was no question that the two were destined to be together forever.

The cracks in Quyhn's dream world began to show with the death of her mother. It was supposed to have been an accident, a horrible accident, but Quyhn never believed. She knew it had something to do with her father's new prize student Irene Drage. Quyhn had watched as Irene stared at her father when she thought no one was looking, how the daggers were in her eyes whenever Irene saw Estelle and Alistair embrace. Other than looks and stolen glances and glares, there was nothing to go on, but Quyhn could never get the feeling out of her gut that where there was smoke, there was certainly fire. But before long, Alistair was spending more and more time away from the Academy of Arcane Arts, and it seemed that everywhere Alistair went, the dutiful little student Irene was only a few steps behind.

For much of her time in the Academy, Irene was an average student at best. In many ways Quyhn was far more advanced than the older woman. However, Quyhn had seen the same glimpses of power in the woman that her father had. But where the fits and starts of progress excited her father, they concerned Quyhn. She knew that Irene was nothing close to stable, and it would only be a matter of time before her vaguest hold on control would slip and she would be the cause of some great accident. But that day would never come. One day it seemed like everything just clicked into place for Irene, like she had become another person. She was confident, in control, and there was a dark edge to her that had not been there before. Or perhaps it had been. Perhaps it had simply been hidden under the veneer of naiveté and puppy love devotion. From that day forward, the skills Irene displayed far outpaced any of the other students her age, and in fact were as advanced if not more so than even the most senior members of the Academy.

That was when the summons from the Imperial Court came. The Crawling Plague had first been spotted in some small farming communities and the powers of the Headmaster of the Academy were needed to help find the cause of the disease and put an end to it. Long late nights were spent studying the disease and those poor souls that fell to its clutches. And no matter what her father tried, the death toll rose. Finally the great tragedy befell the land. Ender Lorien, the great Emperor of Cadaria succumbed to the Crawling Plague, and the whole of the Empire was sent into disarray. When Ender's son Kaitain took the throne, no one realized that the true horror and uncertainty would begin, and Quyhn never dreamed that the pristine if not subtle cracked dream she had been living in would suddenly fall into the worst nightmare imaginable.

One minute, she had a father, a family, and a future. The next, her father was dead, and there was nowhere for her to go. Because of Fiona and Aris, the Academy had fallen out of favor with the Imperial Court, and so the home that she had known since the day she was born had been ripped from her grasp. And so the new Emperor, Kaitain Lorien, in a show of respect for her father, and in a magnanimous gesture to his new subjects, made Quyhn a ward of the Empire, a member of the royal family. And so, in a matter of weeks, she had a new father, a new home, new siblings, cousins, and finally, a new mother. Of all of them, only Dominique, an outsider, showed her true compassion. After her adoption, Kaitain showed little interest in her, and Marlae, her sister in name only ignored her very existence. During the days she took lessons in the great library of Aldere, studying everything that she could. Eventually Irene, who had risen to her father's vacated position of Court Sorcerer, arranged for tutors for Quyhn so that she could learn to be a proper lady of the court. The lessons were mind-numbing in the least and maddening in the worst. She had to learn the names of the royal families of every kingdom as well as everything about those kingdoms. She had lessons in debate and diplomacy, as well as other lessons that a refined lady should take seriously. What was forsaken however was her study of magic. Other than Irene, there were no representatives from the Academy of Arcane Arts, and the Court Sorceress was far too busy to continue the instruction of a novice, despite what her last name might have been.

Then Dominique came into courtly life, and like a breath of fresh air into a sealed room, life seemed to spring up all around her. Quyhn had company in all of her lessons, and the two women together quickly formed a kinship. They were both fish out of water in a manner of speaking, each had far exceeded their depth of experience and were clinging to each other for support in their new lives. Though Quyhn was technically the daughter of Dominique, the two were more like sisters, and once Chelsea joined the fold, the three were thick as thieves. Each had their own torment to deal with, but together they were stronger than whatever the world threw at them. But as it had been for the rest of her world, Quyhn knew that this respite, no matter how needed, could not last forever. Politics would eventually win out, and Quyhn would find herself in a place she never expected.

And so that is how she ended up in a carriage bound for Lordhill. Quyhn understood well the importance of the garrison and mining operations at Lordhill. All manner of precious metals and gemstones flowed from out of the mines at Lordhill, and it was said that the governor of Lordhill was perhaps the second most powerful man in all the Empire. Unlike the Kingdoms, there was no familial claim to the governorship of Lordhill, and each Emperor appointed a man or woman that could be trusted no matter what. For Ender Lorien, the man who had been entrusted with the administration of Lordhill was Connor Peregrim.

Peregrim was an anachronism, a hold-over from a long forgotten age. He was honest and loyal to a fault, and there had never been a single hint that Connor was stealing from the coffers of the Empire as so many previous governors of Lordhill had done. He had been married to the same woman, Gabrielle, for forty years, and there had never been even a single rumor of infidelity from either of them. Connor like many of the men that served him, had risen through the ranks of the Imperial Guard, and had served in some of the most desolate and inhospitable area of the Empire. His last posting before being recalled for the position of Lordhill, had nearly forced the veteran soldier into retirement. Connor had been stationed at the northern tip of Rashaleb, the Kingdom of Ice, where he kept an eye on the trade routes, and insured that no forces could get a foothold there, should the armies of the Dark Gods choose to invade from the north. The post itself was usually reserved for screw-ups and malcontents who had failed over and over again in the execution of their duties. Connor had volunteered for this posting, in an effort to find ways to motivate and reclaim soldiers who by their own misdeeds or simply bad luck had ended up on the scrap-heap of military life. The noble sacrifice had won him many friends in the military ranks, and a good deal of the men that once served in Rashaleb with Connor had been reassigned to work security in Lordhill.

Connor's wife, Gabrielle, was related to the Lorien family, but it was difficult to find out just how she was related. There were rumors that she and Ender Lorien had been first cousins, and that her father had been Victor Maupin, the father of the current Master of Earth Ashinica Maupin. However, that was all conjecture, and no documents had been available to either support or refute such a claim. However, Gabrielle, like Quyhn, had been a ward of the Empire, raised by the Imperial Family, and given the title of Lady Gabrielle. Her marriage to Connor was not one of political opportunity, but one of actual love. Together their reputation was sterling, and their loyalty to the throne was without question. Or was it?

Those thoughts brought Quyhn back to the moment. There were growing voices coming from Lordhill that the Peregrims were growing more and more dissatisfied with the rule of the young Kaitain Lorien, and that they had been gathering forces loyal to the Peregrims. This secret army was said to be small but growing. If Connor and Gabrielle managed to grow enough of a force to isolate Lordhill from the rest of the Empire, the consequences would be catastrophic at best. Cut off from their supply of natural resources, trade and commerce would slowly grind to a halt. Without the valuable ores, equipment needed at the front lines of battle against the dragons and the Dark Gods would start to become scarce, and the ability to repair damaged weapons and armor would dwindle. Now that one rebellion had sprung up in the west, the embattled Empire could little afford a critical resource like Lordhill to become unavailable. Such an eventuality simply could not be allowed to come to pass. So, deprived of most options available to her, Dominique turned to her newly found daughter and conspirator, and sent Quyhn on her first mission for the Throne. She was to find out the nature of the rebellion in Lordhill and bring back any information that she possibly could. Or, if the opportunity presented itself, she was empowered to act as a negotiator in the name of the Empress of Cadaria. At least, her position in that effect would only retain power so long as Emperor Kaitain remained blissfully unaware of it.

Looking away from the window, Quyhn turned her attention to the woman that shared the carriage with her. With the growing trouble in Aldere as well as in the whole of Cadaria, there were no such things as safe roads anymore. In fact, this very route to Lordhill had been beset by assassins that had nearly claimed the lives of Feyd and Felicia Lorien. To see to Quyhn's protection during her travels, Dominique had authorized a full detachment of Imperial Guards to escort her to Lordhill, and Chelsea for her part had hand-picked a member of the Empress's bodyguards to act as Quyhn's personal protector.

When Chelsea had been named to the position of Personal Protector of the Empress of Cadaria, she immediately removed every member of the guard, and rebuilt it from scratch. She brought in a large number of soldiers from her own Army of Fire, and many of them Quyhn was surprised to find, were women. Chelsea always laughed that it was just a coincidence that the only soldiers that she trusted to defend the life of the Empress were women, but the more Quyhn thought about it, the more practical the choices seemed. When men guarded women, there were risks. Men could often not be trusted not to allow their baser natures to override their good sense, and there were always awkward situations when men simply didn't know how to handle themselves without seeming like twelve year old boys. Women on the other hand could be trusted in such situations. For the same reason, Chelsea had selected a young female soldier by the name of Rhionna Winter to act as Quyhn's guardian.

Before Quyhn even met Rhionna, she knew much about the woman who would become her shadow. Chelsea had been very forthcoming with details, as she wanted Quyhn to feel comfortable in the woman's presence. Rhionna was a third generation soldier, and fighting was in her blood just as surely as her long curly blond hair. Her parents and grandparents all served with distinction in various armies over the history of Cadaria, and her parents had actually been on opposite sides of the Saldarine / Thorigald conflict at one point. But they had found a way to put their animosity and enmity behind them, and together they raised a brilliant and gifted daughter. Rhionna was first in her class in the Imperial Military Academy, and was known as much for her tactical acumen as she was for her skill with the bow. She earned the nickname Deadeye during one of the campaigns against the Army of Water by claiming a soldier through the throat at nearly four hundred yards. Rhionna was said to be practical, level-headed, and fierce on the battlefield. For a period of time before her reassignment, Rhionna had even been chosen to join Chelsea's command staff.

Rhionna was beautiful by most standards, and Quyhn had to admit that looking at the slightly older woman made her feel more than a little self-conscious. There was a quiet confidence about her, one that belied her youthful appearance. Rhionna was in her mid-twenties, with a very fair complexion and dark almond shaped eyes. Her lean yet muscular body could be seen quite well even through her clothing, and full lips seemed to always have a pouting quality. In every way, the woman made Quyhn feel like a girl, a small underdeveloped girl.

"It's never polite to stare."

The woman's clipped words shook Quyhn away from her thoughts, and forced her to put an uneasy smile onto her face.

"I'm sorry," Quyhn said after a moment. "I guess I'm a little out of practice at looking without looking. Father always said that it was a very good skill to harness. That way you could know everything that is going on around you without letting everyone know how vigilant you are."

Rhionna turned her face away from the window and looked Quyhn in the eyes for a moment, and then back to the window.

"Your father was a wise man. It's a shame what happened to him."

Quyhn felt her cheeks redden a bit, but then she returned her gaze out the window. The uncomfortable silence held in the air for a long time, but it had nothing at all to do with the mention of her father.

* * * * * * * * * * * *

Connor Peregrim paced around the meeting room, his gait clipped and uneasy. He had not been the same man once he had returned from the far reaches of Rashaleb, and his body was much older than it should have been. Both of his knees ached from dawn till dusk, and he couldn't lift his sword arm above his head any longer. He was an old, broken-down warrior in a time that demanded he be the lion that he was in his twenties. That more than anything grated on him. He had wanted to be there, to do his job and defend the Emperor from those that would do him harm, but now he had been prevented from doing that, not once, but twice. His friend, his patron Ender Lorien had been killed by the Crawling Plague, and his bastard son had nearly been killed by an assassin's arrow. Of course, Connor didn't believe for a moment that the arrow had been fired by Seraph Kore, but that was another debate for another time. But Connor knew that if Seraph had been the one to fire the arrow, it wouldn't have been an attempted assassination, and there would be a new Emperor sitting on the throne in Aldere.

"So what are we going to do?" Arent Fox, Connor Peregrim's right hand in the administration of Lordhill said calmly. "She'll be here before the day is out."

Arent like Connor was a lifetime soldier. From the time he was twelve, he had been fostered to the Imperial Military Academy, and had done his first posting in Galateria, fighting off the hordes of beasts and creatures that called that place home. But like so many of the soldiers that were posted in Galateria, eventually a mistake or failure led to death. Such was the case for Arent as well. He had been on patrol with the rest of his unit when they were ambushed. His entire unit was wiped out, and only Arent made it back to the garrison alive. However, Arent did not make it back unscathed. One of the beasts had raked long nails down his left arm, leaving it nearly ruined. The scars would be deep and lasting, and even now looked as though the wound had been inflicted only days earlier. Despite everything he said, Arent was found to be in dereliction of duty, and charged with responsibility for the death of his unit. Rather than be discharged, Arent was demoted to the lowest rank possible and reassigned to the worst post in Cadaria, the northern reaches of Rashaleb. He had already been there ten years when Connor found his way there. Were it not for Connor, Arent would never have had a chance at redemption. When the opportunity arose, he followed his commander to Lordhill, where he had done nothing short of serve with distinction.

"She is a ward of the Empire," Gabrielle said leaning forward and resting her elbows on the table, "and she must be afforded all of the privileges that that entails. To do otherwise invites more questions, and creates more opportunities for her and her handlers to see more than we want them to."

Connor looked at his wife and smiled. She was a fierce and formidable woman to say the least, and though her hair was beginning to gray slightly, there was still life in the long brown strands that hung about her shoulders. There was also life in her bright green eyes, a fire that could never be extinguished no matter the trial. As usual she wore a dark green gown with long sleeves and the golden bracelets that had once been gifts to her from Ender Lorien on her wedding day.

"But who is she loyal to?" came the deep rumbling voice of Strum Anvilguard, the Peregrims' dark-skinned family guard. "And will she be willing to listen if she does see something she isn't supposed to."

Strum like Arent had been posted in the northern reaches, but his posting was purely out of disfavor. Like many of the people who were born and raised in Galateria, Strum was the subject of mistrust and scorn. Many felt that he had demon blood running through his veins and that he could not be trusted with the defense of the Empire. But Connor knew the man to be fiercely loyal and a good soldier. Strum would never be questioned in the execution of his duties as long as Connor was in charge of Lordhill.

"If she has any loyalty at all to Kaitain, we could be finished before we get started," Arent cautioned.

"There is no indication that she is loyal to anyone other than Dominique. We know for certain that she has no love for Irene, even if she doesn't know the whole truth about what happened to her father," Gabrielle countered.

There was a pregnant silence that filled the room. When Connor had learned that Quyhn Ravenheart was the one being sent by the Empress of Cadaria to inspect their production and act as the Empress's eyes and ears in Lordhill, the chances of her discovering the truth about the true fate of her father became a bargaining chip open to the Peregrims. But it was a dangerous chip to hold, and an even more dangerous one to use. Many suspected that the death of Alistair Ravenheart could not have been one of simple carelessness. Anyone who knew Alistair knew that such things were simply not in the man's character. Perhaps once when he was young and adventurous, but not when the fate of the Empire rested on his shoulders, and certainly not when the fate of his daughter could spin so wildly out of control. No, Alistair was most certainly murdered, and it was made to look like an accident. It had taken considerable amounts of the Peregrims own personal fortune to find a member of the Shadow Guild who was willing to talk, and once he did start talking the words were like poison in Connor's ear. It had been Alistair's own student, the woman who usurped his position, Irene Drage who had been the instrument of Alistair's demise. It had been murder most foul, a murder that was covered up by the Emperor of Cadaria, and was very likely carried out under his orders.

Of course the Shadow Guild member could not be allowed to leave Lordhill, and he could never repeat his story to anyone, or reveal who else knew the truth. Strum had seen to that personally. But that incident was the start of Connor's look into who the new Emperor of Cadaria really was. He had known both Feyd and Kaitain as children, and they were as different as the suns and the moon. Feyd had always been thoughtful, if a little too impulsive. Both were good traits, but Feyd was more of a slave to his nature than he should have been. It actually hurt him in the political arena, and his daughter Felicia was far more practiced a politician than her father would ever be. Kaitain on the other hand was very aware of the limits of human nature, and he made a practice of knowing who was around him, and what their proclivities were. It seemed that Kaitain had an ear for human weakness and learned quickly how to turn those weaknesses into an advantage. In some ways Connor was almost impressed by this ability, as it closely mirrored skills that Connor himself had learned on the field of battle. He had learned to analyze the weaknesses of his opponents and to turn them to his own advantage. However, there seemed to be something much more unsavory about the ability when it was turned in the direction of human emotion. Finding the weaknesses in another person's soul felt dirty and something akin to evil.

"We need to be careful with that," Connor said finally, "if we have no other choice, we can bring that information to her awareness, but only if we have no other choice. The ramifications for us knowing this long and not making it public could turn her against us rather than make her our ally."

Arent nodded and then spoken again.

"Does anyone know anything about this Rhionna Winter that is coming along as the bodyguard? Is she the kind that could be useful to us, or is she just another brainwashed product of the Imperial Military Academy?"

"She's one of Lady Chelsea Zarova's bright stars. She was handpicked for this assignment according to our spies in the Imperial Palace," Strum replied.

Gabrielle smiled.

"Don't worry about Rhionna. She won't be a problem at all. Leave her to me."

Connor was a bit surprised at his wife's words, but he simply nodded in her direction. The conversation was cut off as the doors to the meeting room opened. A page appeared quickly and bowed to the Lord and Lady before letting his voice fill the air.

"The Emissary from the Imperial Court of Aldere, the Lady Quyhn Ravenheart Lorien has arrived."

Requiem for a God

Year Three of the Just Emperor Kaitain "Dragonsbane" Lorien, Creator's Calendar Year 1870

Natalia Pressen stood facing off against the two women, Perseverance held coolly in her right hand while the dagger burned in her left. The woman in the red dress took a step back and recovered a simple silver dagger that was held in a sheath that was indecently high on her right thigh, while the other woman in the simple clothing stood and waited for something. There was a bow standing in the corner opposite the woman but it looked as though it had not been lifted from its spot in years. Equally showing the marks of disuse was a common longsword propped up beside the bow with what appeared to be the symbol of a lion carved into the blade. Natalia remained in battle posture but let her voice break the uneasy silence.

"I am Natalia Pressen, Sunstone Knight of the Flashing Blade and loyal servant of the Emperor of Cadaria, Kaitain Lorien. I have been sent here to dispose of as many of the Dark Gods as possible, and I will not be dissuaded from my task. I would assume as you are lodged in this Citadel that you are to be counted with the number of my enemies."

Natalia was caught off-guard when the woman in the red dress laughed.

"These fools are worse than you and your band ever were, Midarin. The arrogance and disrespect they show your position is unforgiveable. If you or Logan or any of the others would have burst into my palace spouting this nonsense, Grawn would have painted the walls with your blood."

Midarin looked first at the woman in the red dress and then to Natalia.

"At least we had some decency about how we did things. We didn't go barging into people's bedrooms in the middle of the night," she said calmly. "And of course we respected you, Bryn, we knew that even all of us together would have had problems fighting a phase. Just because we got lucky a few times didn't give us the right to be cocky. Even after Gwydeon and Pike killed a couple single-handedly, they didn't let it go to their heads. These Flashing Blade people have been coming here for generations and not one of them has even come close to wounding one of us. And yet each one that comes here is more arrogant and self-assured than the last. You would think they would have learned something by now. They still think their Emperor killed Gwydeon single-handedly. That is the only part of the plan that has backfired on us."

Bryn sat on a cushioned footstool.

"Well, Natalia," Bryn said with venom in her voice, "if you wanted a Dark God, you've got one. Midarin is one of their highest ranking members. Have fun."

Despite herself, Natalia felt her brow furrow with frustration. The banter should not have pierced her calm and practiced mind but something had thrown her senses into disarray. Her mind was on fire and rage crept deeper into her every moment. Midarin stepped forward one pace and turned to face Natalia fully.

"I am Midarin Rice," she said proudly, the sound of her own ancient name empowering her, "former Queen of Brea, wife of the first of the Dark Gods, and general of the armies of the Mythryn. I have fought against gods, angels, demons, and every form of evil that has walked or crawled on this and many other worlds. Lay down your weapons now and I will let you leave here with your life. Persist in this foolish task, and I will make sure that you suffer for every insult that your Cadarian Emperors have ever visited upon us for the last two-thousand years."

* * * * * * * * * * * *

Xaran Firesoul did not have to see to know what had happened. It was entirely possible that the Dark God, the one the woman had called Pike, was going to let the dagger pierce his flesh not thinking that it would cause any real harm. His bold and most assuredly deserved aura of invulnerability had nearly completed Xaran's task for him, but the interloper to their conflict had certainly been intelligent enough to understand the danger that the dagger posed and ended Xaran's assault with a simple push. Now any option for a simple and quick resolution to this conflict was gone. It took only a moment for Xaran to find his way back to his feet, and let his thoughts drift out to the room. The one called Pike stood like a blazing fire in the center of the room. He exuded rage, shock, and disbelief, and those emotions hung around him like a fog. The slight woman opposite him near what must have been a door, was wreathed in a different kind of power, one nearly angelic. The purity and power that rolled from her was like a star had simply chosen to manifest in the room, shining bright and yet threatening to consume the both of them.

"What madness is this?"

Pike's confused voice rang out like a clarion bell. Xaran's ears could detect the shock, horror, and pain that flooded into the harsh, raspy tones. Even though it was obvious that the Dark God's eyes were focused on the woman in the room, his attention was still very much on Xaran and the dagger that suddenly began to warm in his clutched hand. Even more strangely to Xaran was the sudden emptiness coming from his other hand. He still felt the familiar weight and comfort from Faith, but there was something different. The calming influence and the subtle flow of power that permeated the weapon had somehow become muted.

"Time enough for stories and condemnation later, Pike," Eldar chided. "You never were able to think of more than one thing at a time. Perhaps that is why you were so lacking in bed."

If there was playful taunting in the jibe, Xaran could not detect it. The verbal assault was pointed and cruel. The confusion coming from Pike ceased, replaced by a burning hot rage.

"Sadrina has never complained," Pike returned. The ice in his voice chilled the room, and even Xaran could feel the impact from the woman's form. "But you're right, whoever you are, I have no time for you. This so-called knight and his toy deserve all my attention. And unfortunately for him, he'll receive the brunt of the anger you have incited."

* * * * * * * * * * *

Deep in the Pritan Islands, in a small cabin built into the cleft near a waterfall, a gentle breeze slightly stirred the small accumulation of dust that had grown like a shroud on untouched furniture. Then suddenly in the heart of the emptiness a form appeared. As Sabrina looked around the room, it was strangely familiar and alien in the same breath. From the memories she shared with Aerith she knew every inch of this place instinctively as if she too had dwelled here for a hundred years. The hardest part of her shared consciousness with the man who was thousands of years old was not the memories or the awkward relationships that those memories caused, but it was the mass of tangled emotions that played with her heart and with her mind. It was the love that bloomed in her heart every time her eyes floated across Bryn's features, and the heat of desire that flooded through her body, regardless of her attempts to resist it. Perhaps that had been part of the reason for her inability to find comfort in any relationship. Perhaps that had been why she frequently found herself in Serrina's arms on many nights. Many times she had wanted to slap Aerith for that, but she knew in her heart that he would just laugh at her. He had always found the shared memories and emotions one of the more amusing side-effects of the transfer of his mantle. For her part too, Sabrina enjoyed knowing more than her peers.

As she ran her hand across the still tangled sheets of the bed her mind flashed to Aerith and Bryn's last night in that bed together and suppressed a bit of a shudder. This unfortunately was not one of the more endearing parts of the sharing. Shaking herself back to the here and now, Sabrina felt movement behind her, and turned slowly. As she had expected, a large black ball of fur was sitting on the floor beside the door. Within a matter of moments a low deep purr began to come from the creature. Sabrina tilted her head to the side slightly and smiled.

"I know you remember me."

The purring changed pitch slightly, and the creature unfolded itself, revealing a long, whisper-thin tail, two large penetrating eyes, and a mouth full of razor-sharp teeth curled into the most cruel, and yet comforting smile.

"It's nice to see you again too, my little friend," Sabrina cooed softly. "Aerith has gotten himself into trouble again, and he's going to need our help."

The creature covered the distance between them in three long hops, the end of the third perched the Snag on her shoulder. The smile on Sabrina's face widened slightly and she grasped the straps of Aerith's always-packed travel bag from where it lay beside the wardrobe. Sabrina paused for a moment at the open wardrobe door and ran her hand over the black shirt that hung beside a long formal red gown. As if Snag understood her intentions, it bounded from her shoulder to the top of the wardrobe and waited patiently as Sabrina removed her too-formal royal gown and quickly pulled on the man's shirt and pants. Though they were a little snug in the hips, they still fit surprisingly well, with a slight magical modification.

"I don't think Aerith will mind," Sabrina said looking up at Snag.

The answer came as a low purr, before Snag rebalanced itself on her shoulder.

"Now, where should we start looking?"

The purr lowered an octave.

"Right, just look for the most trouble. Aerith is sure to be in the middle of it."

Before Sabrina let her essence fade into the flows of energy to take her toward where Aerith must have been, she caught a flash out of the corner of her eye. A glow that had not been there before, yet it was something that was not part of her normal perception. Her eyes had not seen it. It was her memories that ignited the vision. With a careful pace, Sabrina returned to the wardrobe and easily found the secret compartment in the back wall. Tears welled in her eyes as she looked over the items there. The wedding rings that had been crafted in secret early in their exile on Espre, a set of Gideon's daggers, a small likeness of Ellis. But it was the small golden locket that pulled Sabrina's attention. When she opened it, she saw the likenesses of a young man and a young woman. The young man was Ayden, the girl, Sabrina did not recognize. Aerith had carefully blocked the memories of this red-haired girl from her. Despite herself, Sabrina could not help but smile. Maybe the old man still had some tricks up his sleeve.

"Bryn won't appreciate you going through her things."

The woman's voice was not as much of a surprise as it should have been. Sabrina had sensed the portal open seconds before. No one would have come here that way, except for family.

"Just as Aerith wouldn't have liked you coming here to go through his things, like you always found ways to do when he was off on his supply trips. I guess you have to expect such behavior from the daughter of a thief."

"Touché," Taya's reply came swiftly.

"So I take it you are here because you've heard from either Aerith or Bryn?"

Taya put both hands on her hips and flipped her long blond hair over her shoulder. She had inherited her grandmother's loose sense of morality when it came to clothing, and her father's swarthy nature. Instead of a common thief, Taya had taken it upon herself to become one of the most renowned pirates around the Pritan Islands, preying almost exclusively on Cadarian shipments.

"It was more the point that I hadn't heard from them. It's not like them to miss a delivery of supplies. So I thought I would come and have a look. And surprise, surprise, I find the little tagalong wearing Aerith's clothes and going through my grandmother's private things."

"Things have changed more radically than you could know Taya. I need to find Aerith and help him if I can."

Taya frowned and fidgeted uncomfortably. She had never liked Aerith, and in all their years together, she had never developed a fondness for the overly glib man. He was perpetually a spoiled child in a man's body, and no matter the trial or the irritation, it seemed as though he was utterly incapable of taking any situation seriously.

"Well, you won't find any answers there. Wherever Aerith is, he won't be with his children."

Sparks fired in Sabrina's mind. Aerith and Bryn had two children on Espre. But why had the memory of Ayden remained while the memory of the daughter been hidden?

"Then maybe we should work together to find him?" Sabrina said finally.

Taya laughed and crossed her arms.

"Not a chance. If you want to rescue that derelict, be my guest. If my grandmother wants my help, she knows where to find me. If not, I have my own business to attend to which has nothing to do with the Dark Gods or their stupid wars."

With that Taya turned from the door and started to walk away.

"You'll never get the revenge you're looking for," Sabrina called after her.

Only silence returned.

* * * * * * * * * * * *

Perseverance ached like a cold piece of iron in Natalia's hand, and her heart burned with every racing beat. She tried hard to remember a simple calming spell, but she couldn't calm her mind long enough to find the incantation. Before she knew what was happening, she lashed out in a precise, if clumsy for her level of skill, strike at the woman who had called herself a queen. Midarin side-stepped the strike and landed a quick elbow strike to the side of the knight's face. A cracking sound echoed through the room, and Natalia tumbled away, blood flying from her mouth.

"Midarin!"

Bryn's voice was shrill and impatient. When Midarin looked over, Bryn was backing away from the stool, a line of blood smearing the front of her dress.

"I thought you phasia liked blood," Midarin mocked.

"That was my little sister, not me."

Midarin shook her head and rounded on Natalia who was just finding her way back to her feet. Her mouth hung open unevenly, and it was obvious that her jaw had been broken by the blow. Natalia knew that any attempt now to cast any of her incantations would fail, so she lunged again, this time with a high feint with the dagger, followed by a spinning slash with the blade of her sword. Midarin easily dodged the blow, but was impressed with the woman's skill. She was obviously no match for the power of a Dark God, but Midarin was sure if she was still a mortal, Natalia would have been more than her equal in combat. But, things were not equal. Midarin quickly spun under the woman's guard and landed a hard palm strike to her sternum, shattering it and sending her crashing against the far wall of the room. Natalia coughed hard spitting up massive amounts of blood. The fact that the knight was still breathing was a testament to her conditioning and valor.

"This fight is over," Midarin said coldly, "surrender now, and we'll send you back to your emperor in one piece."

Bryn frowned.

"Maybe we should just kill her now. It would be merciful compared to what Kaitain will do to her. His impatience with failure is well documented."

Midarin shook her head.

"We're not murderers, despite what they think of us. Her fate was sealed as soon as she was sent on this mission. When will they learn?"

Natalia's mind burned. She was filled with hate, and it drowned out any pain that she may have been feeling. With labored breaths, she began to pull herself to her feet. The pain inside her chest was unbelievable and it threatened to force her into unconsciousness, but she was too well trained to let the pain stop her. Perseverance clattered to the ground as she supported herself with one hand on the wall and the other clutching the dagger.

"Stay down, girl," Midarin chided, "don't make me kill you."

Natalia lunged again, the point of the dagger racing for the woman's heart. Midarin easily dodged the attack and grabbed hold of Natalia's wrist, effortlessly crushing it, causing her hand to spasm and the dagger to clatter to the ground. Once disarmed, the woman crashed to the ground in a heap, all of the fight gone from her.

"That was quite interesting," Bryn said finally, looking at the dagger laying on the ground, a slight glow emanating from the blade. "I think perhaps we should go see Pike."

"What about her?"

Bryn regarded the fallen woman for a moment.

"Aren't you a little old for a pet?"

Midarin glowered and set off to alert the guards of their intruder.

* * * * * * * * * * * *

Xaran stood somewhat transfixed, his mind in dozens of places at once, trying to piece everything together. Something was wrong, and it was something far more serious than the Dark God whom he was staring down with his blind eyes. His mind whirled with uncontrolled thoughts, and his normally serene and placid mind was afire with the alien drives of hate and thirst for the death of another. This god named Pike, was the enemy of Cadaria to be sure, but Xaran had never relished the death of any of his enemies in any of the wars he had been involved in. Hate seemed to ooze from the dagger that had been given to him by the Council of the Winds, while at the same time Faith sent calming forces through him. The two were at war and would have cancelled each other out, but the wild card that was the intelligent item known as Kadaan was throwing everything further out of balance inside of him.

He is distracted, Kadaan was saying, you can take him. *You were given this task and shown great trust. Repay that trust now, Knight.*

And yet Xaran took no action. However Pike did not show the same hesitation. From across the room Pike's right hand shot forward and a wave of invisible force travelled the distance faster than a blink and slammed Xaran hard in the chest, sending him against the wall for the second time in the brief confrontation. This time, the dagger clattered to the ground, away from Xaran's grasp. Before Xaran could grab for it again, it was whisked across the room and into the hand of the blond woman.

"Now finish this, Pike," the woman wearing Eldar's face said coldly. "The Cadarians have proven once again they are your enemies. End him and we will take the war to their Emperor and to the dragons that aided his ambition."

Pike hesitated for a moment. Everything about this situation was wrong. The Knight of the Flashing Blade, Eldar, the weapon that could supposedly kill him, everything. For his part, Pike remained where he was and took no action against Xaran. Xaran too took no action and simply remained where he had fallen, clutching Faith and letting its innate powers heal his wounds. Though the attacks focused against him had not been intended to be lethal, they had caused significant damage nonetheless. Several of his ribs had assuredly been broken, and Xaran could feel from the rattle in his breathing that it was possible that one of the broken ribs had caused more significant internal injuries. But he was not going to be out of the fight long.

"There is no advantage in breaking this truce," Pike was saying to the blond woman. "We have turned away every one of their advances. We have crushed their champions time and time again, and we will continue to do so. They can come with their magic and their armies, and even their pathetic dragon-crafted toys, and we will continue to overcome them."

Eldar's hand shot out the next moment and Xaran found himself seized by his throat and lifted into the air. His feet were a hand-span above the ground, and it took only a few moments for his whole body to spasm and Faith to come crashing to the floor.

"This insult to your authority cannot be allowed to stand, Pike. Gwydeon knew what it took to be the leader of the Dark Gods, but you seem to be caught somewhere between your humanity that you left behind on the smoldering ashes of Onea and the god that you have become. You were heroes, you fought against the very darkness that Kaitain Lorien and his followers represent. Don't you realize that they will keep coming for you again and again until you are all dead? Eventually they will find a way to exploit you. They will find a way to hurt you. Don't you realize that you have become what you hated in their eyes. Today, you are Taron."

Pike trust his hand out and sent Eldar flying across the room where she crashed into the stone archway that held the chamber's door and crashed to the ground. The door itself was thrown off its hinges and into the hallway. Xaran, free of the woman's control fell back to the ground hard, his head hitting the cold stone floor, but he remained conscious. However, he felt more like he was in a dream than in reality. The Dark Gods had once been human? They had once been heroes? Pike moved around the table toward the fallen woman, his right hand wreathed in a white mist. He placed himself between Eldar and Xaran, with his back to the knight.

"How dare you!"

Pike's mind whirled. He saw the woman lying on the ground before him, but he knew despite her visage that she was not Eldar. The woman that he had loved and married would not have said those words to him. She was a mask, a shell, something evil wrapped in a pleasing form. She pulled herself to a semi-sitting position, blood trickling from her nose and from the corner of her mouth. But instead of a look of defiance, or shock, or disappointment, there was a faint smile.

"Lashing out at those who don't agree with your judgment, Pike," the woman taunted. "How very phasia of you...."

Pike lashed out that next moment, a spray of razor sharp ice shards erupting from his outstretched hand. There was a flash of light from where the woman lay, and a set of leathery wings appeared wrapped around the woman the next instant, deflecting the assault. When the attack was at its end, the wings retracted revealing a new set of features. It was no longer Eldar, but a young woman who could have been in no more than her late teens, extremely fair, but her cruel smile belied any beauty held by her face. She rose easily to her feet, with seemingly no effect from either of the attacks directed at her. The vile dagger was in her left hand, clutched tightly.

"Thank you for being every bit as gullible as you were made out to be, Pike," Seraphina Masile said in an evil and foreboding voice. "Though I was hoping you would be stupid enough to kill this puppet first. You know we can get to you now. You know we can hurt you and you would never see us coming. And what's even better is that you don't know who your enemies or your friends are any more. Dorovar, Kaitain, even your own fellow Dark Gods...how many battles can you fight at the same time, Pike? How many of your friends are you willing to sacrifice for this stupid dream of yours?"

She held up the dagger and waived it slightly.

"Just think about who I'm going to use this on first. That should help you sleep tonight."

The next moment she was gone.

* * * * * * * * * * * *

When Midarin made it to Pike's chambers, Bryn was already there with Sadrina. Pike was sitting on a somewhat broken chair and the door to the chamber was still laying in the hallway. What was the most shocking was that across from the table in another chair sat a blind man clutching a staff. He wore the symbols of allegiance to the Empire of Cadaria. Sadrina was standing beside Pike, her hand on his shoulder, while Bryn had not moved past the doorway.

"So the dragons put you up to this? You weren't acting as an agent of the Emperor of Cadaria?" Pike said in a surprisingly even tone.

The blind man frowned.

"While I may not have undertaken the mission on the direct order of my Emperor, I am quite sure that he would have sanctioned it. His hate for the dragons is strong, but his hate for the Dark Gods, even more so."

"And don't you fear the repercussions of this failure? Especially after what happened to your colleagues?" Sadrina asked.

"Our Empress, Dominique Lorien, seems to have a much clearer head than her husband, and perhaps he will still be recovering when I make my return. As for reprisal from the dragons, I am afraid that before long they will have far more concerns than a simple blind man."

Midarin entered the room and stood opposite Xaran while still across the table from Pike and Sadrina.

"And what about your fellow knight Natalia? Was she also working for the dragons, or was the timing of your attack a coincidence?"

The aura that wafted from the man was all the answer that Midarin needed. She recovered the pouch from her belt and laid it on the table in front of Pike. Once opened, the pouch revealed the glowing red dagger, the one that could kill a god.

"Be careful with that weapon," Xaran said after a half-caught breath. "It has a mind of its own and all it knows is hate for those it was crafted to destroy. It is single-minded in its purpose and desires only to taste the blood of the Dark Gods."

Pike looked at the dagger and then up to Midarin.

"Perhaps you should take this Natalia with you when you go to negotiate. It may strengthen your position or at the very least gain us some information about the true motivations of the Cadarians. Xaran, you are welcome to accompany Midarin back to your home."

Xaran shook his head.

"I will need to answer for my actions to my friend Khalas. He needs to know that the dragons themselves were manipulated. There is a dark cloud descending on this world, and I am afraid that if we do not discover the truth as to who is truly behind these manipulations that we may all suffer."

The blind man rose, nodded and effortlessly made his way from the room, a guard waiting for him in the hallway.

"So what now, Pike?" Bryn said from the doorway. "Seems we have some other enemies to hunt down."

Pike closed his eyes for a moment and then shook his head.

"I think I need to seek some advice from an old friend. Bryn, you're going to lead the hunt in my absence. We need to start turning up the pressure. Our enemies are getting bolder in their attacks on us, and now we know they have access to weapons they should not have."

Bryn just stared. Pike's eyes met hers after a moment.

"You said it yourself Bryn, you're here for your own reasons, but I need you to be what you were bred to be. I need the ruthlessness and disregard for humans that Shau-ling created within you, and I need you to make our enemies pay."

A smile grew on Bryn's face, an evil smile dripping with malice.

"My pleasure."

Dark Vendetta

Year Three of the Just Emperor Kaitain "Dragonsbane" Lorien,
Creator's Calendar Year 1870

Felicia Lorien woke with a start as she felt a hand cover her mouth. Her eyes darted back and forth, until she saw Wynne's concerned face above hers. He wasn't looking down at her, but rather his eyes were scanning the tree line at the edge of the clearing where they had made camp. The last few days of travel had been slower than they all had wanted, as Feyd's injuries seemed to limit their pace far more than Wynne expected. The herbal mixtures had been nothing short of miraculous though, as Felicia knew, because under normal circumstances, her father probably would have been long dead without them. As it was, he would probably never walk straight again, and his back would most likely always pain him. However, her father was strong, and he battled through the best he could, regardless of the constant pain that ravaged him. Wynne on the other hand was very nimble and spent most of the day either scouting ahead, or falling behind the father and daughter to disguise their trail and plant false clues for the force that was obviously pursuing them. They had done well to make it this far without being overtaken, and they were no more than two days travel from the family's holdings in eastern Pellatori. Once within the keep's walls, they would at least be safe. There was always a standing regiment of Imperial Guards on site, and they would hopefully be a match for any intruders who meant harm to the Lorien family.

Wynne's eyes continued to scan for another moment, and then he removed his hand from Felicia's mouth. She sat up slowly and as silently as possible, her eyes going to where Wynne was looking. The man had proved to be full of surprises in their time together, and he was possessed of a great many skills that would make him invaluable in their weeks together. He was a more than impressive swordsman, and Felicia had taken every opportunity to learn his unique style. There was no doubt that he was superior to her in skill, but he constantly slowed himself down so that she could learn from him and not be completely overwhelmed. In addition to his skills with a sword, he also had incredible tracking and hunting skills. They ate very well during their travels, and he was more than a fair wilderness cook. Despite his military skills, it did not seem likely that he was ever a member of the Imperial military, but a sword master such as himself would never be just a member of a local militia. It was as if this man wanted to stay hidden no matter the cost, and didn't want to be part of the world that was going on around him. Luckily for the Loriens, Wynne had broken his seclusion and isolation to save them from their would-be assassin. Finally Wynne straightened, and held his hand out to help Felicia get quickly up to her feet.

"What is it?" Felicia whispered.

"One of the traps went off in the distance. It was probably a wolf or something that size, otherwise the trap wouldn't have triggered. But I didn't hear any cries."

Wynne's voice was hushed, but Felicia could feel the man's concern radiating through him. His eyes never left the direction of the tree line, and his other hand tightly gripped the hilt of his sword.

"So we're still being tracked."

Wynne nodded.

"And you thought they would stop chasing us?"

Felicia frowned. She knew he was right, but certainly didn't like the fact put so bluntly. The assassin had only been the start. There was a plot at hand that threatened the entire Lorien family. It had started with the attempt on Kaitain, and continued with the attempt on Feyd and Felicia. It would only be a matter of time before the targets included Dominique and Marlae.

"We need to move," Wynne continued, "and we can't afford to stop again until we've reached your keep. Otherwise there is far too much of an opportunity for whomever it is that is following us to finish what they started back in Aldere."

It took only a few minutes for Felicia to wake her father and get him ready for travel. It was uncomfortable for him to sit on horseback, and any pace over a trot was nearly enough to make him pass out from the pain, but there were no options left to take such things into consideration. As soon as Feyd was in his saddle, Wynne came over and began to lash Feyd into the saddle. Once Wynne was sure that the Prince was secure, he handed Feyd another herbal concoction. Feyd took a look at the dark liquid, and then took a quick smell. The look on his face told Felicia everything she needed to know about the contents of the drink.

"What is that?" Feyd asked with irritation.

"We can't afford to have you slowing us down," Wynne replied, any attempts of graciousness repressed from his voice. "This will put you to sleep for a few hours. You're tied into your saddle and should not fall out, no matter how fast we have to move. If our pursuers overtake us, you won't be much good in a fight anyway, so I should be able to hold them at bay while you and Felicia make it to the keep."

Feyd regarded the man for a moment. Despite the situation, he could not help but trust Wynne. He had done everything in his power to keep Feyd and his daughter alive, and thus far he had made no overtures about wanting a reward for his deeds. Perhaps that was reason enough to have a little doubt about the man's motivations. Feyd was raised to believe that no one did anything purely out of the goodness of their heart, especially where the royal family was concerned. There was always some sort of ulterior motive, some thought of advancement or the betterment of ones station to consider. No matter how altruistic the deed, Feyd could never relieve himself of the anticipation of the request for compensation. Despite it all though, Feyd had hopes that this Wynne was exactly what he appeared to be. A genuine hero in a time of darkness. Without another word, Feyd downed the contents of the drink and felt the liquid burn his throat as it went down to his stomach. His stomach heaved and then before he knew what was happening, the blackness began to eat at the edges of his vision.

Felicia watched as her father slumped in his saddle, the reinforcement that Wynne had applied holding him upright. Wynne took another moment to ensure that Feyd was held firmly in his saddle, and that the now dead-weight would not put too much of a strain on the restraints during the ride. Satisfied with his handiwork, Wynne moved to where Felicia sat in her saddle, and wordlessly pulled himself into the saddle with her. She passed him the reins and let her arms fall around his waist. Feyd's horse was secured to the saddle of Felicia's and as Wynne set the group into motion, Felicia had the sinking suspicion that they would not make it to the keep without their pursuers overtaking them.

* * * * * * * * * * * *

The campsite was the first clear clue that Alise had run across in her tracking of the Lorien father and daughter, as well as the mysterious interloper that had done nothing but make her life difficult since his murder of Cole Breon, the somewhat skilled assassin from Geoffry Aramour's ranks in the Shadow Guild. Of course, Emperor Kaitain never should have entrusted something as important as the death of his brother and niece to someone as incompetent as Geoffry Aramour. The man may have been a competent minstrel and poet, but his ability to kill was often overridden by his artistic flair. Alise did not believe that an assassin could be an artist. It was too much work. Killing itself was an art, but the art could not override the act. Geoffry wanted each assassination to be perfect, that death could be used to remove obstacles from the path of those in power without the blood coating the wrong hands. Deaths were made to look like accidents, or others were framed with the deed. Such skills were not the ones that Alise prided herself on. Killings should be used to send messages. They should invoke fear, nothing more, nothing less. The more brutal and visceral the killing, the more fear it invoked. What's more, Alise enjoyed killing. She loved the feel of her claws ripping through vital flesh. She thrilled at the smell of freshly drawn blood, and the cries of the dying were music unrivaled to her ears. But there was one thing that she enjoyed far more than any other aspect of her many murders. The look in the eyes of her victims the instant before they felt the cold steel of her talons ripping into them. The mix of horror, hatred, fear, and most of all, regret. In those final moments, she could practically taste all of the regrets they held from their lives. All of the things that they would never get to do, or never get to set right. The unclean parts of their souls that had probably led to their untimely demise sung out to her in those final heartbeats of life.

For the first time in their long cat and mouse game, Alise felt close to the throat of this wild card who had become such a thorn in her side. His traps had been little more than annoyances at first, and his false trails could be seen through with a minimum of effort. But soon she had begun to see that she had underestimated the skills of the man. The realization hit her when all of a sudden the trail that she thought so obvious and clear disappeared right before her eyes. The distraction cost her several hours before she was able to find the real trail again. Then the second surprise hit in the form of a very lethal trap that claimed the lives of one of the soldiers that followed with her. From that moment on, Alise felt her respect for her quarry increasing. She would enjoy ripping this man limb from limb, after the Loriens had been eliminated. For days now she had dodged increasingly lethal traps, and the numbers of her force had dwindled with every near miss. But this morning, she knew something was different when the man-trap that a soldier triggered barely missed severing his head. Their quarry had not taken the kind of time and care that he had the previous days when hiding his traps or his trail. He was starting to feel the pressure of Alise's pursuit, and was starting to make mistakes.

Alise moved from the remainder of the small fire to the hoof prints that led away from the campsite. The first set of tracks were pressed deeper into the earth. The horse was obviously carrying a much heavier load than its companion. The tracks of the second animal were not as precise or ordered, and it took only a few moments of tracing the path and pattern of the tracks to know that the second horse was not being led by a rider, but was instead following the first horse through a lead line. Obviously they knew how close the pursuit was to them now, and they were taking all of the steps to increase their rate of travel. It was a desperate act. Alise felt herself smile. If her reading of the tracks was as accurate as it usually was, then they could have no more than a two hour head start. If there were no surprises along the way, Alise and her group would be able to overtake them well before they reached the family keep. But then again, even if Feyd and Felicia made it to their keep, they would live long enough to see it brought down around them stone by stone.

* * * * * * * * * * * *

The ride was hard, but finally the Lorien family keep was within sight. Felicia could see the small detachment of Imperial Guards that was on patrol at the edge of the keep's grounds. However, her feelings of relief were immediately robbed from her when Wynne jumped from the saddle and immediately drew his sword. Felicia looked over her shoulder and felt her blood freeze. Emerging from the trees hot on the trail that they had left in their haste emerged several dozen figures clad in dark robes. In the center of the group was a small woman in a ghostly white dress with long curly blond hair. She was obviously the leader of the contingent.

"Go, as fast as you can," Wynne was saying as he struck the horse on its flank with the flat of his hand, "and don't stop no matter what until you are inside the keep."

The horse lurched forward, and Felicia was barely able to control the charging beast. She was able to look back and see Wynne take a fighting stance and dig in for the battle to come. She returned her gaze to the road before them, and searched for the Imperial Guard patrol that had been within sight only moments ago. Finally she saw them, and they were aware of the approach of the two horses. Before the patrol could issue a challenge to the approaching steed, Felicia let her voice catch the air.

"Guards, defend us! Defend the Lorien name!"

No one would have used that phrase unless they were members of the Imperial family or under the protection of the Imperial family, as to do so falsely was an act of treason that was punishable by death. A cry went up from the patrol a moment later, and they charged forward toward the two rapidly approaching horses. Three of the four member patrol ran past the horses, heading toward where Wynne must have already been engaged with the pursuing force. The fourth ran alongside.

"Lady Felicia," the guard said quickly. "Where is your escort?"

"Murdered," Felicia managed. "The assassins still keep pace with us, and our defender faces them alone. Call out the guard and defend the keep. My father has been gravely wounded and we must get him to safety."

The guard nodded and sent up a cry as they approached the keep's main gate. It took only a few moments before Felicia was safely off the horse and felt the cobblestones of the keep's inner courtyard under her boots. Two guards were helping to pull Feyd from his saddle, and the keep's healers had already been summoned. More of the Imperial Guard detachment was flooding out of the main gate to engage the assaulting force, but Felicia's only thoughts were for Wynne, and the improbability of him surviving against so many.

* * * * * * * * * * * *

Wynne held his ground as the black robed figures surrounded him. His eyes never left the young blond woman with the vicious looking talon laden gauntlets. The others were no matter to him, not now. Everything hinged on ensuring that this woman was dealt with.

"So you are the one who has been causing all this trouble?" the woman said with a reptilian hiss. "You have to know that you haven't prevented anything by getting them here. The Imperial Guard is no match for my men, and the keep itself is just the shell of a nut waiting to be cracked. Before dawn of the next day, the Prince and Princess will be dead, and there is nothing that you can do to prevent it. But, you have proven yourself to be a more than adequate opponent, so I will give you the option to relinquish your sword, and to surrender the sword that you stole from the other assassin, and then simply walk away. I give you my word that you will not be hunted and that there will be no reprisal for the crimes that you have committed."

Wynne lowered his sword slightly.

"As I see it, the only crimes being committed here are the attempted murder of members of the royal family. I don't think you are in much of a position to judge another's behavior."

The young woman shook her head.

"You are aiding the activities of a known criminal and his daughter. Feyd Lorien has been branded a traitor to the Throne and has been ordered executed by Emperor Kaitain Lorien himself. For you to harbor and to assist him in his endeavors is tantamount to treason as well. Show the level of intelligence that you have proven to possess, and walk away while you still can."

Wynne seemed to ponder the woman's words for an instant before responding.

"If the Emperor has indeed decreed that his brother is a traitor to the throne, then show me the order of termination with the Emperor's signature."

There was a long pause, and the cold and vicious look from the young woman didn't change.

"I didn't think so. You Shadow Guild people don't like any records of your actions, and Kaitain is too much of a coward to put his hand to anything that scandalous."

The woman frowned.

"The Shadow Guild," she hissed with disgust. "Those amateurs could barely fumble their way through opening a door let alone handle any real work. They have been too concerned with keeping their secrets all these years, rather than sharpening their meager skills. Even their masters are nothing compared to me. I am Alise Modrall, the destroyer of dreams, and the black hand of the Emperor. My only desire is to see his enemies die in the most painful way possible. Right now, you are standing in the way of my work, and if you do not exercise a little wisdom within the next few seconds, I will ensure that you never breathe again."

Wynne raised his sword again.

"Well, Alise Modrall, you'll find I am much harder to kill than any of your previous victims."

Just then the cry went up from behind Wynne. Three members of the Imperial Guard were charging toward the mass of black-robed figures. Alise looked passed Wynne for a moment and then snarled.

"Destroy them, and the keep, but no one touches the Prince and the Princess. And leave this one to me; he has caused me too much irritation to be ignored."

The ranks of black-robed figures flooded past Wynne. Many of them drew long cruel-looking curved black blades, while others held no weapons at all. But Wynne did not pay the figures much more attention than what his peripheral vision was able to collect. He knew the woman who called herself Alise Modrall was far more dangerous than all of the others in her company combined. A moment later it began as Alise darted in quickly, slashing towards Wynn's face with one of the sets of steel talons attached to the back of her fist. Wynne was able to bring his sword up in time to block the blow, but he had underestimated the power of the smaller woman. He was driven back half a step, but that proved to be a lucky accident. Alise's follow up blow with her other hand would have sliced through his abdomen had he been able to hold his ground. As it was, Alise's miscalculation only bought him a heartbeat before the second gauntlet struck out again, this time the points were jabbed straight at his heart. Wynne whirled away from the smaller woman's strike, and kicked with one foot. The blow landed but not with the power that Wynne had hoped. Alise's leg absorbed the blow, and she countered with another hard slash from her right hand. This one connected with Wynne's flank, drawing a plume of blood. The strike reopened the wound from the battle with Cole Breon, and blood flowed freely. Wynne didn't cry out, but instead dropped his sword and took hold of Alise's wrist before she could withdraw her hand from the strike. He pulled her in hard, and struck her across the face with his elbow before burying the talons of her own weapon into the exposed flesh of her thigh. Alise howled in pain and fell back, her leg partially crippled and blood flowing as freely as it did from the wound on Wynne's side. But the assassin was not done yet. She tested the strength in her wounded leg briefly before launching into another assault against the unarmed man. The first slash was a hard feint that Wynne overcommitted his defense too, and so was unprepared as the other set of talons ripped across his chest, leaving three bloody gaping wounds. Wynne fell back for a moment, but then dove forward, driving his shoulder into the stomach of the smaller woman, and propelling them both forward to the ground. Alise ended up flat on her back, all of the air driven from her lungs, and momentarily stunned. That was all the opening that Wynne would need. He drove his knee into her wounded thigh to give himself a clear path to her throat, and with a single deft motion took hold of her head at the back and at the brow and twisted. There was a sickening crack as Alise's neck broke under the pressure. Her body spasmed and flailed for a moment before falling limp. Wynne pushed himself from his fallen opponent and sat on the blood soaked ground breathing heavily. But there was not time to rest. He collected his sword and charged toward the keep.

* * * * * * * * * * * *

Felicia watched the siege from the battlements, bow in hand. The men attacking in the black robes were more than just soldiers, as they had the power of the arcane at their disposal. Bolts of lightning flashed across the sky and then struck the stone walls, sending pieces of rock flying in all directions. Huge gouts of fire assaulted the structures within the keep. Even the very ground beneath the foundation of the keep seemed to turn against the structure. The small keep was dying under the relentless assault, and no matter the valiant efforts of the Imperial Guard, they were no match for the onslaught. All of the guardsmen who had met the black clad force's advance had been slain within the first few seconds of the siege, and it seemed that only the archers on the battlements remained. However, they were too exposed to last very long, and they had not been able to thin out the numbers of the attackers. Felicia herself had only been able to kill half a dozen of the attackers, but had been forced to find shelter as the crackling bolt of lightning had missed her by only a few feet. She had only dared another look over the edge of the wall when she heard the assault lessen for a moment. Then she saw him. Wynne had a sword in each hand, his blade and the blade he had taken off of the assassin after their quarrel. He had waded into the black-clad ranks chopping them down two at a time. The shock and surprise at his assault had given him enough time to slay a dozen before their turned their arcane powers against him. But with him among their ranks, the risk of the use of their abilities was much more hazardous. An errant bolt of lightning vaporized a dozen of the attackers, and seemed to break the will of a large number of them. Many turned and fled, and the ones who did not were swiftly dealt with by Wynne's steel. However, as the assault ended, the damage had clearly been done. The keep had been damaged perhaps beyond repair, and all of the Imperial Guard who had been entrusted with its defense had been slain.

Felicia rushed to the courtyard and arrived just as Wynne was limping his way through the gate. He had been badly injured, and huge wounds were evident on both his side and his chest. However, blood no longer poured from the wounds, and it looked as though he had stuffed mud into the wounds to arrest the bleeding.

"Are you alright, Princess?"

Felicia almost laughed in relief.

"My father and I are both fine, thanks to you, and thanks to the soldiers who gave their lives to defend us. But there is no safety here any longer."

Wynne looked back out the gate and shook his head.

"Pursuit may not come swiftly, but I have a feeling it's only a matter of time before another takes up the work of this group. I fear that all of the places that you would go for refuge will be watched."

Felicia nodded.

"Then where can we go?"

Wynne thought for a moment. Felicia could tell that he clearly had an idea, but it was not one that he was willing to give voice unless there was no other choice. Finally he nodded as though he had come to a decision.

"I think I know a place where we can be safe, at least for a little while."

* * * * * * * * * * * *

Night had fallen on the site of the battle, and the convocation of crows and vultures had begun to descend on the bodies of the dead. Farthest away from the rest of the carnage lay a small woman's body. A large crow landed beside the body and pecked cautiously on the wounds on the body's thigh. A hand darted out and seized the bird by the throat, crushing it with little effort. Alise Modrall sat up slowly, her hands finding her distended neck and wrenching her head back into place. After a moment she was standing again, hate filling her eyes and her blood boiling with it. Looking down at her steel talons, she brought one to her lips and let her tongue gather some of the ichor that clung there.

"I have the taste of your blood now," she said to the silent night, "there is no where you can go that I cannot find you. And this time, you will not get away."

Chapter LVII

Awakenings

Kaitain Lorien sat on his throne looking out at the empty hall around him. For what seemed like years he sat, waiting, looking, and watching everything around him with a detached air that had begun to grate at him like a fly buzzing endlessly in his ear. Month after month he sat, watching, waiting, without hunger. Hours passed slowly without a single pang of thirst striking. And still, the Emperor of Cadaria sat, motionless. The stench of death filled his nostrils with every breath, and no matter how he tried to escape this wall-less prison, he found himself chained to it with every heartbeat.

"Oh how the mighty have fallen," a voice said from the doorway to Kaitain's right.

Kaitain wanted to crane his neck to take in the full features of the person who spoke, but he knew that he could not move. Only his eyes could dart in that direction, his impotent body rebelling against the directions of his perturbed mind. He could not even speak a response as his jaw and tongue had long since ceased functioning. Kaitain was only a will trapped inside a useless shell.

"Poor little emperor," the distinctly female voice said from the darkness at the edge of a torch's flickering illumination, "trapped in the husk of his own body, unable to act, unable to save his empire from the plague that slowly kills it."

Finally the speaker came into view. She was not beautiful, and yet at the same time she was captivating. Her features were cruel and cold and the darkness around her eyes seemed to be pools of evil that directed you to stare into those heartless depths. The woman exuded hate, disgust, and rage. Her black and gold garments clung to her gaunt frame, and her pale almost dead-white skin seemed to absorb the ambient light of the chamber. Gloom and fear trailed off her like a cloak, and her steps were light but still echoed through the chamber like the tolling of the undertaker's bell.

"Look upon your savior, Kaitain," the woman said slowly and pointedly. "You were trapped here because of the machinations of misguided fools who want to turn your pathetic empire into a haven for fanatics and zealots. Those mongrels want nothing more than to impose their beliefs upon the whole of the world."

The woman approached him slowly, seemingly judging each of her steps, her hate-filled eyes never leaving his, sending nearly imperceptible shivers through his uncooperative body. Cold had begun to fill him, the cold of the grave, a cold that penetrated flesh and bone and could never be sated until it gnawed through every last visage of warmth, hope, and love.

"You are betrayed, Emperor," she said finally, stopping less than a foot from the dais. "You are betrayed by a beast of your own making. It is not the fearsome dragons that roam Cadaria, or even your Dark Gods of Mythryn that are the downfall of your precious empire. It is the servants that claim to protect you with their last breaths, it is the daughter that you brought into this world of your blood and seed, it is the wife that you have taken to your bed, and the brother that shares your very essence. These waiting vipers, these jackals in the night; they are the true threat, and they must be extinguished if the Empire of Cadaria is ever to truly rise as the dominant power it is meant to be."

Anger flared in Kaitain's heart unlike any he had ever known. It swelled in him like a fire gorging itself on black powder. It burned hotter than the stars and yet it was impotent within him. It consumed and grew, without outlet, without possibility for release. The rage consumed him so fully that tears began to leak from his eyes.

"That's right Emperor Lorien...or do you even have the right to be called that? You are just Kaitain, the frightened boy that used to hide from his father when he was going to be punished for some misdeed. Your brother Feyd was always the strong one. Always the best at everything he attempted, and you, Kaitain were the oldest and assured of your ascension. You hid from the challenge, from the competition because you felt it was beneath you. Or so you told everyone. Why should a prince dirty his hands with such things? Why should a prince debase himself by socializing with mere commoners and soldiers? The truth was that you were afraid. You were afraid to fail. You were afraid to be shown to be the inferior child. The wrong Lorien is sitting on that throne Kaitain, and you know it."

Kaitain was screaming in his mind. Screaming at this woman to shut up, to show respect, anything that would drown out the words that were digging into his heart and soul like a dagger. She was flaying him open and dragging the worst of him to the surface.

"Pestilence did you a favor by killing that father of yours. In time you would have shown yourself to be inferior to others who were vying for your position. In fact, your sainted father was on the cusp of naming Gregor Quicksilver to be his successor, not you. The Lorien line would have been broken and it would have been because of your failure as son and heir. You were weak...you are weak, a pale shadow of the great Ender 'Justhand' Lorien. Put on the throne by a stroke of fate, put into this state of torpor by a stroke of betrayal."

The woman took a half-step forward, a cruel smile twisting onto her lips.

"You are a failure. Do you really think that you are strong enough to defeat the dragons of Cadaria? Do you think you have the kind of power that it will take to defeat the Dark Gods? Can you even stand against your own Knights of the Flashing Blade as they threaten to tear Cadaria apart with their treasonous rebellion? Can you even subdue your own wife who even now plots to keep her position of power after engineering your demise? What kind of emperor cannot even keep his wife in her place? You are less of a man than I thought you were Kaitain. You are a mute fool, a bleating lamb surrounded by wolves."

The woman turned away from Kaitain after a dismissive wave of her hand. Kaitain wanted to scream, wanted to curse her for her insolence, for her vanity and pride, but his voice would not break through the veil. Then his mind trailed away from the abuse of the dark woman's words and to the thing that he wanted the most. The Dragon's Tear. Its power consumed his mind, and he could see himself standing upon the bodies of his enemies, rending them one after another. Even the Dark Gods and the dragons could not stand against his might. No one could stand against him. Even the Creator would tremble against his power. The hate and the rage the woman had stoked fueled this desire and thirst for power to new heights, as Kaitain envisioned the reshaping of the entirety of reality to his whims. There would be no corner of the living universe that would be outside his dominion, and no force on this world or any other would be able to stand against the will of.... the will of......suddenly his mind went blank. The name that he had been given upon his birth would not come to his mind, and even as he saw the visions of his conquest run through his thoughts, the name upon the banners was hazy, even the symbol itself seemed to have no meaning. Finally, a name entered his mind.

Dorovar.

The woman stopped in her tracks and turned to look Kaitain in the face. His eyes seemed to have glazed over and he was no longer looking at her, but no longer was he seeing anything in this prison of his mind. The long poison-induced slumber had nearly shattered his mind and made him susceptible to the kinds of suggestions that she was going to hammer into him, but it seemed to also leave him open to the manipulations of others with power who could feel his presence. Dorovar was a force to be reckoned with to be sure, but she would not allow Dorovar to take her prize away, not as long as she still had power within her.

Dorovar.

The voice stung Kaitain's mind again. There, just at the edges of his perception he could see a figure in the blackness. A gaunt figure of a man in tattered white robes, but a man whose power could be clearly felt stood in the darkness, a green glow surrounding him. His long, thin, bony fingers arched into a steeple before him, and the heavily pointed chin seemed to perch there like a hawk waiting to swoop down on its prey. If the woman before Kaitain was hate personified, then this man was the personification of fear.

"Do not listen to the witch" a raspy voice came from the gaunt man, though his lips did not move, *"you are destined for a greatness that you cannot know. You will be my final herald, the final cog in the wheel that will grind our enemies to dust. You will be the extension of my great fury that will bring a war of such magnitude to this world that it will burn itself to a cinder before the fires of conflict are finally doused. Then my chorus will be complete and you shall stand at my right hand with the rest of my heralds as we take the war to the heavens and displace the vile Creator and remake everything in my image. Come War. Come and stand beside the will of Dorovar and take your vengeance on all those who have betrayed you."*

The woman waited, hearing Dorovar's evil voice whisper its poison into Kaitain's mind. Finally she seized her opportunity to reinforce her claim on the fragile man's mind.

"Would you be used by this creature as you were used by the Flashing Blade, the Dark Gods, your wife, your father, your daughter, your brother, and court sorceress? Would you allow your will to be subjugated by this beast when you have the method within you to rise to a level of power above even that creature? Think Kaitain! Think about what it is you really want and know that it is well within your grasp. Expel this demon and fight for what is rightly yours."

Kaitain was transfixed, fighting a war with a will that had nearly been ripped from him by a combination of the poison and the crushing hatred he felt for those who had betrayed him. His pride and strength had been sapped from him, but the one thing that remained was his hate. His hate burned strong, and amid the torrent of insults from the mysterious woman, it only grew stronger. He would have his revenge on all of those who tried to manipulate him. He would have his revenge on all of those who used him for their own gains. And most of all, he would have his vengeance upon those who took the only thing from him that he had ever loved.

Yes, Dorovar called into his mind, *know the same fury that has kept me alive for thousands of years. I drifted in the coldness of the space between worlds, alone, helpless, and yet I did not give up my hate. The dragons that put me into this never-ending prison of flesh; the Creator who locked me away in this hole in the center of your world, none of them defeated me. My hate is stronger than all of them combined. Your hate, in my hands can be that strong. You too can live forever and defeat your enemies. See them crushed at your feet. See them beg for their lives with their last breaths and bathe in their blood. As my disciple there is nothing you won't be able to accomplish, and I shall give you a portion of the universe to rule as your own, to remake in any way you see fit.*

"Why should you bow to Dorovar and rule only a portion of the universe when you could have it all for yourself. You could be the Creator, little emperor. You could be the one who remakes all of creation in your own image. Think of the possibilities, think of the power. Do not give up what you could have simply because you do not think you have the strength to take it for your own."

Something in Kaitain snapped at that moment. He would no longer be pulled into a direction that was not of his choosing. He would not be manipulated by Dorovar, or by this insane woman any longer.

"ENOUGH!"

The voice tore from Kaitain like a breaker slamming against the rocks. Power flooded through Kaitain and he felt his life and strength return to his ravaged body.

"No one uses the Emperor of Cadaria for their purposes, no matter how powerful they think they are. I shall find the Dragon's Tear, and I alone shall be sitting in the heights of the heavens when this war is over. The universe shall bend its knee to Kaitain Lorien, or it shall burn for its ignorance!"

With those words, the visage of Dorovar disappeared from the chamber, and Kaitain too winked out of existence leaving Talisia Masile standing alone in the construct of dreams. Her domain was now empty, and she felt the cruel smile deepen on her lips. Things had gone much better than she had anticipated.

CHAPTER 57

* * * * * * * * * * * *

The darkness closed around Dorovar, and for the first time, he began to feel the walls of his supposed eternal prison press in on him. For thousands of years he had dreams of the moment when he would have the final revenge on the dragons that stole his life and his world. Once he had been a priest, a dedicated servant not unlike the human who called herself Hannah Ironheart. Above all others on his world, Dorovar longed to feel the embrace and love of his goddess enter him and make him complete. But once the oversized lizards came to his world his dreams would never become possible. They had perverted his vision of a perfect life. They had taken from him the blind belief in his perfect savior, and he knew from that moment his insignificant place in the cosmos, and his insignificant place in the mind of that which he worshiped. The Creator loved the Dragons more than he loved man, and he loved some men more than he loved others. Dorovar was a footnote and nothing more. However, that had all changed when the dragons were forced to break their deal to protect their lives. Dorovar had been tricked in the estimation of the dragons, but the final joke would be on them. It would be their gift of immortality that would eventually be the death of the entirety of their breed. But Dorovar had made another discovery that day, he had seen for the first time the man that would become his nemesis. His polar opposite in every way, Evan Sinn was the man that Dorovar most wanted to destroy, even more than he wanted to crush the Creator and take the reins of the cosmos.

Evan Sinn had been loved by the Creator since his birth. He had been given every advantage, had been showered with love and acceptance, and had attained the position of Voice of the Creator. Their war would stretch over countless decades and across the dying husks of a dozen worlds, and eventually Dorovar would win the first battle against his hated rival. Evan's wife was struck down in the conflict that put Dorovar into his prison. Dorovar's victory had been two-fold that day. Meredith had been killed by his hand with very little effort, and in doing so; Evan had been convinced that Dorovar's capture had been a hard-fought victory and not a cleverly designed fabrication. Dorovar had learned about the dangerous tools that had been stored in the Vault of Terrors, and knew the only way that he would gain access to them was if he was captured and imprisoned. He had already devised a method to escape; he only had to wait until some mortal was foolish enough to discover the location of the Vault. Then his manipulations would fully come to fruition, and he would use the powerful weapons and tools of chaos at his disposal to unmake the very fabric of reality. What were a few years in the life of Dorovar to wait for the mortal to find his prison? He could have waited a thousand years if it would have gotten him closer to his goal.

But now he felt something had changed in the world above his prison. Evan Sinn could no longer be felt on this plane of reality, and there was a new player in the game. This man called himself Aerith Seth, and he too was a touched of the Creator. A god who was not a god. Death had tangled with this creature and had met with defeat, but it was not without its little victories. Dorovar had learned over the millennia that information was the greatest power that existed, and the true power was in that of manipulation of those who had weaker minds. This Aerith Seth could be useful in the long run, and all Dorovar had to do was make sure he remained pointed in the right direction.

Irritation gnawed at the edges of Dorovar's consciousness. If Evan Sinn was no longer the power that he once was, there was no longer any rush to Dorovar's schemes. He could let things play out over another millennium if he wished. He could let this world bleed itself dry, and let the dragons suffer ignominious defeat after crushing failure. While that would be entertaining to watch, it would not be nearly as gratifying as crushing the life out of every single winged lizard that drew breath. Suddenly Dorovar realized that he was no longer alone in his prison. The Grey Man Pestilence knelt several feet away, just outside the circle of greenish light that always radiated from Dorovar. Dorovar stood for another moment in the silence of his reverie before fixing his eyes on his servant.

Pestilence had succeeded in his tasks in a far greater manner than the two creations that followed him. He had struck terror into the hearts of the entire world and had added thousands upon thousands of souls to the choir. The Crawling Plague had been a master-stroke that had paved the way for the instability of the ruling family and the eventual provocation of the so-called Dark Gods and the dragons of the world. Famine had done her job quite well, and her targeting of the agriculturally rich regions of Cadaria had created an additional problem of resources to the already taxed physical cost of the pain and suffering of those who died from the Wasting Disease. The sheer terror and heartache caused by families literally starving their loved ones to keep them alive was a delicious, if not unforeseen effect of the affliction. Death had nearly exterminated an entire kingdom had it not been for the meddling of the little winged dark goddess, but that was of no consequence. Death's next attack would be enough to bring another once proud kingdom to its knees. The master-stroke would come in the naming of the fourth of the heralds. The one known as War would cause the whole of the world of Espre to be at each other's throats, vying for the opportunity to kill one another until there was nothing left but demolished armies, broken kingdoms, and rivers of blood flowing freely in every corner of the world.

"You have summoned me, my master?"

It is time for you to bring my word to the one that will become War. He may not hear my word at first Pestilence, and he may wish to strike you down, but if you do not relent in your belief of our quest, he will fall to our wishes and lead the thrust against the empire of Cadaria, and the Dark Gods of Mythryn. We will take one of their own and make him into their greatest enemy. We will make sure that everything comes crumbling down upon the paper emperor.

"It shall be done, my master."

With that, Pestilence was gone, and Dorovar was left to ponder how best to first use his fallen knight.

* * * * * * * * * * * *

Talisia Masile returned briefly to the world of the mortals and sat looking over the great kingdom of Albitonin and the nearly impregnable fortress known as the Heart of Stone. This would be the site of her greatest victory against those who had forced her expulsion from the heavens. She would soon have her revenge upon the self-righteous Dark Gods, and would reclaim her name and her rightful place at the side of the Creator. Unlike Kaitain or Dorovar, or the other dark gods, Talisia did not want the Throne for herself. All she wanted was to go home.

Once, long ago, she had been the most loved of all of the beings brought to life by the Creator. She had been his voice, and his emissary to hundreds of worlds, worlds that she alone was given the ability to mold and cultivate. But that was before, before her wicked siblings had been given their bauble to fight over. That was before the mortals became a new distraction for the Creator. So-called heroes had been plucked from one of the many failures of mortality and ascended to lauded positions within the cosmos. She had been disgraced by their mere presence and would never allow herself to be pushed out of the radiance of the Creator's love. The ignominy was too much for her to bare and she began to organize the original gods of the heavens into a coalition that would expel the ascended mortals from their spot in heaven. However, she had underestimated the power of the ones known as Pike and Gwydeon. They had handled her rebellion with little effort, and as she was one of the few of her ranks who survived the attempt, she suffered the most as the leader. Her name was stripped from her and she was rendered formless and impotent. It took centuries for her to learn how to take mortal form again, but the effort was so taxing that she could only manage it for a few minutes at a time. However, she knew that she could influence weaker minds and make them do her bidding.

That was how she had maneuvered and manipulated Irene Drage into her position as the Imperial Sorceress. The girl had power to spare, but she was neither smart nor confident enough to use her powers. However, with slight manipulations and whispers from Talisia, Irene eventually became the most powerful sorceress in the whole of the empire. It was through Irene that Talisia was able to set most of her schemes into motion, and soon, they would come to fruition.

"Hello mother," a young woman's voice said from behind Talisia.

Seraphina Masile was Talisia's daughter in name only. Seraphina was Talisia's second in command during the rebellion and had taken a familial role during the turbulence that followed. Seraphina was easy to manipulate because of her fanaticism and total trust in everything that Talisia said. She was the perfect instrument for Talisia to use in her formless state.

"Seraphina my lovely child. It is time for us to strike at the heart of this empire and begin to expose it for what it is. In a matter of hours, the Lorien girl will proclaim herself the rightful empress of the lands, and I want to make sure that Xavier is there to tear her down. Make sure that he and Dimitri are in the crowd turning the sentiment against her. However, watch out for Gregor Quicksilver, and those meddlers Gabriel Shadowfall and Aerith Seth. Once the seeds of discourse are planted here in Albitonin, we will make for Aldere."

"So it is almost time?"

Talisia smiled wickedly.

"Yes my wonderful daughter. Within a matter of days, the Emperor will be waking from his little slumber, and when he does, the wrath that he will loose upon this empire will be unlike any scourge Dorovar could see fit to release. The killings will be in the hundreds of thousands, and even more will suffer. We shall ignite a war the likes of which have never been seen, and then we will have our revenge."

"What about Tess and Camille?"

Seraphina's voice was filled with venom that could kill a thousand men. She had an utter hatred for the children of the Dark Gods and wanted nothing more but to exterminate the lot of them.

"Tess is to remain unharmed. However, the Camille girl is yours to do with as you please. Take Syren and her brood with you, as you may find yourself against numbers you wouldn't expect."

Seraphina bowed.

"And what are you going to do mother?"

Talisia smiled again. There has been a number of unexpected circumstances since the fall of Evan Sinn, but now was the time to make things more interesting for the Dark Gods of Mythryn.

"I am going to make Pike's life miserable, little one. My old friend Evan Sinn's fall from grace has made it possible for me to turn the sins of my brothers Halicon and Emries into a weapon for us to use. I go now to loose this weapon upon Cadaria."

When Talisia's form disappeared from view, Seraphina stood at the edge of the cliff and looked down upon Albitonin. In a few hours, she would crush the Heart of Stone, and the blood of Camille Renar would be on her hands.

From a Certain Point of View

Year Three of the Just Emperor Kaitain "Dragonsbane" Lorien, Creator's Calendar Year 1870

Escaping Hedorah proved to be more problematic than it should have been, even with everything that had gone wrong. The Flying Guard proved to be incredibly competent on this occasion, and were to the scene of the conflict within a matter of minutes. The dragon hunters and their newly minted accomplices had barely left the scene when an entire detachment appeared. Dane had hurried them all along into one of the many winding alleyways while Blade held back to get a feel for the opposition that might await them. They all knew if something went wrong, that they would split up and make it the best way they could to the Temple of the Creator. If they had to split up, they would hide until nightfall. Whoever didn't make it after that would be considered lost. While only the dragon hunters currently had death warrants against them, if anyone was caught aiding them, those people would share the same fate. Jillian though had a feeling that Blade and Dane had been on the wrong side of the law before. Blade for his part seemed to be the only one of them that had been prepared for everything going wrong. There was a small cart left in the closest alley, laden with supplies, as well as a few cages and some thin crates, which Jillian could only imagine held weapons of some type or another. Minutes after his departure, Blade returned, and the look on his face could only be described as irritated.

"Well," he said stroking his beard and grimacing, "you've certainly gone about stirring up a hornet's nest."

Jacqueline was the first to respond. The skin around the woman's neck was raw and red from the assault of the blood-like tendrils, and a few spots had raised blisters that would grow to be painful in a matter of days if they went without treatment.

"What the hell is going on? Who were those people, and why are we running?"

There were similar statements coming from Angelina and Kiara, but it was Dane not Jillian who put the questions to rest.

"Best I can figure," he said wiping a bit of blood from the corner of his mouth, "your Lady Jillian here did a better than average job of annoying the Emperor, and so now you have all been sentenced to execution. And honestly, that is the least of your problems."

There were shocked glances all around, and before the next round of questions could hit the air, Blade cut them all off.

"This is not the time. The Flying Guard is here, and they are looking. Far too efficiently if you ask me. If I knew that these lazy beasts had this kind of motivation hidden in them, I might not have been so eager to open my business here."

Dane shook his head.

"That would be Jerah's doing."

All eyes were on the monk.

"The woman in white with the icy disposition. Her name is Jerah, and the other three are members of the Hand of Chaos. If they're here, then it would benefit them to motivate the Flying Guard to help either find us or drive us. We'd be better off with your Emperor's justice, I'm afraid, then if they get their hands on us."

Jillian's head was swimming.

"They were after you, Jillian," Kiara added in quickly. "They were happy to kill us, but you they wanted. Someone named Dorovar."

Dane put his hand on Jillian's shoulder. Normally she would have swatted it away, but in that moment in time, she didn't overly mind the contact.

"We'll have time to figure out why Dorovar wants you later. For now, if we don't get out of Hedorah, there won't be a later. Kiara, take the lead. Get everyone to the Temple, and I'll keep up. Maybe I can give the Flying Guard something else to pay attention to. I've been known to be persuasive from time to time."

* * * * * * * * * * * *

The Temple of the Creator was a welcome sight as the small band emerged from the twisting streets and alleys. Apparently Dane had done a good job of leading the Flying Guard on a wild goose chase, and after a few hours it appeared that they had given up the search altogether. Kiara approached the doors to the temple and was met by a woman in robes. The two spoke briefly, and the robbed woman disappeared into the temple. It took only another few moments before three more white-robed women appeared and Kiara motioned for the others to approach. Kiara quickly made introductions.

"This is Reverend Mother Amallia. She has been kind enough to help me continue my training while here in Hedorah. While she must abide by my expulsion from the order, she is willing to share the same teaching with me that a non-ordained acolyte would be eligible for. She has also been willing to help me keep my stocks of supplies fresh."

"Kiara is a good student," the Reverend Mother said after a slow nod to the rest of the group, "and I am sure that her soul will find its way back to us before too long. These days, I fear we can use all of the willing souls we can gain in the order."

It was then that Dane came around the corner, the hood of his simple cloak pulled back, and a bright smile on his face. The Reverend Mother scowled as soon as she set eyes on the man.

"Dane Dark-Omen. I should have expected to see you mixed up in all of this. Were it not against the teaching of the Temple, I would have helped the Flying Guard put an end to you and to your entire Order, not that I have ever seen any of them other than you."

Jillian balked a little at the name given by the Reverend Mother, and the venom that had entered the older woman's voice. Dane to his credit seemed to embrace the label.

"Mother Amallia, you are looking as radiant and misled as usual. I'm sure the Creator is more than pleased with your steadfast, and may I say sheep-like devotion to dogma."

Blade laughed loud and deep, and the color deepened in the Reverend Mother's cheeks. The two initiates with her put their hands to their mouths in shock.

"Kiara, you and your companions may enter, but this non-believer and the criminal may not cross into the Temple. There are limits to the charity that the Creator will extend. The unrepentant non-believers will not be welcomed into the Creator's House with open arms."

Jillian looked back at Dane and Blade. Blade had folded his arms across his chest and glowered at the Reverend Mother. Dane on the other hand simply laughed and moved to the other side of the street where he sat on a stoop and pulled out a simple leather book and began to read.

"I will lead you to the river, and you may collect your unfortunate companions a mile down river where it turns away south from the city walls."

Blade turned back toward his cart and started pulling it in the direction that the Reverend Mother indicated. Dane watched as the four women entered the Temple. The Reverend Mother hesitated for a moment at the door looking out at Dane before shutting it with a shake of her head. As she returned to the group, and motioned for them to follow, Kiara spoke up in a hushed tone.

"I've never seen you have such a reaction to anyone, Reverend Mother."

The older woman sighed hard.

"Dane is a trouble-maker. What's more, he is a corrupter of souls. He blasphemes the name of the Creator and perverts its teachings through the words of his Order. He claims to know the mind of the Creator, and claims that his way is a better way to live. Were he not obviously learned and well-spoken I would say that he was a madman and have him removed for the good of society. But Dane knows just how far to push his teachings, and where they will be listened to. He does not force anyone to contribute, but his charisma is not without some power. More than a few members of our flock have been lost to his petulant scheme."

Angelina spoke up next.

"He saved our lives."

Angelina was the most practical member of the group, which was a bit surprising considering Jacqueline's considerable military experience.

"Which does not excuse his blasphemy. He does not do anything without thinking about how it benefits himself or his order. That is the most unfortunate thing about him. In the end, all of his good works will mean nothing when he stands before the Creator and is made to account for all of his sins."

Silence held them all as the Reverend Mother led them down a long flight of stairs to the river access that would help take them out of the Flying Kingdom.

* * * * * * * * * * * *

Traveling from Hedorah to Iltorp was problematic at best. The bay that surrounded the southern tip of Hedorah was a major trade route, and probably was a close second behind the Pritan Island trade routes to the south. However, with the increase of piracy in the south, the Hedorah Pass seemed to be the only secure way to move large amounts of goods. The major port in the Hedorah pass was Misthaven, in the northern reaches of Aldere. Misthaven was also the home of the Imperial Navy, and was perhaps the third most impressive stronghold in the whole of Cadaria behind the Imperial Palace of Aldere and the Heart of Stone in Albitonin.

There were three garrisons of Imperial troops in Misthaven, as well as separate detachments from the Army of Steam and the Army of Blood. Misthaven sat on the border between the Kingdoms of Iltorp and Zevarit, which made it an important strategic resource as well as a political necessity to continue to maintain a strong presence. However, on the Iltorp side, there was a smaller fishing village called Seacrest. Very few vessels made berth there, except in the first few days of spring for the festival of floating lights, when the Emperor of Cadaria would make the trip to the little village to float a lantern into the bay in memory of each of the Emperors that had come before him. However, the festival had not occurred this past spring due to the Emperor's incapacitation, and the security concerns for the safety of the Empress after the attempts on the lives of the Emperor and members of his family. It was considered a bad omen in the village, and the lower than usual catches had been attributed to the spirits of the dead who lay restless in the dark waters. While it created serious misfortune for the village, in terms of the needs of Jillian and her companions, it was certainly a favorable circumstance. They would be able to put into port without too many people asking questions, or even worrying about their arrival. That was the theory anyway. However, theory has a way of being proven completely inadequate for the time when it is depended upon.

As Blade steered the lead boat into one of the docks of the little fishing village, everyone was shocked to see a group of armed warriors waiting for them. As the second boat was pulled and lashed to the dock, the regiment from the Army of Steam parted, and a brown-cloaked figure emerged, leaning heavily on a long staff taller than himself. The staff itself glimmered in the moonlight, its dark, almost black wooden length covered in a wax-like sheen. His face was obscured by the hood of his cloak, but the black beard that was closely cropped to his chin and ran down his long throat was quite visible. He appeared to look over the faces of the six people in the boats as well as the cargo, and then his gaze settled back on Dane.

"I thought you were told to never come back to Iltorp."

There was no anger in the man's voice, nor was there any levity. The statement was one made calmly, as though communicating a fact that everyone knew without question.

"I was under the impression," Dane said after a moment, "that it was more of a polite suggestion than an order. Besides, as I recall, you were quite happy to have me here during that outbreak of the Crawling Plague."

The cloaked man reached up and gently lifted back the hood of his cloak. It was then that Jillian for the first time saw the bright yellow eyes of the man who could only have been Vallic Ultiv, the Serpentine Knight of the Flashing Blade. As soon as she saw him, her heart sank, and she could almost feel the noose tightening around her neck.

"It's not like you to sneak around, Dane," Vallic said finally, "even if you are keeping unfortunate companions. But you also had to know that you couldn't come ten miles from the border of Iltorp without my knowing. You make far too many ripples in the pattern for me to not notice."

Dane nodded.

"Believe me, old friend, if I had any choice in the matter, I would not have come by this route. I'm afraid you could be in more trouble than we are if you let us pass through your territory without stopping us."

Vallic motioned to the guards on either side of him. They saluted quickly and then turned and marched in step away from the docks.

"Trouble follows wherever your feet tread," the Knight said slowly, "but I fear that your brand of trouble is the only kind that may bring light along with its darkness."

* * * * * * * * * * * *

The home of the Serpentine Knight was not a grand keep, or even one that could compare to the royalty for the Kingdom of Steam. It was modest, like the man that inhabited it, full of plants and flowers, and very few of the fineries that would attach itself to a man of his station. Half a dozen servants ran the entire household, and though Vallic had never married, he had been in a long relationship with the woman who called herself his concubine, Isa Shar. Vallic believed that one day his marriage could help to settle a dispute with one of the other Great Kingdoms, and so he sacrificed a bit of his own happiness to ensure that political avenues would remain available for those whom he served. But that was the reputation of the Serpentine Knight. There was nothing that he did without thinking forward several dozen moves. He believed in balance in all things, and was not taken in by the trappings of power or religion, but despite all of that, he was a practical man in a time where things tended to spin out of control without much effort. If anything Vallic was a holdover from a previous time, when things were simpler, and the baser desires of powerful men held less ramification for those they had power over. It seemed as the years went on, the specter of power had a longer and longer shadow.

The group was led to a large dining room on the far side of the keep, one that was kept clean and free of any clutter in case the Serpentine Knight had to entertain members of either the local or Imperial royalty. Despite his isolationist nature, Vallic knew his role, and played it when necessary. Though as impressive as the formal dining room may have been, what the keep was known for above all else was the sprawling library. It was said to rival even those found in the Academy of Arcane Arts, or in the Halls of Knowledge in Menoris. When they were all seated around the dining table, three servants appeared with trays of food and drink, and began to serve the guests. Vallic and Isa sat last, and Vallic kept his eyes trained on Dane until finally the younger man relented and began to speak.

"I won't repeat the part of the story you already know, Vallic, and I won't insult you by asking that you keep our visit here to yourself."

Vallic nodded, and Isa chuckled a little to herself.

"It was Jerah. She's the reason we came this way."

Vallic seemed to tense at the name.

"I thought perhaps she would reappear after the disasters in Rashaleb and Albitonin. Dorovar must be marshaling all of his forces if she has reemerged."

Dane nodded.

"And it seems that she has been recruiting. We ran into a few new members of the Hand of Chaos, and they were nasty customers. And they knew me by name, which is not a very good sign either. I think perhaps that you and Orren need to watch your steps for a while."

Jillian had stopped chewing and just stared.

"How is it you are on a first name basis with two members of the Knights of the Flashing Blade?"

Blade grumbled.

"I told you he was trouble."

Vallic seemed to brighten a little at that.

"Ah yes, the famous Blade. Or at least that is what you are calling yourself these days. It is said that your works rival that of the great Arturious Demascious. It is a pleasure to have such a master craftsman in my home. Perhaps you would have some time to bring your talents to bear and help outfit the guards of my keep. I fear that our weapons and armor have fallen into a little disrepair after having to break up the latest clashes between our noisy neighbors."

Jacqueline shook her head.

"So Thorigald and Saldarine are at it again?"

Vallic nodded solemnly.

"I wish it were not the case. However, it seems that the latest decree from the Imperial Court naming Seraph Kore as the one behind the assassination attempt on the Emperor has driven the Army of Water into a bit of a frenzy. They are looking for blood, and there is no better place to start than their ancient enemy. I suppose we should all count ourselves lucky that they would rather settle old vendettas than turn their attention to Aldere."

"They wouldn't!" Kiara replied shocked.

"Do not underestimate the power of rage and thwarted ambition my young cleric. It is only going to be a matter of time before Seraph reemerges at the head of the Army of Water, and once he does, you can only imagine the hell that he will unleash. In his mind, everything has been taken from him, and unfortunately, he is the type of man to try to take things back by force, rather than through good sense and well-planned action. Seraph is the kind of man that believes a square peg will fit in a round hole once enough force is applied."

There was silence around the table for a long moment, but Vallic continued.

"But in answer to your question, Lady of Cadaria," the last stilted words pointed toward Jillian, "Dane and his order have been very active in trying to treat the effects of the Wasting Disease and the Crawling Plague, and I dare say that most of their efforts have been far more effective than anything the healers from the Temple of the Creator have been able to manage. He has even been able to show me a few herbal remedies that have been quite effective in dealing with most of the smaller outbreaks. Provided we get to the infected in time. It was Dane here that actually first brought my attention to the actions of the Grey Man Pestilence and his twisted associates."

Dane continued after a moment.

"These illnesses are all the creation of a being known as Dorovar. All you need to know about him is that he is the kind of evil that you've only ever read about in fairy tales. The creatures that serve him want nothing but death and destruction, and they aren't shy about making it happen."

Dane turned back to Vallic.

"The three that attacked in Hedorah were after Jillian. They said that Dorovar wanted her."

Vallic's head drooped for a moment.

"So you had no choice but to leave Hedorah, but why come here? You had to know that Iltorp will be no safer for you than Hedorah was."

Blade was the one who spoke up.

"None of the Imperial Kingdoms are safe."

The implication was clear, but Blade was obviously wise enough not to state it more fully. Their only destination was the rebel kingdoms, and the fastest route to the Kingdom of Stone was through the Plains of Steam in the southern reaches of Iltorp that ran along the border between the Kingdoms of Thorigald and Saldarine.

"I see."

Vallic's words trailed off to nothing.

"You can stay here for a few days," he said after a moment, "until you've recovered your strength and your wounds have healed. I can make sure that you are re-supplied and that you have horses for the rest of the journey. I'll also make sure you have travel papers in case you are stopped by Imperial Magistrates. Unfortunately, it is a likely occurrence this close to Aldere. You'll have nothing to fear from my men, however. The royal families trust my judgment and I can convince them that you are no threat, so long as you make quickly for the Plains of Steam. Though I fear you may not like what you find there, and your path between Fire and Water may not be as smooth as you would wish for."

"There's been nothing at all smooth about this journey," Angelina added in.

"Please," Vallic said standing, "enjoy the rest of your meal. Once you are finished, Isa will see you are well taken care of."

He moved away from the table with a quick backwards glance in Dane's direction. Wordlessly, Dane wiped his mouth and stood, following the Serpentine Knight away from the table. Jillian started to stand to follow, but Isa motioned for her to keep her place.

"I'm afraid that conversation is not for your ears, child."

Isa was a woman probably in her late fifties, but she still had a very youthful glow to her skin despite the flowing silver hair that framed her face. Though Jillian bristled at the thought of being called a child, she understood the implication of the words. She was a guest, and she had to play by the rules, at least for now.

* * * * * * * * * * * *

Deep in the keep of the Serpentine Knight, Vallic Ultiv stood next to a small fire, looking down at where his guest sat. The two men had known each other for a long time, longer than anyone could have ever imagined.

"We agreed you would never come here."

Dane looked down at his feet, and then back up into the yellow eyes of his long-time friend.

"You know if I had any other choice, I wouldn't have. But you needed to know about Jerah, and I needed to keep Jillian out of the hands of Dorovar. There is obviously something special about the woman, and we need to keep everything that we possibly can out of Dorovar's hands."

"Do you think that she is the Tear?"

Dane shook his head.

"I don't know, but anything is possible. It's only a matter of time before Dorovar escapes from his prison, especially since three of his minions are already out causing problems. And now that Evan has fallen, I can only imagine what that is going to mean once he's free. If he manages to get his hands on the Dragon's Tear, we're all in a serious amount of trouble."

Vallic nodded finally.

"Be careful passing through the Plains, there is more to fear than just the two armies."

Dane nodded.

"Nessus acting up again?"

"She's never liked people encroaching on her territory. I had hoped once Xaran returned, we would have a better negotiating position with the dragons who have made Cadaria their home, but he is long overdue, and the last time I saw him, he was very troubled."

"If he's been sucked into the politics of the Dragon Council, you may never see him again."

The two men were silent for a long time. Dane finally stood and started toward the door of the library.

"Pike sent word that he wanted to see you."

Dane turned and frowned.

"Did you tell him where I was?"

Vallic nodded.

"And here I thought you were my friend."

"Shadows have never liked the light cast by a Phoenix."

The Road to Rebellion

"That arrogant, overbearing, ignorant, lout!"

Marlae's voice pierced through what remained of the quiet morning air as she slumped down on the cushions of her litter. She had had yet another unsatisfying exchange with the man who called himself Aerith Seth, the man who had supposedly saved them from the minion of Dorovar known as Death.

"He has got to be the most insufferable man that I have ever met in my life. He had the audacity to tell me to shut up! Can you believe that?"

Rhain sat and listened dutifully. Though she did not share Marlae's opinion of Aerith Seth, questioning Marlae when she was in the middle of one of her rages was not an advisable course of action. As Marlae continued to question Aerith's parentage, Rhain looked down at her hand and flexed her fingers. For all of Aerith's quibbling about his lack of healing ability, he had done a fine job in restoring her hand to perfect working order. When she had tried to thank him, he just smiled with this odd lop-sided grin and returned to speaking with Gabriel. Those two had become quite a pair, discussing the state of Cadaria as though Aerith had been out of touch for the entire life of the Empire. However, while Aerith seemed to soak up any knowledge he could about what was going on in the world around him, he was very slow to give any details about himself. The only thing that Rhain had been able to discover for Marlae was that he had been living in the Pritan Islands with his wife until recently.

"Are you listening to me?"

"Of course, my Empress…"

Rhain's reply sparked another tirade from Marlae. And Rhain settled in for another long day of travel with her lover and charge. Luckily they were almost to their destination.

* * * * * * * * * * * *

"You enjoy doing that, don't you?"

Gabriel tried hard to keep the humor out of his voice, but it was no use. For years he had seen everyone from nobles to common foot soldiers bow and scrape at the feet of the Celestial Princess Marlae Lorien, accepting any manner of unacceptable behavior minute by minute. However, for the first time ever, Gabriel watched as Aerith and Marlae went at each other like starving jackals. The more Marlae would fuss and rage, the more Aerith would taunt and jibe. It was as if the man had no grace at all, either that or he had no time to waste on the niceties of life. Aerith struck Gabriel as a lifetime soldier who had little patience with anyone who had never borne arms against an enemy and ordered others to do so in their stead. He seemed more civil when the puzzling Rhain approached him, half on a mission of intelligence gathering for Marlae, and half with genuine thankfulness for Aerith's multi-faceted assistance, but still guarded and somewhat adversarial.

"Spoiled girls are spoiled girls, no matter which world I'm on. Believe me, I have seen princesses like her come and go. Those that are willing to take the chance to use their power to make the world better get my respect. Those who plot and plan who to make others do their bidding aren't worth my time or energy. Like your Marlae. She wants the world to bow to her and lift her up on a pedestal, and maybe she deserves it, but because she isn't the kind to get her hands dirty, or gods forbid break a sweat, then she'll always find others to do her work for her. It's those people who will be dying and killing, so they get my respect, not the spoiled little rich girl."

"You never know, Aerith," Gabriel said shrugging, "Marlae may surprise you."

Aerith stopped in his tracks and rounded on Gabriel.

"Ok, now I've got it. You're in love with her!"

Gabriel couldn't stop the crimson color from filling his cheeks, but threw his hands up and shook his head in a weak attempt at a denial.

"Don't even try to say you aren't, boy. It's obvious, it's painted so clearly on your face. Any rank-and-file like you who isn't busting a gut laughing at someone who takes a cut at the pompous royalty is either in love or too stupid to get the joke, and you don't strike me as the stupid type. And you better watch your back, that Rhain girl could be more of a handful than even your princess."

Gabriel smiled.

"Thanks, I think."

Aerith fell back in stride with Gabriel and clapped him on the shoulder.

"Don't mention it," Aerith said smiling. "Wish you would have known me back when I first met Bryn. I was a lot like you. Trying to do my duty and be a general of the army, while at the same time trying to be in love with the Lady of the kingdom. Wouldn't have been so bad if we weren't in the middle of a war, and she wasn't married."

Gabriel had been in the middle of taking a drink for the last part, and nearly choked.

"It's ok, kid," Aerith said walking ahead of Gabriel a few paces, "I have that effect on lots of people."

* * * * * * * * * * * *

Aerith went scouting ahead shortly before sunset, leaving Gabriel to set up camp. Though the travel seemed to be going a lot faster now that the company had been shaved down to four, Gabriel's tension and discomfort seemed to grow with every passing mile. Rhain's hunt earlier in the evening had turned up a nice sized deer, and Gabriel was in the process of roasting it over the fire when the Celestial Princess and her guard emerged from the litter. Marlae's mood had been sour most of the day after her repeated confrontations with Aerith, but now it seemed as though she had calmed somewhat, and the three of them fell into the routine of a nearly wordless evening meal. Marlae and Rhain would speak to one another of course, but Gabriel tried to tune out as much of that conversation as possible.

"What have you been able to learn about our savior, Gabriel?" Rhain asked about half-way through the meal.

"Not much I'm afraid. I know that he was once a general of a great army serving under a woman known as the Lady Fox, a woman that would eventually become his wife. I know that he is older than the Empire of Cadaria, and he came to Espre about the same time as the Dark Gods, but he isn't a Dark God himself."

"Then what is he?" Marlae demanded.

"I'm not sure, princess, but whatever he is, he is not someone to be taken lightly to say the least."

The three stayed silent for several long moments before Marlae spoke again.

"Do you think he can be trusted? Is he on our side?"

Gabriel shook his head.

"One thing is clear. Aerith is on his own side, and his goal is to destroy Dorovar and all those who follow him. As far as if he can be trusted, it seems as long as we have a common enemy, then we have nothing to worry about, but I think her could just as easily be counted as an enemy as he could be counted a friend."

"Then that leaves just one question, Gabriel…."

Marlae's statement cut into Gabriel's heart like a knife.

"I will do my duty," Gabriel said finally. "If Aerith Seth becomes a threat to your life, princess, then one of us will meet their end."

* * * * * * * * * * * *

Aerith Seth stood at the edge of a small cliff looking down at the town of Stone's Throw, a border town at far eastern reaches of Albitonin. The trip with the so-called Celestial Princess was drawing to a close, and Aerith's chances to stay in the shadows were also coming to a close. Back on Onea when he was a member of the Army of the Fox, and again when he was being used as propaganda for the Hand of the Light, Aerith was ever in the public eye, either for his leadership or for his abilities. But, that could all change now. If Aerith were to show up in Albitonin at the side of the woman who was in some circles referred to as the Empress of Cadaria, it would not take long before Aerith's name and abilities would be widely known. Then, would he be an enemy of those who he had once counted as allies? Would Pike and the others hunt him down for being allied, even in theory, with the Empire of Cadaria? But, none of that really mattered now. Aerith had been responsible for the death of his only real friend, and it was only a matter of time before the agents of the Creator and the agents of Dorovar were fighting for the right to kill Aerith.

"Well, that could be an interesting fight," Aerith said to the sky. "The Dark Gods, the minions of Dorovar, the envoys of the Creator, all coming after little old me."

Aerith laughed into the silence.

"Arrogance was never one of your more redeeming qualities, Aerith."

Aerith spun around to find himself face to face with a blond woman who he never thought he would lay eyes on again in his lifetime.

"Meredith?"

Meredith Sinn was supposed to be dead. No, not supposed to be, she was dead. Dorovar had killed Meredith prior to his imprisonment over two-thousand years ago. It was her death that caused Evan to spiral out of control. It was her death that caused the death of thousands of others on hundreds of different worlds because Evan was too distracted by his wife's death to do his job properly. Ultimately, it was Meredith's death that led Evan to his own.

"In a manner of speaking," the woman said calmly, stepping closer to Aerith.

When he was able to see more clearly, Aerith could see the patchwork of scars and burns on the woman's face, as well as the willowy and gaunt expression. Meredith was far paler than Aerith remembered seeing her, and some of the spark of life had gone from her eyes.

"How are you alive?" Aerith said, his disbelief building.

Meredith smirked, looking more like an expression of pain than as one of jubilation. Moving slowly, she sat on a large tree stump and fixed her cold blue eyes on Aerith. She looked like a ghost in the moonlight, pale white skin, piercing blue eyes, sunken cheeks, dark circles under her eyes, and a light blue tinge to her lips.

"How are you alive, Aerith?"

"Didn't your mother ever teach you that you shouldn't answer a question with a question?"

"Apparently yours didn't as you are guilty of the same offense."

Aerith grimaced and then chuckled. Apparently some of Evan's dry wit had rubbed off on his wife over the years.

"I'm alive because the Creator has a sick sense of humor. It was supposed to be a reward for my years of service in his name, but I thought Bryn and I would grow old and die together, but we have just kept going. Year after year we have lived on that little island unchanged, just as we were two millennia ago on Onea. And now, I'm put in a position to get my powers back, as well as the powers of my wife, and so we keep on living."

Meredith sighed and shook her head.

"They even lied to you...."

Aerith felt his heart catch in his throat. He knew that he didn't know everything about what had occurred in his life, and he had always been at the beck and call of the Creator and his agents. Now perhaps this former agent of the Creator had information that could help Aerith put his life into focus.

"Who lied to me?"

Aerith took an involuntary step forward and instantly regretted it. He wanted so much to know what was happening in his life, why he was over two millennia old, why he always made it through every battle, why he came back from the dead.

"Relax Aerith," Meredith said with a wave of her hand, "no one will come looking for you for some time, we have plenty of opportunity to answer the questions you need answered."

＊ ＊ ＊ ＊ ＊ ＊ ＊ ＊ ＊ ＊ ＊ ＊

In a small cabin outside the Heart of Stone, Tess Annis tossed and turned in her small yet comfortable bed. It had taken her hours to make the right mattress, the right pillows, the right frame that didn't squeak. And now, even with the perfect bed, in the perfectly decorated room, she could not sleep. The powers in her seemed to be growing day by day, and still she did not know what to do with them. It had all started when she brought Camille back from the dead. Ever since that moment in time, it seemed as though reality was a piece of paper that could be folded and changed to fit whatever pattern and shape she wished. Time, reality, space, even life and death were not out of her range of ability to change. Suddenly, Tess felt something, like a great shudder in time. She sat bolt upright and threw a blanket around herself before running out the door and heading for Camille's cabin. She threw the door open and shouted for Camille. A few seconds later, Camille emerged from the bedroom, her hair mussed, and her robe barely pulled over her naked body.

"It's late, Tess, what's the matter?"

"Did you feel that Camille? Did you?"

Tess was frantic. There was a wild look in her eyes, like she had just been scared out of sleep.

"Feel what, Tess? What are you talking about?"

Camille finished pulling the robe about herself and went to Tess's side. After a moment, Tess had calmed down enough to make sense.

"Just for a moment, out in the woods, there was a feeling like someone had stopped time, just for an instant. But then it was gone."

Camille looked puzzled but smoothed Tess's hair, and tried to comfort her.

"I didn't feel anything, Tess. Are you sure that you felt something?"

Tess stood up and glowered down at Camille.

"Of course I felt something, Camille. It was just like a bubble burst in my ear. How could I miss it? I can't believe you didn't feel it! I have to go tell Aunt Hannah and Aunt Leonora. Something is coming, and it isn't good. We could all be in danger."

With that Tess was out the door and stalking her way half-dressed toward the Heart of Stone. Camille looked out the door for a long moment before closing it and heading back toward the bedroom to get dressed before following her charge. When she entered her bedroom, she found Devlin was already dressed.

"Something wrong?" he said shortly, quickly buckling his sword-belt around his waist.

"I'm not sure," Camille said finally, "but whatever it is, it doesn't seem good."

* * * * * * * * * * * *

Aerith sat down on a log across from Meredith and waited. If this was going to be a story, he would at least be comfortable for it. Meredith took a long time before she spoke again, but when she did, it shook Aerith to the very core.

"When you were tapped as the first Chosen One of the prophecies, it was not random, Aerith. The Creator had a plan for you long before the moment of your birth. Long before your parents even met. Did you think that you were picked by accident? Did you think that you were accidentally the father of the first Coromor? Do you think it was an accident that you fell in love with the one woman who would have such a pivotal role in the battle between light and dark? And did you think it was an accident that you were able to defeat Evan and rekindle the Blaze?"

"So what is the Creator's plan? Why me?"

Meredith laughed.

"Why do you think it's the Creator's plan now? The Creator was done with you the moment that Cedric was born. Since then, there have been other powers that have taken an interest in you. Whether it was Shau-ling, or others in the hierarchy of gods, someone has been pulling the strings to put you in the right place at the right time."

"Who was it?"

Meredith's face was stone.

"Tell me who it was, Meredith?"

"You know who it was, Aerith, you just don't want to admit it."

Aerith's head spun, and yet anger began to boil.

"Dorovar."

The name tasted like acid in his mouth, but at the same time, he knew he couldn't be wrong.

"Dorovar's plan to get his revenge on the dragons and the Creator go back a very long way, and he learned after his centuries of destroying worlds that it went farther to manipulate and hurt the Creator more when his own creations were responsible for the downfall of his little playthings. So, what better way to get his revenge than to set a plan in motion that would not only cause the downfall of the Creator, but aid in his own ascension to the position. Luckily for you, Evan was able to help engineer the fall of the Dark Gods."

Aerith's blood froze. Evan?

"What are you talking about, Meredith? How did Evan engineer the fall of the Dark Gods?"

Meredith leaned back, and let the question sink in for a moment before answering.

"Gwydeon and Evan had a plan. When Onea fell to fire, they both realized that the Creator allowed it to happen, no matter the interference by Halicon or Emries. So, Evan and Gwydeon decided to learn everything they could about the Creator and how things worked. It was that time when Evan learned about Dorovar and the dragons. The dragons mattered more than any other race, and Dorovar killed hundreds of worlds trying to get back at the dragons. Onea was an experiment, an experiment that failed. And so the Creator wanted to start over, with more control, and less interference by those the world would see as gods. But in order to draw Dorovar out into the open, Evan had to trap the dragons on a world and give Dorovar the method that he needed to get back at the Creator. So, Gwydeon engineered a little rebellion and the Dark Gods were cast down. However, Gwydeon's plan went further than Gwydeon ever expected. He didn't think his insurrection would spread as far as it did. Pike, ever the hothead took up the banner beside Gwydeon and led the charge against the angels and the other gods. A great many of the other gods fell under the might of the heroes of Onea, until the envoys and heralds of the Creator got the upper-hand and assisted in the expulsion of the so-called Dark Gods. It was Evan that cast Gwydeon down, but the two knew it would come to this, so Evan targeted the one man on Espre that should have never been targeted, the man who made the deal with the dragons for asylum on Espre. The second act was when Gwydeon sacrificed himself to Terrik Lorien to seal the deal between Cadaria and Mythryn."

"And what about Dorovar?"

Meredith smiled.

"Now that the dragons were trapped on Espre, Dorovar allowed himself to be captured, knowing that his prison would be on the world of Espre. Of course he had to put up a convincing fight. In that fight he killed several dozen of the Creator's envoys, including myself, or so Dorovar thought. Evan knew that he could not continue with his plan if he were still the Evan from Onea. So, we agreed that I would be the one sacrificed to take him down the right path."

"So it was all an act?"

Meredith smiled.

"A very good act. Evan needed to seem out of control, someone who could not be brought back from his grief and pain. The very qualities he needed to lure one of the Dark Gods to start the next phase of the plan."

"The murder of the envoys."

"Very good," Meredith said slowly. "If the envoys are murdered, both factions, the Dark Gods and Dorovar could both succeed. No matter what, if all of the envoys are killed, Pike and the others can go back to the heavens and finish off the Creator and make things right. All of the Dark Gods will be able to either go back, or to finally die. You and Bryn can grow old together, just like you always wanted."

"Evan needed me to start it off. He needed me to kill him, because I was the only one who could strip away his powers."

Meredith nodded.

"Right again. Evan knew about the Dragon Sword from Gwydeon, and knew that eventually it would fall into your hands and that you would use it in the manner that you already have. The accidental re-kindling of the Blaze was an interesting byproduct. But Evan knew what he was signing up for. But we've planned for all contingencies."

Meredith stood and started to walk away.

"Wait," Aerith said quickly, "how are you still alive? What happened to Evan?"

Meredith turned and smiled.

"There are some secrets that need to remain secret a little longer, old friend."

Aerith watched as Meredith walked away, sorrow in his heart, and anger filling the rest of him. It had been a plan, a reckless and ambitious plan to say the least. But, perhaps Aerith had new reason to go on, and a new target. He would find a way to bring down Dorovar, but would find a way to get his rest as well. Laughing to himself, Aerith walked back toward the camp, knowing that he would have to endure Celestial Princess for a few days more. As he made his way back to the edge of camp, he saw Rhain out gathering firewood. He thrust his hands in his pockets and walked in her direction.

"Watch your back, girl," he said in a nearly whispered tone as he passed by, "there are lies and phantoms in the woods tonight. Not everything is as it seems."

Rhain smiled to herself and purposefully let her elbow find his ribs.

"You worry too much, old man."

Aerith frowned.

"Is that any way to talk to your father..."

* * * * * * * * * * *

Deep in the wilderness, Seraphina Masile waited, her long blond hair shimmering in the moonlight. From the east, another woman entered the small clearing, and the two blond women stood eye to eye for a moment before the thin, gaunt form of Meredith Heron laughed.

"Report?" Seraphina said quietly.

Meredith smiled, and then shook her head slowly. Her blond hair shifted to red, and her sunken features filled out to a more healthy weight. The visage of Meredith Heron had disappeared and the beautiful pale features of Kyrie Tensas stood opposite Seraphina.

"Aerith Seth is on the path we want him on," Kyrie said smiling. "He will now work toward defeating the remaining emissaries, just as the Dark Gods will. We can now move with relative impunity. All of the wildcards have been dealt with."

"Not all," Seraphina cautioned. "But they will be shortly. Pike and the others are stirred up now, and they will accelerate their time table. In a matter of days, Tess Annis and her precious Camille will be dead, and the whole of the royal family of Lorien will be dead as well. Only Kaitain will be left, and through him we will make the Creator pay for what he did to us."

Fate's Last Sigh

Year Three of the Just Emperor Kaitain "Dragonsbane" Lorien, Creator's Calendar Year 1870

Moonlight sparkled off a small lake in the center of what most would call a forgotten forest. It had been generations since any humans had set foot on the grass of this land, and it would be generations more before men remembered that such a place existed. Small animals ventured out, though they were wary of the larger creatures that called this ancient place home. Dragons did not usually settle to dine on rodents and small mammals, but it was not unheard of. Wariness led to survival far more often than complacency and recklessness did. In the stillness of the night, a small point of blue light appeared, hanging in the air like a will o' the wisp. Slowly the edges of the blue point of light expanded outward, and the swirling heart of the portal began to display itself to the invisible audience. Once the portal had reached its full size, it lingered for only a moment before a form stepped through. The blind man had barely cleared the event horizon of the portal before it began to contract behind him. In a matter of heartbeats, the portal had contracted back to an insignificant point of light, and then was gone.

Xaran Firesoul the Tiger's Eye Knight of the Flashing Blade stood for a long time, simply breathing and listening to the world around him. Traveling through a portal created by one of the Dark Gods had been nothing like he had ever experienced before in his short existence, and he wondered at the marvel of it. Xaran, due to his blindness and his connection with all things unseen both within his soul and outside of his body had a connection with the spirit that belied description. There were times when he felt he could almost see the spirit world, wrapping around him like a cloak and changing the very patterns of fate that Orren Eldrath was always talking about. Most of his discussions with Orren had been contentious when the subject of fate came up. To Orren, fate was this immutable thing with a will and a goal. To Xaran, fate was a breeze. Fate wrapped around all things, sometimes pushing, sometimes guiding. Fate could erode the greatest of men as the wind made mountains tremble, or fate could be steered around those who chose not to be guided. Fate was not a master. Orren would say that ignoring fate could only bring pain and suffering to the one who fought against its mandates. Xaran felt that fate respected those who charted their own path. Where fate became the vengeful thing that Orren perceived was when a man became arrogant enough to believe that he could steer the course of fate itself. Those men found themselves broken and destroyed by their own hubris.

There was movement in the distance, and Xaran kept as still as he could, broken from his reverie. Xaran knew that not only was he being watched, but that the steady eye of a marksman of incredible skill was locked upon him. He didn't have to hear the groan of the bowstring or the aching stretch of the wood to know that an arrow was trained directly at his heart.

"You are known to me, human," a voice called from a great distance, perhaps a thousand yards, "and you know that you are not allowed upon these lands without the permission of the Council of the Winds. This is the only warning you will receive, and if you take so much as a step forward, there is nothing that will save you from my arrow."

There was no bravado in the man's voice, he was speaking fact. Even at this distance, there was no doubt in the unseen man's voice that his shot would be true.

"I have been recognized as a guest of the Council of the Winds, under the protection of Khalas. I am returning with a report for Lord Tarot."

Xaran kept his voice even, and tried to remember if there was any protocol that he had to abide by. This man was obviously one of the four guardians that Khalas had eluded to on his last visit to this ancient and protected land. The sense of danger that filled Xaran did not abate, and he knew that the man's aim had not shifted from his lethal intention. There was another sound from behind Xaran, movement that could only be from a pair of human legs. The footfalls were solid but light, and seemed to show some level of reverence for the land. The figure wore a heavy cloak, that much was clear from the rustling sound of the fabric, and the hood was pulled up and the fabric was bristling up against hair, and unless Xaran missed his guess, a short beard. The man's pace was slow, almost ambling and casual. His footfalls were uneven, as though he was favoring his left side.

"Halt," the archer's voice came again as the cloaked man moved to within a few steps of where Xaran stood, "if you take another step, you will not live to see another sunrise."

The cloaked man came to a stop nearly parallel to where Xaran stood and turned his head first to regard Xaran and then back to the woods where the archer must have been perched somewhere in the heights of the trees.

"You are known to me, Jander Eveningstar," the stranger's voice called out.

There was gravel in his voice, and a pain that Xaran could practically feel. It was an old voice, but there were notes of youth still hidden within it. This was a man who was much older than his years. But there was a quality to the man's voice that stirred something within Xaran, as though he had heard the voice before.

"Your prowess with a bow is well known," the man continued, "and your eyesight even more so. But your careful and practiced aim will fail you this evening, no matter how many times you draw back your bowstring. Fate is not your ally so long as the moon hangs in the night sky."

Strange though the man's words were, they seemed to hold meaning for the archer. The sense of danger that held in pit of Xaran's stomach suddenly disappeared. It was then that he heard the bow and bowstring relax in the distance. There was a soft sound of boots hitting earth, and then soft, almost silent footfalls approaching where Xaran and the stranger stood. Were it not for Xaran's enhanced hearing, Xaran was sure that no ordinary person could have heard Jander's approach. Within a matter of moments, Jander Eveningstar had come within a hundred feet of the two men, but he would come no farther.

"State your intentions in this holy place," Jander said slowly. Xaran could feel concern and what could have been fear radiating from the man, but none of it was focused at Xaran.

"As I have said," Xaran replied in a cool even tone, "I am here to deliver a report to Lord Tarot. Should he be unavailable, my intention would be to speak to Khalas Skydancer."

Jander's attention did not leave the cloaked man.

"Your intentions are unimportant, Knight of the Flashing Blade, they are being dealt with."

The cloaked man chuckled slightly.

"You have nothing to fear from me, Jander; I simply intend to wait with Xaran until Khalas comes. He is coming this way after all, isn't he?"

There was hesitation coming from the guardian, but nothing came of it, as Xaran heard the familiar beating of massive wings against the wind coming toward them. Absently, Xaran heard the guardian withdraw slightly from the area, and then the great bulk of Khalas Skydancer settled into the clearing. The cloaked man moved away, and sat gingerly on the edge of a great clump of roots. Xaran inwardly marveled as he always did when he heard Khalas fold his wings back and then sit up, straight backed, his talons pulling through his long white beard.

"Your timing is interesting, my friend," Khalas sighed, "and I am sure by your appearance here that your intended goal did not meet with the success we had hoped for."

Before Xaran could even respond, the cloaked man spoke.

"No need to be cryptic in my presence, Khalas."

Khalas looked at the cloaked man as though he was seeing him for the first time. It was strange that the normally observant Khalas would have ignored the man's presence until he had spoken. It was almost as though the cloaked man did not want to be seen by the massive dragon until just that moment. There was a resounding feeling of shock and confusion that filled the air, and then the sensation shifted to one of malice, as a roar ripped from the great dragon's throat.

"Enough of that!"

The man's voice was filled with a power that Xaran had never felt before, and it burst out of him like a great gout of fire. It washed over everyone in the clearing, and Xaran felt as though all of the breath had been stolen from his lungs. If the voice had a tone, Xaran could not find it. There was only one ingredient to the voice, and it was power. Khalas's growl died.

"Now," the cloaked man said, his voice going back to a normal tone, "I could carve my way through you and all four of the guardians if needs be, but I don't want to do that unless I have no choice. My words are not for your ears alone Khalas Skydancer, and there is nothing you can do to prevent me from speaking to the whole of the Council."

Khalas seemed to regard the man's words for a moment, and then after another pull of his beard finally relented.

"But first, conclude your business with Sir Firesoul. There are other matters that he is called to. A budding rebellion will soon need his council, and he must stand witness to what will happen next. Fate has put you on a strange and dangerous road Xaran, and I hope you have the strength and bravery to see it to its end."

Xaran, though confused by the man's words quickly began to recount his failures on the Dark Continent of Mythryn and his encounters not only with the Lord of the Dark Gods, but also the emissary of the forces of the being known as Dorovar. Khalas listened through the entire tale, his countenance as calm as he could manage given the circumstances. Finally when the tale was done, and Xaran had fallen silent, Khalas considered his words for a long moment before speaking.

"I cannot say that I am surprised by your defeat at the hands of the Dark Gods, Xaran," the great dragon spoke with a grave and remorseful tone, "and there is providence in how you managed to survive the encounter. But as you have said, the truest threat is not the one posed by the Dark Gods, though I have no doubt that their retribution will be swift and harsh, but the fact that the Emperor of Cadaria somehow came into possession of one of those wicked daggers... It appears that the Council of Winds has been a pawn in a greater game being played between Dorovar and the Dark Gods. And my greater concern is that some members of the Council were aware that we were being manipulated."

The cloaked man had stayed silent though the entirety of Xaran's tale, but now chose to lend his voice to the conversation.

"The dragons will never see themselves as pawns in a greater game, Khalas, and that is the reason they are so easily manipulated by the forces that understand them best. Dorovar manipulates you because you feel his hate blinds him and his prison is absolute. But Dorovar is much more than hate and madness. He was and always will be a zealot with utter and total devotion to the goddess that you stole from him. He still waits for the day that she will return and save him from the destruction you and your kind wrought upon his world. Hate is a powerful motivator, but true faith is the most dangerous force in the whole of the universe."

Xaran took in the man's words, but no matter how many questions the words evoked within his heart, part of Xaran knew that it was not his time for answers. His small part in this act of the play had been fulfilled, and the introspective knight felt as though he had been used and discarded. As though feeling Xaran's thoughts, the cloaked man turned his attention to the Tiger's Eye Knight.

"We are all used, Xaran," the man said in what could have passed for a caring and sympathetic tone, "some of us are the kindling to fuel a greater fire, and our only reward is to be the ashes upon which the new worlds are built. But sometimes, a few of us are used to be the spark of a greater fire, and we are carried through that fire on the winds of chance and fate, the thing you call destiny, and stand atop a new world, instead of being crushed by it. But we choose, Xaran, we choose whether our path takes us through the fire, or just deeper into it. Dorovar chose to be an instrument of destruction, his hatred burned hotter than any fire that creation has ever seen. But if Dorovar is successful, and his crusade remakes the whole of creation according to his vision, what will be left? His fire of vengeance and faith will have long since gone out, and all that will be left is Dorovar, alone, in the cold empty husk of what remains of the universe. Faith can be shattered by knowledge, Xaran, and Dorovar is only dangerous so long as his faith is true. Perhaps this is true for more than just Dorovar and his supplicants."

There was something in the man's words, a quality Xaran didn't recognize until the cloaked man finished speaking. Xaran felt as though he had just been told a great truth, as though the secrets of the universe had been laid at his feet for the barest of moment before being pulled back into the mists of mystery. Before Xaran had much of an opportunity to consider the man's words more fully, he snapped his fingers and another of the dark blue swirling portals appeared to Xaran's left. Xaran was shocked at the appearance of the portal, but strangely not surprised that the man possessed this power.

"This will take you close enough to the Heart of Stone in Albitonin that you will not have a hard journey, but far enough away that no one will question how you came to be there. Go now, and remember what I have said to you Xaran. There are still many battles ahead and still many choices to be made. One day you will need to choose whether you will be consumed by the fire, or whether you shall walk through it to the other side."

Xaran nodded and turned to the portal.

"And perhaps you must consider whether or not there is an Other Side to cross over to."

Xaran was half-way through the portal before the cloaked man's words hit his ears. Confusion held him through the short journey to Albitonin. With the Tiger's Eye Knight gone, the cloaked man turned back toward Khalas and regarded the larger creature for a long moment.

"Take me to your Council, Khalas," the cloaked man said coldly, "perhaps I can save them from themselves."

* * * * * * * * * * * *

Rashaleb had once been a thriving city filled with artists, families, the laughter of children, and a sense of hope and purpose. That had all changed the day that Famine had walked through the streets of the capitol and spread her evil tainted touch through the populace. Every man, woman, and child that had once called the frozen city their home suffered and died on that same day. And now, Rashaleb was a tomb, a monument to the day that evil had touched Cadaria in a way that could never be erased. Rashaleb had become the indelible mark that would symbolize for the rest of time that evil was a real thing that did not care who you were or what kind of person that you were. To evil, you were a victim, and would only ever be a victim.

Orren Eldrath walked through the city, his head low, the landscape lost to him. He could have walked through the city blindfolded. Once the walls of every building practically breathed with the life that inhabited them. Now there was only silence. It seemed that even the wind did not wish to blow through the empty streets, as not to disturb the sanctity of what the city had become. Orren kept his hands in the pockets of his cloak, one hand wrapped around the symbol of his position as a member of the Knights of the Flashing Blade and the representative of this wounded kingdom. In the other hand he clutched the parchment that contained his latest assignment for the Cadarian Empire. The Empress had called him away from his tracking of the creature calling itself Death in order to track down a mercenary band on behalf of the Throne. The Empress believed that some of the members of this band could be of use to the Empire, but Orren had his doubts. Those doubts aside however, he would fulfill his duties. But he had wanted to come home first, to see the place that he had been born one more time. Even if one day people returned to Rashaleb, it would never be the same. The specter of what had happened there would never disappear.

Orren continued to walk through the streets of the city, turning down familiar corners until he stood in front of his favorite tavern. He had good memories of taking up three tables with books for study while flipping coins to help himself concentrate. There was a little serving girl that worked there that always marveled at the number of books that he read, and he would always try to teach her something in a few stolen moments. It was not love, but Orren felt in those moments as if he was more than he was before and after those moments.

"You're not what I was expecting."

The voice caught Orren completely by surprise. He spun quickly, feeling like he was screwing himself into the ground hunting for the voice that had spoken. Courage was in his hand, and in his heart he almost felt as though he would need every bit of the Sacred Weapon's abilities. Finally Orren found the source of the voice, as a man stepped out of a dark alley, his right hand held out at his side. The man's left arm had been severed just below the shoulder, near the middle of the bicep, and a cruel scar stretched the length of the bicep to the shoulder. The man wore no armor, nor did he wear a sword belt either on his hip or across his chest, but there a danger in the man, that much was clear, armed or not.

"Sneaking up on a member of the Knights of the Flashing Blade is not an advisable past-time if one wants to keep their health."

The one-armed man smiled.

"You have nothing to fear from me. I'm just another ghost touring the graveyard."

While Orren should have been insulted by the man's words, he wasn't. Orren too felt like a ghost. Like part of himself had been left in the wreckage of Rashaleb. That he was much less than he once was after the touch of Famine had robbed so many of the fate that had been carved out for them. And then there was the one-armed man. Orren had been touched with the gift to sometimes see the strings of fate that held people together. He could see if two people were destined to spend their lives together, or if one person was fated to end another's life because of the way their threads of fate crossed in the pattern, but this man was an enigma. He had no string of fate, as though he was exactly what he said he was; a ghost.

"So," Orren said playing along, "are you a benevolent ghost, or a malevolent one?"

The blond man put his hand behind his back in an almost military rest position, and then seemed to chew over the words in his mind.

"I've been both, I'm afraid, over the history of my life. I've killed in the name of good, evil, and everything in between. But I have never killed without purpose, and I have never killed without feeling something about the person or thing that I have ended the life of. Ending the fate of a person is a great responsibility, one bourn only if one understands the true meaning of life, death, and fate."

Orren was struck by the plainness and the depth of the man's words. It was as though the ghost had stared into his soul and known exactly what to say to shake him to the core; to the heart of every belief that he held dear.

"But I was a soldier, Orren," the one-armed man said finally, "in the end that is all I was. I was not strong enough to make my own fate, and I was only a participant in the story that others created. You are fortunate enough to be on the stage with some of those men and women now Orren, and you, as some of your brothers and sisters in the Knights of the Flashing Blade, have their own verses to add. But you, Orren, you are important in a way that you can't even begin to understand."

Orren's mouth felt dry.

"It's said," Orren's voice came, raspy and uncertain, "that I was born under powerful signs. That I would be touched by the Creator and be the instrument through which great things would come to pass."

The one-armed man took a long step forward, his brilliant blue eyes disarming and haunting in the same breath.

"In the end, Orren," the man said firmly, "that is for you to decide. I have been the instrument through which the fate of great men have been launched, and I have been there in the end when great men rose above their own failings, or fell to their own vices. A dark time is coming, one which you could have never predicted, and one that you may not be prepared to face. But that is why I am here."

The man stopped and held out his hand again, this time in front of him. After a moment, a single brilliant emerald green flame appeared on the man's palm. It danced there, almost hypnotic in its simplicity and power.

"What is it?" Orren asked, his mouth going dry again, but this time with excitement and anticipation.

"This is power," the one-arm man said finally, "in the truest sense. It is the power of life, and the power of death, and the very thing that all of this reality is built upon. In some ways, it is my life, and what ties me to this world, and in some ways it is everything that ties me to everything I have ever been and ever done. But soon, this power, will be needed to save this world from the darkness that is coming, and this power, this Blaze, will be needed to light the way into a new tomorrow."

Orren's eyes were filled with the dancing green glow. He knew the man's words were true, he knew that he was looking at a power unlike anything he had ever experienced before, but he did not hunger for it.

"Some of us have known for a very long time that the day was coming in which we would be given a choice. We would be allowed to walk away from this conflict. Walk away from the choices we have made in the past, and give our places to those who can fight for a better tomorrow. My choices have never been the best, and I have made more than my share of mistakes. I've tried to do right through my failings, and I have tried to do right by those that I have led down terribly dark paths. I've watched friends, family, and even my own children subjected to horrors that no person should. And finally, now I see what I must do."

The man drew himself up. For the first time Orren paid attention to what the man was wearing, and at one moment while it was a commoner's shirt and pants, it began to shift to something else. In a matter of moments, he was wearing a full set of armor, the form of a springing lion on the breastplate. Stretching behind him was a black cloak that fluttered softly in the slight breeze that had started to blow. His left arm had incredibly been restored, as though it were never gone, and his left hand was encased in a glowing golden gauntlet. On his right hip had appeared a sword and scabbard, and the man was possessed with such an ominous and impressive aura, that Orren almost lost the grip on Courage.

"This is how I choose to remember myself Orren," the man said proudly, "in the days before I brought a young farm boy a message that would change so many lives. The days after I had redeemed myself from needless darkness that may have condemned us all."

The imposing figure took another half step forward, the dancing green flame on his palm pulsing with power and meaning.

"And so now, the choice comes to you. I offer you all that I once was. Once I was the child of a god, and once I was a savior of the helpless. Once I was Sir Aryx Terian, and once my enemies trembled at the sound of my name. They called me White Lightning. If you take this gift I am offering you, all of my skills, all of my knowledge, and everything that I was then will be yours. Through it you will be given the ability to forge a new world with others who will take up similar mantles, and through it you will have a chance to undo the misery that I have helped to create."

Orren hesitated. He didn't know what to do, what to say, how to answer. Everything in his being wanted to honor this gift, and at the same time he feared it. He feared its power, and he feared what he could do with it. Perhaps that is why the gift had been offered to him. Perhaps it had been because this Aryx knew that he would not abuse it. Finally, he set his feet firmly and reached out with his left hand and plunged it into the Blaze.

Orren felt the burning course through him in a way he never could have expected, and his eyes squeezed shut with the pain. It pushed into every corner of his frail mortal body, saturating every pore, duct, and cell. He felt in that moment that he would have been burned to a cinder, or even just ripped asunder by the amount of power that was flowing into him, and if it were not for the way that Aryx was letting the power flow into him, the unbridled power of the Blaze would have destroyed him. Panic set in as Orren felt his blood boil and his tortured heart began to slow. It was agony that radiated through every part of him, and he could hear the beating of his weakening heart begin to slow. And then suddenly, the life of Orren Eldrath, the man that he had once been, was over. Orren Eldrath died. But the silence in his chest lasted for only a few moments before the heart began to move again, began to force blood through the body again. This time though, the slow, calculated, cold rhythm of his heart would mark the passage of time for the rest of his days. No matter the exertion, no matter the trial, and no matter the emotion, the rhythm would never change. When his eyes opened, the man who had called himself Aryx lay on the cold hard ground, his breathing raspy and slow. Orren knew the man was dying. He fell to his knees at the side of the once legendary knight and held fast to his right hand. Aryx looked up, a faint smile gracing his lips.

"Your path is different than any I could have ever charted for myself. Soon you will know what you must do. That much has already been set into motion. Make the most of what this day has brought to you, and above all, remember that all power comes with a price. I forgot that for a long time, and I cannot begin to know what it has cost."

Aryx Terian closed his eyes for a moment, and then opened them again. This time he looked past Orren Eldrath into the sky. His skin was growing colder and the fierce light in his eyes was slowly beginning to fade.

"I'm so proud of you, Aerith," his faint voice said into the still air, "my son."

And with his final words, Aryx Terian closed his eyes for the last time.

Chapter LVIII

Aggressive Negotiation

Empress Dominique Lorien sat on the throne and shifted uncomfortably, but tried not to let any of her discomfort make it to her face. This round of petitions had become exceedingly tedious, as the crackdown from the Imperial Guard was starting to border on the level of oppressive. Chelsea had warned her that things would start to move in this direction. The rebellion against the banner of the Just Emperor Kaitain Lorien was intensifying as the days rolled on, and more and more partisan bands of warriors began cropping up throughout the kingdoms. Whispers of dissension and disloyalty were rampant, and the Imperial Guard under the direction of the newly appointed Head of the Guard, Korin Melcab, their reaction to these whispers had been swift and brutal. Dominique had not known about Melcab's ascension to the position until the two had been introduced at a recent inspection of the palace's garrison. Irene Drage had seen to the man's promotion, and it was unclear what his background was, other than he was a thug from the Pritan Islands. Apparently the man had been dispatched as a counter to the increase in piracy in the islands, and his record contained as many citations for bravery and success in the face of long odds, as it did for brutality and malice in the execution of his duties. He had never risen above the rank of Lieutenant in his career, mostly due to a series of demotions for failure to adhere to orders, or the methods in which he followed those orders. How such a man could find himself as the head of the Imperial Guard was beyond all comprehension, except when looking at who signed his papers of promotion. Irene was putting yet another piece in play to undermine Dominique's authority. Now, no matter the good will that she engendered through her kindness and fairness with the people, this thug would be a blot on the reputation of her rule. Chelsea had wanted to demote the man, find a way to send him back to the islands, but that was impossible. To overrule the appointment would make public the rift between the Throne and the Court Sorceress, even more than it already was, and would give some hardline elements the opening they needed to attempt a coup and remove Dominique from her position. If Irene could tip the tables and cast light on Dominique as a usurper, then it would be an easy trick for her to have the Empress imprisoned and protect Kaitain's rightful rule. The sorceress had proven to be a quite astute opponent, and it had been everything that Dominique could do to continue countering the woman's maneuvers.

Thoughts of the woman made Dominique's head hurt. She wanted to rub her temples, but she sat as still as possible, pretending to pay attention to the farmer who was lodging a complaint against the over-zealous guards who seized his livestock and all of his money in response to what the captain of the guard had called a 'pattern of behavior that supported rebellion'. She had heard this same story a dozen times already this morning. Those people originally from the rebel kingdoms that openly displayed the crest of those kingdoms were considered supporting rebellion, and the policy had been disseminated by the Imperial Guard after the attempt on the lives of Feyd and Felicia and Dominique's public declaration of Seraph's complicity in the attempt on Kaitain's life. The Imperial Guard was right in their enforcement of these laws of course, but it was their methods that Dominique found repugnant. Korin Melcab did not understand the meaning of the word warning.

However, even as those thoughts entered Dominique's mind, she reflected on the briefing that Chelsea had given her early that morning about the state of rebellion across Cadaria. Aldere was in an increasingly tenuous position. Situated in the center of the lands of Cadaria, it was a landlocked kingdom bordered by four of the great kingdoms. To the southeast lay the loyal Kingdom of Iron, Pellatori. The staunch men and women of the Iron Legion had been incorporated into the Imperial Guard and the Imperial Army upon Bernhardt Yeoman's ascension to the position of General of the Imperial Armies. To their east lay the loyal kingdoms of Bellnoc, Celidar, and Rashaleb, ensuring that they Pellatori would be a stronghold of support of the Imperial lands. To the northwest of Aldere lay the still loyal Kingdom of Steam, Iltorp, and beyond Iltorp to the west was Saldarine, Chelea's home and staunch supporters of the Imperial Family and Dominique's current rule. However, to Aldere's northeast lay the Kingdom of Blood, Zevarit, whom Dominique had delivered into the hands of the rebellion through Gabriel Shadowfall's engineered defection. And to the southwest lay the now rebel Kingdom of Water, Thorigald and beyond to the west, the core of the rebellion, Albitonin and Galateria. Thorigald had immediately defected to the rebellion after the decree of Seraph's role in the assassination attempt and the labeling of him as a traitor to the Throne. Word had spread to Dominique's ears that Seraph had returned to the Kingdom of Thorigald and was gathering an army to use to bring down Kaitain's reign. But such a scenario could not be avoided. Now five of the Kingdoms of Cadaria had fully thrown in with the rebellion, and the word coming out of Menoris was that they would be joining with their sister kingdom Oradrim in the rebellion very soon.

As if in a dream Dominique worked her way through another dozen nearly identical petitions, and then called an end to the session. When the last of the men and women had exited the audience chamber, Dominique slumped against the unyielding iron back of the throne and rubbed her temples hard. The headache had just gotten worse. Thirty complaints against the Imperial Guard. Twenty complaints of cruelty and unnecessary violent force. The details were too sickening to attempt to remember. Unfortunately in only one case could Dominique levy any discipline upon the Imperial Guard for their actions. One of the young guardsmen had assaulted the daughter of one of the farmers and was intending to elevate the simple assault to a rape had the farmer not smashed the soldier's head in with a shovel. Of course the farmer had been killed for his assault on a member of the Imperial Guard. Melcab had been unrelentingly cold in his description of the events, his stern features showing nothing but contempt through the retelling. Cold grey eyes that smoldered with nothing but hate, features set as though they had been carved from granite, and a speaking voice that could curdle milk and make the bravest man cower. In the end, all Dominique could do was to extend the protection of the Throne to the wronged girl and ensure that her lands and all seized belongings were returned to her and that she would be exempted from Imperial taxes for the span of two years, or until she was married, whichever came first. That last was a concession that would surely be viewed as a woman's weakness. Melcab was completely unaffected by the decrees, and what was worse, seemed to take no pleasure when the petitions against his soldiers were dismissed. He was totally and completely dispassionate about everything it seemed, except for inflicting pain and suffering.

My husband will love him, Dominique found herself thinking. This was just the kind of severe creature that Kaitain would use to punish his enemies in the most expedient way. Kaitain had a myriad of tools at his disposal, and where Geoffry Aramour was an elegantly crafted blade, this Korin Melcab would be a wicked and gnarled club that could be used to bludgeon the populous.

"I don't think I like this anymore," Dominique said finally, turning to look up at Chelsea who stood at her left shoulder.

Chelsea's look was impassive.

"I would be worried if you did," she said after a moment, "and I wish I could say that it was going to be better soon. The more people openly support the rebellion, the more drastic measures are going to be taken to ensure the safety of the Imperial family. Worse still will be what happens when your husband wakes up."

Dominique knew in a moment what Chelsea was referring to, as it had been a topic of conversation late one night when both women had had far too much to drink after a trying day. They both had needed some respite and knew they could let their guard down a little in each other's company. Chelsea had been postulating what would happen when Kaitain found out that Marlae had defected to the rebellion and would be vying for his throne. The unspoken answer was that Kaitain would see his daughter broken at his feet and that he would most likely want to be the one to end her life. Neither Chelsea nor Dominique could see any mercy or forgiveness waiting for the severe young woman, were she to ever be captured and brought before her father. It had been Chelsea's off-hand comment about the lack of another heir that made Dominique shiver. That would be the next expectation on her shoulders. All would be watching and waiting for the royal heir to be born.

"We can only hope that these situations will be resolved long before that happens, and that cooler heads will prevail."

The look shared between the two women had only one meaning. There was no chance such a miracle was even still possible.

* * * * * * * * * * * *

Irene Drage waited in the antechamber for Korin Melcab to emerge from the morning petitions. Irene no longer attended these audiences, largely because it was more advantageous for her to do every subtle thing possible to undermine the rule and authority of Dominique Lorien. Appointing the wicked general of the Hand of Chaos to the head of the Imperial Guard had turned out to be a master stroke however. Thanks to Seraphina and Xavier, it had been easy to invent the man's service in the Pritan Island chain, and Torda had been able to forge all of the documents necessary to prove the man's military linage. Ensuring that no one would be alive to disprove the service of Korin in the Imperial Army had been left to Syren and her brood, and they had done a masterful job. Of course it had taken burning several strongholds to the ground, but that was easily blamed on the female pirate captain who continued to make a nuisance of herself. Finally Korin emerged from the audience chamber, and his attention was suddenly drawn from where Irene stood to another figure that Irene was sure had not been there before.

The man stood in the shadows, and try as she might, Irene's eyes would not lock onto the man's form, they seemed to just slide past as though he was part of the shadow. The essence of the dark goddess that inhabited Irene allowed some information to pass into her mind, and it was then that Irene knew the identity of the obscured man. He was known as Dimitri Sulano, commonly known as the Voice of the Lost. Generations ago he had been a general serving in the Imperial Army, a man of some stature and some accomplishment. But he fell in battle through the machinations of one of his subordinates who coveted his position. As he lay dying from poison on the battlefield, darkness fell over the land and when the light returned, Dimitri's body had disappeared. Under orders of Dorovar, Dimitri had been recovered by Syren and given a chance to serve. Dimitri was given the gift of hearing the voices of the dead and damned. It was said that he could feel death before it happened, as the souls of those who were about to cross to the other side called out to him. Others said that Dimitri had been driven mad by Dorovar's chorus of souls, and that he now could not distinguish what was on the living side of reality, and what was on the side of the dead.

Irene blinked, and suddenly Dimitri stood beside her.

"Death comes to this house," he said in a whisper that sounded like a snake's hiss, "and a fallen one brings it."

Korin's eyebrows twitched.

"A Dark God? Here? Impossible."

Irene leveled a stare in the general's direction. The implication was clear. For the Dark Gods, nothing was impossible. Moreover, Irene knew better than anyone through Talisia that the Dark Gods could have crushed the Cadarian annoyance any time they wished, and it was only their mercy that stayed their hand. Perhaps Kaitain's recent machinations had been enough to push them past that restraint. It was then that Irene felt it. There was a power within the palace that had not been there before. It was hiding as best it could, but it was still there. Suddenly rage exploded within Irene, and Talisia exerted full control over the frail girl's body. To Korin and Dimitri's eyes, Irene seemed to grow in height and her terrible visage was filled with such hate and power that even Korin felt the icy tendrils of fear gripping his heart.

"Find it!" Irene bellowed. "Tear this palace apart stone by stone if you have to!"

* * * * * * * * * * * *

Dominique and Chelsea were still chatting when they reached the door to Dominique's private chambers. There was so much that was not going well, that Dominique had tried to find as much solace in the company of the one person she trusted in the world. They spent nearly every hour of every day together, and some nights since the attempts on Feyd and Felicia, Chelsea had taken to sleeping in a chair beside Dominique's bed. Dominique admired the woman's strength and tenacity, and knew very well that as dangerous an opponent on the battlefield as the Wolf of Saldarine was, she was even more loyal as a friend. Chelsea opened the door to the chamber, and then quickly scanned the interior before letting Dominique move past into the room. This time though, when Chelsea had finished closing the door and turned into the room, she was shocked to see a woman sitting in a chair on the far side of the room who had not been there a moment earlier.

Instantly Chelsea's mind became a whirl of conflicting and colliding thoughts. Had the woman been there and Chelsea had not seen her? No, that wasn't possible. Her skills could not be fooled that much, regardless of how tired she was. Besides, the abilities granted to her by the Sacred Weapon Tenacity made her even more acutely aware of everything. She knew the smell of every servant who had worked in the room over the last day. She knew that a bottle of scented water had been spilled during the morning cleaning. She could even tell that one of the chambermaids who had been in the room that morning had made love that morning before fulfilling her duties. Her eyes saw every crease in the coverlet on the bed, and even the slightest veneer of dust that had been left behind by a hurried and carless cleaning of the wardrobe. And yet she had not seen this woman.

The second set of thoughts were the practiced military drill of assessing the opponent. From the look of the woman and the way she held herself, she was high-born, but the rough edges of her fingernails, slight fraying of the cuffs of her pants, and scuffs on one of her boots marked her as a more active participant in life, not a spoiled aristocrat. The shirt she wore was a man's by the cut, and hugged her form if not indecently, certainly without modesty. This was a practical woman, someone who brooked no nonsense. Her posture was perfect, breathing calm and regular, not a single ounce of disquiet in her manner. Even though she had broken in to the private chambers of the Empress of Cadaria, she showed no outward sign that she was anywhere other than where she was supposed to be. Chelsea also knew that this woman was a cagey opponent. She had not moved an eyelash since Chelsea and Dominique had entered the room, and her expression was certainly one of expectation, colored perhaps with a little annoyance. Chelsea could feel Dominique's shock resonate through the room. But there was something more to this scene than a mystery woman. There was someone else in the chamber, someone familiar. A smell that Chelsea knew. The mystery woman had obviously caught the look of understanding in Chelsea's eyes as she looked to her left and nodded slightly. It was then that Natalia Pressen entered the room.

At Natalia's appearance, Dominique's concern softened slightly, but Chelsea's was still sitting on a razor's edge. The smell of blood and sweat was thick on Natalia. She had been in a battle, and she had not fared well. And yet there were no visible signs of injury on the woman. But from the smells that were invading Chelsea's nose, the knight should have been lying unconscious on the floor barely hanging on to life.

"Chelsea," Natalia said finally, "thank the Creator it is you."

Chelsea eased in front of Dominique, Tenacity in her hands. While she knew that Natalia was a fierce opponent, and not one to be trifled with, Chelsea knew that her experience with combat far exceeded the younger woman's.

"Natalia," Chelsea intoned coldly, "you shouldn't be here."

The look of acknowledgement was quick and clear.

"It was the only way," the young Knight of the Flashing Blade said finally, "we could not come through the front door. There are too many problems."

The woman sitting on the chair exhaled sharply, and stood in one smooth motion. There was practiced, nearly unconscious grace in the woman's movements, and a regal nature that cast a huge shadow. Dominique was a child in this woman's presence, regardless of her title. But Chelsea could feel Dominique steel herself from the fear and awe that had raced through her. She laid an easy if a little unsteady hand on Chelsea's shoulder and moved passed her in a practiced, if slightly clumsy regal stride.

"Lady Pressen," Dominique said, trying to keep the waver out of her voice, "I trust there is a good reason for this unconventional audience."

The annoyed exhalation from the mystery woman was quickly followed by her voice hitting the air for the first time in the tense confrontation.

"Enough of this," she said abruptly, "I have neither the time nor the desire to observe ritual and pomp with little girls who should be scrubbing linens instead of wearing lace."

Dominique inhaled sharply, but it was Chelsea who responded first.

"How dare you speak to the Empress of Cadaria with that tone!"

The mystery woman stared down Chelsea, and despite herself, Chelsea flinched. It was then for the first time that Chelsea saw the sword at the woman's hip. She was sure that it hadn't been there before.

"In my day, this girl could not have been called an Empress of anything other than her little cottage in a farming village somewhere. She would be a nice bauble for some lucky farmer and nothing more. And trust me girl, I know all about you and your bed-hopping habits."

Chelsea was incredulous, but Dominique seemed to have recovered her footing.

"You seem to have me at a disadvantage. You know who I am, and you know how it is that I rose to my position. I do not and will not say that I have earned this title, but I have it, and I am doing my best to make the best of the situation. There are those, even in my own adoptive family who have said that my advancement was only though my ability to spread my legs, but we can all aspire to be more than our circumstances have dictated."

The mystery woman looked Dominique dead in the eyes, and then smiled.

"You are everything I heard that you were, Dominique," she said after a moment. "You are guided by your heart, and you do your best to be more than you once were. There was a girl that I met once, and she would have been your same age, that despite the fact she was born and raised in a backwards farm town, she aspired to be more than that, and had the stubbornness and drive to stare down the embodiments of evil and follow the love of her heart to the ends of the world and back again. She and I were from different stations in life, and under ordinary circumstances, we would never have become friends, but I count myself lucky every day of my life that that stubborn farm girl found her way into my life. And she was my best friend until the day she died. I would like for another farm girl to be my friend, Dominique, but I have no time for gilded empresses."

Dominique smiled.

"My heart will always be what guides me, and no amount of finery can change what lies beneath my skin."

The mystery woman nodded.

"Very well then, Dominique. I am Queen Midarin Sandar, formerly of Brea, wife of Gwydeon Sandar, formerly the Brother of Angels and First of the Dark Gods. I am the leader of the armies of the dark continent of Mythryn, and I have come here to deal with you, Dominique, in an attempt to avert possibly the greatest catastrophe that had befallen Espre since the Dark the Heavens Fell."

* * * * * * * * * * * *

The search had taken too long, but finally Irene had tracked the source of the presence she felt to the private chambers of Dominique Lorien. There was no doubt now that the power was coming from a member of the Dark Gods. Perhaps this was the opportunity that Irene was waiting for. If indeed there was a Dark God on the other side of that door, Irene could execute both Dominique and Chelsea and blame the Dark God for the assassination. All of the obstacles facing Irene would be removed in an instant, and the Throne of Cadaria would be hers. She reached in that instant for the handle but a hand took firm hold of her shoulder and spun her around. The man that stood before her was no more than twenty if he was that old, but there was a gravity to him that said he was much older than his youthful appearance betrayed. There was nothing about his face that was remarkable, save his dark brown eyes that had a seductive softness to them. He seemed to be an average person, common build, common height; the last man that one would focus on in a crowd. But Irene knew him immediately and she smiled.

"Not so hasty, sister," Emries' rich baritone said softly, "there is a great opportunity here to exploit, if we choose to be very careful."

Each Draws Water...

Year Three of the Just Emperor Kaitain "Dragonsbane" Lorien, Creator's Calendar Year 1870

Seraph Kore stood looking out of one of the large bay windows onto the square of the capitol city of the Kingdom of Water, Thorigald. It had scarcely been two weeks since the leading members of the royal families of Thorigald had been executed for their traitorous allegiance to their own greed. What Seraph had not expected however was the series of riots and outright rebellions that his actions had touched off. Returning to Thorigald was supposed to be a grand event, and he should have been embraced by the people of the kingdom as a kind of savior, but that didn't happen, not in the slightest. The Army of Water was certainly loyal to him and him alone, but the people were a different story. The people of the Kingdom of Water were sick of war, they were sick of the death and destruction, and a large portion of them saw the alignment with the rebellion against Emperor Kaitain was inviting more destruction on their heads. What was under the current of resentment was the genuine fear that had come from what happened in Rashaleb. The entire capitol city had been scoured clean of all life, and it had been reduced to a ghost town. The devastation had only taken a matter of minutes, but the impact would last for hundreds of years. The Emperor had done nothing to prevent it, but then again, neither had the vaunted members of the Knights of the Flashing Blade. If someone other than Kaitain had been in charge of the Empire, would the thousands of people of Rashaleb still be alive today? If there was no Kaitain, would the Empire still be in one piece rather than teetering on the very real brink of all-out civil war? There were too many questions and not enough answers.

But the bloodshed had already started in the south. The Academy of Arcane Arts was under siege by the Iron Legion. There were mixed reports coming from the front. Some said that the Jade Army had engaged the Iron Legion. Some said that the whole of the Imperial contingent had been wiped out by some arcane force coming from the Academy. Others said that everyone had been wiped out exactly like Rashaleb. Whatever the truth was, and the horror of all the possibilities were almost too much to take in, the Academy may well have been lost to both sides, as well as a sizeable part of both sides' military. The Iron Legion was the most numerous of the Imperial Armies, with perhaps the possible exception of the Army of Blood in Zevarit. However, there was not a trained military man left to lead that army, now that Gregor had crossed over to the rebellion. Some said that the new Ruby Knight, Gabriel Shadowfall could have been a decent military commander, but he was busy running errands for Dominique. Seraph caught himself smiling at the thought. Dominique ordering around members of the Knights of the Flashing Blade.

On the side of the rebellion, the Army of Stone was impressive, as was the Jade Army, but now that the Army of Water had joined their ranks, Seraph's military skill and leadership on the battlefield rivaled that of Gregor Quicksilver, and he would put his troops up against any that Kaitain and his loyalists could manage. However, that certainly would mean going head to head with the Army of Fire, and that meant that Seraph would one day have to cross swords with Chelsea. All of the times they had clashed before, it had been over some imagined slight, or the flexing of impudent and arrogant royal muscle. The stakes had changed a great deal, and Seraph would not have to look across the battlefield and see Chelsea as a real enemy. Would he have what it took to strike her down in combat? Would he be able to draw her blood? Deep in his heart he knew that whatever doubts he might have, once the battle was joined, the famous Wolf of Saldarine would not hesitate to kill him if it meant doing her duty. Perhaps that was one of the reasons she was so much better than he was. She understood and accepted duty, and was not ruled by her passions the way he was. It would not have been her choice to marry him had her duty not compelled her. She would not be acting as the bodyguard of a woman she should have hated if it were not for her duty. Chelsea would never still be at the side of that pig Kaitain were it not for her adherence to her duty not only as a member of the Knights of the Flashing Blade, but as a loyal member of the Imperial Army and representative of an entire kingdom. Chelsea would never be royalty, but she had more integrity and passion for the fate of the Empire than a thousand royals.

Seraph shook away thoughts of his wife and looked back out at the courtyard. A small scuffle had begun to break out amongst the people. The division between those who supported Seraph's cause and those that supported peace was becoming more emotionally tense, and before too long the isolated pockets of violence would grow, and the Army of Water would have to deal with it. This caused two major problems. The first would be that the army would be taking direct action against the populous which would erode support of the army and of Seraph's leadership. The second problem was that as the violence worsened, the Army of Water would become more deeply entrenched in policing the populous and be less able to take the fight to Kaitain and his forces. The Army of Water would be immobilized, and would be an easy target for either the well-trained Army of Fire, or the lethally efficient Imperial Army. He would have to put a stop to this now, if he was going to have any chance of pulling his people together and stopping Kaitain. Taking a deep breath, Seraph Kore opened the doors leading out on to the third floor landing of the palace of Thorigald and waited for the shouting and confrontation below to subside. There were some shouts in his direction, but when he put one hand up, most of the shouting and cheering faded. Seraph swallowed hard. Public speaking was never his strong suit, and in a situation such as this he worried that he might do much more harm than good. But he had taken the steps that had touched off this situation, and he would have to make it work, no matter what.

"My fellow citizens of the great Kingdom of Thorigald," he began, trying to keep his voice as calm and even as possible, "this is a troubling time for the Empire of Cadaria, and so it is a troubling time for all who dwell within her borders. All of you know by now that I have been branded a traitor to the Empire. Many of you I'm sure believe the charges that have been levied against me. You feel that I am a criminal, not only for my attempt on the life of Emperor Kaitain Lorien, but also for my actions here against the royal families of Thorigald."

"Murderer!" one man cried out from the throng.

"Traitor!" another called.

Seraph raised his hands, and the shouts calmed again, but the mood of the crowd was on a knife's edge. Seraph could feel the tension rising, not only from the crowd, but from the soldiers that ringed the courtyard. They would act to put down any threat to their lord, and would not hesitate in the execution of their duties, no matter how unpleasant that duty might be. It seemed that the whole of the city had now become surrendered to the moment, fate perching on every word he would utter.

"You call me a traitor! You scream for justice to be visited on a murderer!"

There was some sporadic cheering, but Seraph continued through.

"But where is the justice for those who died in Rashaleb? Where is the justice for the hundreds who have lost their lives in this futile war against the dragons who had lived here peacefully on this land for thousands of years? Where is the justice for the men and women who are dying now in Jelan?"

A hush fell over the crowd. They all sensed something was about to happen.

"My duty as a Knight of the Flashing Blade was to protect the Emperor, but moreover, my duty was to protect the Empire. All of the Knights of the Flashing Blade are duty-bound to protect the Empire of Cadaria from all threats against her borders. But what if that threat is posed by the man sitting on the throne? What if the greatest danger to the lives of the people of Cadaria is the man who was entrusted with their care? I put to you that Kaitain Lorien is responsible for all of the ills that now befall this land, and the three years of his rule have been marked with nothing but blood and misery."

Some supporting shouts started now, and Seraph seized on them as he continued.

"Some of you say I'm a traitor, but what would I have been if I did not attempt to stop the threat that Kaitain has become? It was my duty to come to the defense of the people of Cadaria. It was my duty to take the fight to Kaitain and those who are loyal to his banner! It is my duty to protect you and to protect Cadaria!"

The small pockets of cheers grew. More of the crowd had been enthralled.

"Is Gregor Quicksilver, the hero of Cadaria a traitor for standing up against the tyranny of a villain like Kaitain?"

"No!" the crowd surged.

"Is Hannah Ironheart, the High Priestess of the Church of the Creator a traitor for following the teachings of the church and defending the innocent from Kaitain's wicked crusade?"

"No!" the crowd called nearly in unison.

"Are the people of Albitonin and Galateria traitors for wanting to defend their homes and have peace returned to their lives?"

"No!"

"Then are the people of Thorigald, their soldiers, and their leaders traitors for wanting to bring an end to Kaitain Lorien and his cruel and irresponsible rule?"

"No!"

The single word shouted in unison dissolved into a chorus of cheers and chants and applause. Many chanted Seraph's name, while others chanted the name of the kingdom. They blurred together into an almost unintelligible mess, but what was clear was that sentiment had shifted fully in favor of Seraph's carefully crafted vision, and even the members of the Army of Water who had been on the edge of deadly action had visibly relaxed and taken up with the cheers for their commander.

"My people," Seraph started again, and waited until the cheers had faded so that he did not have to scream over the din. "We have come to a crossroads in the history of Cadaria. A call has gone up from the people that the Lorien line has failed us. Kaitain Lorien has failed his people, and so must be removed from his position. But our fight is not with just Kaitain Lorien, it is with the years of neglect and self-indulgence that has corrupted the leaders of the kingdoms. They remain loyal to Kaitain because it keeps them in power. They back his wars and help spread the misery he breeds through their greed and inaction. Our brothers and sisters in the kingdoms still chained to Kaitain's will are the victims, not our enemies. We must take the fight to the royalty that helps Kaitain to enact his evil whims. We must chip away at the armor that protects the Emperor and free our fellow Cadarians from their bondage. They may not be in chains, but I say to you that they are just as much slaves to Kaitain's will."

There was another cheer that went up.

"Death to Kaitain!"

The voice was a single one at first. Then another joined the call, and another. The chant spread through the crowd, until they all chanted it as one.

"We must free our brothers and sisters," Seraph continued, "we must help them see that they are held under the thumb of a madman. We must start this quest with our ancient enemy, the people of Saldarine. If the rest of Cadaria sees us help them shed their yoke of fealty to this tarnished throne, there can be no doubt as to the sincerity of our cause."

The chant turned to another chorus of cheers, the infectious frenzy spreading like wildfire. The courtyard had continued to fill as word spread about what was happening, and the streets and pathways were packed with people.

"In three days," Seraph called, his voice beginning to waver and rasp, "the Army of Water shall begin the march to the Plains of Steam. We will bring this revolution to the doorstep of our brothers and sisters in Saldarine, and we will help them into the bosom of our cause. Together we will take Aldere by force, and we will bring an end to the cowardice and the vice. We will bring an end to the injustice and death. Once again we will have peace in Cadaria, and once again the people of Cadaria will be able to trust that the Emperor is their protector and not their oppressor."

The crowd exploded in another round of cheers, and Seraph waved to the people before stepping back into the room and shutting the doors. He could still clearly hear the chants, alternating between calling his name and shouting for the end of Kaitain's rule. Seraph was exhausted, but he could not help smiling. When he turned away from the window, he saw a man standing across the room. When the visitor locked eyes with the new Lord of Thorigald, he began clapping slowly.

"A very nice speech," the tortured voice said after a moment, "very nice indeed."

Seraph took hold of the hilt of the Sacred Weapon strapped to his hip and fell into a defensive posture. The figure of the Grey Man Pestilence did not move or react, and simply allowed his head to lull slightly to the left with an amused grin.

* * * * * * * * * * * *

Jerrard Mistic and his wife sat at the small table in an anteroom to the kitchen in the depths of the palace of Celidar quietly eating their dinner. Like most of the royal palaces across the face of Cadaria, the palace of Celidar also had a formal dining hall as well as a smaller royal dining room, but when days were difficult and the Lord and Lady of Celidar wanted to distance themselves from the titles they had been granted, they found solace in the simple table near the kitchen. The room was most often used by the cooks and the servants, but more often than not, the simple table had far more refined occupants. Since the visit from their wayward daughter, Jerrard and Erika found themselves wanting the seclusion of the simple life more and more. Both felt the changes on the wind, and both knew that the wars that were to come made the bloodshed happening at that moment across Cadaria but a trickle in the face of the coming tidal wave. If any of them survived the carnage that was on the horizon, it would be a miracle. There was a brief knock on the door to the anteroom, and by the time Jerrard had looked in the direction of the door, it had opened and a page rushed through. He faltered for a moment before coming to attention and waiting to be recognized.

"Yes?" Jerrard said casually.

"I'm terribly sorry to disturb you my lord, my lady, but there are visitors at the gate, and they request an urgent audience."

Jerrard looked down at his plate and then to his wife. Her face painted the picture that was being played out in his mind. It was certainly unusual to receive audience requests at that late of an hour, but those circumstances were reserved for the gravest of situations. The page reached forward and handed a scrap of cloth to Jerrard.

"The visitors gave me this to present to you," the page said finally.

Jerrard opened the piece of fabric and felt his heart sink.

"Let the visitors in and have them brought to the audience chamber. Make sure to take them through the back corridors, and also clear the audience chamber of all servants and guards before they are brought in. I want as few people as possible to know they are here."

The page nodded and scurried off to fulfill his orders. Erika met Jerrard's eyes the next moment and her puzzled glance caused him to press the piece of fabric into his wife's hands. Her eyes widened too with realization. On the simple piece of cloth was the crest of the Lorien family, specifically the personal crest of Prince Feyd Lorien.

* * * * * * * * * * * *

Feyd hobbled noticeably, but Felicia helped her father keep as much of a regal air as possible as the three weary travelers were led through the royal palace of Celidar for their audience with the Lord and Lady Mistic. Both were surprised at how empty the palace seemed. Wynne kept pace with the Prince and Princess, his distance respectful of their station. Though the page had wanted him to surrender his weapons, it had been Feyd and not Wynne whose objection caused the page to color with embarrassment. The journey from Pellatori to Celidar had been difficult to say the least, and Feyd was still in a great deal of pain. He had no patience for the niceties of court, especially at this late hour, and he would not stand for Wynne to be insulted as though he were a common thug. The man had more than proven himself worthy of the respect a royal guardsman would be afforded. The important thing now was that they had made it to Celidar, and if Wynne was right, this was the safest place they could be right now.

Upon entering the audience chamber, Feyd and Felicia were kept waiting only a matter of moments before Lord and Lady Mistic entered the room. Felicia watched as the surprise blossomed on their faces, but it took her a moment to realize that the surprise was not from the appearance of the Prince and Princess Lorien in their court, but rather for the attendance of Wynne. There was certainly recognition there, as Felicia had expected, but not what she saw in the eyes of Lord Mistic. However, the look was quickly suppressed.

"Prince Feyd, Princess Felicia," Jerrard began, "we're both relieved you are safe. When we heard the reports out of Lordhill of the attempt on your lives, and then your disappearance, we feared the worst. Then when the reports came about your personal guardsman Galen being found barely alive, many believed that you had both been killed. Then of course when Galen was later found with his throat slit, the fear was that much greater."

Felicia was shocked to hear about Galen. She had watched him fall at the hand of the assassin, how did he walk away from the ambush? Why had he not been with them during their escape? How was it that he was later assassinated? She shook the thoughts away as she heard her father speak.

"We would have been the victims of the assassin's blade had it not been for our savior here. Wynne believed that we would be safe here for a time, until we can discover the source of this plot against our lives and take a more offensive posture. I must admit I am not a proponent of running from a fight, no matter how injured I may be."

"My father will require your best healers, Lord Mistic," Felicia said, taking a more diplomatic tone. "And any hospitality you can offer would be welcome."

Jerrard nodded.

"The palace of Celidar and the whole of my kingdom is at your disposal."

Feyd and Felicia both bowed, though Feyd's bow was much shallower than his daughter's. Jerrard then moved his gaze to Wynne.

"Wynne, is it?" Jerrard said slowly. "I thank you for your service in the name of the Empire of Cadaria, and I'm sure that you will be generously rewarded for your deeds of bravery in the defense of the Lorien family. Surely your family awaits your return?"

Wynne smiled.

"My wife would certainly not be happy if she knew where I was."

Felicia felt her heart sink.

"And there is no need to trouble my family," he continued. "If the Prince and Princess would have me, I would like to continue to see to their safety, at least until we're sure that their attackers have been truly dealt with."

Felicia answered, trying not to clench her teeth.

"We could scarcely want for a better defender."

Jerrard nodded.

"I shall see you well bestowed, Wynne," he said flatly, "and I look forward to hearing more about your adventures."

* * * * * * * * * * * *

Pestilence kept his hands at his sides, the look of pure amusement on his face. Seraph made no moves other than to draw his weapon. For some reason he hesitated. He knew that he should strike the demon down as quickly as possible, but hadn't that already been done? Pestilence was already defeated, so how could he be standing in the royal palace of Thorigald?

"You speak well, Lord Seraph Kore, but how do you intend to make good on your promises? How do you intended to free your brothers and sisters from the grip of the evil Kaitain? And what will you do if those brothers and sisters do not see the enlightened view that your crusade offers to them? What if they take up arms against you? What will you do then? Will you shed the blood of innocents who know no better? All those poor souls lost…"

Seraph snarled.

"You don't give a damn about the people you demon. You've killed more than I could in ten lifetimes of honest warfare."

Pestilence laughed.

"What is honest about your brand of warfare? The dead are dead no matter how much honesty and honor you approach the killing with. And yes, I have killed, but I care about the souls that I welcome into the service of Dorovar. They serve a higher cause, and they sing once released from the mundanity of their petty lives."

Seraph became aware of a green glow filling the room and a chattering sound filling his ears.

"Many will lose their lives in your crusade," Pestilence continued, "so much blood and so many lost souls. And for what do they die? This is not a conflict of their making, but they are victims of it nonetheless. You know the evil of men like Kaitain. You have seen it all your life, Lord Seraph."

Seraph could not help but nod. The chattering in the back of his mind was maddening, but he was starting to hear something in it. Something like singing, or maybe chanting. There was a low rumbling beneath it. Something primal. Something ancient and cold.

"You could help erase that evil," Pestilence said taking a step forward. "You could help save the souls of those you spoke so highly of. Help them serve a higher purpose than simply the defeat of one corrupt man. What is to stop the next man sat upon the throne of Cadaria from continuing the horrors that Kaitain began? Is it not possible that the next man is worse than Kaitain?"

Seraph had not thought of the possibility before. Pestilence was right. Kaitain could just be the beginning. The primal rumbling was getting stronger. It was almost like it was saying something.

"But are men to blame for this? Are men to blame for power bringing out their baser natures? Or is it something else? Someone else?"

Seraph's mind swam. He should not be listening, but the Grey Man was making too much sense. It was all wrong, but all right at the same time.

"The Creator made you this way, this fragile, and he lets these atrocities take place. Dorovar can make the pain go away. He can save the lives and the souls of those you love the most. He can see that they never feel pain again."

For the first time, the primal voice broke through the chorus. Seraph heard it clearly.

Dorovar....

"The souls you will save can help bring the Creator crashing down from his throne in the heavens. He can be made to pay for all the suffering he has caused by allowing evil beings such as Kaitain to exist. Greedy men who take what they want, even if those things belong to others."

Seraph sneered.

Dorovar....

The green glow intensified, and Seraph became aware of another presence in the room. It was ancient and powerful, but at the same time, Seraph felt the being's need. A need to take revenge for the wrong done to it. To take revenge for the needless suffering. A need to topple the very Creator who made it all possible.

Dorovar....

"Come to us, Seraph Kore. Bring us the holy war that will swell the ranks of the Choir of Souls. Bring us a war that will set fire to the heavens and bring them all crashing down as the Dark Gods once fell. Become a whirlwind of retribution for all those wronged by the Creator. Become Dorovar's War."

The Grey Man extended a hand. Seraph didn't hesitate before reaching out and taking the demon's hand. Pestilence smiled and the green glow pulsed.

"Soon you will be one of us," Pestilence said smiling.

"I must fulfill one final task," Seraph said finally, "and then this whole world shall burn."

Iron and Jade

Year Three of the Just Emperor Kaitain "Dragonsbane" Lorien, Creator's Calendar Year 1870

From where she stood in the Master's Council chambers, Jastra Mythryn watched as the first hail of arrow rained down on the courtyards of the Academy of Arcane Arts. Before the negotiations had begun, Aris and Fiona had made sure that all of the students were in the safest places possible, and the only people left in the courtyard were the detachment of the Jade Army under the command of Rory Blackrock. They were clinging to the inner walls of the courtyards to avoid the incoming fire, but were preparing for their opportunity to fulfill their role as defenders of the Academy. Ashinica and Rory had returned from their unsuccessful negotiations only minutes before the bombardment began, and as the doors to the Master's Council chambers opened, Jastra, Fiona, and Aris turned to welcome the Master of Stone. Fiona approached the smaller woman quickly and wrapped her arms around Ashinica. The embrace was short but meaningful. However, when Fiona pulled away and looked into Ashinica's eyes, there an expression closer to triumph than to dejectedness.

"There was nothing you could have done, Ashinica," Aris said in a supportive tone, "this invasion was inevitable. The important thing now is insuring that the students and the records of the Academy are safe, and are not allowed to fall into the hands of the Imperial forces."

The front lines of the Imperial forces were advancing cautiously, their initial charge seemingly blunted by the superior tactics of the defending army's leader. Falling in waves upon the walls of the Academy while there was a defense force may not have been the soundest tactic, but it would have worked as a brute force solution. However, there would have been considerable losses. This more cautious and reserved advance allowed for two possibilities. The first possibility was that the general of the Imperial Army, Bernhardt Yeoman believed that help was too far away to be an issue. If this was the case, Bernhardt would not feel pressured to overwhelm the Academy in one swift thrust and could try every way possible to prevent as much bloodshed as possible. The other possibility, and the one that Jastra believed to be the most likely was the Bernhardt Yeoman was worried about a possible counterattack of magical means. What was not common knowledge was that the Moonstone Knight had a very pronounced mistrust of magic and those who used it. This was both the worst and best responsibility for Bernhardt. The best because he had the possibility to eliminate that which he did not trust or understand, and also the worst because it was the one fear that nagged him deeply.

"The important thing now is to determine what we must do to defend the Academy," the Master of Energy said, steel filling her voice. "We cannot depend on the full Jade Army arriving to defend us, and we know that the few soldiers that are here under the command of Commander Blackrock will not be enough to turn back the assault of so many troops. We must consider using our abilities to defend these walls."

Fiona turned sharply, the anger rising to her face.

"What you are suggesting is against the highest tenants we hold as the Masters of the Academy of Arcane Arts, and I as the acting Headmaster of this Academy forbid you to even mention such things."

Jastra turned away from the window, and smoothed her dress.

"Our rules allow for those of us who are threatened with violence to defend ourselves by any means necessary. I'm not talking about going on the offensive, or using the abilities that we have to strike out at the army directly, but we have many powers at our disposal that could be used to aid in the defense of the Academy grounds itself. The Master of Stone could create a trench around the grounds, the Master of Air could create a dense fog to obscure the vision of the archers. The Master of Fire could burn the arrows out of the sky as they approached. There are many possibilities that would not violate out laws."

Fiona seemed to consider the words for a moment, when Ashinica chimed in.

"The Master of Stone would not be opposed to the measures that the Master of Energy is suggesting, provided that no offensive measures were taken against the members of the Iron Legion. And that any actions taken are taken by the members of the Master's Council alone; that no acolytes or initiates are involved."

Fiona didn't have time to look back at Ashinica before Aris added her voice.

"The Master of Air will consent to these measures, under the terms outlined by the Master of Stone."

Shock filled Fiona's heart, and she looked at her daughter. For the first time Fiona didn't see the girl that she had raised. She saw a mature woman who had stepped into her role as a Master of the Academy of Arcane Arts. While all at once she was proud of her daughter, Fiona inwardly wished that Aris had picked another time to take a stand.

"The Master of Energy consents to these terms."

Fiona sighed and shook her head. Though the measures suggested by both Jastra and Ashinica did not violate the letter of the law of the Academy, in some ways it did violate the spirit that the law was meant to embody. Part of Fiona wondered what Alistair Ravenheart would have done if he were standing in the room with them now. Would he feel that it was more important to protect the Academy and the students, or more important to protect the spirit that the Academy stood for? As the acting Headmaster of the Academy, it didn't matter how many of the Masters voted for something to take place, she could still override them. However, in a tense situation like this, she risked the others taking independent action and involving some of the students in their plans. This way, any actions taken in the name of the Academy would be taken by the Masters alone, and so any responsibility would fall on the Masters, sparing the students should things go badly. Finally, Fiona nodded.

"Under these terms, the Master of Fire agrees. The Creator help us."

* * * * * * * * * * * *

Bernhardt Yeoman, the Moonstone Knight stood at the crest of the hill looking down on the Academy of Arcane Arts and inwardly dreaded what was happening. The small group from the Jade Army would be no match for the Iron Legion once the full charge had been ordered, and the archer fire was just setting up for the inevitable. Any resistance would be crushed in the first charge. The Academy was in a very defensible position, but nothing was invested to take advantage of the landscape or the lack of good approaches. But then, this place was designed to be a school, not a fortress. By nightfall, the entire Academy would be under the control of the Iron Legion, and then if the rest of the Jade army did appear, it would be too late, and they would have to invest in a prolonged siege at the cost of many lives and perhaps the whole of the Academy itself. Bernhardt would burn the whole place to the ground before he would allow it to be taken by the rebellion.

"General!" one of his lieutenants cried out.

Bernhardt didn't have to ask what had captured the man's attention. He saw it with his own eyes, and even still he did not fully believe it. He should have known that this siege would not have been as easy as simply walking through the front gates. The challenge would never have been the number of men or arms that were brought to bear by the Jade Army or any other force that would have chosen to defend Jelan. The worry was if the Masters of the Academy chose to use their abilities to defend what was sacred to them. Now, as Bernhardt watched an entire wall of arrows vaporize in mid-air, he knew that the chances for a quick and relatively bloodless occupation were gone. Even as the archers prepared for another volley, a large bank of fog rolled in on the valley. It was a massive bank of dense fog that obscured most of the buildings of the Academy, and made precision targeting, or even seeing what was going on in the courtyards impossible. Then there was a rumble from somewhere. It seemed to be coming from the direction of the Academy but it rose and fell, seeming to come from everywhere and nowhere all at once. Fear set in for Bernhardt after a moment, wondering whether the whole of the hillside would crumble. But the rumbling stopped a minute after it had begun, and there appeared to be no adverse effects to Bernhardt's troops. But an upheaval like that couldn't just be for show. Something had happened.

"Sir," the lieutenant said after a moment, "what are your orders? The target is completely obscured, and there is too much danger that the volleys will hit something unintended. But after what happened to the last volley, the master archers aren't even sure that their arrows will get through. Shall I order the charge?"

Bernhardt pondered for a moment, and then shook his head.

"Order a slow advance," he said taking Gravity into his hand, "scout in front. I have a feeling the Masters have left a few surprises for us on the approach to the Academy. I have no doubt that once our soldiers are in the valley they will barely be able to see their hand in front of their face, let alone the enemy sneaking up on them."

"Surely the enemy would be at the same disadvantage, sir."

Bernhardt looked at his subordinate, and then sighed.

"I only wish I could be as sure about that. Remember, we are dealing with the most powerful wielders of arcane power in Cadaria. I would not put it past them to have some ability to grant their allies ways to see through their tricks. Even if only a small group were able to see clearly in that soup, they would be able to kill perhaps twenty or thirty of our men before we got one of theirs. And not only that, once engaged, how could our men even know if they were striking the enemy or one of their own. All that valley has become is a death trap."

"And yet we still advance."

The implication was out of line, but Bernhardt would not chastise his subordinate for saying exactly what he was thinking. But time was not their ally. The more they were delayed by these tricks, the more time the Jade Army under the command of Leonora Wastri had to box them in. Once that happened, even the Iron Legion would have difficulty withdrawing from the field. They were isolated, too far away from secure supply lines, and in the very heart of what was now enemy territory. If Bernhardt did not think it would mean his execution, he would order the retreat now. So, he couldn't go back, he couldn't stay where he was, therefore the only option was to go forward.

"We serve at the pleasure of the Emperor of Cadaria, and he orders that we take this rebel stronghold at all costs. They have thrown down the gauntlet and so we must be strong enough to pick it up and strike them down with it if need be. Order the advance, and I shall lead our troops on the field."

The lieutenant looked shocked for a moment and then snapped a quick salute before running off to relay the orders to the rest of the men. As the word circulated that Bernhardt himself would take the field, a huge cheer ran through the ranks. The longer this went on, the more would die, and Bernhardt would not allow himself to leave the field of battle disgraced, cowering in his command tent. He would meet the enemy with Gravity in his hand and his troops at his back, and if he were going to leave the field, he would walk off victorious; otherwise, he would be buried where he fell.

* * * * * * * * * * * *

Leonora Wastri watched as the fog rolled in around the Academy of Arcane Arts and smiled. She had not thought that the Masters would use their abilities to defend themselves, but she was happy with the choice they had made. Rory Blackrock, one of her trusted commanders was on the grounds of the Academy, and he would be starting to send small groups of his soldiers to defend key positions around the perimeter of the Academy. The Iron Legion was immense, and with a single full charge, they could level the school and cut through any opposition that got in their way. But now the sides were more even. Leonora looked back down the cliff and saw her troops moving steadily through the ravine. In a matter of two or three hours they would be in a position to mount a rear charge on the Iron Legion's command group. Such a tactic was not without risk though, and Leonora knew that she was matching wits with one of the greatest military minds in the Empire. Bernhardt had been wise to take the high ground closest to the Academy. It cut off most of the escape avenues, as well as gave him a nearly unlimited view into the grounds of the Academy. The problem was that his rear flank was totally exposed. The ravine that the Jade Army were currently advancing through ran to the base of the hill where the Iron Legion command post had been set upon, and then out to the sea on the northern and southwestern flanks of the Academy. However, though his flank was exposed, Bernhardt's army was not without the tactical advantage of the high ground. The hill was steeper on his flank, and to charge up it would expend a great deal of effort and take much longer than it should. This would give the Iron Legion time to prepare for combat, and if they had taken any steps to ready anti-siege or anti-charge provisions on that side of the hill, such an advance could be catastrophic. But the defense of the Academy was worth the risk. It could not be allowed to fall into the hands of the Emperor, no matter the cost. Such power could not be perverted. Even if it meant that the whole of the Academy would need to be sacrificed for the greater good. Leonora made her way easily down the cliff and rejoined her troops. By morning, the fight for the Academy of Arcane Arts would be decided, and the only true outcome was that death would be the victor.

* * * * * * * * * * * *

The scouts found the trenches long before advancing lines of the Iron Legion made it to the walls of the Academy. It would slow the advance, but it did not make things impossible. However the hit and run assaults from the small detachment of the Jade Army had proven to be even more bothersome than Bernhardt had anticipated. Another of the green-clad soldiers had fallen under the weight of Bernhardt's strike when a huge cry went up from behind him. It came from the direction of the hill where the archers and a large portion of the Iron Legion still waited. It was the reinforcements and the second line. It took only a moment for Bernhardt to place the cry, it was a charge order, but not directed toward the Academy. Another force had taken the field, and it could have only been the Jade Army come to aid their fellows in defense of Jelan.

"Fall back to the command post!" Bernhardt yelled out.

He heard his order echoed through the ranks, and the advance portion of the Iron Legion surged back toward the hill as fast as they could manage. Speed however did not equate to care, and more than one soldier found himself at the bottom of one of the randomly placed ditches that had been carved by the Masters. When Bernhardt and his soldiers did manage to make it back to the top of the hill, he found that the reserves were fully engaged with the elite members of the Jade Army who had taken the perilous charge up the far side of the hill. Many were already dead on both sides, but the Jade Army was gaining ground, and a group had already burst up into the encampment. That was when Bernhardt saw her. Leonora Wastri was at the head of a small group of soldiers, cutting her way through his troops as though they were so much wheat in the field. The long elegant Sacred Weapon, Wisdom, arced and struck with amazing precision for a weapon its size. The two-foot long blade attached to a five-foot haft flowed smoothly from strike to strike, a credit to both the design of the weapon and the skill of the woman who wielded it. The blade darted between plates of armor, severing limbs, ripping at throats, and creating massive amounts of carnage. Bernhardt gripped hard to the haft of Gravity and charged forward. He swung two steps before he would come in contact with Leonora, but the momentum of his charge carried him forward and the two Sacred Weapons met in mid-air, the head of Gravity colliding with the finely polished and curved bladed of Wisdom.

A sound came from the colliding of the two weapons, and many soldiers would have nightmares for the rest of their lives with that sound tearing through their minds. It contained the screams of thousands of dying men and women, the screams of loves lost, and the sound that a heart must make when it breaks, a thousand times over. The force of the two weapons colliding forced both Leonora and Bernhardt had to fall back a few steps. More members of the Jade Army surged forward, and the numbers were looking more and more even as the moments passed. Bernhardt charged forward again, this time his strike was aimed at the ground at Leonora's feet. As if she sensed what was coming, Leonora leapt into the air and almost floated back several feet. Gravity hit the ground and the hillside groaned with the impact. A huge fissure opened, and the crack extended several feet in all directions like a sunburst radiating from the head of Gravity. A few soldiers found their footing suddenly robbed from them, and more than a few found their lives ended a moment later by an opponent who had been able to keep his feet. Blood flowed freely on the hilltop. Leonora struck down two more members of the Iron Legion before Bernhardt had recovered his weapon. This time instead of charging, he whipped the hammer up around his head and then let it fly in the direction of the Jade Knight. Rather than attempt to block the strike, Leonora rolled out of the way, and then charged where Bernhardt stood. But Bernhardt was ready. As if commanded, Gravity stopped and hung in mid-air, and then changed directions. The tactic surprised Leonora, and she caught a glancing blow on the shoulder from the massive weapon. She was thrown ten feet across the top of the hill and crashed into a knot of Iron Legionnaires. But even in her surprised state, the five soldiers were no match for her superior skill. They fell swiftly, and Leonora was back on her feet. The piece of armor that had shielded her shoulder was a ruined mess, and a large crack now ran down the front of her breastplate. Gravity had returned to Bernhardt's hands, and he settled himself for another assault.

Leonora darted forward, the tip of Wisdom at ground level, when she suddenly stopped a few steps from Bernhardt and pulled the blade of Wisdom up in a long arc as though she was trying to strike at something in the sky. A wave of force erupted from where the weapon's blade passed, and it slammed into Bernhardt's chest. He was thrown from his feet, and he knew in an instant that several of his ribs had been crushed by the blow. He coughed and rasped, and could taste blood in his mouth. Perhaps more had been damaged than just his ribs. But Gravity would help him heal, and after a moment he was able to force his way back to his feet. Leonora was not going to give him more time to breathe and recover than she had to, and she was on top of him the next moment, bringing the blade of Wisdom down hard. Bernhardt was able to get the haft of Gravity up in time to block the blow, and pivoted his hip with the strike, causing Leonora to shift to his left, and allowing him to bring the head of Gravity around in a low-power strike to her exposed left ribs. She cried out in pain as the blow struck, and Bernhardt could hear the sound of breaking bones. But Leonora would not allow herself to be taken out of the fight so easily. As the force of Bernhardt's blow propelled her away, she twisted and brought the blade of Wisdom back to bear. It flashed upwards toward the Moonstone Knight's face. The razor-sharp blade found his chin and tore up through skin, tendon, and muscle; ripping open his cheek and digging a deep furrow into the cheekbone itself before continuing up to his left eye.

There was still enough force in the strike for the tip of Wisdom's blade to rupture the soft tissue of his left eye, and then carving a notch in his brow. The whole left side of Bernhardt's face was a ruined mess, and he cried out in pain. Both members of the Knights of the Flashing Blade fell, neither of their wounds fatal, but more than enough damage had been done to take a great deal of the fight out of them. Soldiers from their respective armies rallied around their fallen leaders, and it was as though the conflict had taken a long breath.

It was then that fate would intervene. Leonora watched as heads began to turn away from the conflict and horrified gazes shifted to the direction of the Academy of Arcane Arts. The Jade Knight forced herself back to her feet and turned to look at the Academy, her blood immediately feeling as though it had been replaced by ice. The fog had cleared from around the Academy, and the great trenches that had been dug by the Masters were now apparent. There were small groups of members of the Jade Army that still held key positions around the walls of the Academy, but what stood between the hill and the Academy could barely be believed. What must have been hundreds or perhaps thousands of swirling blue man-sized ovals had appeared all over the grounds outside the Academy, and many of them in the air as well. As soon as the ovals had finished forming, creatures began emerging from all of them, until the whole of the valley was filled with ranks and ranks of the tall, lean, red-skinned creatures. Leonora had seen the creatures many times on her tours through Galateria, and she knew that they were called Jeresei. From the portals that floated in the air, great winged beasts with metallic skin poured through, their massive bat-like wings beating against the air. There could have been a hundred of the Shadowwalkers there, and tens of thousands of the Jeresei on the ground. Inside the grounds of the Academy, five larger portals appeared, and out of them stepped massive creatures made of Stone, and they stood at the walls of the Academy like great colossi, ready to crush anything that wandered too close. At the crest of the hill, perhaps twenty feet from where Leonora now stood, eight more of the portals opened, two a foot in front of the other six. From the back row of portals, six animals emerged, large and vicious looking. Three were white tigers, with black stripes, while the other three were black panthers, all with golden eyes and snarling faces. Their bright white fangs gleamed in the retreating sunlight. Finally two figures emerged from the foremost portals. The man was dressed all in black, with long black hair and a jet black goatee. The woman was dress purely in white, her red hair long and hanging to her shoulders. Both of their eyes were as blue as the sky on a rainy day.

"Representatives of the Empire of Cadaria acting in the name of Emperor Kaitain Lorien," the man began.

"And representatives of the Empire of Cadaria acting in the name of Empress Marlae Lorien," the woman continued.

"You are hereby ordered to withdraw from this field," the man concluded, "or you shall forfeit your lives. The Academy of Arcane Arts is now under the protection of Lord Rael and Lady Trece Starlin."

Chapter LIX

Melodious Silence

Year Three of the Just Emperor Kaitain "Dragonsbane" Lorien, Creator's Calendar Year 1870

Jillian sat, her mind troubled, as conversation continued around the table. Dane's words haunted her, and no matter what was being said around her, all she could hear ringing in her ears were his simple words. 'Dorovar wanted her.' In the time since the Grey Man Pestilence had made his first appearance, there had been many whispers about a creature named Dorovar. It was apparently the force behind all of the terrible things that were happening around Cadaria, and was the master of Pestilence, Famine, and Death. It was after the disaster in Rashaleb that the name Dorovar began to be whispered like a curse in the night. And now, this creature whatever it was wanted her. There was a roar of laughter around the table, and Jillian realized that she had been missing out on one of Blade's famous stories, and even the reserved Isa was chuckling along with the rest of the group. Jillian also realized that the food sitting on her plate had barely been touched and was now long cold. But there was a stone in the pit of her stomach, a cold hard stone that robbed her of all hunger, and that stone was one of fear and uncertainty. She wanted so much to hear what Dane and Vallic were talking about. But now the rest of the group was breaking up, and the few servants that tended the house were showing the guests to their rooms. Jillian lingered at the table until it was just she and Isa sitting there.

"It's unfair for those your age to be thrust into these kinds of situations without knowing everything that you should," the older woman said after she was sure that no one else would hear her words. "But the longer you are alive, the more you will realize that the world simply is not designed on any level to be fair."

Jillian regarded Isa for a moment and expected to see a smile on her face. When people said that life wasn't fair, it was supposed to be a joke, or an attempt to bring levity to a situation that shouldn't have a bright spot. But there was no such attempted joviality on the woman's face. There was sorrow there, and perhaps a bit of pity. While normally such expressions would have raised Jillian's ire, she could not help this time but feel the genuineness of the woman's words.

"It took me a very long time to realize that truth," she continued in the same somber voice. "And it made the first several years with Vallic difficult. He is a private man, and a man that is possessed with such secrets that he cannot share with even those closest to him. It creates a very isolated existence for him, and though there is little I can do to help him, I try my best to be here when he needs me. However, there are some people, like your friend Dane there, who do seem to share a level of understanding of what Vallic is burdened with. I'm not sure though whether that makes Vallic's life better or worse."

Jillian listened intently, but Isa stopped speaking and looked in the direction that Dane and Vallic had gone. Jillian herself turned and saw Dane walking back, his head down, and his hands thrust into the pockets of his simple pants. There was a frown there that did not fit his demeanor, and Dane suddenly seemed much older than he had in the moments previous to leaving the table. Vallic had not returned with Dane. Isa and Dane locked eyes for a moment, and then Isa quietly excused herself from the table and moved in the direction of the library. Dane sat down in a chair across from Jillian and took a long drink from one of the wine glasses before pouring himself another full glass.

"I take it your conversation with Vallic didn't go well," Jillian hazarded.

"Went as well as can always be expected," Dane replied after another long swallow of the sharp liquid. "Vallic and I have a complicated relationship. Always have."

Dane fell silent and reached for the mug of wine again.

"I never would have expected that you knew a member of the Knights of the Flashing Blade, or that we would be staying in a place such as this while on the run from the Imperial Guard and this Dorovar creature."

Dane cocked his head to the side and gave a languid smile.

"It's amazing the places you find yourself when fate takes a guiding hand."

There was nothing condescending in his tone, but Jillian could not help but feel that in a way Dane was mocking her with his words.

"So what is it you're not telling me?"

Jillian didn't have many tactics to leverage against Dane. She didn't know him very well, other than he was something of a holy man who had the habit of not acting like one. He showed all of the traits of a warrior, one that had seen a great many things, but he held himself in such a way that he could have been a farmer or something else common.

"More than you can imagine."

His tone was flat, matter-of-fact, and irritating. Jillian could feel her teeth grating together, but she was surprised the next moment when he asked a question of his own.

"What is it you're not telling me?"

With this question he looked up, right into her eyes. There was something there that she hadn't seen in his eyes before. It was a power that had been hidden, a power that should have inspired, but caused her to shiver deep in her core. She felt her head swimming; like she was lost in an ocean of sensation, but the only thing she could focus on was his eyes.

"I don't know what you're talking about."

Her own voice sounded so distant in her ears, like she was shouting down a long tunnel. Her field of vision was empty except for his eyes. Those deep mysterious eyes and the sparkle of green at their core.

"Who are you and why does Dorovar want you?"

His voice was so soothing and melodic. Like the sound of the rain on the roof, lulling her to a quiet slumber. She felt so calm and at ease in his presence, and trusted him implicitly.

"I'm Jillian Corven, though that wasn't the name I was born with," her voice had dropped to nearly a monotone. She didn't know why she was telling him this, but she trusted Dane and wanted him to know everything about her. She needed him to know the truth. Those bright eyes of his beckoned the truth and he deserved to hear it.

"And what was the name you were born with?"

His voice was so kind and reassuring.

"I was born Jillian Feris, my mother was Jehna Feris, the Dark Seer. But she was taken by the Demon Dragon Shadowweaver when he burned our village to the ground. I never saw her again. That's why I hunt dragons, because they destroyed everything I knew and loved, and stole my mother from me."

There was a new edge to Dane's voice when he spoke again.

"Your father. Who was your father?"

Something in her mind cried out. It felt like she was being shaken to the core. She wanted so much to answer Dane's questions, she needed so much for him to know everything about her, all of the secrets that she had buried deep in her soul. Her mouth worked, but no sound would come out. She tried to make the thoughts form in her mind, but they would not.

"Who is your father?" he repeated again.

She couldn't answer, and she felt the pain and the regret of it begin to build inside of her. She couldn't disappoint him, but she couldn't make herself answer.

"Dane!"

The voice from outside destroyed the peace and blackness that held her, and Jillian found herself sitting at the table again, looking into the now very ordinary dark eyes of Dane Rhuiden, the simple monk who had been their savior back in Hedorah. There was a haze that had descended over her mind, and suddenly she felt very tired. Before she knew what was happening, Isa was at her side, helping her to her feet, mumbling something about getting her into a fresh warm bed. The thought of laying down and going to sleep filled Jillian with a sense of peace, and she allowed herself to be led wordlessly to her room.

＊ ＊ ＊ ＊ ＊ ＊ ＊ ＊ ＊ ＊ ＊ ＊

"That was unwise."

Dane sat, watching Jillian be led away, and as soon as she was out of his line of sight, he swung his glance to Vallic Ultiv, who stood with his arms crossed at the edge of the dining room. Finally, Dane shrugged his shoulders.

"It may have been unwise, but at least I have a little bit more information than I had before tonight. If Jillian really is the daughter of Jehna Feris that would explain one of the reasons he wants her. Dorovar has never been able to perceive the future, no matter how many of the forbidden tools have been at his disposal. And now that the talents of the Dark Seer and the Maldovrin Triplets are out of his reach, the only option left would be Jehna's daughter."

Vallic frowned.

"But you don't even know if the girl has any talent."

Dane looked away from his friend, toward the stairs.

"She had talent, otherwise the identity of her father would not be as protected as it is. There is more to this than any of us knew, except perhaps for Dorovar. He may know who she is."

"Or he may be guessing who she is," Vallic countered, "just as you are. He may think she is the Tear, or he may simply think that she is someone who he can leverage in his war against Pike and the rest of the Dark Gods. But regardless, if you keep going at her mind like that, there may not be anything left for either side to use. You were never that practiced with your abilities, and I never should have encouraged you to learn how to manipulate the minds of others."

Dane looked back at Vallic and grinned.

"Didn't have them long enough to be practiced with them," he said finally. "I should get some sleep. As much as I appreciate your hospitality, I don't think it benefits us to stay in Imperial held territory for longer than we have to."

He moved away from the table, and walked slowly toward the stairs.

"And what are you going to do about Pike?"

Dane stopped briefly and looked back over his shoulder.

"One of these days, I won't have to worry about ever answering that question again."

* * * * * * * * * * * *

Early the next morning, the dragon hunters and their companions were assembled outside the gates of the Keep of the Serpentine Knight, resupplied with fresh horses and as much fresh provisions as the animals could handle. The Serpentine Knight himself was conspicuous by his absence, but the lady of the keep, Isa, was there ensuring that everything was taken care of with grace and speed. Dane gave the older woman a long hug before mounting his horse, and the entire band was back on their path to the Kingdom of Albitonin before the sun was fully into the morning sky. Together the six fugitives rode in silence until nearly midday when it was Angelina that let her voice find the wind.

"I still don't understand why we couldn't have stayed there a few more days to rest and recover our strength. Sir Vallic seemed perfectly willing to extend his protection and hospitality."

Blade answered in his typically gruff voice.

"Protection is easily and quickly offered when the one offering it doesn't think it will be needed. The more the need presents itself, the less readily you will find it offered."

Dane laughed.

"Remind me not to take many chances today. Blade becoming a philosopher is too much for my good fortune to handle."

The group continued through the countryside of the Kingdom of Steam, keeping to the routes that Vallic had suggested for them. The patrols of the Imperial Magistrates and their detachments were easy to predict, and by keeping to the forested paths and off the main trade routes, most possibilities for intervention were avoided. The first night, the group found a small pond to camp by, and most of the night was passed by telling stories and swapping tall tales. The second day of travel was not nearly as conducive to keeping a good pace as the first day was. The sun beat down with little to no cloud cover in the sky, and the horses had to keep a much slower pace in order to keep from falling ill. The riders too found themselves drained of most of their energy, and there was little banter or stories during the day's long ride. As night began to set in, and temperatures cooled, tongues loosened, and the dragon hunters began to tell stories about their most difficult hunts. Blade and Dane were both impressed with the stories, but Dane seemed to be less forthcoming with his amazement than Blade, which Jillian found both curious and alarming. The more the night deepened, the more distracted Dane seemed to become. When they decided to stop for the night to make camp, it was Dane who volunteered to gather firewood, and did so quickly. Unlike the previous evening however, Dane did not seem all that interested in telling stories, and the reverie that had held the night before never materialized. Before long the six had settled in to sleep for the evening.

Dane lay silently on the ground, listening to the fire as well as to the breathing of the rest of his companions. He had felt a presence shadowing them for quite some time, but he didn't want to alarm the other members of the group. There would have been nothing they could have done even had they known. As quietly as possible, Dane sat up and waited until he was sure that no one would notice his departure. Confident in his ability to silently move away from the campsite, Dane moved silently but quickly deeper into the woods. Several minutes away, Dane found a clearing with a large log in the center of it. After a moment of looking around the clearing and ensuring that he wasn't followed, Dane moved to the log and sat. He knew he wouldn't be waiting long, and still he felt impatience rising in him.

"Isn't this a little cliché?"

Dane knew the voice before he saw the man. Pike Rhuiden was not a man easily forgotten, and now that he was the leader of the Dark Gods, he was perhaps one of the most well-known and feared men on the face of the planet. Dane thought perhaps that he enjoyed being notorious far too much for his own good, or for the good of those who followed him. But Pike was a complicated man with simple problems.

"What isn't cliché for us these days? Meeting out in the woods, fighting against unbeatable foes, overthrowing lords and emperors? Seems pretty pedestrian for us. Guess the only thing left to do is take down a few gods."

There was a slight pause.

"Oh wait," Dane said finally. "We've done that too. I suppose there isn't much left to do."

Pike moved closer to where Dane sat.

"Only one thing."

The smile was disturbing and expected all in the same breath. This was the conversation that Dane had been dreading for quite some time.

"So you're still serious about this?"

Pike's smile faded.

"Why wouldn't I be? This is the only way. After all of the things that have happened; Gwydeon, Evan, all of the things we lost."

"And no matter what we do now," Dane countered, "we're not going to get those things back. I loved Gwydeon like a brother, but I think even he began to see the error of his ways after the Fall. That's why he made the deal with the Cadarian Emperor to give the Dark Gods peace, so you could all just live out your lives. And as far as Evan, you can't blame anyone else for that but yourself."

Pike's frown deepened.

"What do you mean by that?"

"What do you think I mean?" Dane said standing, pointing an accusatory finger into Pike's chest. "Aerith and Bryn were perfectly happy living out their days in seclusion. You knew what would happen if Aerith went toe to toe with Evan, and you were counting on it. That is why you baited Aryx into approaching him."

Pike put his hands up and opened his mouth to give a defense.

"Save your lies for your wife, Pike," Dane interrupted. "I know the way you think, and I know just what you are willing to do to get what you want. How Midarin and the others have let you get away with this for so long I will never understand."

This time Pike rounded on the taller man, any joviality gone from his features.

"I am the leader of the Dark Gods," Pike thundered, "and it was me that Gwydeon trusted when he made the decision to extend his olive branch. But Gwydeon knew what he was doing would only be perverted by the Cadarians, which is why he left me in charge instead of Midarin or one of the others. There needed to be a warrior in command, someone who would not lose sight of the ultimate goal. Someone who would not forget who the true enemy in all this is. And that is why I wanted to talk to you, old friend, because I thought you would be willing to help us now that the covenants have started to break. But I see you're still the same self-deprecating and doubt-filled coward you've always been."

"And you've learned nothing from the sacrifices that were made when Onea burned. Don't you remember standing toe to toe with yourself? Don't you remember the Lord Pike Rhuiden who came to power with all the advantages and everyone wanting to bow and scrape at his feet? And you, you were the one who had to struggle, who saw what darkness had done, saw the death and destruction that a world without heroes had brought. You and Gwydeon and me, we stood shoulder to shoulder against the gathering darkness, and it was the three of us that turned the tide. We ended the game that Emries and Halicon were playing with millions of innocent lives. But you became everything that you fought against. You became exactly what you once destroyed. Petty, cruel, misguided, and arrogant. And Pike, if I ever had doubts about anything, I should have had doubts that you would ever end up as anything other than what you have become."

Pike raised his hand as though he were going to strike Dane, but Dane held his ground. After a moment he lowered his hand and turned his back on the taller man.

"So you won't be helping us with what is to come?"

Dane shook his head.

"I'm sorry Pike. I can't be with you this time. I know what is at stake, and believe me; I wish I could ride alongside you one more time to do what's right. But I don't think you can even see what's right any more. This isn't what Gwydeon would have wanted, and this certainly isn't what Eldar would have wanted. You can't make it right, not this way."

At the mention of his lost-love's name, Pike spun, but the fury that was in his eyes melted immediately, replaced only with sorrow.

"That won't work with me anymore. She's dead and gone, and I won't be manipulated with her memory ever again. This is the path that I have to walk. And I'm sorry you won't be there to walk it with me."

Pike turned back away from Dane and took two long steps forward before stopping again.

"Of all the names you could have picked from, why did you have to choose mine?"

A moment later a portal had opened, and Pike had stepped through, leaving Dane alone with just the night.

"I thought maybe I could help you remember what it used to mean," Dane said into the night air.

It was then that Dane heard rustling from the tree line behind him. Jillian emerged from the undergrowth with her sword raised and a combination of shock and horror painted on her face.

"Who the hell are you?"

Dane didn't have to ask how much she had heard, it really didn't matter now. The time for secrets was rapidly nearing its end, and before long they would do nothing to shield them anyway.

"I hardly think that's the question you really want to be asking me," Dane said after a moment. He found his seat on the log again. "Even if I told you what my real name was, it wouldn't mean anything to you. What you really want to ask is who was that who just left, and was it really the leader of the Dark Gods. The answer to the question is yes, that was the leader of the Dark Gods, and his name is Pike Annis, but he once went by the name of Pike Rhuiden."

Shock burned in Jillian's eyes, but Dane continued.

"Yes, I'm using his last name, and we used to be very close friends. But that was a long time ago, and we don't exactly see eye to eye any more. But then again, you heard that part."

Jillian continued to point the tip of her sword at Dane's chest, but her arm was starting to shake, and Dane could tell that she was doubt the veracity of the betrayal that she thought she was feeling. Finally she lowered the blade, but didn't return it to the sheath.

"I still want to know who you are, and why you're helping me."

Dane nodded.

"I'm helping you because it is the right thing to do, that much has been the case since the moment those creatures attacked you. But I'm also helping you because keeping you out of Dorovar's hands is probably more important than you can even imagine. If he wants you, it doesn't mean good things for you, and it doesn't mean good things for this world. The easiest way to look at it is that anything Dorovar wants, he can't be allowed to have."

Jillian hesitated for a moment.

"Why does he want me?"

Dane scratched his chin.

"The best I can tell, it has something to do with your father. The fact that your mother is Jehna Feris is of course important, because a part of you has the power of prophecy within you. But the more I think about it, the more I think it's whatever the information is about your father that is hidden within you."

Jillian felt her jaw open, and knew she was staring agape in shock. How could he have known who she was?

"I never knew my father," she said, finally able to find her voice again, "it was always just my mother and I, at least until she was taken."

The two just stood alternately looking at each other and the ground, before Dane stood up and started walking back toward where the rest of the group was camped.

"We should get back before someone else realizes we're gone."

Dane started to pass by Jillian, but with her free hand she took hold of his arm.

"I may not recognize your name, but I want to know what it is anyway. I know some of your secrets, just like you know some of mine."

Dane nodded.

"My name is Logan."

Reversals

"**W**ell, this is not at all what I expected," Aerith Seth said over his shoulder as he stood back to back with Gabriel Shadowfall, surrounded by two-dozen paladins of the Army of Stone.

* * * * * * * * * * * *

Forty-eight hours ago......

Aerith Seth watched the fanfare and the banners as Gabriel Shadowfall led the litter through the streets of Albitonin. The princess, soon-to-be empress, to her credit hid much of her selfish and arrogant tendencies during the parade, and seemed genuinely touched and grateful for her welcome. When they finally reached the steps that led to the great chapel at the center of Albitonin, Aerith could see four people standing at the top of the steps. The two in the middle could only have been Hannah Ironheart and Gregor Quicksilver, two of the most well-known and powerful people on the face of Cadaria. Of course, Aerith had to chuckle at the thought of either of the two thinking they were truly powerful in the grand scheme of things. In truth, for mortals they were exceptional, and from the stories, Gregor could have been the equal of Gwydeon Sandar before he achieved his immortal gifts. However, as Aerith reviewed the knowledge granted to him by all of those who held his mantle, Gregor seemed to be more like Korrd Ranthall. Gifted with some divine power, but without the vicious edge to use it to its full capability. Being touched with true divinity made two kinds of people: the kind that avoided using their gifts whenever possible, and those that used their gifts to excess. There was rarely a middle ground.

With Gabriel's help, Marlae descended from the litter flanked by her ever-present bodyguard Rhain Feirbran, and took long, slow, measured steps up to the top of the long set of stairs. Aerith had to admit Marlae looked the part. Her gait was flawless, and she never seemed to make a single effort. When Marlae reached the top of the stairs, all four people bowed slightly and then went to one knee. The woman in the middle, Hannah Ironheart spoke clearly over the quickly hushing crowd.

"Celestial Princess Marlae Lorien. Due to the recent events in the Imperial province of Aldere and throughout the Empire of Cadaria, Albitonin and several of its allies have had no choice but to declare themselves apart from the empire ruled by your father and step-mother Kaitain and Dominique Lorien. Their irrational rule and constant war-mongering have brought this empire to the brink of extinction, and we believe that only a drastic change in rule will bring us back from the precipice of destruction. For that, we, the collected kingdoms of this rebellion bend our knee and proclaim our allegiance to the rightful Empress of Cadaria, Marlae Lorien."

A great cheer went up from the crowd, and Marlae turned to soak in the adoration of the crowd. After a moment Marlae turned back to the still kneeling quartet.

"As four of the rebel members of the Knights of the Flashing Blade," Marlae said quickly, "you have been marked for execution should the forces of my insane father lay their hands upon you. In the old Empire of Cadaria, your lives are forfeit. However, in the Cadaria that will be led by Marlae Lorien, your value is clearly seen. From this day forward, the order of the Flashing Blade will be returned to their rightful place as the icons of virtue that they have always been. All people shall aspire to their example, and they shall serve no other master but the rightful ruler of Cadaria. I put out a call to all members of the Flashing Blade who still live. Any who will willingly bend their knee to this rightful court will be cleansed of all their deeds while serving under the perverse rule of Kaitain Lorien, and will be granted their place within this new order. Any who remain with my father in his service will be branded traitors to the empire and their positions and lives will be forfeit."

There was an uneasy hush that radiated through the crowd. Marlae soaked in the silence for a moment before turning back to the assembled onlookers. She held the crowd in the palm of her hand, and she was doing a masterful job of controlling both their emotions and their enthusiasm.

"People of Cadaria," she said after a moment, "a new day is dawning. The plagues, famines, and wars have gouged deeply into the heart of this eternal empire. Only by working together, noble and commoner alike, can we heal this gaping wound and create the tomorrow that we all wish for ourselves. We must have peace, but not peace at any price. There will be struggles, there will be battles, and there will be death around the corner for both ourselves and our enemies. But hear me now. The enemies of this Empire will not be victorious!"

A great cheer went up from the crowd.

"The Empire of Cadaria will vanquish our enemies and we shall know peace and victory!"

The cheer rose in magnitude until it reached a near deafening pitch. Finally, Gabriel's voice rose above the din.

"Long live Empress Marlae Lorien!"

The call was echoed through the crowd and rose and fell in waves on the wind. Marlae soaked in the attention for a moment before turning back to the assembled members of the Flashing Blade.

"Rise my friends," she said after a moment. "You are all returned to your rightful positions as members of the most elite fighting group ever assembled and my personal protectors. Rhain here will act as my personal protector, and the captain of my personal guard. Hannah, you will continue to act as the High Priestess of this kingdom and church, and will take your place as the spiritual advisor for the empire, a post you should have had many years ago."

Hannah bowed.

"Thank your Empress, I will endeavor to live up to this great responsibility that you have bestowed upon me."

Marlae smiled and turned to Gregor.

"My father has always counted you as his most staunch competition to the throne, and he worried for the entirety of his rule that you would usurp his power. I have no such fears Sir Quicksilver, as I know you are an honorable man. I hereby return you to your position as the Ruby Knight of the Flashing Blade and grant you the command of all of the armies that swear their loyalty to my empire. My companion, Gabriel Shadowfall has your sword and is ready to surrender it to you at your leisure."

Gregor bowed slightly and then locked his eyes upon the new empress.

"My Empress, I thank you for your gift. There will be many challenges in the days to come, and I would be honored to help prepare for them. Your step-mother may allow this ceded government to prosper for some time, and may even try to open diplomatic relations, however, in time your father will awake, or Irene Drage will wrest power from Dominique and we will be in a full civil war. Most of my time will be spent mobilizing the armies, and unless Bernhardt decides to join our fold, I shall be on the front lines more often than not, and as such I may not be able to fulfill my duties as your protector. The word coming out of Jelan is not encouraging, and Bernhardt may be lost to us. To that end, I would request that I be named your Master-at-Arms, and the general of your armies, but that the young knight Gabriel Shadowfall retains the position of Ruby Knight. I believe he has earned distinction enough in his life to use the title to its best ends, and in the battles to come, a title will mean little on the field upon which I shall tread."

Marlae seemed to ponder this for a moment before smiling and nodding.

"I cannot argue with your wisdom, Gregor, and while selfishly I would love to be able to count on you being at my side to fend off all dangers, I know that your skills will be far more valuable to our cause on the fields of battle that await our future."

Gregor bowed again.

"I will be at your side should the need arise, my Empress, of that you can be assured."

Marlae nodded and smiled, knowing that she would be safe no matter the circumstance. After a moment of pondering, she turned to face the Tiger's Eye Knight, Xaran Firesoul whose head remained respectfully bowed.

"Xaran, your wisdom is renown through the empire, as are your fairness and attention to every detail. Some say that you have sight into a world that most of us will never be able to perceive. I need that kind of wisdom if I am going to steer our fledgling empire through the turbulent times ahead. As Rhain will be acting as both my Court Sorceress and bodyguard, I am in need of a chief advisor. I would very much like for you to take that post."

Xaran lifted his head and nodded quickly.

"It would be my honor to serve as your advisor, my Empress. Any experience and sight that I have are fully at your disposal."

Marlae smiled wider and turned to face Devlin Rannoch. Aerith looked him over from the distance and could not help but feel slightly uneasy at the visage of the large man. But after a moment, he knew it was not the look of the man that truly disturbed him, it was more the aura that surrounded the knight. There was something familiar about it. Something familiar and terrible all at the same time.

"Devlin Rannoch, the Onyx Knight. You showed great determination and courage in your rescue of Gregor and Leonora from the dungeons of the Palace of Aldere and even more in disobeying the decrees of the Emperor. Perhaps in another life that daring would have gained you nothing more than a traitor's death, but in this case you are to be commended for your foresight and bravery. In time, I will find a way to thank you more fully for your efforts, but for now I have another task which every bit of your bravery will be needed for. As for now, we are unsure as to where the loyalties of our great general Bernhardt Yeoman lay, as Gregor alluded to. Before too long, the attacks of the dragons of Cadaria will move into the regions that are loyal to this empire, and we will need to strike back. I believe your past and your abilities make you singularly qualified for leading this endeavor, Devlin, and I would be grateful if you accepted the charge of leading our counter-offensive against the dragons."

Devlin nodded his head solemnly.

"Though I do not relish the death that will come from this course, my Empress, I know it is my duty to follow your orders and to take this burden upon me. However, I will promise you that before the last breath escapes my lips, you will have victory over the dragons, and they will regret the day they cross the Celestial Empress Marlae Lorien."

Marlae nodded once more and turned to the crowd. She said more to them over the next few minutes, but Aerith did not hear any of those words. His eyes and his fears were locked on the man known as Devlin Rannoch, and he could not help but feel the impending doom creeping up around him.

* * * * * * * * * * * *

The broken bodies of paladins and priests lay all around Aerith and Gabriel. The fight had been short and totally unnecessary. If they had only listened to reason. But the time for talking was long since past. They would not listen no matter what was said, and no matter what reasons would be brought to bear. The sounds of clanking armor could be heard around the corner and Aerith knew that it would only be a matter of time before they would be knee-deep in another phalanx of soldiers. Though it was well within his capability to take on the whole of the Army of Stone himself, Aerith knew that Gabriel would not be able to keep up, and Aerith felt a certain kinship to the boy. They had both been placed in an unwinnable position.

"This is getting out of control, Aerith," Gabriel said panting. "I know Gregor and Hannah are hunting for us right now, and I don't want to fight them, no matter what that means. They are too important."

"I'm kind of fond of being alive, kid. And if I have to carve through two members of the Flashing Blade, then that is what I'm going to do. We can't very well win if we're dead."

Aerith knew that last part wasn't essentially true, but it sounded good when talking to someone who hadn't ever had the privilege of dying.

"Well," Gabriel said after a moment, "we better pick up the pace if we are going to catch up with Devlin and Camille."

On a dead run, the two warriors rounded the corner into another group of paladins. They were all heavily armed and armored, and looking for a fight. Aerith stopped short, took a half step back, and held both of his swords to bear, and smiled.

"Hang back for this one, Gabriel. Its time these pups saw what real power looked like."

As Gabriel watched Aerith wade into the ranks of troops, he found his mouth dropping open. He knew that Aerith had power at his disposal, but the way he took apart those troops was unbelievable. Godly would not have been the word that sprang to mind. Aerith fought like a demon.

* * * * * * * * * * * *

Twenty-four hours ago......

In some ways, Aerith felt like a hypocrite. Check that. In every way, Aerith felt like a hypocrite. The new Empress, fresh off being proclaimed the savior of the empire of Cadaria was set to officiate her first mass to the Creator at the side of the spiritual leader of the empire, Hannah Ironheart. As the savior of the life of the Empress, Aerith was granted a front row seat to the proceedings. All Aerith wanted to do was crawl under the pew and die.

When Aerith was human, he never had much use for the trappings of religion. Sure he believed in the Creator, and for a time he even believed in some of the old gods and their influence over the daily lives of the mortals of the world. But as he got older and he saw the abilities of creatures like Saurn, Basille, Jeroch, and the rest of the phasia, the power of those beliefs began to wane. Then he died for the first time. Dying has a way of opening up one's perceptions on the universe. It is one thing to say that you believe in the Creator, or even simply believing that he exists. It is quite another thing altogether to be shown that not only does he exist but he has the capability to shape all of reality at the snap of his fingers. Believing is one thing, but knowing is something else entirely. Most days, Aerith wished he didn't know half of what he knew.

So, as Aerith sat in the first pew along with most of the high level priests and nobles of Albitonin, Aerith found his mind wandering. The sermon meant nothing to him. He no longer had faith. Faith was not a factor when the Creator was something real, something that he had stared into the face of many times. All he felt was empty, and a little sad. Having faith was a luxury now. As he looked to his left, he saw Devlin Rannoch sitting by a woman who he had been introduced to named Camille Renar. It took Aerith only a second to place the woman's name, but he tried hard not to let the familiarity show. Camille was the daughter of Midarin and Gwydeon. A touched child to be sure, one who carried a piece of the Creator's powers that had once inhabited her father. Obviously Aerith's name didn't mean anything to Camille when they shook hands cordially before entering the Heart of Stone, or if it did, she did an admirable job of hiding it. Conspicuous by his absence from the proceedings was Xaran Firesoul. Aerith knew it was because he was looking after Pike's daughter Tess, who could not show her face at these functions, at least not yet. It was said that Xaran was supposed to become a sort of tutor for the girl, but deep in his heart Aerith could not shake the feeling that there was another reason. Gabriel had said that Tess and Marlae were scheduled to meet later in the day to begin negotiations for peace between the new Empire of Cadaria and Mythryn, and that Xaran was going to act as a mediator of sorts. If such a deal could be brokered, then it would go a long way to establishing Marlae's legitimacy as the true Empress of Cadaria.

Half-way through the sermon, Aerith knew that something was wrong. There was a presence in the hall that was familiar, one that could be felt by anyone who had known the touch of the Creator. Looking to his left, he locked eyes with Camille, and he saw the fear in her eyes as well. A few moments later, there was a bright light on the dais that caused Hannah to break off mid-sentence. When the light finally receded, a form floated inches off the floor to Hannah's left. It was instantly familiar to Aerith. Its armor glistened with an other-worldly brilliance, and the flaming crystal sword clutched in its right hand radiated divine power. There was no physical form visible under the armor or the heavy helm, simply energy. Raw energy that served the Creator.

"I AM THE WILL OF THE CREATOR," the empty metallic voice boomed from beneath the helm of the creature. "AMONG YOU ARE PRETENDERS TO THE DIVINE POWER OF THE CREATOR AND THOSE WHO WOULD USURP THE CREATOR'S GOOD WORKS AND PERVERT THEM TO THEIR OWN BLASPHEMOUS GOALS. THE ONE NAMED AERITH SETH IS ONE OF THE FALLEN DARK GODS AND CANNOT BE ALLOWED TO HAVE A VOICE IN THIS PLACE. HE MUST BE EXTERMINATED. RENOUNCE HIS EVIL AND RETURN TO THE TRUE PATH OF THE CREATOR. THE WILL HAS SPOKEN. YOU HAVE ONE DAY TO BOW TO THE WISHES OF THE CREATOR."

The bright light flashed again, and the Will was gone. Seconds later all hell broke loose.

* * * * * * * * * * * *

Aerith was starting to get tired. They had fought together back to back for the last two hours through the dungeon of the Heart of Stone and through the main levels where the parishioners had mobbed them when the Will first made its proclamation. Every battle was taking its toll on Gabriel, and now even Aerith's immortal might was beginning to feel the drain. It had been too long since he had full command of his powers or remembered what it took to fully command them for so long. What made matters worse is that for some reason his ability to use portals had somehow been halted. It was like someone reached into him and turned off that power. It was quite aggravating.

Another soldier ducked out of a passageway and was quickly cut down before he even knew what was happening. Aerith braced himself to charge into another open passage, but Gabriel took hold of his shoulder and pulled him into an antechamber. Gabriel was panting and was covered head to toe with blood, most of which was not his own.

"I thought you said getting out of here would be easy," Gabriel said slumping against the wall for a quick breath.

"It would be, but for some reason I can't use most of my powers."

There was a rustle from the darkness at the other side of the chamber and a female's voice broke the silence.

"Neither can I, and I imagine I know why."

The voice was from Camille, and as she emerged from the shadows, Devlin was a pace behind her. He folded his wings back, and pulled his sword from the sheath. Somehow his wings had bent the dim light to create a pocket of shadow in the corner. Camille must have known that this would have been a good place to rest and recover.

"How?" Aerith said quickly.

"Tess," Camille answered half in sorrow and half in anger. "Her powers are so much greater than any I have seen from any of the Dark Gods, and I guess she has learned how to suppress the powers of the others who have fallen. The only powers I have left at my disposal are those I got from my father, and I assume the only ones you have are the ones that you had before your ascension?"

Aerith smiled a wry smile.

"So you did recognize me."

Camille nodded.

"Mother was quite thorough in her descriptions of all the major players in this little game. Information is the only advantage we have going for us right now Aerith, so we must make the most of that advantage."

Aerith smiled despite himself.

"I knew I should have taken the stones...."

Devlin frowned.

"So, how do we expect to get out of here alive and without having to take on half the Albitonin military including Hannah and Gregor?"

Gabriel wiped his brow and looked down at the ground. How had everything gone so far out of control?

* * * * * * * * * * * *

Six hours ago......

"I don't see where we have any other choice," Gregor said shaking his head.

Hannah was troubled. She had seen the good that Camille Renar had done, and from Marlae's own mouth she had heard the tales of Aerith Seth staring down the creature known as Death and winning in single combat. But the Creator had been firm in his decree. The one known as Aerith Seth had to die. Right now, Aerith was locked in a cell in the dungeon, and part of Hannah knew that he was there only because he chose to be. If he had wanted to strike all of the guards dead who escorted him there, he would have. He was humoring them. Part of that made Hannah's skin crawl and left the pit of her stomach feeling empty.

"We can't kill him," Devlin said finally. "He has done too much for us, and could do more than we could ever imagine. With the battle against Kaitain and his forces on the horizon, we need every advantage we can get. Not only that, in the negotiations to come, it would be advantageous to have every one of the Dark Gods we can get on our side to prevent a war. Tess and Camille are nice to have, but they are children of the Dark Gods, not gods themselves. Aerith by his own admission is not part of their council, but his voice would be respected were it to champion our side."

Hannah shook her head.

"We cannot sacrifice our soul to save our lives."

The finality of the statement ended all debate. A moment later Empress Marlae Lorien issued a termination order for Aerith Seth.

* * * * * * * * * * * *

"Regretting busting me out of prison yet?" Aerith asked, looking at Gabriel.

Gabriel smiled.

"It was wrong what they were going to do to you, Aerith," the Ruby Knight said finally, "and they all know it. Hannah is trying to protect her position and the position of the new Empire they are trying to build. If there was any other way…"

Devlin sighed hard.

"Wish I could agree with you, Gabriel. Hannah made the wrong choice. And it's a choice that could damn us all in the long run. But the question still remains…how do we get out of here?"

Suddenly a great explosion ripped through the city. The palace shook violently, and it took Aerith a moment to recover his hearing.

"Well," Aerith said after a moment, "our luck may just be changing."

Things Left Undone

Year Three of the Just Emperor Kaitain "Dragonsbane" Lorien, Creator's Calendar Year 1870

Seraph Kore moved silently through the halls of the Imperial Palace of Aldere, his mind on fire with the possibilities that had been presented to him. The impending doom that faced the Cadarian Empire; the threat that Dorovar and his children posed, as well as the Dark Gods who were about to launch a multi-tier offensive, created a level of forced attentiveness that also engendered exhaustion and carelessness. The world was spinning more and more out of control, and if the creature calling itself Pestilence was to be believed, the worst cataclysm was still to come. Kaitain would awaken at any time, and the misery he would rain down upon his people would be unparalleled, and even that was not the worst that was to come. Pestilence had spoken of a time of unparalleled darkness, one that could not be averted by any means. But Dorovar had offered Seraph a choice. He would be able to save those that he loved, he would be able to take control of the scattered forces of the world and unite against the evil of the Dark Gods, and the horrors that followed in their wake. Seraph would become War itself, and the broken bodies of his enemies and their freed souls would be testament to his love and devotion not only for the empire, but to his wife and his lover.

It had been easy to elude the patrols around the Imperial Palace, just as it had been the day Seraph should have ended the threat that Kaitain posed once and for all. But now he realized the folly of even that simplistic plan. Obviously there was a much greater role that Kaitain was poised to play, and his removal from the game too early would have tipped the balance of power too far in the favor of the Dark Gods. The world would have shattered under the weight of their unopposed rule. And though the suffering of the people may have been lessened, the chance for salvation would have been removed completely. Only because of the misery and pain that Kaitain would cause could come the hope of a future.

Slipping in wearing the garb of an Imperial guard had been easy enough, but with his knowledge of the layout as well as the never-changing patrol structure made it that much more simple. This new captain of the Imperial Guard had been easy to predict. He obviously had a rigid military mind, but that mind was being bent to other purposes. The hand of the Imperial Sorceress could be seen everywhere, and the carelessness that the guards showed in their protection of the halls of power of the Imperial Palace would not have been tolerated if an unfettered military professional was allowed to do their job. How easy it would have been to slip into the bedchamber of the Emperor and end his life once and for all. Only six guardsmen were on duty in the hall that led to the heavy wooden door of the Emperor's bedchambers, and the anteroom that connected to that hallway could not have held more than four more guards, and at this time of night, it was more likely to only be two. Any Knight of the Flashing Blade alone would have been able to overcome such odds, and it would have been no effort for one of the Dark Gods. Even the guards standing in the corners of the room would be no match for Seraph's skill. It was as though Irene Drage wanted someone to finish off the wounded Emperor. But Pestilence had warned Seraph against such action. Kaitain still had a substantial role to play in the grand scheme, one that would benefit the world. Seraph could not see anyone that caused as much suffering as Kaitain had or would becoming a benefit, but Pestilence was privy to more information than Seraph.

Creeping through the darkness, Seraph found his way to the antechamber that connected to the suite of the Empress of Cadaria, Dominique Arias. Seraph refused to call her by her married name. Any time he tried, his mouth felt as though it was full of slime and ash, and before long he could taste the blood from his teeth cutting at the fleshy insides of his cheeks. She would never be a Lorien in his mind. She would never be the property of another man. He could have easily slipped through the door, knelt at the side of her bed and watched her sleep for a moment. He could have sated the desire of his heart to lay his eyes upon her once more. But that part of his heart was too wounded to be embraced. His arrogance and petty jealousy had ended that part of his life. Dominique would never, could never, be his again, and perhaps she was better without his trauma and damage in her life. A life in the finery of the Empress of Cadaria strangely suited her, and she had grown into the role, despite the pain she had to endure at Kaitain's hand.

She had been a beautiful and free spirit when they met, regardless of her squalid surroundings. No one would know that her father had tried to sell her into slavery. There would be no record that her father had beaten her mother to death, or that her older sister had taken her life rather than work in a brothel to pay the father's substantial debts. No one would have to know the terrible things she had been subjected to in the name of survival, or the blood that would forever stain her hands. Seraph had seen to that personally. Her past had been erased and reconstructed the way he felt she deserved. He had unwittingly paved the way for her to become the Empress of Cadaria, and it brought a smile to his lips at the same time it turned his stomach.

His heart beat fast as his eyes were drawn back to the door that separated him from the woman who had shared his bed and stolen his heart. No, his task this night lay elsewhere. He moved through the darkness from shadow to shadow until he reached the private quarters of the Captain of the Empress' guard. Seraph didn't dare cast any of his silencing spells this deep in the palace, for fear of alerting Irene Drage to his presence, and this close to the Empress, it would draw too much attention too quickly. So, instead Seraph had to rely on a practiced hand and good reflexes. The old wooden door to the chamber was heavy enough that it only creaked slightly, and Seraph passed through with little effort into the darkness of the room beyond. For days he had studied Chelsea's increasingly erratic behavior and he knew that she slept less and less these days. Her nights were spent sitting in a chair at the bedside of her charge, most nights sleeplessly. However, one night per week she would allow herself a few hours in her own bed, both a submission to Dominique's will and to her own physical needs. Tenacity would keep her on her feet far past any human definition of exhaustion, but even the power of the Sacred Weapon would not be enough to stop her body from simply shutting down if sleep was ignored for too long. Chelsea was a proud woman, but her practicality won out when necessary.

Little moonlight trickled in through the high narrow window. The chamber itself was more spartan than Seraph had expected, but then again, the room's occupant was never one to indulge in any kind of luxury. Finery was unknown to the woman who would rather share a bedroll in the middle of a field the night before a battle than on a feather bed with silk sheets. The moonlight arced over the bed like a canopy, creating just enough glow in the blond hair of the woman who lay there. Her normally hard and impassive features were soft and inviting in the unguarded moments of sleep and peace. Seraph felt as though his heart was being pulled forward toward the woman, his chest aching from the exertion. Softly and silently, Seraph approached the bedside, and knelt just at the edge of the bed, his own face only inches from that of his wife. Wife…the word was hollow in his mind. What kind of husband had he been? They played at marriage for a while, played at trying to have a life. But his will was for duty, for service, and not to be in the bed of a woman whom he was bred to see as his enemy. She was from Saldarine. She was the embodiment of everything that those from Thorigald found abhorrent. Their marriage was political, an attempt to forge a peace that could never exist. And yet, despite the desert around them, a rose bloomed, a life, a shred of happiness. Their daughter had been a beauty, but she lived only long enough to have one beautiful dream of the future that could have been. When her chest rose and fell for the last time, and chance at a future, a marriage, a life, or a peace was shattered.

He was so close that he could feel her breath and smell the sweetness of her body. He ached to touch her skin once more. Their marriage had never been one of love and devotion, but Seraph loved Chelsea in his own way, a way that he could honestly say that he never shared even with Dominique. He had been unfaithful in every way it was possible for a man to be, and yet he remained inexplicably devoted to Chelsea. While he stayed kneeling there for only a few moments, it felt to him like an eternity. The seconds were filled with love, hate, sorrow, and more pain than he had expected. Finally, he rose from his crouch and moved silently over to the table in the corner of the room. In one deft motion, Seraph retrieved a sealed letter from the pouch on his belt, and laid it on the table. He turned to leave, and then stopped. No, if he was going to take this course of action, he could take nothing of his old life with him. He removed Patience from his belt, still in the scabbard and laid it on the table beside the letter. There was a moment that he could feel the weapon reaching out for him, trying to convince him to not take this course of action, but his mind was made up and the matter was closed. Patience would have to serve another master in the execution of his duties, and perhaps this time its wielder would be more worthy than Seraph had been.

As he turned back to the door, he caught a small glint of light from his finger. The wedding band sat on his finger, half mocking him with its continued presence. Without thinking, Seraph removed it from his finger and turned back toward the table, fully intending to lay it upon the letter. But as he turned the simple piece of metal in the moonlight, he could not let it go. He would just as soon cut out his heart and lay it on the table as let go of the ring. He closed his eyes, turned to the door, and slipped it back on his finger. Whatever fate awaited him in the service of Dorovar, he would meet it with Chelsea in his heart.

* * * * * * * * * * * *

Chelsea knew the moment someone had entered her room, and though she was shocked to see that it was Seraph, she kept her breathing measured and calm, not wanting to disturb him from whatever task he was on. Her hand was stretched above her in her normal sleeping posture, under the fluffy pillow, where her dagger lay. It was a common practice she had learned to live with her first years in the military. Better to learn to sleep with your hand on a weapon than be caught unawares and never wake again. Her senses burned as he knelt beside her and watched her sleep. She could sense everything about him. The smell of sweat on his skin, the smell of the wind that had ruffled his hair, and the dust on his clothing from the travels through the oft-unused forest paths in Aldere. There were no words for the risk he had taken just to get this far.

Her mind flashed back, to the first weeks of their marriage, and the uncertain fate of their union. She remembered a night when he knocked on the door to their bedroom and then pretended that he had the wrong room. How she would cuddle up with her head on his chest as he gently hummed a tune. Then he would stroke her hair and gently sing to her, lulling her to sleep. How for a time she thought she would never be able to sleep again without him by her side.

Through mostly-shut eyes she watched him watch her, the expression on his face full of sorrow. Her own sorrow built as she watched him place the letter and the Sacred Weapon on the table. When she saw him pull the wedding ring from his finger, it was all she could do to keep herself silent and still. She felt as though her body and soul would shatter if he placed the ring upon the table. When finally he turned and returned the ring to his finger and left the room she could breathe again. She waited several full minutes in agony before she dared move. But when finally she felt it safe to move again, she sat upright on the edge of her bed, clutching the wedding ring that hung from a chain around her neck, her eyes stinging as hot tears filled them, blurring her vision. She tried to find her feet, tried to will herself to stand, but the sobbing and soul-wrenching sorrow robbed the strength from her body. Chelsea fell to her knees, tears streaming down her face, her vision gone. Hanging from the back of the chair beside the bed were the scabbards that held Tenacity, and she wanted to reach for them, wanted them to help her bring some sanity back to the moment. Her hand found the weapon, but instead of being flooded with the normal sensations of power and stability, Chelsea felt nothing. Her soul cried out, drowning out any power the Sacred Weapon may have conferred upon her. The emptiness won out, and the woman, not the proud knight, lay curled on the cold stone floor, and cried herself to sleep.

* * * * * * * * * * * *

Deep in the heart of the Citadel of the Dark Gods, Sadrina Annis sat on her cold iron throne, looking out at the emptiness of the chamber, lost in thought. She wondered about her children, Tess and Darrien, as well as their protectors, the children of the Dark Gods who had grown up together on this world destined for self-destruction. Sadrina had been an acolyte of the Church of the Creator once. She and her sister Hannah had promising futures in the service of the Creator, and from all records, Sadrina could have outpaced her sister, and perhaps it would have been Sadrina and not Hannah that would have ascended to the ranks of the Knights of the Flashing Blade. But fate had conspired to ensure that Hannah and Sadrina would take very different paths indeed.

Sadrina was in her last year at the temple, and was about to take her vows, pledging her life to the service of the Creator. But as was the custom in the church, each acolyte took three days away from the temple to ponder their fate and ensure that it was their soul's desire to give up the distractions of the worlds in favor of a life of service and servitude. But the first night in the common room of a tavern at the edge of Albitonin she had met the man that would change her life forever. He was all rough edges and hard muscle, but his eyes were so full of playfulness and charm that they were intoxicating. He sat at the edge of a small stage, singing along with the minstrels, changing words to tunes that everyone knew, making them mocking, lewd, and utterly delightful with every turned phrase. Ale and wine flowed like a river and the patrons laughed and danced. The common room was full until dawn, and when the beautiful man retired for the evening, Sadrina wished he could have stayed for just a little while longer. The next night was the same, but this time Sadrina worked up the courage to say hello to him.

All of her life, she had been the meeker sister, the more accomplished one, but more awkward. She had few if any friends among the other initiates, and even Hannah was not considered a confidant. It was just as well that she was going to become a devotee of the Creator, as her faculty with talking to men was non-existent. But that night, in the common room, his smile and eyes inflamed her. They danced and laughed and carried on as though there would never be consequences for their actions. When they made love that night she felt as though she was flying and that she would never come down. They spent the whole of the next day in his bed, laughing, talking, and entwining both their bodies and souls. They had food brought up from the kitchen, and he fed her three meals there in bed. The night in the common room was more of the same, and she felt that every glance, every word, every song was meant for her alone, and nothing else existed except the two of them. The next morning she could not pull herself free from his arms, and she confessed that she never wanted their time together to end.

"Then you would be marrying a Dark God." He had said. She should have thought he was joking. She should have protested or said anything other than what she said. "You could be the Great Dark One, and I would marry you anyway."

The rest seemed like a dream now. Coming to Mythryn, meeting the Dark Gods that she had been taught to fear since the moment she could understand the words being spoken to her.

"This place seems empty now."

Ivan Quicksilver's cold voice shook Sadrina from her reverie. For a man of his size, Ivan could move silently when he wanted to, and had the unnerving tendency to do so even when it was not intentional.

"I can't say I'm accustomed to this few of the Dark Gods being about. Everyone is either off on some mission or they are attending to matters in preparation for the invasion. Pike and Midarin are gone, so are Serrina and Sabrina, and that Bryn woman is as well. Though I can't say I'm sorry to see her go. With Darrien, Tess, Alderin, and Camille all in Cadaria as well, Lissa is left in charge, but she has Wolf and the girls to take care of. I'm not sure where Aryx and Diana are."

Ivan seemed to ponder that for a moment.

"I wasn't aware that Pike had gone as well. Where did he go?"

Sadrina shook her head.

"Something about meeting with an old friend to get some advice. That could mean anything or nothing when it comes to Pike. You know how fond he is of his walkabouts."

Ivan smiled and nodded.

"Pike is very fond of taverns and tavern girls."

Sadrina felt her heart sink, and the anger began to rise. Pike's dalliances were well documented, but no one had the gall to mention them in front of Sadrina. Looking in Ivan's eyes, he knew exactly what he had said, and there was no trace of remorse for it in his features.

"If only he would confine his wandering eye to the serving girls, it would make matters so much easier. But, he seems to take great joy in impugning the virtue of noble women as well, just as he did with you, Queen Annis."

There was venom in his voice when he uttered her title. There was a difference about Ivan. He had been such a staunch supporter of the goals of the Dark Gods ever since his ill-fated mission to kill Pike, when he learned the truth about what the Dark Gods were and the level of power that they possessed. Before Sadrina could give her objections to his tone or his manner voice, Ivan had crossed the length of the chamber and was on top of her. The blade of his knife was at her throat, and his cold hard eyes stared down at her.

"I've waited and waited for the perfect opportunity to get my revenge for everything that bastard husband of yours took away from me. He shattered my marriage, my position, my future, and stole everything that should have been mine in this life. I wasn't just given the assignment to kill Pike by chance all those years ago. I begged for it. Not because I thought that I could get a dagger to his throat, but because I wanted to kill everything he cared about. Everything he loved. I wanted to take from him all of the things he took from me. And I'm starting with you."

* * * * * * * * * * * *

Lissa Aerol, once Lissa Terian, then Lissa Ranthall sat looking at the window at the low hanging mist that encased the island continent of Mythryn. For so long she had been here in the Citadel of the Dark Gods, wondering what the next day would hold for her, and whether or not she would get her life and her husband back. Their twin girls had been born not long before their expulsion from the heavens, but her husband Wolf had been robbed of watching most of their maturation. Now, as she turned back to look at the body of her husband, she knew that another presence inhabited the cold eyes that stared back at her.

"You don't like me very much, do you?"

Lissa laughed to herself. The rest of the Dark Gods had gone, and she was left alone in the Citadel to oversee all of the plans that had been set into motion. She was not what one would call a skilled administrator, and were she given a choice, she would much rather be hunting with Bryn and Midarin or even looking for the ever-troublesome Aerith Seth with Sabrina. Anything was better than staying put in the Citadel, especially now that she had to babysit the interloper who was wearing her husband's body.

"Is there any particular reason that I should?"

Basille looked at her and then suddenly turned his head toward the door.

"Because in about five seconds I'm going to save your life."

Lissa felt the shockwave erupt through the floor before she had a chance to retort. The entire Citadel of the Dark Gods shuddered from the power of the explosion that erupted from somewhere deep in the palace itself. A huge piece of the ceiling fell the next moment, and Basille leapt from the bed where he sat and tackled Lissa, pushing her out of range of the debris and the flash of pure white light that erupted through the door the next moment as it was thrown off its hinges. Stone boiled when contacted by the light, and the Citadel groaned as though it were dying. Lissa looked up into the man's eyes again. The cold emotionless eyes were no longer there, only a caring, if not confused look stared down at her.

"Lissa," Wolf's confused voice pierced the sudden stillness, "why are we on the floor?"

* * * * * * * * * * * *

In the darkness of the forest outside the Imperial Palace of Aldere, Seraph Kore looked back toward the gleaming towers, pain still filling his heart. It had been a simple matter to get back out of the palace, and he didn't even take great care to avoid being seen. It was as though he knew that he would not. He felt the presence behind him, and knew immediately that the creature calling itself Pestilence was there. This was where they had agreed to meet once Seraph had concluded his business.

"You are a man of honor, Seraph Kore. Others in your position would have thought better of the bargain they have made and attempt to cheat their fate."

Seraph frowned.

"I keep my bargains," Seraph said coldly, turning to face the figure wreathed in sickening green light, "so long as the other side keeps their part."

Pestilence smiled.

"Come," its cold voice echoed into the darkness, "let us go make the Kingdom of Fire burn."

Chapter LX

Shattered Heart, Broken Soul

Year Three of the Just Emperor Kaitain "Dragonsbane" Lorien, Creator's Calendar Year 1870

*T*hree *hours ago...*

Marlae Lorien stalked around her chambers deep in the Heart of Stone, the echoes of her footsteps sounding hollow to her ears. Rhain sat on the bed, strangely placid. Rhain was never one to sit quietly, and she was never one to keep her council to herself in the presence of her lover and now her Empress. She had been silent ever since the decree of The Will, and the imprisonment of Aerith Seth. It was as though she was taking the punishment of this man as a personal affront, though Marlae knew deep down that Rhain had no fondness for men, and enjoyed when they found pain either by her hand or some other method. But, Hannah and Gregor's council had been sound. Only Xaran had cast a dissenting vote, but he kept his reasons for that to himself. Finally Marlae stopped pacing and stood in front of Rhain locking her eyes on the older woman. Rhain did not look up to meet her eyes, instead continuing to look at her feet.

"What?"

Marlae's tone was a mixture of wrath, frustration, and genuine concern, but it came out more like a bark. The newly minted Empress had always considered herself able to easily control and shape the emotions of the moment to fit her needs, but in this case, the level of frustration and stress was starting to crack her controlled shell. Finally Rhain looked up, and Marlae could see the echoes of tears in her eyes.

"This is wrong, Marlae," Rhain said finally, her normally submissive tone replaced by something harder. "We wouldn't be alive if it wasn't for Aerith Seth, and now you have sentenced him to death. I think he deserves better. Hannah and Gregor are locked into their stupid dogma, and it seems that only Xaran has the fortitude to think."

Marlae started to speak, but Rhain stood, cutting her off.

"I have been a whore for a long time," she said, steel in her voice, "and I have knelt at the feet of unscrupulous men to fulfill their egos. Gregor and Hannah are no better than whores themselves, falling on their knees and opening wide to receive the Creator's blessing."

Rhain turned and made toward the door, but Marlae caught her by the arm.

"And just where do you think you're going? This is no way for the Court Sorceress and the consort of the Empress to behave."

Rhain turned into Marlae and held her by the shoulders. Suddenly Marlae began to realize how much taller and more muscular Rhain was. The red haired woman stood a head taller than the diminutive Empress and could have easily lifted her and tossed her around like a child. In some moments there was a softness and demure quality about the woman, but in others she could be as hard and dominant as any man. At this moment, there was a fire in her eyes that Marlae found equally intoxicating and frightening. That next moment, Rhain leaned in and kissed Marlae full on the lips, but hard and forceful. The shock caused Marlae to resist the dominating grasp, but when Rhain's soft probing tongue forced its way between her lips, Marlae could feel herself melting. The passion of the kiss overtook her, and her head began to swim. She was barely aware of a sharp quick pain in her shoulder where Rhain held her. Suddenly her head felt heavy and though she tried to fight against her eyelids, her eyes would not open. Marlae suddenly went limp in the stronger woman's arms. Rhain finished the kiss slowly, her unconscious lover in her arms, and then gently picked her up and tucked her under the covers of her spacious bed. The poison stored in the secret compartment of the ring that her mother had given her had been delivered through a thin sharp needle that protruded from the side of the stone setting. Marlae would not wake for at least twelve hours, and it would give Rhain plenty of time to ensure that her father was well away from Albitonin.

Setting out through the door to the Empress's chambers, Rhain nearly ran headlong into Gabriel Shadowfall, who also seemed to be moving with purpose through the halls of the Heart of Stone. For a moment the two figures stood looking at one another, their hands hovering near weapons. Gabriel sidestepped slowly, keeping his face to Rhain.

"Shouldn't you be attending to Marlae?" Gabriel said shortly.

"Shouldn't you be planning an execution? You were chosen to wield the blade weren't you? Marlae thought you would be a good executioner."

Gabriel grimaced.

"Don't you mean the Empress?"

Rhain smirked.

"I don't recall you using her title. I know that sharing the Empress's bed allows me some latitude, but unless I missed something, I don't think you've earned that right. Much though I know you've thought about it."

Gabriel could fell his cheeks burn, but he was sure that they did not color.

"I must be attending to my duties."

Rhain watched as Gabriel turned. She had taken in the state of the hallway and knew the rotation of the guards. In an instant, she had drawn a small thin silver dagger and ambushed Gabriel from behind, the blade of the dagger quickly finding its way to his throat. The taller man reacted as she expected and tried to turn and slam backwards into the wall, in an attempt to dislodge the woman, but Rhain was more than prepared. She got her feet up onto the wall, and pushed off at a high angle, propelling the two of them forward. Gabriel smashed face first into the stone floor, while Rhain flipped away, turned in one deft motion and was on top of the Knight of the Flashing Blade the next moment, the dagger again at his throat.

"I won't let you kill him, Gabriel," Rhain said finally. "If I have to carve my way through all of you to insure his safety, I will."

Gabriel grunted a reply, but the dagger was pressed too firmly into his throat and he could not form the words properly. Finally he was able to force out a single word.

"Pocket."

Rhain was caught off-guard by the word for only a moment before she used her off-hand to pat Gabriel's pockets on his right flank. Something hard and metal was there, and when Rhain recovered the item, she saw that it was an iron keyring. The same keyring that held keys to the cell where Aerith would be held. Rhain eased the pressure on the blade for a moment, allowing Gabriel to catch his breath.

"I'm going to help get him out of here," Gabriel said, finally able to bring his voice to bear. "I couldn't kill him after what happened on the road, and it doesn't seem that you want to either."

Rhain scrambled off of Gabriel's back but kept a defensive stance as the much stronger man found his way back to his feet. Where Rhain expected Gabriel's face to be twisted into a snarl of anger, his features were amazingly placid and understanding.

"If you would be so kind as to go to the western gates and insure that the guards remain distracted for a little while, we'll see if we can't get our friend out of here alive."

Rhain smiled and tossed the keys back to Gabriel before sprinting toward her new objective. Despite herself, Rhain found herself laughing.

* * * * * * * * * * * *

Two and a half hours ago....

CHAPTER 60

A portal opened at the edge of a cliff that overlooked the bridge that led across the great chasm that separated the Plains of Stone from the Heart of Stone. The great Temple of the Creator loomed in the distance, and as Sabrina Binosear stood looking over the vista, she was at the same time awestruck and confused. The portal should have taken her directly to where Aerith Seth was, but she knew that she was still quite a ways from him. The connection between them seemed to be getting stronger the closer they were together, but at the same time there seemed to be some kind of interference that was dampening not only his powers, but now seemed to be having an effect on hers. It was a strange sensation. Within her, three torches burned. The first was the powers that she had been granted after her ascension to the status of a god. The powers granted to her by the Creator were a fraction of what they once were before the Day the Heavens Fell and her expulsion from the heavens, but those powers were still potent and frightening to ordinary mortals. The second was the now brightly burning torch that was the powers given to her as the Chosen One, the mortal fated to carry the mantle passed by Aerith Seth following his death at the hands of Shau-ling. The powers open to her through that connection with Aerith had been dim and nearly non-existent since her ascension after the death of Onea, but now that Aerith had reclaimed his powers from Evan Sinn, she was beginning to feel the vigor and life from the mantle coursing through her. But it was more than just power that the mantle brought her. It was a vast knowledge of tactics, battle strategy, martial prowess, and a belligerence that could only be described as Aerith's style. One thing that Aerith could never be called was a subtle man. The last of the torches burned green at the edge of her mind, and she knew it to be the Blaze. Once it had been the lifeblood of not only Onea, but the child of the Creator once known as Shau-ling, but whose true name was Halicon. Those powers lay just beyond Sabrina's grasp, but she knew that should she need them, they would be there for her to draw upon.

Snag bounded from her shoulder that next moment and sat at the edge of the cliff, looking down. Obviously the ancient creature felt something odd too. There was a sound of falling rock behind her, but Sabrina didn't turn. She didn't need her eyes to know that three men approached, and from the sound of them, they were fully armored and had weapons drawn and ready for a fight. Sabrina had known she would be walking into a warzone, but then again, she hoped that she would be with Aerith for most of what would happen next. She had been feeling his troubled and worried emotions for the past two days, and it was only though those strong flashes that Sabrina had been able to track him. Now that she was this close, it was easy not only to pick out his powers, but the powers of Camille and Tess, as well as those of the daughter that Aerith had tried to hide from her mind. There were other powers here too, they felt like Alderin and Darrien, but she couldn't be sure. She knew that the lovers had been dispatched to return Tess to the Dark Continent of Mythryn, but Sabrina had thought that their task would have been long accomplished by now.

The sound of the armored men drew closer, and Snag turned, but Sabrina sent the creature patience. She turned slowly, keeping all expression from her face, and her hands open and away from her sides.

"What is it we have here?" one of the soldiers said viciously. "Are you lost, little girl?"

Sabrina tried not to frown, but she could feel it curl her lips anyway. She did not like to be called a little girl, despite her appearance. She was only in her early teens when her world died, and the Creator saw fit to insure that she would always be that physical age after she ascended. It was maddening on many levels. She was not as physically developed as some of the other young women who were members of the Dark Gods, and her figure was still slightly boyish. At times she resented this part of herself, especially when she saw Lissa who should have been nearly her same age, but who was a voluptuous, adult-looking woman. She was more than a bit ashamed of her body, and perhaps it was that, and not Aerith's mentality that kept her from finding love and acceptance in the arms of a man.

"Not lost. Just a little off course," Sabrina said finally. "I'm here to see a man who has been like a father to me, and I have a feeling he may be in trouble."

One of the guards snickered.

"Lost your daddy, huh? What's his name, maybe I can help you find him."

Sabrina exhaled softly, trying her best to keep herself calm.

"Aerith Seth."

The flurry of action the next handful of moments was both what Sabrina expected and had resigned herself to. The men to either side to her fell back into a defensive posture with the tips of their spears pointed at her, but at a pace away so that they could take full advantage of the length of their weapons. The man in the center who had spoken drew his sword in one deft and well-practiced motion but took no recognizable fighting stance. He obviously did not appreciate the threat that Sabrina posed to them, nor should he have. Sabrina made no motion, but took a moment to take in the look of the men. They wore full armor with the sigil of the Hand of the Creator on their breastplates, marking them as paladins of the Order of the Creator. They were soldiers under the command of the great Gregor Quicksilver. In recent years, Gregor's father Ivan had been a 'guest' of the Dark Gods, and he had been willing to share a great deal of information about their armies and their tactics. While Ivan had not been the pious man that his son was, the two men were nearly equals in both tenacity and tactics. A dangerous combination. However, Ivan had made it clear that the zealots that flocked to the banner of the Creator were not pious men, or even virtuous ones. They were simply frail men, men of weakness and vice, who chose to hide behind the law of the Creator. One was rarely held subject to laws they were entrusted to enforce.

"I'm sorry little girl," the guard in the center said coldly, "but you're going to have to come with us. Speaking the name of that condemned man may well land you in a cell right beside him. And if you are lucky, you may only spend the rest of your life there."

Sabrina shook her head, and felt the ripple of hate from behind her.

"I should have known that he would have gone and gotten himself into this kind of trouble again. I wonder if he'll actually wait for someone to rescue him this time, or if he'll just find his way out yet again the hard way."

The guards seemed puzzled by her words.

"There is no rescue or escape from the Heart of Stone…"

Sabrina cut him off hard, the words both her own and coming from somewhere else.

"Yes, yes. Impregnable, inescapable, cannot be done, rot forever. Why is it always the same thing? Do they actually, honestly believe that a man who can move mountains with a thought can actually be held in a little cell made of iron and rock? The stupidity and arrogance of the human race never ceases to amaze."

In spite of herself, Sabrina laughed, a reaction which brought flickers of annoyance to each of the guards' faces.

"Now see here…."

"No," Sabrina cut him off again, suddenly deadly serious. "I don't want to have to kill you, but I really don't have time for this. I'll give you to the count of three to turn around, run back to your impregnable fortress and warn them that I'm coming for Aerith, and I will crush anyone who stands in my way. Don't irritate me, or I will show you why the Lioness is the symbol for my house."

There was stunned silence for a moment and then the three guards laughed nearly in unison. Sabrina hung her head in resignation for a moment and then shook it slightly. They never listen, she thought to herself as she imparted instructions to Snag who was crouched and ready to strike behind her. The attack came and went, the two guards with spears dead before they knew they were struck. Snag bounded over Sabrina's left shoulder, the razor sharp tail spinning like a scythe and claiming the first guard through the throat, severing his head without effort. The other guard was not lucky enough to see the strike as Sabrina reached out in the man's direction and with the sheer force of her will crushed his heart within his chest. The two suits of armor clattered to the ground, leaving the third guard standing with Sabrina to his front, and the Snag coiled behind him waiting to lash out again.

"Now," Sabrina said, a small smile on her lips, "go, before I forget I'm a lady."

The guard turned to run, but Sabrina's attention was turned elsewhere as a familiar feeling swept through her. Aerith was embracing his powers, and it was only a matter of time before he would be making his way toward the western gate of the palace. The black Snag bounded back to Sabrina's shoulder without urging and the two of them leapt from the cliff face and soared toward the palace.

"I should have known he couldn't wait."

* * * * * * * * * * * *

Two hours ago…

Camille sat on the edge of her bed and could not get the sick feeling out of the pit of her stomach. She should have tried to fight harder for Aerith, but she knew that no amount of pleas from her would reverse the decisions that Gregor and Hannah made. The Will had seen to that. Even though Hannah and Gregor were no zealots, they were believers. Sometimes that was more dangerous. Hannah and Gregor had no reason to not have faith in the Creator, no matter what the Dark Gods said. After all, the Dark Gods were evil. Even though Camille had sacrificed herself to save the whole of the Heart of Stone and all the people who dwelled within it, she was still an evil Dark God. She looked up at Devlin who sat on the other side of the room sharpening his sword nervously.

"You know that sword doesn't need sharpening," Camille said with slight annoyance in her voice.

Devlin looked up at Camille for only a moment before returning his focus to the blade. The Sacred Weapon Discipline felt cold in his hands, and for the first time since he had taken up the position of Onyx Knight, he felt unworthy to even hold the blade.

"We can't just sit here while Aerith is killed."

The statement was cold, calculated, and totally true. There were no words that Camille could put together that would make Devlin's assertions false. The problem was magnified when Camille considered that Devlin had absolutely no reason to make the statement.

Oh, he has plenty of reasons my dear, the voice that was as much a part of Devlin as his dragon heritage said. *Devlin and I have discussed this quite a bit, and we believe that Aerith would be an asset in the war to come, and that he should not meet his end here. Besides, there are more dangerous creatures afoot in this world than Aerith Seth, no matter what he himself may believe.*

Camille frowned.

"You speak as though you know the man."

I do. He is insufferable, inconsiderate, pompous, brilliant, and terrifying. There is no better ally or worse enemy to have in a fight. But the man is as unpredictable as the wind. He has and always will follow his own path, and for a time you may be lucky enough to be going the same direction he is. But make no mistake, no one, not even the Creator tells Aerith Seth what path to walk. Not even his wife, no matter what Bryn may think. Your father and mother never trusted him either, but in all fairness they never really got a chance to know him. He's not much for the company of others.

"With Bryn as a wife, who could blame him."

Camille's jibe met with empty air. Then she felt it. There was a surge of power from inside the Heart of Stone, and it came from below, in the dungeons. As if on cue, Aerith was making his own escape attempt. Perhaps he didn't need rescuing after all. It fit his character.

"Perhaps we should do something to help him," Devlin said, reading not only the intentions of the voice in the back of his mind, but also the look on Camille's face.

"I know just where we can meet him," Camille said, grasping her sword and heading for the door. The knot in her stomach was still there, but no matter the outcome, at least she could sleep soundly, if she survived the night.

* * * * * * * * * * * *

One and a half hours ago….

Tess stood looking out the window, a frown painting her face. She watched Camille and Devlin rushing out of Camille's little cottage toward the Heart of Stone. She knew that Camille had felt Aerith Seth beginning his escape attempt, but she was probably unaware that Sabrina was there as well trying to aid Aerith. But it wasn't Aerith that bothered Tess. She just stared as the two ran, Devlin's hand brushing Camille's briefly. The tears ran down Tess' cheek after a moment, the anger and hurt and tumult growing inside her.

"You can't have her," she whined, tears streaming down her face. "She's mine! She's mine!"

The cottage was in an upheaval around Tess. Wall, floor, and ceiling colors shifted and surged through an ever-changing kaleidoscope of colors. Furniture moved itself all around the room, crashing into each other like drunken sailors in a bar brawl. The hurt and anger built inside the young girl as the moments passed, a storm raging inside her was soon matched by a storm raging in the cottage. Thunder shook the walls, and rain fell from the ceiling, coating everything. Tess stood, still staring out the window, her lithe form soaked in the cold rain, her white dress clinging to her. Suddenly the pain lost out to the anger and she snarled.

"I won't let you ruin my Camille. I won't let anyone take her from me again."

She reached into her mind and found the essence of the powers the Dark Gods were given by the Creator. They were bright and powerful like bolts of lightning barely contained. She reached for the ones that were part of Aerith, Camille, and Sabrina, and she held them firmly in her hands. They burned her to the core, but her will did not allow for her to relent. With great effort she severed the strands, temporarily robbing the three of their powers. Camille would have to come to her senses now. There was nothing more she could do. She would have to come back to her cottage and just leave Aerith to his fate.

"She'll come back to me now," Tess whispered into the air. "She has to. I can't live without her."

∗ ∗ ∗ ∗ ∗ ∗ ∗ ∗ ∗ ∗ ∗ ∗

Moments ago….

Darrien Annis and her protector and lover Alderin Parran appeared at the foot of the Heart of Stone and looked up unimpressed at the massive fortification. After all, it was only stone, no match for the powers of one of the children of the Dark Gods, let alone two. They had delayed too long in coming straight to the Heart of Stone, instead taking time to gather information about the rebellion and how it had affected the political climate in Cadaria. Tess would be fine, she had Camille with her, and a few days delay would not incite Darrien's father if they came back with valuable information. Then they had gotten word of the attack by the creature Death and the apparent sacrifice of Camille. But the stories after were confusing, first Camille was said to be dead, and then miraculously she was alive again. But that was another mystery for another day. Now, Darrien's mission was clear. She had to bring her sister back, and in one piece.

"I don't know why Tess was even sent on this mission. It should have been you and I to come to deal with Aunt Hannah and that bastard Kaitain. If we would have come here, there wouldn't be any of these problems. I'd have killed their Emperor and their whole army if they stood in my way."

Alderin nodded.

"Don't you think that is why your father sent Tess?"

Darrien scowled in Alderin's direction. She had a retort ready for him, but the wall of the fortress before them exploded, sending shards of stone and metal flying in all directions. Alderin stepped in front of Darrien, shielding her from all of the impact, his arm flung over his eyes, to protect them from the brightness of the explosion. When the light had faded, and Alderin was able to see again, he had no time to react before the blow struck him on the side of his helm, and sent him sprawling toward the edge of the ravine. He was barely able to grab ahold and right himself. Darrien didn't move from her spot or attempt to help Alderin. Her eyes were locked on the woman who had delivered the blow. The pale blond woman stood proudly, a full set of armor made from the bones of fallen beasts wrapped her form, a huge dragon-head helm sitting atop her head. Leathery wings extended from her shoulders, and she clutched a cruel looking black blade in her right hand. There was a cold smirk on the woman's lips.

"I had wanted to kill your pathetic little sister," Seraphina Masile said icily, "but I guess I will have to suffice with you for now."

Escalation

Year Three of the Just Emperor Kaitain "Dragonsbane" Lorien, Creator's Calendar Year 1870

Dominique tried hard not to stare at the woman who had just named herself as a member of the Dark Gods, but she could feel her own tension rooting her to the spot and preventing her from doing anything but stare. Behind her, she could feel Chelsea stiffen slightly, but there seemed to be more of a resignation in her than worry. While in the Imperial Court Dominique had heard the tales from both Gregor Quicksilver and Leonora Wastri, arguably two of the most powerful members of the Knights of the Flashing Blade, detailing their utter defeats at the hands of children of the Dark Gods. This woman standing mere paces from the Empress of Cadaria could have killed both of them with a thought, and yet, the woman seemed to be just like them. She had a rugged if refined look to her features, and though she was clearly a noblewoman, she had seen many battles in her time, and her features spoke of pride and loss. Finally finding her ability to move again, Dominique motioned for Midarin to sit again, and when her uninvited guest sat, Dominique too found her way into an unreasonably comfortable chair.

"Queen Sandar…." Dominique began.

Midarin held her hand up quickly, cutting off Dominique's sentence. Dominique felt her mouth dry immediately and her voice shriveled in her throat as though it had been cut off by the woman's motion. But no such sorcery was at play. Nervousness had robbed the voice, not any extension of the Dark Goddess's power.

"Any kingdom that bowed to me has long since been ground to dust under the boot of the Creator and his machinations. And as for my name, Midarin will do. The Sandar name was robbed from me when we were cast down to this rock, and any ties that I had to the great Sandar linage died with my husband in the throne room of this palace."

Dominique inclined her head for a moment.

"I wish that I could extend you the same courtesy, Midarin," she said finally, "but my station requires that if I am to negotiate for the whole of Cadaria that I adhere to some level of protocol."

There was a slight look of annoyance on Midarin's face, but it faded quickly into a chuckle.

"Very well, Empress Lorien," Midarin said, stressing the last name. "You are quite fortunate that it was myself and not Bryn who came for this negotiation. She would have insisted that protocol demanded that you address her as Goddess Bryn."

Dominique made mental note of the name, and then felt the sour taste in her mouth at the idea of referring to anyone as 'Goddess'. It made Empress sound hollow in her ears. It was then that the completely ridiculous nature of this negotiation hit her.

"Please," Dominique said finally, "call me Dominique. I can't stand to be called Empress Lorien, especially when you attach that tone to it."

Midarin nodded.

"Will you please ask your guardian there to sit down. I know she can't hurt me, and she knows it as well, so her posture is nothing short of insulting."

Dominique looked over her shoulder at Chelsea, and the two women's eyes met. So much could have been said in that brief moment. Midarin's own posture was an affront to every level of decorum that should have been afforded to the Empress of Cadaria and her personal guard, but this was not a normal situation. Chelsea relented and sat to Dominique's right, her hands finally straying from her weapon. Natalia too found a seat and seemed completely relieved to be off her feet.

"Would you like to begin?" Dominique offered.

Midarin nodded.

"My husband, Gwydeon Sandar, was the first of the Dark Gods, and he sacrificed his life to broker a truce with the first Cadarian Emperor. That truce was to be binding for the rest of our existence here on this world, but of course we knew it would not be. However, I want to make it clear now, I will not be laying down my life as Gwydeon had. If there is blood required for this truce, I am under orders from the Council of the Dark Gods to ensure that it is Aldere that pays that price."

Midarin's eyes were stone, and her voice shook Dominique. The threat was more than clear, and there was no hyperbole in her statement.

"The Dark Gods have their own agendas," Midarin continued, "and they do not include the petty lives of Cadarian people or their politics. It was the forces of Cadaria that made war on us, not the other way around. And yet we have forgiven, time and time again. We spared the life of Gregor Quicksilver when he came to our island and killed dozens of our soldiers. There was cause then to loose our forces on the shores of the Empire of Cadaria, and yet we stayed our hand, knowing that you stood no chance against us. But still you came, sending not one, but two more of your Knights of the Flashing Blade against us, and both failed. This one here, Natalia, one of Kaitain's assassins brought with her a dagger that could have ended the life of one of us, but she made the mistake of drawing it against me. I could have killed her, but not only did I spare her life, but I healed her extensive injuries and brought her with me."

There was something that resembled shame in Natalia's eyes, and she hung her head and nodded softly.

"Emperor Kaitain gave me the dagger and ordered me to kill a Dark God."

Midarin continued before Dominique could react.

"Such orders constitute a clear breach of the truce between the Empire of Cadaria and the Dark Continent of Mythryn, and stains the honor of the Lorien family. It is also an act of war."

Silence hung heavy in the air. The last word had been spoken in almost a matter of fact tone, but it was pregnant with meaning. It would not be so much of a war as a slaughter. The best warriors in the whole of Cadaria had been defeated with minimal effort, and to think that anything would reverse that course was foolish. Midarin saw Dominique's hesitation and continued.

"Before I left Mythryn, orders had also been given to Bryn, and she was going to begin making Cadaria pay for its insults. And believe me when I tell you, that she does not have nearly as much patience as I, and she is far more practiced in the inflicting of suffering than the rest of the Dark Gods combined. She's been doing it for several thousand years, and she enjoys it far too much to be palatable."

Dominique shuddered involuntarily.

"How can we prevent this reprisal?" Dominique said, her voice wavering slightly.

Midarin eyed Dominique for a moment and then steepled her fingers under her chin.

"Are you in a position to make such a deal?" Midarin questioned finally. "Or once your pig husband wakes up, will he reverse any bargains you make here and punish you for your impertinence?"

Dominique considered for a moment. Kaitain hated the Dark Gods, and hated them in a way that defined any rationality. There was a very good chance that even if Dominique were to create some truce with the Dark Gods, Kaitain would simply ignore it, if not completely overturn it. That put Dominique in a dangerous position to say the least. There would be no grounds for her to attempt to enforce the truce, no legal grounds. As if reading the thoughts in Dominique's mind, Midarin leaned forward and smiled slyly.

"Or are you prepared to stop him?"

* * * * * * * * * * * *

Deep in the woods outside of Aldere, a form stood, his cold shadow casting a pall on the land, and causing the plants and grass to wither and die as he passed. Death focused his eyes on the gleaming beacon of the Cadarian Empire, the Imperial Palace at Aldere and felt the cold smile peal back his lips. Dorovar had wanted to make a statement, had wanted to make the whole of the Cadarian Empire shiver and cower in fear. This would be Death's greatest act, and it would pave the way for the coming of War. While Death did not want to sacrifice itself in the same manner that Pestilence and Famine had, he knew that it was necessary to help shepherd in the darkness that would mark the beginning of Dorovar's reign. This one action, the fall of the capital of the Cadarian Empire would cause the rebellion to burst throughout the countryside and give War all of the tools he needed to make everyone suffer. Hundreds of thousands of souls would find their way into Dorovar's Chorus of Souls, and it would only be a matter of time before Dorovar was freed from his prison and the choir would sing him to the heavens to unseat the Creator and remake the universe in his own image. Death and the rest of Dorovar's heralds would sit at the right hand of the Creator, and bring his love and mercy to all of the worlds under his command.

A moment later there was another form in the woods, and Death knew her before her form had settled. Jerah stood looking as he had at the palace, her gaze cold and isolating. Images formed in Death's mind, the images of women, soldiers, men in black robes who bent the arcane forces to their will. One woman in particular came to death's mind. A warrior woman with a bow and a green cloth holding her hair. It took only Death a moment to know her name, and his smile deepened.

"I should like to kill a Dark God."

Death did not feel the blow, but after it struck Death knew that Jerah had not moved to deliver it. She had simply exerted her will and he had been pummeled under the weight of her desire. The implication was clear, the woman was not to be harmed, no matter the cost.

"As Dorovar wills," Death intoned coldly.

Jerah lingered for only a moment and then an item formed in her hand. It was a coin, roughly the size of her palm, and it floated smoothly from her grasp and landed in the black icy gauntlet that covered the rotted flesh of Death's right hand. Jerah wanted to make sure that the token was found, though it did not matter who it was recovered by. That next instant Jerah was gone, and Death looked down at the coin. It was completely made of silver, and on the face of the token was the open-mouthed head of a wolf.

* * * * * * * * * * * *

Emries pulled Irene into a side corridor and waited until he was sure that none of their words could find their way to unintended ears. It had been many centuries since he had laid eyes on any of his siblings, and it had taken this long since his defeat at the hands of Evan Sinn to heal from those wounds. But Emries was a child of the Creator, and he could not be defeat by a mortal, no matter the power he may have thought he had at his disposal. The brush with mortality had taught Emries many lessons, and the centuries after had given him the patience to take his revenge.

"That is quite a shell you have chosen for yourself, sister."

Irene frowned.

"Young girls are not to your liking any longer, Emries? The years have obviously dulled your edge."

The venom was playful but palpable. Together Emries and Talisia had watched as the Creator formed the universe. Together they had battled against their siblings in an effort to prove themselves superior. They had caused wars on thousands of worlds, and brought humiliation on Halicon and the others time and time again. But their greed had gotten the better of them. Emries fell because of his own carelessness, and Talisia fell because of her misguided greed and impatience.

"You centuries of imprisonment may finally be at an end, my lovely sister. The Creator is destined to fall soon, and whether or not we are the instruments of his fall is immaterial. We will be in the position to profit from his destruction. Pike and the others are fools if they think that the breaking of one of the covenants is going to bring them anything other than suffering."

"One of them is here now," Irene said quickly, "if we rob them of their numbers, they are even more sure to fail."

Emries smile was wicked and knowing.

"As much as it would fill me with delight to pull Midarin limb from limb, it will please me more to make her suffer in the hell that is to come. Your Kaitain is very close to wakening now, and I have been attending to his madness. Now that Dorovar's influence has been cleared from his mind, he has been very open to suggestion. The chaos that he will create once he is back on his feet will break the back of any resistance and give us the chance we need to take possession of the Dragon's Tear. With that power, we can rewrite everything; unmake these pathetic heroes and take back what was ours. Not even that meddler Aerith Seth will stand in my way this time."

Irene smiled and opened her mouth to speak, but Emries shook his head.

"Have your dog Korin stir up some trouble at the western gate. It will give Death the opening he needs."

With that, Emries leaned in, kissed Irene passionately on the lips and then walked off in the direction of the eastern exit to the palace. The woman smiled and brought her fingers to her lips, memory of many such kisses filling her mind, and turned down the passage toward where she knew Korin would be waiting. This was going to be a very eventful day after all.

* * * * * * * * * * * *

Deep in the bowels of the Imperial Palace, behind a wall that no one but the initiated knew to be false, the Shadow Academy continued it work.

Under the watchful eye of Jaccob Aldora and master Yaron Telsin the recruits continued to work on more and more deadly and destructive spells. Ayden Seth stood on the opposite side of the chamber from the two masters, watching more than practicing. In the weeks that he had been part of the Shadow Academy, he had learned much about the makeup of the recruits. A full ninety percent of the students in the Academy were men, and most of those had been expelled for one reason or another from the Academy of Arcane Arts in Jelan. Most of them had little in the way of ability, but had been corrupted by the teachings of Yaron Telsin into thinking they were more powerful than their potential. Ayden had recognized Telsin's purpose from the first lesson, and when he had tried to question Jaccob about it, it became clear that however gifted the Topaz Knight may have been, the years of drinking and whoring had rotted his ability to think of anything past his own desires. It was a pity really. Ayden had come to think fondly of Sir Aldora, but if he could not be brought to see the wrongs that were being perpetrated on the members of the Shadow Academy, he would have to suffer for the error of his shortsightedness.

Telsin was another story altogether. The man was too vigilant, too studious, and saw everything as though he knew it was going to happen before it did. Ayden had learned quickly that nothing escaped the man's eyes, no matter how deft one was at obfuscation. Above and beyond his attentiveness and attention to detail, Telsin was tireless and single-minded toward the training of the recruits. He taught them all how to embrace powers that should have been beyond them to create terrifying wonders. Ayden knew that Telsin had taught the students to create these terrors by drawing on their own life-forces, sacrificing a bit of themselves with every spell cast. He was preparing them to sacrifice themselves in a battle that could not be won, to make casualties of themselves before they could suffer from the effects of their own destruction. These recruits would die by the dozens in their first battle, and it was unlikely that any of the survivors would even realize why their classmates had died.

The lessons for the day had come to an end, and the students of the Shadow Academy carefully left the hidden training grounds. Ayden waited for them all to go and followed Jaccob back into the hallways of the Imperial Palace. Ayden had never seen Telsin outside of the training room, nor had he ever seen the man leave the palace. It was as though he was always there, a construct of the training grounds themselves. Though Ayden knew better. He had felt the flows of power as he was leaving the room one day, and knew immediately that the man had created a portal. That ability should have been beyond a simple trickster like him, a man who was possessed of only enough power for the simplest of spells. Though he hid his lack of ability behind nearly encyclopedic knowledge of the arcane arts. Together Ayden and Jaccob walked, avoiding any subject that the wrong ears could have misinterpreted. They were coming close to the eastern exit of the palace. Jaccob's need for drink and company after the long morning of training were driving his feet in an almost unnatural speed. The addictions were as amusing as they were pathetic to Ayden. Walking together, they passed a man who was bound in their same direction. It was only for the briefest of moments that Ayden looked over his shoulder, his intention to wish the man a good day. But once his eyes found the other man's, his blood froze in his veins. He was saying something to Jaccob, but the words died in his throat, and any recollection of the subject matter was gone from his mind in that instant. A full five paces ahead of the man, Ayden stopped and turned to face the man whom he had never met, but knew in an instant. Jaccob too had stopped, puzzled by his younger friend's actions. The other man had stopped dead too, but no recollection was in the man's eyes, more puzzlement than anything else.

"Something bad is about to happen, Jaccob," Ayden was saying, throwing the black cloak over his shoulder. You'll want to be out in the courtyard now."

The next moment, Ayden's hands were filled with two blades, one crackling with lightning, the other smoking with the cold of ice. Jaccob opened his mouth to question, but with a single twist of his head in Jaccob's direction, the older man found himself propelled out the eastern entrance into the light of the day.

"Should I know you, boy?" Emries said in a cold smooth voice, letting a pure crystalline blade form in his left hand. "I should at least like the pleasure of the name of those I kill."

"You don't know me, world-killer, but I certainly know you. My father has told me all about you, and it will please me to no end to tell him that I struck down the greatest enemy he has ever known. And as for my name, it's Ayden Seth."

Emries smiled despite himself and eased back into a fighting stance, reveling in his good fortune.

* * * * * * * * * * * *

Chelsea sat, her hands gripping tightly to the arms of the chair, watching the sparring session between Midarin and Dominique. Had this been a physical confrontation, Dominique would be lying on the floor bleeding and begging for mercy. Her inexperience with negotiation was being seriously exposed by the far more experienced woman, and the doubt and worry were starting to creep into Dominique's voice.

"The Empire of Cadaria cannot capitulate to such demands," Dominique said, not nearly as convincing as she wanted to be. "The kingdoms have existed for generations under the direct command of the hereditary families appointed by the first Emperor. To ask them to give up their titles and their lands to members of the Council of the Dark Gods would start a more far-reaching rebellion than already exists in the countryside. Instead of two people claiming to be the rightful rulers of the Empire you would have dozens. Every lord and lady throughout all of Cadaria would be staking their claim and the chaos would be unimaginable. And even if they accept the rule of a Dark God over their lands, they would not accept any commands from the Emperor. It would be clear that any Lorien Emperor would be seen as a puppet serving the whims of the Council. This will be made even clearer since you refuse to allow the Dark Gods who control those kingdoms to swear fealty to the Emperor."

"The only way that the Dark Gods will swear fealty to the Emperor of Cadaria is if the head of the Council of the Dark Gods is sitting upon the throne."

Dominique shook her head.

"Then there can be no accord. It will be war."

Midarin sat back, and exhaled slowly.

"You still haven't answered my earlier question Dominique, and you have been quite masterful in avoiding the subject whenever I have tried to steer you back to it. The matter is clear, and no matter how long we sit here talking, there is no other resolution to our conflict that the Dark Gods will accept. There can be no peace so long as a member of the Lorien family is sitting on the Throne of Cadaria. The Loriens forged the peace with the Dark Gods, and it was the Loriens who arrogantly broke that peace. The family must be made to suffer for those crimes. And whether a peace is brokered that removes the Lorien family from the Throne, or we are made to do it through force, the outcome will be the same. How much death is your Kaitain worth, Dominique?"

Dominique fell silent and her features fell. That was the crux of it all. Kaitain. Could she really sacrifice him? Could she, in this room, be the instrument that would seal his fate? She knew what kind of man that he was. She knew the cruelty and the savagery of his heart, but could she, knowing the evil that lurked inside of him, give the order that would end his life? Would she then be any different than the one she was replacing? What then? Would she give the order to have Marlae killed as well? And then Feyd and Felicia? When would it stop? How many would she have to order to their deaths to forge this peace with Midarin and the Dark Gods? But then, how many would die if she didn't make this deal? Would there be a Cadaria left to any of them if the Dark Gods chose to unleash war upon them?

Before Dominique could say another word, Midarin's eyes shot toward the door, and in a moment she was on her feet, her left hand falling to the hilt of the sword on her hip and a bow of brilliant crystal appearing in her right hand. Chelsea and Natalia too, shot to their feet, the practiced instincts of warriors taking over. However, Dominique had expected the two members of the Knights of the Flashing Blade to advance toward the Dark Goddess in some vain attempt to protect their empress from a fate worse than death, but Chelsea spun to face the door, and Natalia ran toward the window. Chelsea looked back over her shoulder and her eyes found Midarin's.

"You sense it too?" Midarin's question was cold.

"I smell death," Chelsea answered. "Death on the scale I haven't smelled since the rotting corpses on the battlefield in the Plains of Steam during the last great war."

"Arcane forces are being brought to bear," Natalia said, her eyes scanning the courtyard through the thin glass, "power that could consume the soul."

Midarin's brow furrowed.

"There is a presence here that shouldn't be here. That bastard is dead, and I'm going to see that he returns to the grave."

An explosion rocked the palace, coming from somewhere in the direction of the eastern gate.

"Get her out of here," Midarin said looking at Chelsea. "No good will come of any of this if we lose her now. Trust no one."

Midarin didn't wait for a reply as she moved past Chelsea toward the door. Before she got there, the door exploded inward, a shockwave knocking Chelsea off her feet and sending Midarin stumbling backwards. The chair that Dominique was still perched on was rocked off its feet and sent toppling, with Dominique sprawling to the ground. Midarin took only two steps backward before her feet reset, and saw the two black robed forms move into the doorway. The bow was up in a second, and the whisper-thin nearly insubstantial crystalline bowstring was pulled back and released before either of the men could know what was happening. A needle-thin arrow seemed to coalesce out of nothing a fraction of a second before it collided with the first man's forehead. The force of the impact threw him through the door a fraction of a second before the second twang of the bowstring signaled the impending death of the second interloper. Both men were dead before Chelsea was able to get back to her feet and her attention immediately went to helping Dominique back to her feet. Chelsea looked over her shoulder to call for Natalia, but the assassin was already out the window, her new goals unknown. Midarin hesitated for only a moment before starting for the door.

"It seems that your Court Sorceress is making her move now," Midarin said. "Those lackeys were meant to take care of the two of you before they fell at my hand. After, any excuse could have been created, the most logical would be that these black robed men were followers of the Dark Gods. You see now the treachery we have stomached for generations of you Cadarians. There will be no peace."

With that, Midarin raced through the door, tracking her query. Dominique clung to Chelsea, a trickle of blood running down from her forehead to her cheek where her head had struck the hard floor. This would not be the only blood spilled this day, and Dominique wondered if all of this war and death could have been prevented if she could have only brought herself to do a little evil.

Elements of Faith

Year Three of the Just Emperor Kaitain "Dragonsbane" Lorien, Creator's Calendar Year 1870

Aerith Seth looked up the hallway at the phalanx of soldiers that had taken station there in an attempt to cut off their path to the western gate. Behind them he heard the clattering of more armor, and knew that they had been herded toward this trap. Unfortunately this was the only direct path to the western gate, as any other path would have lead through the center of the Heart of Stone and more confrontations and death than even Aerith was ready to stomach. Had it been him alone in the fight, the path would not have mattered. But for this fight he had Gabriel, Devlin, and Camille in tow. Camille he knew by reputation, and if she was half the warrior that her mother and father were, then she would at least be useful in a fight. Gabriel had skill, but at the end of the day he and Devlin were both mortal, and mortals had their limits. They would be a liability in a pitched battle. As it was, Aerith had already had to slow his pace considerably to make sure that Gabriel had survived this far. The annoyance was rising in Aerith. Patience was never a quality that Aerith had in abundance, nor would there be an opportunity for him to exercise it here. What made matters worse was that he wasn't even fighting at full strength. If Camille was right, and Tess had shut off a portion of their powers, things just got a lot harder.

"You know, we may just be doing Kaitain a favor if this goes on much longer."

Camille balked at Aerith's mistimed attempt at humor. Devlin to his credit smiled and braced himself for the fight that was going to be upon them in a moment. Gabriel seemed to let the comment pass through him as though it hadn't been made. Obviously Gabriel had been around Aerith long enough that the man's humor was simply an extension of his coping with the stress of the moment. As Camille looked at the arrayed forces, she saw the glimmer of truth in Aerith's comment. How many had they killed already? What kind of toll was this little escape attempt going to take on the state of the rebellion if the forces of the Cadarian Throne decided to descend upon Albitonin? Would there be enough troops left between Aldere and Albitonin to make a difference against a coordinated strike? The row of troops in front of them parted after a moment, and the hulking figure of Gregor Quicksilver stepped through, an impressive-looking broadsword in hand. It was not Valor to be sure, but in Gregor's hands it was surely a formidable weapon. Behind them, the ranks parted to reveal Hannah Ironheart. She was carrying Faith, and the weapon made her more impressive of a warrior than she would have been otherwise. This was the very thing that Aerith had wanted to avoid, but deep in his heart, he knew it had to be this way.

"Aerith Seth," Gregor said firmly. "You have been judged an abomination by the Creator himself, through his emissary on the mortal plane, The Will. You shall surrender now and end this chaos. If you willingly submit to this judgment here and now, we will spare the others that you have swayed to your camp. They will be given the opportunity to freely leave Albitonin. However, Devlin and Gabriel will have to surrender their swords and their positions as Knights of the Flashing Blade. Regardless of your decision, you have to know that you will be dying here, today. Ask yourself whether you want to take your three companions down into the depths of hell with you."

Aerith stood straight and let his swords fall from his grasp. Instead of clattering to the ground, they hung in mid-air beside him, as if waiting to be taken back into his hands. He took a step forward, away from his three companions, and the swords followed, keeping their position relative to their master.

"I didn't want it to come to this Gregor," Aerith said finally, "and you have to know that's the truth. But if you think I'm going to lay down my swords and let you take me to some dungeon so you can cut my head off, you've got a serious issue with reality. Once, a very long time ago, before this world was even in the imagination of the Creator, I was captured and paraded in front of my enemy. I was forced down to my knees and killed like a lamb. Never again. Never again!"

The hall seemed to reverberate with the power of Aerith's words, and Gabriel could feel the shivers going down his spine. Some of the soldiers seemed to shudder as well, and a few looked as if they were going to break and run. But Gregor stood firm, and his strength bolstered the strength of those around him.

"Now, you stand before me, gangs of dead men at your back, threatening me with words from some puppet creature calling itself the Will of the Creator." Aerith spoke in a cold and serious tone, the kind Gabriel had never heard come from the man, and for the first time since their meeting, Gabriel feared the man calling himself Aerith Seth. "I've stood face to face with the Creator. I've heard his words with my own ears."

There was a ripple of uncertainty that came from the soldiers, and even Hannah seemed to take a sharp breath. Of course the Dark Gods had been cast down from the Heavens, everyone knew that, but no one spoke openly of their relationship to the Creator. It was the dirty little reality that no one wanted to accept. Truth could never intrude on the beliefs of the faithful if their faith was to continue unstained. Sensing the shift in the atmosphere, Aerith pressed forward, his voice booming so that he was no longer speaking just to Gregor, but all of the soldiers as well.

"You are here, all of you, giving your lives and your wills to the great and wise Creator. You feel his touch, imparted through priests ordained by service and loyalty to a calling. You hear the words of love, devotion, and forgiveness from the lips of your unimpeachable leaders like Gregor and Hannah. And you take those words as the great truth, something that never needs to be questioned. But it's the questions that make faith possible. If you simply believe, blindly believe, you are no better than the animals of the field who look on you as if you're gods. To most men, Gregor, you are a god. You are divinity through your power, your prowess, and your benevolence. Yet you surrender the very thing that makes you human by worshiping this fraud."

The word 'fraud' hit all of the soldiers like a sledgehammer to the chest. Fear melted away to anger and they wanted to charge. Gregor and Hannah's will was all that held them back. Undaunted by the display, Aerith continued, his eyes piercing Gregor's soul.

"You've fought a great many battles, Gregor, but how many have you fought for your faith? How many have you fought in the name of the Creator, but at the behest of corrupt and unworthy men? You go into bloodshed with the name of the Creator on your lips, but it is really the Emperor sitting on his throne in Aldere that put you there. So is that really an exercise of your faith? Or is it sanctioned murder?"

For the briefest of moments, Gregor faltered. His shell of strength cracked for a moment, but only Aerith saw it. He pressed on, taking a step forward.

"Have you ever truly fought for your faith, Gregor? Have any of you ever truly fought for your faith, or were you just following orders? Were you just doing the bidding of greedy men who used your faith for their own gains? I have fought and died for my faith. Though I have been touched by the Creator, I am not divinity. I'm flesh and blood the same as all of you. You say the Will of the Creator calls me an abomination. The embodiment of evil. But doesn't the Creator teach that to know evil is to know the depths of your own soul? That within each of us is the capacity for goodness and evil? The difference between me and the rest of you is that I know the evil of my soul. I have confronted it, and I have embraced it. I have done what the Creator will not do. I have looked inside myself and I have understood the truth."

Aerith took another step forward, and the shaky spears of the Army of Stone were only a long pace away from him now, but Aerith didn't see them. His path was clearer to him now than it had ever been.

"All men, no matter how holy, are touched by evil. All men, no matter how evil are touched by the divine. There cannot be one without the other. And to deny that, is to deny everything that faith is. We all touch the divine every day. It is the unbridled love in our hearts for a total stranger, it is the inextinguishable light in the eyes of a child. It is the unerring hope that tomorrow will bring something better than today. We are divine, our hearts are divine, our love is divine. Divinity and holiness are within us."

Aerith was now nearly face to face with Gregor. The two men stood nearly the same height, with Gregor only a fraction taller than the much older man. Camille felt herself tensing now, as though she knew what Aerith's next words would be, and the reaction that would be sparked from them. Devlin seemed to sense her trepidation and tightened the grip on the hilt of his sword.

"I have heard the words spoken from the Creator's lips. I've read the Creator's words from the Book of the Creator. I've seen how his words have been turned into the goals of the wicked, and I have seen worlds burn because of misguided faith. I've seen the children of the Creator squabble over who is the greater, and I have watched millions die at the Creator's command. The Creator doesn't care about the fate of men. The Creator doesn't care about the fate of this world any more than he cared about the fate of mine. You are not his children. You were created by a misguided, power-mad fool who wanted to prove a point. A man named Emries created man, and we are the embodiments of the chaos that he chose to release into the Cosmos."

"Liar!"

One of the guards from behind Gregor thrust his spear forward, claiming Aerith in the shoulder. Aerith didn't move, he took the blow and held firmly his ground as blood flowed from the ugly wound. Gregor raised a hand, preventing the charge that was about to come.

"I know this to be the truth, as I have heard it from the Creator himself. Just as the Dark Gods were once mortals who rose up to defeat the very Emries who created them, the Dark Gods rose up in an attempt to prevent an even greater catastrophe than the one that occurred on their world. You should embrace them as leaders, and use the wisdom they have within them, not cower in fear. But as long as you listen to the lies of the Will and the others that serve the Creator, you will never know the truth."

Gregor's voice was cold.

"The Creator is the truth. His servants are the heralds of His word, and those who receive their words are the most blessed."

Aerith smiled.

"Then why was it the Will of the Creator who delivered this message and blessing. Why wasn't it the Voice?"

That was it. Camille knew where this was going. Aerith was about to detonate this conflict. She didn't need to see his face to know that he was smiling.

"Do you know why, Gregor?" Aerith leaned in conspiratorially. "Because I killed him."

* * * * * * * * * * * *

"So you're the one who's been causing all of the trouble for us," Darrien Annis said, her cloak gently disengaging itself from her shoulders and falling to the ground, a brilliant crystal axe forming in her hand. "I'm sure father will be happy when I report that you're dead."

Seraphina laughed slightly and shook her head.

"I should have expected nothing less from Pike's daughter. Defiant glare, axe in hand, and absolutely nothing between her ears that would be considered intelligence."

The winged woman struck the next moment, the black sword colliding with the haft of the axe in a sound that was both unnatural and horrifying. The air screamed with the impacted, seemingly tortured by the very passage of the blade. Darrien spun into the strike and extended a hand into Seraphina's chest, exerting her power and landing a blow hard into the woman's breastplate. Seraphina was struck soundly, and was propelled backwards, her wings beating to keep her upright, and then charging forward again. The two weapons found each other once more, but this time Seraphina had the advantage. Darrien was almost taken off her feet.

At the edge of the ravine, Alderin was finding his way back to his feet, and pulling his sword from the sheath at his hip. Unlike Darrien, he liked the feel of a real weapon in his hands, and had never mastered the art of conjuring one from thin air. Instinct told him to hit the ground before he knew he was doing it. The blade that would have claimed him through the throat passed through empty air, and when Alderin scrambled back to his feet, he was face to face with a pale man. The man wore a baggy red tunic with sleeves several inches too long for his arms, but the hem of the shirt stopped just under his ribcage. The collar too seemed odd, as it billowed and flowed around his neck. Jet black hair fell around the young man's face in an organized mess. His pants too seemed out of place, too low on the hips and loose as though they would fall if he moved the wrong way, but tight everywhere else as though they had been made to fit his form. His feet were bare, but he stepped so lightly as though the terrain did not bother him.

"I can't have you interfere," the stranger spoke, his voice melodic and strangely soothing. "Seraphina has been waiting for this for a long time."

Alderin scowled behind his faceplate.

"You've made a mistake thinking that you can prevent me from assisting my charge," he said coldly, his voice modulated as it passed through the helm. "Unless you have the power to challenge a Dark God, you should withdraw now, or be destroyed."

"Lucian Vispilio, the Thief of Hope and Love, withdraws in the face of no challenge."

Alderin didn't wait for the man to finish his words before he lashed out, a feint of the blade the elicited the response he wanted. Lucian dodged to the right, an attempt to avoid the fast strike, but Alderin extended his right hand and a bolt of lightning erupted from his gauntlet, striking the lithe man hard in the chest, scorching his tunic and sending him sprawling to the ground. The man obviously had not been killed by the strike, but it would put him out of commission for several minutes. Alderin turned to where

Darrien and Seraphina were still engaged in combat. The two lovers caught eyes for a fraction of a second and the plan was hatched. Seraphina lashed out with a hard strike from her sword, which Darrien blocked easily. Instead of countering with the axe, Darrien extended her fingers, and a torrent of water sprang from her fingertips. Seraphina was quick, her wings wrapping around her like a shield and deflecting most of the harmless assault. Before Seraphina could take any other action, Alderin let loose with another lightning strike, aimed not at the winged woman, but at the growing puddle at her feet. Sparks lit up the night sky, and Seraphina howled in pain. But she would not be disabled by the tactic, and her wings beat wildly trying to find enough air to pull her out of the trap. Darrien lashed out again, this time with a spray of razor sharp needles of ice that penetrated the thin spaces of the woman's armor drawing plumes of blood. Finally Seraphina was able to extricate herself from the lightning filled puddle, and found the air, her scowl clear.

"This isn't over Darrien," Seraphina cursed. "Your whole family will soon be dead."

Darrien and Alderin's full attention were on the sky-bound form of Seraphina Masile, and they had both lost track of Lucian who had made his way back to his feet. In a single deft motion, he pulled a black dagger from his pouch and threw it with great accuracy at the gap between Alderin's helm and the back plate of his armor. The blade of the dagger struck true, and Alderin fell to the ground. Darrien rounded, hearing the sound of Alderin's armored form crashing to the ground. She saw Lucian for only a moment before he disappeared into the darkness of the Heart of Stone. The next moment she was on the ground beside Alderin, gently pulling the helm from his head and cradling him in her arms, tears welling in her eyes.

* * * * * * * * * * * *

Sabrina had crossed the distance to the western gate of the Heart of Stone as quickly as she could manage, but it had not been an easy crossing. There were far too many guards, and while she could have carved her way through them and drawn attention to herself as would have been Aerith's preferred method, she wanted to exercise a little more strategy. That was one of the things that always bothered Sabrina about Aerith. He had the reputation for being a tactical and strategic genius, but the actual accounts of his battles showed little in the way of strategy other than charging forward with a quip on his tongue. Granted there was a certain purity in his methods, knowing only how to go forward, but it was not always the subtlest of approaches. Sabrina had had generations to study strategy and tactics, and had learned from a myriad of different masters. Sabrina found herself leaning more toward Midarin's style of leadership, never plunging into a conflict until there was no choice left, but once engaged in battle, end it quickly. If the killing of one target could end a battle, the best method was to eliminate that target as quickly as possible and limit the carnage. That flew in the face of the way that Aerith approached battles. He chose to wade in, cutting a bloody swath. If he could not reach his target, he would inflict as much damage as possible. The fear created by his rampages was legendary.

"Sometimes fear is a better weapon than a sword."

Sabrina smiled to herself as she heard the mixture of Aerith's voice in hers. He was close now, closer than he had been in far too long. It would be good to see him again, even if she would not be able to gloat about actually saving him.

There was a large knot of guards, perhaps thirty on the approach to the western gate. There was going to be no going around this obstacle, and she would have to end the battle quickly, otherwise the patrols that were in the area would be drawn and could create a problem. Sabrina had to admire the discipline of the Army of Stone. Even though a powerful man was trying to escape their dungeon, and there had been an explosion from the other side of the palace, these men held their ground and kept to their posts. Obviously, Gregor Quicksilver had trained them well and instilled an impressive level of discipline. Time for a very Aerith approach.

Sabrina stepped out from behind the rock outcropping and began a very calm, casual stroll toward the gate. Her hands were behind her back, and she had her palms up so that Snag could sit comfortably. Just before the guards saw her, she started whistling a tune softly to herself, drawing attention quickly. All of the guards fell into alert postures within an instant. The lead guard did not move, but issued his challenge.

"This gate is off-limits, and the Heart of Stone is not open to visitors. If you are a parishioner, please return to the city and offer your prayers at the Temple of the Creator there. There is nothing to fear."

Sabrina continued moving towards the guards. Whistling slightly louder, an image forming in the back of her mind, one that curled her lips into a smile.

"I said turn back!" the guard growled, drawing his sword.

Sabrina stopped and cocked her head slightly.

"I've always wondered," she said wryly, "does that armor protect you from fire, or does it just get hot and cook you?"

There wasn't enough time for the guard to respond or even form the quizzical look that his mind wanted. The ball of fire exploded from behind the knot of guards, sending them flying in all directions. Snag bounded from Sabrina's hands the next moment, and without a thought the twin swords formed in Sabrina's hands. One was thin, crystal, and delicate. It formed in her right hand, while the more substantial heavy onyx blade formed in her left. Though she had a large measure of Aerith's fighting prowess, she still had weakness in her form. She compensated for this by allowing a lighter blade to form in her weaker hand. But once in battle, Sabrina flowed through the ranks of her opponents like water. As the onyx blade found the first of her victims, Sabrina saw the faintest trail of the red-haired woman as she dove into the right flank of the soldiers, beheading two of them as they struggled to recover their feet after the explosion. Where Sabrina flowed like water through a river, Rhain crashed like waves against the shore. Her brute force laid waste to the ranks of the guards, and she liberally applied both the sword and flames to her victims. Screams of the dying soldiers resounded from her side of the battlefield, while those that fell to Sabrina and Snag did so with largely stifled gurgles. Their strikes were precise and meant to kill swiftly. Rhain wanted her deaths noisy and brutal. When finally the last of the guards had met their end, the two women stood face to face. Snag sat between then, a wave of emotion rolling from it like confusion and irritation. Rhain looked first to Snag and then to Sabrina.

"You are the absolute last person I expected to see here. Well, maybe Bryn more than you, but you are certainly a surprise."

Sabrina scowled.

"I'd be surprised to see you to, if I had even known you existed. Though I suppose your father has quite a few things to answer for today, if we get him out of here in one piece."

Rhain smiled, and Sabrina knew the smile. It was the deadly yet intoxicating smile that Aerith had seen on Bryn's face a thousand times. Rhain was her mother's daughter, that much was clear from just that look.

"The only thing that Aerith excels at more than getting into trouble, is finding ways to get out of it again."

Epilogue

Blood Calls for Blood

Year Three of the Just Emperor Kaitain "Dragonsbane" Lorien, Creator's Calendar Year 1870

Midarin stepped out of Dominique's chambers, her bow ready. The ground shook with another explosion, and plaster and rock fell from the ceiling. The Imperial Palace of Aldere was dying under the strain of what could only be a battle of power from deeper inside the palace. The presence she had felt could not have been there, it was impossible. Emries was dead, killed by the hand of Evan Sinn at the fall of Onea. But the purity and strength of the powers she felt could belong to no one else. Two Imperial Guards stood at the end of the hallway, and they started their advance as soon as they set eyes on Midarin. She had no time for this. The arrows were off the bowstring and both guards were down before they knew what was happening. Midarin barely had to break stride to end their lives. This should have been an easy mission. Dominique proved to be more reasonable than she had any space to be, and it would only have taken a few more hours to convince the woman that the deaths of Kaitain and Irene Drage were the only way to ensure the peace between Cadaria and Mythryn. But that possibility was gone now. Midarin would have to do the unpleasant work herself, no matter what it would mean. War was inevitable now. Suddenly Midarin stopped short of the door. An unpleasant memory twisted at the back of her mind, and she saw herself in a very different role. One she had been in the position that Chelsea and Dominique found themselves in. Railing against those with power who they had no chance to truly defeat. It sickened Midarin to think of herself in the same way that she had thought of the phasia on Onea. It took a moment to shake herself from those thoughts, and just in time for three more guards to meet their end from her deadly accuracy. If her memory of the layout of the palace was accurate, it was only a few turns and corridors to where Kaitain slept. Then it would be only a matter of time before she tracked down Irene Drage and end this once and for all.

* * * * * * * * * * * *

Aerith fell back, the first strike of Gregor's blade coming slightly faster than it should have. The man was possessed of great strength and ability to be sure, but he should not have been able to move that fast. Maybe Aerith was just losing his touch. The twin blades were back in Aerith's hands the next moment, and he lashed out, as the soldiers flooded around where he and Gregor crossed swords, trying to overwhelm Gabriel and the others. Camille had broken off from Devlin and Gabriel and was turning to face Hannah. Devlin and Gabriel stood back to back, their immortal weapons ready to taste more blood in the coming conflict. Aerith and Gregor tested each other, probing the defenses of the other, waiting for a mistake. There was something different in the way the man was fighting, something different and yet familiar in those moments. His eyes were different too.

Hannah waited for Camille's strike, sure that it would come high, but cursed inwardly when it was merely a feint and the true strike came low. When Camille's sword met Faith, Hannah was unprepared for the force with which the woman struck, but still held her feet. One of the guards flashed in with his sword, a strike that would have severed a normal woman's head from her body, but Camille had already spun away from the engagement with Hannah, and severed the guard's arm at his shoulder. She jumped back nearly ten feet, carried by the invisible air currents in the passage. A dozen crystal swords appeared around her, and they hung like a halo around her body. Camille smiled slightly, the smirk just raising the left corner of her mouth for an instant before the wreath of swords lashed out. As the swords moved away from Camille's body, a shadow appeared with the weapons, as if phantoms appeared out of the nothingness at her bidding to act as her guardians. The phantasms engaged the paladins of the Army of Stone, and suddenly the odds were less in the favor of the righteous.

Gabriel and Devlin were struggling against the mass of enemies, but they were doing their best. Even with the abilities granted by Valor, Gabriel was having a hard time keeping up. Already three strikes had gotten through his defenses, and he was bleeding from two vicious wounds. The third had merely been a glancing blow that left a cut on his right cheek. It probably would scar, but that would be the least of his concerns if he made it out of this conflict alive. They had done well to get this far, and had killed a great many men, but the odds were finally starting to catch up with them. Devlin too seemed to be having difficulty, and Gabriel could see from stolen glances that he too was bleeding heavily.

An explosion ripped down the hallway, a sheet of fire clinging to the ceiling, sending almost everyone scattering to the floor to escape the flames. Only Aerith and Gregor seemed to keep their feet, smoke rolling around both of the men as they continued their duel. It was as if the rest of the battle didn't exist for them. From beyond where the two men fought, a whirling black ball plunged into the ranks of the enemy soldiers, and where it passed, plumes of blood erupted. A dozen men died in the first pass. Behind the whirling ball of death came two women, one of which Gabriel immediately recognized as Rhain Feirbran. The odds were starting to even a bit, and with Rhain's liberal application of fire and steel, the two women made their way to reinforce Gabriel and Devlin's position. Aerith stole a look over his shoulder as Sabrina and Rhain passed, the barest of smiles coming to his lips. He pushed back hard after his blades met Gregor's leaving a little distance between the two men.

"Alright," Aerith said letting the blades fall from his hands again. This time instead of remaining at his sides, they dissolved into nothingness. "Time to get serious now. This is a little trick I learned from an old friend. Though he never allowed himself to do what was necessary."

Sabrina knew what was going to happen an instant before it did, and it was all she could do to get the bubble of power extended over Gabriel, Devlin, and Rhain before it happened. Had she not been as connected to Aerith as she was, there would have been no time at all to defend. Sabrina didn't need to see to know that Aerith was smiling widely as he extended his hands and bolts of white hot lightning sprayed from his extended fingers and filled the entire hallway with their crackling power. The bolts jumped from solider to soldier, drawing cries of agony. The deaths were slow, brutal, and merciless. Dozens died in the blink of an eye, the echoes of their screams overwhelming the din of the sizzling armor and crackling lightning. Several of the bolts struck Gregor, but he stood firm, scorch marks on the breastplate of his armor. Smoke rolled from him, his hair crackling as though it had been set ablaze. Camille had been able to defend herself by wrapping her wings around herself, and Hannah it seemed had ducked to the ground, Faith slammed into the ground acting as a makeshift lightning rod. She had not escaped damage, as there was a scorch mark on her left arm as well as her right cheek. The arm hung useless at her side, and it looked to Camille as though the woman was using all of her might just to keep from passing out. This battle was over, that much was clear, and only Gregor's unreal fortitude was a beacon of resistance. When Sabrina turned back to where Aerith and Gregor stood, she watched with horror as the man levitated slightly off the ground, his body wreathed with angelic fire. His eyes had gone white, and the broadsword in his hands had been replaced with a sword made of pure crystal.

"I should have known you couldn't stay dead," Aerith said after a moment. "The Creator doesn't know when to stay out of things."

"THE VOICE OF THE CREATOR WILL NEVER BE SILENCED, AERITH SETH. YOU HAVE NEITHER THE POWER NOR THE WILL TO END MY EXISTENCE. NO MATTER IF YOU DESTROY THIS BODY, I WILL RETURN TIME AND TIME AGAIN UNTIL YOU ARE MADE TO PAY FOR THOSE CRIMES YOU HAVE COMMITTED AGAINST THE CREATOR."

Aerith knew that Gregor had ceased to be at that moment. The man was still inside of course, but the power of the Voice had taken over completely. Bright white wings sprouted from Gregor's shoulders, and the scorched armor melted away to be replaced with gleaming crystalline plate mail. Aerith took another step back and rolled up his sleeves.

"Sabrina," Aerith said over his shoulder, "get them out of here. You know where to go."

Sabrina nodded and pulled one of the stones from Aerith's travelling bag. It took only a moment to form the portal, and Snag quickly bounded through as though it understood that it needed to ensure the other side was safe for the rest. Sabrina helped Gabriel to his feet and steered him toward the portal.

"I'm not going," Gabriel said in the firmest voice that he could manage. "Aerith is going need all the help he can get."

"You'll just get in his way," Rhain said after a moment, "this is his fight, no matter how it ends."

Rhain could see the look on Gabriel's face; she shook her head and smiled.

"Don't worry, Aerith comes back from the dead better than anyone I know."

Gabriel balked at the quip, whatever humor should have been there lost on him. The scene was too fantastic and ridiculous to be believed. Dark Gods, Emissaries of the Creator, Knights of the Flashing Blade, and whatever Aerith was. Rhain was steering Gabriel toward the portal when he felt a tug at his back. Valor pulled at its sheath, as though the blade wanted to be drawn. Looking over to Devlin, Gabriel could see the same puzzled look. Gabriel pulled away from Rhain's grasp and reached back to pull Valor from its sheath. The blade was alive in his hand, more alive than it had been in all the time it had been in his possession. The weapon almost thirsted for battle now, but it rebelled in Gabriel's hand, as though it did not want to be with him any longer. On a hunch, Gabriel opened his hand and Valor hung there for a moment, suspended by its pure will in mid-air. The blade hovered through the air and stopped at Aerith's side, almost as if it had been bidden there. However, it seemed that Aerith was surprised by the event. Taking his cue from Gabriel, Devlin too relinquished his Sacred Weapon, letting it join Valor at Aerith's side. Willing to leave the mystery for later, Gabriel allowed Rhain to push him through the portal, and Devlin followed. Sabrina lingered for a moment and turned toward the portal, but a surge of power stopped her in her tracks. Camille was rocked off her feet by an explosion, one that left her crumpled to the ground, feathers from her wings scattering in all directions. The woman's breastplate had been shattered, and her blade broken. In front of where Hannah Ironheart knelt, the form of The Will materialized with an incredible burst of power. The bolt of pure white energy erupted from The Will's outstretched hand the next moment claiming Sabrina full in the chest, sending her tumbling to the ground like a broken doll. Aerith barely turned in time to see the assault, and he roared in a mixture of pain and anger, a stream of bright green flame erupting from his hand, forcing The Will backwards.

"Get them out of here!" Aerith yelled to Rhain who stood dumbstruck by the turn of fortune.

Camille had somehow forced her way back to her feet, but she was very much worse for wear. Rhain picked up Sabrina from where she lay and leapt through the portal after she was sure that Camille could make it under her own power. However, the second that Rhain passed through, the portal closed, and Camille collapsed to the ground, defeat filling her. Aerith backed up two paces, until he stood directly between the two Heralds of the Creator, and Camille lay at his feet. She was hurt badly, barely hanging on to the last threads of life, and if she did not get help soon, she would surely die. In spite of himself he could not get the smile to leave his lips. Exhilaration filled him, and he let his hands find the hilts of the two Sacred Weapons that floated beside him.

"Finally," Aerith said to no one in particular, "a challenge."

* * * * * * * * * * * *

In her little cottage in the middle of the woods, Tess stood looking out the window, her eyes locked on the Heart of Stone. She could not see the battle, but she could feel every moment of it. She could feel the horror and the death and the pain, and no matter how hard she tried, she could not stop the tears from flowing down her cheeks. She could not stand the death. She felt each and every scream of pain in her mind, and no matter how she tried she could not shut them out. Finally she pulled herself away from the window and lay on her bed, a pillow over her head. She tried to think of Camille, of her face, of the way that she smiled and how the touch of her hand always took all of her fears away. But all she could see in her mind was Camille with Devlin. Their hands touching, him holding her, kissing her. Her mind went places she did not want it to go, and her stomach turned. Then suddenly the pain hit. Camille was hurt. Tess could feel it in her chest as though she had been hit herself. Camille was dying. The cottage around her exploded in a wreath of golden flames. Furniture twisted and groaned as though it was burning alive. The walls and ceiling melted away to vapor, and in a matter of seconds Tess was standing amongst the ruined foundation that would be unrecognizable as a cottage. Her white nightshirt was tattered but she paid it no mind. A storm had begun around the Heart of Stone, hard rain beating unrelentingly at the ground. But as Tess walked, almost in a trance toward the Heart of Stone, the sheets of rain seemed to part, allowing her passage. However, if anyone would have been there to look closely, they would have realized that the rain actually vaporized before it got close enough to hit the young girl. Her hate and anger had formed a pocket of superheated air around her body, hot enough to boil water at a touch.

It took a much shorter time than it should have, and Tess was standing at the walls of the Heart of Stone. It was as if the distance between the countryside cottage and the palace itself simply ceased to be. Tess took another step forward toward the wall, and the stone before her melted away as though it were not even there. The halo of heat around her was melting a path through the fortifications.

"I'm coming, Camille, my love."

∗ ∗ ∗ ∗ ∗ ∗ ∗ ∗ ∗ ∗ ∗ ∗

Ayden stood looking at Emries, hate filling him in a way he never knew possible. Emries lashed out without a word, his form tight and precise. The battle ebbed and flowed quickly, the two men not bothering to test one another, as if they knew each other's abilities despite never setting eyes on one another before. Both Ayden and Emries were masters with the sword, but as they began to apply their powers into the duel, each move and maneuver became more deadly. They crashed at each other with speed that belied the human eye following the movements. Emries was the first to lash out with a direct use of power, a ball of energy erupting from his free hand. Ayden was able to block the blow with one of his swords and sent it crashing into the outer wall. It collided and exploded with such force that the stones were blown outward, creating a massive gaping hole. Emries became less shy with his assaults at that point, hurling bolt after bolt of power at the young man. Ayden was up to the ever-increasing challenge, blocking and redirecting the strikes into the superstructure of the Imperial Palace. Walls groaned and shook as supports and buttresses were damaged and broken by the errant blows. But Ayden was not content to be on the receiving end of the assaults. He too lashed out, waves of fire and streams of ice alternately erupting from the blades of the swords in his hands. Where the two met, huge gouts of steam flared, the first such assault exploding into Emries' face. The god's face boiled, and skin sagged from the heat. Blisters formed and his right eye swelled shut. Emries fell back, his hand instantly going to his ruined face.

"Well at least you'll look better once this fight is over."

Ayden could not resist the insult. He had a lot of his father in him, but there was no time for gloating, not now. Emries was too dangerous of an opponent to be underestimated. A few burns would not prevent him from continuing.

"Simple tricks will not win this battle for you, boy," Emries growled. "You have some skill, but you are no match for me."

Ayden didn't feel the strike coming. Suddenly Emries was just behind Ayden, and the blade of his crystalline sword entered Ayden's back and erupted from his chest. Blood streamed from Ayden's mouth and nose, and he choked on the thick viscous liquid with every tortured breath. Disbelief filled Ayden.

"You're not your father," Emries growled into Ayden's ear. "And he would have to be at his best to defeat me, so what chance do you, a petty and tainted imitation have? My blade could have pierced your heart just now little boy, but your death would gain me nothing. If you survive, tell your father that I'm coming for him. I'll make him pay for every insult that his lackey Evan Sinn visited upon me, and every indignity that I have had to suffer since that defeat."

Emries leaned in, so that his mouth was as close to Ayden's ear as possible.

"Oh, and as for your whore mother," Emries said coldly and cruelly, "it will be my pleasure to make her suffer and beg for death. The humiliation that I will visit upon her will make her wish that my brother had never given her life."

With that, Emries was gone, and Ayden fell to the floor, the sword still impaling him. Ayden was not sure how long passed before he finally lost consciousness. The last thing he remembered before his eyes closed the last time was Jaccob Aldora's shocked voice.

＊ ＊ ＊ ＊ ＊ ＊ ＊ ＊ ＊ ＊ ＊

Irene Drage ran toward the room where Kaitain slept, her mind whirling not only with her own thoughts, but with the thoughts of the goddess that called herself Talisia Masile. The boundary between her identity and that of Talisia was starting to erode, and before too long there would not be a separation between the two women. They would be one and the same. For now though, there was only one purpose propelling her feet. She had to ensure the safety of the Emperor. The way that the Imperial Palace was shuddering and shaking, it could only be a matter of minutes before the whole thing came crashing down around them. Finally she arrived, the small group of Imperial Guards holding their positions at the door, regardless of the mounting chaos.

"The Imperial Palace is no longer safe," Irene called out, "secure the Emperor and withdraw to the village of Coventry. Take a full detachment of guards and meet with Korin Melcab at the western gate. There is no time, make haste."

The guards sprang into action with no further bidding, and Irene turned back in the direction of the Throne Room. There was little time to do anything of consequence before having to retreat from the palace, but the Imperial Seal needed to be saved. If plans went to form, and the Empress was indeed dead, if Irene was going to stake her claim of leadership, she would need the Imperial Seal to ensure the loyalty of those who would be looking for a voice to lead them out of the chaos. She could not allow more kingdoms to slip to the rebellion.

＊ ＊ ＊ ＊ ＊ ＊ ＊ ＊ ＊ ＊ ＊

Midarin stood in the center of the great Throne Room of the Imperial Palace of Aldere and could not help but take a moment to take in the place where her husband and the love of her life had been killed. The throne stood gleaming golden, the Imperial Seal on one low table, while the Sword of the Cadarian Emperor lay beside it. They were symbols of the leadership of the whole Cadarian Empire. Part of Midarin wanted to smash them, to destroy them. But they were just things, symbols. Once she had killed Kaitain, they would be needed to ensure that Dominique could unite the shattered empire. Dozens of guards lay dead around the throne room, the unfortunate few who had decided to attempt to prevent her from achieving her goal. The doors to the throne room were broken and barely hanging from their hinges, and through the shattered opening, a black clad figure emerged. His armor seemed to drink in all light, and the air around him chilled into a haze. The pale face with sunken cheeks and dark eye sockets could only have belonged to the creature that had become known as Death, a herald and servant of Dorovar.

"Fitting that you will meet your end here," Death said, drawing its sword from the sheath on its hip. "Your Gwydeon threw his life away kneeling at the feet of the first Cadarian Emperor. His voice was lost to the great Chorus of Souls. But you, the warrior queen, your voice will be one of the strongest to ever join Dorovar's choir."

Midarin's answer came in the form of an arrow. The pure crystalline arrow struck Death in its right eye. The creature howled in pain and fell to its knees, the sword clattering from its grasp.

"You mock me?" Midarin growled, drawing the ancient sword from her scabbard. "You are a puppet on a string, and your death means nothing. Dorovar has been waiting for this moment, waiting for someone stupid enough to take your head so that his next pet monster can punish the Cadarians and collect souls. I should kill you so that we can be closer to ending this."

Midarin stayed her hand and with a thought flung Death across the room, where it burst through a wall and toppled into the hallway at the feet of Irene Drage. The sorceress in her blue and white gown stepped through the hole in the wall and regarded Midarin for a moment. Power flashed from Irene the next moment in the form of a wave of pure white power that swept like the blade of a scythe toward Midarin. The older woman let her blade catch the wave of power. The two weapons flared against one another, and Irene kept the pressure up, urging the weapon forward, wanting to end the battle quickly. Finally Midarin got the upper hand, batting the blade of energy to the side, sending it back toward Irene. She ducked the blow and it slammed into a wall, obliterating it completely. Midarin pressed the advantage, her will replacing her bow. Arrows appeared from thin air and rained down upon the sorceress. Dozens hit the ground where the woman stood, and Irene rolled away, several of the arrows just missing, cutting her dress but not her skin. Irene was up again, looking less elegant and more haggard, but she was not done, not yet. She extended both hands forward, and twin gouts of flame erupted. This flame however was colored with black. Midarin countered with flames of her own. Using the techniques she had picked up from Lissa and Bryn, Midarin poured all of her hate and rage and sorrow into the strike, her emotions feeding the attack. She had never been gifted in this kind of application of her powers, but she would not be out-fought by this woman, no matter the cost. More and more the two women poured their powers into the growing battle of wills. What neither woman saw was the creature Death pulling its broken form back through the hole in the wall. Its armor was shattered, one arm completely severed from its body, and both legs mangled and nearly useless. The crystal arrow still protruded from what had been its eye, and it pulled itself along the floor, using what little strength it had left. Agonizingly it pulled itself past where Irene stood, and made it half-way across the chamber to where the two massive waves of power vied against one another for an advantage.

"For Dorovar!"

Death forced its way to its feet the next moment, piercing the stalemated powers. The explosion that erupted the next moment engulfed the whole of the throne room in flames, smoke, steam, and unbridled power.

* * * * * * * * * * * *

Dominique and Chelsea had gotten clear of the Imperial Palace of Aldere without much difficulty, thanks to Chelsea's enhanced senses and what Dominique could only credit to a massive amount of luck. They were making their way toward the little village of Coventry on the outer edge of the Imperial City of Aldere, as it would be the safest place to plot their next move. Dominique looked back when she heard the explosion. It was louder than anything she had ever heard before, and with it came the unearthly sounds of stone, steel and wood being contorted and tortured in a way that even the Creator couldn't have dreamed. The two women watched, transfixed as the Imperial Palace of Aldere shook and crumbled in on itself, completely destroyed by the conflicts that took place within its walls.

* * * * * * * * * * * *

The Imperial litter that held the slumbering body of Emperor Kaitain Lorien moved slowly toward the village of Coventry. The Imperial Guards had taken great care even in their haste to ensure that no harm came to their charge, and Kaitain lay comfortably on a soft mattress within the enclosed litter. As the moments stretched on, the guards heard the conflagration behind them and all watched in horror as the Imperial Palace collapsed in on itself, the cloud of debris and fire rising high into the darkening sky. What no one saw was the eyes of the Emperor flutter for a moment and then open.

EPILOGUE

Appendicies

Dramatis Personae

The Knights of the Flashing Blade
Bernhardt Yeoman
The Moonstone Knight
Kingdom of Iron, Pellatori
Wielder of the Hammer Gravity

Chelsea Zarova
The Garnet Knight
Kingdom of Fire, Saldarine
"The Wolf of Saldarine"
Wife of Seraph Kore
Wielder of the Katars Tenacity

Devlin Rannoch
The Onyx Knight
Kingdom of Night, Galateria
Half-Dragon
Wielder of the Kopesh Discipline

Gregor Quicksilver
The Ruby Knight
Kingdom of Blood, Zevarit
Husband of Hannah Ironheart
Paladin of the Church of the Creator
Son of Ivan Quicksilver
Wielder of the Greatsword Valor

Hannah Ironheart
The Celestine Knight
Kingdom of Stone, Albitonin
High Priestess of the Church of the Creator
Wife of Gregor Quicksilver
Wielder of the Mace Spirit

Jaccob Aldora
The Topaz Knight
The Flying Kingdom, Hedorah
Former Member of the Academy of Arcane Arts
Wielder of the Double Sword Temperance

Leonora Wastri
The Jade Knight
Kingdom of Soul, Oradrim
Wielder of the Naginata Wisdom

Natalia Pressen
The Sunstone Knight
Kingdom of Gold, Bellnoc
Master of the Shadow Guild
Wielder of the Rapier Perseverance

Orren Eldrath
The Sapphire Knight
Kingdom of Ice, Rashaleb
Former Member of the Academy of Arcane Arts
Wielder of the Long Sword Courage

Seraph Kore
The Emerald Knight
Kingdom of Water, Thorigald
Husband of Chelsea Zarova
Wielder of Twin Sword Patience

Tolon Morr
The Amethyst Knight
Kingdom of Steel, Celidar
Former Gladiator
Wielder of Battle Axe Strength

Vallic Ultiv
The Serpentine Knight
Kingdom of Steam, Iltorp
Wielder of Scythe Harmony

Xaran Firesoul
The Tiger's Eye Knight
Kingdom of Knowledge, Menoris
Blind Since Birth
Wielder of Staff Faith

Ivan Quicksilver
Former Ruby Knight
Father of Gregor Quicksilver
Advisor to the Dark Court

Tutio Illik
Former Onyx Knight

Heremon Tal
Former Amethyst Knight

The Seers
Jehna Feris
The Dark Seer

Jania Maldovrin
Oldest of the Maldovrin Triplets

Jerrica Maldovrin
Youngest of the Maldovrin Triplets

Jordyne Maldovrin
Middle of the Maldovrin Triplets

The Academy of Arcane Arts
Alistair Ravenheart
Grandmaster of the Academy of
Arcane Arts
Master of Water
Imperial Sorcerer
Husband of Estelle Ravenheart
Father of Quyhn Ravenheart

Estelle Ravenheart
Sorceress
Wife of Alistair Ravenheart
Mother of Quyhn Ravenheart

Fiona Ebonsight
Master of Fire
Mother of Aris Ebonsight

Aris Ebonsight
Master of Air
Daughter of Fiona Ebonsight

Jastra Mythryn
Master of Energy

Ashinica Maupin
Master of Stone
Member of the Imperial Family

Ayden Seth
Son of Aerith Seth and Bryn Aplee

The Dragon Hunters

Jillian Corven
Self-Titled Lady of Cadaria
Wielder of Scaleripper
Leader of the Dragon Hunters

Kiara Aren
Dragon Hunter
Former Priestess of the Creator

Angelina Lynn Sydor
Dragon Hunter

Jacqueline Escandi
Dragon Hunter
Former Member of the Iron Legion

The Chorus

Dorovar
The Destroyer of Worlds

Pestilence
The Grey Man
Carrier of the Crawling Plague

Famine
Formerly Isabel Relin
Carrier of the Wasting Disease

Death
Formerly Ardis Franel
The Collector of Souls

Jerah
The Woman in White

The Hand of Chaos

Dimitri Sulano
The Voice of the Lost

Syren Belloch
The Priestess of Blood

Torda Safrick
The Master of Secrets

Xavier Cormea
The Corruptor of Souls

Erik Relcan
Pursuer of Lost Love
Former Personal Assistant of Hannah Ironheart

Seraphina Masile
Second in Command of the Hand of Chaos

The Children of the Creator

Emries
The First *Coromor*
Creator of the *Erieal*

Halicon
Formerly known as Shau-ling
Master of the Shadows
Father of the Phasia

The Court of the Dark Gods

Sadrina Annis
Queen of Mythryn
Wife of Pike Rhuiden

Darrien Annis
Half-Dark Goddess
Daughter of Pike Rhuiden

Tess Annis
Half-Dark Goddess
Daughter of Pike Rhuiden

Alderin Parran
Dark God
Son of Aryx and Diana Terian
Protector of Darrien Annis

Camille Renar
Dark Goddess
Daughter of Gwydeon and Midarin
Sandar
Protector of Tess Annis

Serrina Mistic
Dark Goddess
Voice of the Dark Council
Daughter of Jerrard and Erika Mystic

The Dark Gods

Aryx Terian
White Lightning
Fire *Erieal* of the First Generation of
the Prophecies
Husband of Diana Geoffry Terian
Father of Lissa Terian
Father of Alderin Parran
Former Host of Nightwing

Diana Terian Geoffry
Wind *Erieal* of the First Generation of
the Prophecies
Sister of Arathorn Geoffry
Wife of Aryx Terian
Mother of Lissa Terian
Mother of Alderin Parran

Pike Rhuiden
Water *Erieal* of the Second
Generation of the Prophecies
Refugee from the Dark Mirror
First Cousin of Logan Ranthall
Eldar Merin's Former Husband
Husband of Sadrina Annis
Father of Darrien and Tess Annis

Gwydeon Sandar
Brother of Angels
Husband of Midarin Rice Sandar
Father of Nathaniel Sandar
Father of Camille Renar

Midarin Rice
Wife of Gwydeon Sandar
Mother of Nathaniel Sandar
Mother of Camille Renar

Lissa Terian
Fire *Erieal* of the Third Generation of
the Prophecies
Daughter of Aryx and Diana Terian
Wife of Wolf Ranthall

Sabrina Binosear
Third *Chosen One* of the Prophecies
Refugee from the Dark Mirror
Daughter of Cairyn Binosear

Wolf Ranthall
Son of Logan Ranthall and Elwyne
Tamerlane Ranthall

The Forgotten
Aerith Seth
The First *Chosen One*
Husband of Bryn Aplee
Father of Ayden Seth, Cedric
Binosear, Anabel Binosear, Gideon
Viruci

Bryn Aplee
The Lady Fox
Member of the Brotherhood of Phasia
Wife of Aerith Seth
Mother of Gideon Viruci
Mother of Ayden Seth

Taya Viruci
Daughter of Gideon Viruci and Erika
Belnosian
Refugee from the Dark Mirror

Jerrard Mystic
Son of Basille Mystic
Husband of Erika Belnosian
Father of Serrina Mistic

Erika Belnosian Mystic
Wife of Jerrard Mystic
Mother of Serrina Mystic

Other Cast
Cole Breon
Freelance Assassin
The Living Shadow

Liandra Nightshade
Freelance Assassin
Death Blossom

Alise Modrall
Assassin

Wynne
Farmer

Dane Rhuiden
Monk
Leader of the Order of the Flickering
Flame

Blade
Merchant
Purveyor of Oddities

Isa Shar
Companion of Vallic Ultiv

Evan Sinn
Inheritor of Aerith Seth's power
The Voice of the Creator
Husband of Meredith Heron

Meredith Heron
Emissary of the Creator
Wife of Evan Sinn
Murdered by Dorovar

Tera Dawnrunner
Guardian of the Council of the Winds
Guardian of the East
Last of the Tigrelle

Jander Eveningstar
Guardian of the Council of the Winds

The Council of Winds

The Elder Dragon Tarot
Leader of the Council

Mariti Brightblade
Second in Command of the Council
Companion of Tarot

Khalas Skydancer
Friend of Xaran Firesoul

The Demon Dragon Shadowweaver
Chief Opposition to Tarot

Krangoth Granitewill

The Arcane Dragon Serentis

Brux Mightytide

Charnada Ivorytooth
Ally of Shadowweaver

Stormbane the Traitor
Ally of Shadowweaver

Sheyruushk Bottomdweller
Ally of Khalas Skydancer

About the Author

Brian Kershner is a life-long dreamer, writer, and problem-solver. He grew up absorbing anything and everything he could get his hands on, and as a child of the Star Wars era he constantly wanted to see the worlds beyond the little Indiana town he grew up in. There was no adventure too far, and no problem too big.

Emboldened by parents who always supported his curiosity and his thoughtfulness, Brian found himself bounding from Space Camp to Laser Summer Camp to Athletic Training Camp to Piano Lessons to Football Practice to Basketball Practice to Choir Practice and back again. Despite all of the roaming and traveling, his family remained close-knit and supportive.

Though he flirted with the idea of becoming a doctor, Brian's attentions always fell back to the computer world. He got his first computer when he was six, and not long after found his way into a word processing program and began crafting his own fantastic worlds and even more fantastic characters.

As he has grown and changed and experienced life, so too have his characters. He continues to write, craft, and create; whether it is websites for his customers, or characters and worlds for his audience.